Seventh Daughter

Ronnie Seagren

WolfSinger Publications  Security, Colorado

ACKNOWLEDGMENTS

I'd like to acknowledge the historical figures who made cameo appearances in *Seventh Daughter.*

Lorenzo Hubble did, indeed, run a string of trading posts across Arizona and New Mexico. A colorful and legendary character larger than life in more ways than one. I first discovered him in *West of the Thirties* by Edward T Hall.

D. Owen Stephens accompanied the Grace/Hayden expedition to Peru, hired to paint the eclipse because photography wasn't considered accurate enough to capture the subtle hues of the sun's corona. He died of a cerebral hemorrhage in Panama on the way home.

There's also the trekkers who hiked the Andes and came home to publish their journals. When I started *Seventh Daughter* in the '90's, there was no Google Earth to show me the way. My favorite was Dervla Murphy's *Eight Feet in the Andes*, the journey of a forty-three year old woman, her eight-year-old daughter, and a mule named Juana.

Oh, and that archeologist who first discovered Killichaka? I always fancied his last name was Jones.

Prolog
June 8, 1918

AMANI

"It's a girl!"

Amani blinked to focus on the infant raised before the open window as if in offering. Beyond, sun embraced moon amid stars come out in the midday sky, a wedding of light and dark. Cold dread seized her as she beheld the ring of pale blue fire like a halo around her new daughter. She reached for the infant, desperate to shelter her from the destiny ordained by the Vision.

"A seven daughter, Amani! You've done it!"

Amani released her breath slowly. The pain eased, but not the fear. This house did not welcome her. Too many shadows prowling the edges, too many whispers behind its walls. She did not belong here.

But Denver was in the path of the eclipse, and home was not. So with her sisters and oldest daughter, she had come. She had used herbs and medicines and her own strength of will to delay labor, regardless of the risk, and then held off the contractions until the eclipse had begun, so that her daughter might be born in moon shadow, possessing the power needed to fulfill the family's mission.

"She's beautiful, Mama," Petra said in hushed awe. Amani's oldest daughter stood beside her, her gaze fixed upon her newest sister.

Amani offered a weak smile while her sisters busied themselves counting fingers and toes and caressing dark, wet curls. She alone could appreciate the mystical beauty of the eclipse, now that her part was over. The gentle aura touched her like a blessing.

Vera, the youngest of her sisters, leaned over her and whispered, "You have your seventh now. Are you pleased?"

Amani heard the envy beneath her sister's words. If not for a stillborn infant, Vera would've been the seventh. The honor would've been hers. *If honor this could be called*, she thought wryly. Vera wore her bitterness like a woolen cloak, heavy and scratchy, keeping herself within and alone.

1

Still breathless, Amani answered back in short, broken phrases. "Be glad it wasn't you. I would not wish this ordeal on my worst enemy." But what Amani served as reconciliation, Vera tasted as bitter offense.

"So I am now your enemy," Vera stated, her tone as twisted as her smile.

"You're my sister and always will be."

Vera grimaced as if biting into bitter fruit. Once they had been close, and no one loved Amani more, save that she was seventh and Vera was not. The envy that fact had sown grew as each daughter was born—the seven that might have been Vera's—until the weight of her bitterness had crushed the bond the two had shared.

Amani turned from Vera to face again the preternatural twilight. Moonshadow weighed heavy upon her, and she longed for the return of the sun and its clean, pure light.

Quickly, before the other comes. The thought came abruptly, so alien, she could not believe it her own. Before she could ponder it, though, the pain of labor returned with sudden and insistent ferocity. She tried to curl around it, to contain and deny it. Young Petra stroked the sweaty hair from her face.

"It's all right now, Mama. It's over."

Amani shook her head. "No," was all she could gasp as another contraction possessed her. She let loose a cry as if the mere sound of her voice could make the pain stop.

The others came to her, once more murmuring encouragement and concern. She looked past them to the window, to the dark hole of the eclipse.

As she bore down, she sought to embrace that dark promise, to tumble into the emptiness at its center and take refuge there. But her sisters held her, gently pressing her back into the bedding, and the moon was too far away.

Her muted groan burst into a scream as she felt something tear. The second baby slid free, slick with blood. In that instant, beads of brilliant crimson broke out at the moon's rim, corrupting the delicate aura. A blaze of white fire heralded the sun as it emerged from the moon's custody. Amani collapsed back onto the pillows, drained of energy, emptied of will, gasping for breath that would not come.

"Another girl!" someone cried out. "Twins!"

Amani shuddered.

"What do we do now?" another asked.

"There's nothing in the legends about twins."

"This changes everything. Our mission is corrupted."

Amani didn't care who said what. It didn't matter. She wanted only to sleep. She drifted off listening to the strained, whispered argument as her sisters cleaned up the room, the bed, and her own exhausted body.

~ * ~

When Amani awoke, the curtains were drawn against the natural darkness of night. She was alone except for the two infants—one in the cradle prepared for her, the other in a drawer hastily emptied and lined with blankets. She moved her hand across her abdomen, feeling its new flatness, the emptiness within.

Someone entered and slipped across the shadows to hover over the cradle and makeshift bed. Amani struggled to sit up, and the figure turned, hugging a white bundle close to her bosom.

"Vera?" Amani asked in dazed concern. "What's wrong?" The question echoed in her mind like the pealing of funeral bells. She began to tremble.

"What is it, Vera? Is something wrong?"

"Shh. Go back to sleep."

Amani listened to the whisper of silence beyond the door, laden with guilt and mourning.

"What's wrong, Vera? Is it one of the babies?" Her heart lurched with fear. *Please, let them live. I cannot do this again!* She struggled to sit up, but her limbs felt as fluid as quicksilver.

"Your daughter is fine," Vera insisted, but Amani would not believe her. Vera crossed the room.

"Rest, Amani," she said with her persimmon frown. "Your work, at least, is finished." She leaned forward to bestow a kiss on Amani's forehead. The bundle shifted, and Amani saw the face of her new daughter. *Which one?*

Without another word, Vera left.

Even the distant, heavy closing of a door could not break the grim silence that settled upon the birthing room. Amani wrestled free of the bedclothes, then stood panting, clinging to the bedpost. Her skin itched as blood ran down her thighs, and she pressed a hand against the sharp, deep pain in her empty womb.

She made her way to the bedroom door, then the hall, and finally leaned heavily against the parlor doorway. Her sisters, seated on sofa and chairs as if at a wake, kept their gazes nailed to their laps. Only Petra dared to look up, and her face was streaked with tears.

"What have you done?" Amani cried out to them. "Oh, dear God, what have you done?" she murmured as the walls circled around her and the floor rose up to embrace her in darkness.

Part One

New Moon on the Horizon

MOONRISE: 4:25 a.m. CST ~ MOONSET: 7:35 p.m. CST
SUNRISE: 4:37 a.m. CST ~ SUNSET: 6:59 p.m. CST
Monday, May 10, 1937

GALEN WILLIAMS

"Miss Orlov, is that you?"

A shadow flowed across the campus quad, all but opaque against the glare of the lowering sun. Galen Williams could barely discern the figure standing at its heart, but there was no mistaking that plume of red hair. He waved hesitantly at the student, but she appeared not to notice. She was staring into the bushes on her left, a tangle of naked twigs and branches bearing only a few dried leaves. Galen could see nothing there of interest and stepped closer. He stopped where the shadow spilled across the walkway, reminding him of blood.

Edward's blood. Eight years later, it still haunted him. He hugged his books against his chest, hesitating to enter the shadow's realm, lest he choke on that darkened air.

"Miss Orlov?" Galen called a second time. Still, she did not answer. He normally would not associate with students, maintaining a professional detachment stoic in its intensity. Yet he could not ignore the student trapped at the shadow's core. *And why should he consider her so,* he wondered, for she was only a woman standing alone. Yet a certain tension framed her posture and a sense of menace breathed chill upon the nape of his neck. "Miss Orlov, is something wrong?"

GIL ORLOV

Gil Orlov heard someone call her name, but found herself unable to respond.

Something waited here. Not the Other—that presence she knew too intimately. No, this felt different, ancient—the dust of catacombs, feral and potent. Its dark hunger frightened her. Something that wanted that fiercely could not be good.

She had sensed it the moment she entered the shadow that hung like a veil across the campus sidewalk—familiar and alien

6

and utterly pervasive. A presence ignored until called to notice, colored by an overwhelming sense of *wrong*. She raised her hand against its influence.

I am the seventh daughter of a seventh daughter, she thought, but could not give the words voice. That frightened her as much as whatever lurked in the bush. *I should have power over this, and I don't.*

It swept such thoughts aside, leaves skittering on the pavement. In the sudden void, whispers hissed in her mind, water on flame. Sweetened lies, silken deceit.

I'm not prepared for this, she thought, and quickly pushed that doubt aside. Yet its echo persisted. *I'm not prepared, and I should be.*

She shuddered, yet failed to banish its presence, overwhelmed by its potent lure. Its passion summoned her.

Curious, naïve, unprepared, her spirit began to yield. Incarnate now, the entity emerged from the core of the shadow and stood before her. She drifted toward it.

GALEN

At first, Galen thought the animal a mere dog, but the fur, dun colored and coarse, and its feral crouch set one thought against another.

A coyote? argued one side.

It can't be. This is Chicago, countered logic.

But it is.

The beast paced back and forth, ears laid back and teeth bared. Still, Orlov did not move.

Holding his breath, Galen lunged across the shadow's edge. Eyes adjusting to the dimmer light, he watched Orlov reach out her hand. The animal crouched back on its haunches, preparing to spring. Galen tried to yell. Words wouldn't come, some bit of darkness clogging his throat. He sought a weapon, but found none at hand—not even a stone—only the books he carried. Hefting the largest, he hurled it at the beast as it sprang.

The heavy tome glanced off the animal's flank. With a yelp that was more surprise than hurt, it twisted in mid-air, snapping at the fluttering pages. Dropping the rest of his burden, Galen charged forward, waving his arms and yelling. The beast turned toward him, hackles raised and a low growl issuing from its throat. The two faced one another like competing suitors. The animal's gaze held a startling malevolence, marking Galen down to the very core of his being. A snarl vibrated deep in its throat.

Abruptly, the beast shook itself, shedding the darkness. The savagery left its eyes. With a whimper, it cowered then turned and ran, dragging the shadow in its wake.

Galen leaned forward, hands braced on shaking knees, the reality of what had just happened overwhelming the rush of the moment. Orlov was still staring after the animal, and Galen wondered at her calm. He touched her shoulder lightly. She started, then turned to gaze at him, blinking.

"Are you all right?" he asked.

Her mouth opened and closed wordlessly. Her fingers trembled as they scratched at the air. Galen feared she might faint, and then what would he do? He glanced around to see if anyone witnessed this encounter, but the campus quad was unusually empty.

"Professor Williams," she answered at last, with a deep sigh as if she'd been holding her breath. "I am fine." And then she began to tremble and rubbed her arms as if chilled. She cocked her head to one side and regarded him with a slightly bemused expression at odds with the pale terror still lingering in her eyes.

"Thank you, Professor. You may have saved my life—or at the very least, my soul."

Galen arched an eyebrow at such melodrama, yet shivered at the possibilities. To avoid the measure of her regard, he turned to retrieve his book from the grass where it had landed, glancing at its spine.

"Hmm, saved by Malthus, actually. There must be some irony in that." He turned to gather the other books.

Orlov stooped to help him. "Still, you have potential."

An odd thing for a student to say to her teacher, and Galen wasn't sure if he were offended or amused. But the remark seemed more curious than critical, a mere and casual observation. Did it mean he was forgiven past failures?

Then she added, "There's a touch of hero in you after all."

Galen frowned. "I don't want to be a hero." Heroes took chances; they risked their security. Heroes didn't let their brothers die. To avoid the topic, he asked, "Are you certain you're unharmed?"

Orlov nodded, shook her head, then shrugged.

"Perhaps I should escort you home," Galen suggested, gesturing toward the row of dormitories where he assumed she lived. He ushered her towards them. After a period of awkward silence, Galen commented, "A coyote in Chicago." He shook his head, still not willing to believe what he had seen. "Have you ever seen one?"

Orlov nodded absently, as if distracted by another conversation. "In New Mexico we call them tricksters."

"New Mexico?" The coed now seemed as out of place and exotic as the coyote. "I had no idea. What brought you to Chicago?"

She merely shrugged. "The curriculum suits my purpose. There's much I need to learn."

A distant howl shivered the air. Galen wondered if there might be more than one animal. Didn't coyotes hunt in packs?

"But how did it get here? I suppose it's possible, via the Midway. But I've never heard of such animals approaching people, especially in broad daylight." He paused to consider the failing light and realized he was on the verge of senseless babbling, and swallowed hard the lump of lingering fear. "What do you suppose it was doing here?"

"It wanted me," Orlov murmured, and even more softly, "I wonder why." Galen thought she'd not intended for him to hear.

"Perhaps it's rabid," he observed, then hastily added, "Though I'm certain it must be far away by now."

They had reached the dormitories, limestone faced and ivy cloaked. Orlov stopped, gazing in the direction the coyote had fled, then shook herself as if shedding the entire incident. "Thank you, Professor. I'm quite safe now, and I don't believe it'll return."

Galen nodded, keeping a respectable six feet from the young woman. Better not to be seen escorting the woman into the building—it might start a compromising rumor. Its Gothic façade seemed to glower down at him. "I'll see you tomorrow in class, then."

He didn't wait to see her enter. Instead, he hurried on his way, paying close attention to the shadows bleeding across the lawns and pavement and whatever they might hide.

MOONRISE: 5:17 a.m. CST ~ MOONSET: 8:46 p.m. CST
SUNRISE: 4:35 a.m. CST ~ SUNSET: 7:00 p.m. CST
Tuesday, May 11

GALEN

"Miss Orlov, are you with us today?"

Galen stood behind his lectern with arms crossed as he regarded the young woman. He considered Orlov a most promising student, if only he could convince her to continue beyond this basic course. But now she sat staring out the window, her chin resting in the cupped palm of her hand, her focus elsewhere. His gaze shifted to see what might distract her so, a quiver of expectation stirring within him. *Something waits,* a voice not quite his own murmured in his mind. *It's coming.*

Spring fever, he thought. It swept the campus, more virulent than influenza. He considered opening the windows to let in fresh air, thinking that might revive his listless students. But more likely, their thoughts would simply escape into the sunlight, and he'd lose them entirely. Fantasies lurked beyond that glass barrier, whispering of adventure, romance—anything but the cold, harsh reality of Economics 101.

Galen, himself, felt a gentle pressure, his center of balance shifting sunward. Spring. Each pregnant bud a promise. *Something's coming.* He frowned at such whimsy. His expression mistaken for disapproval, a ripple of motion flowed across the room, a subtle tensing and shifting accompanied by barely voiced murmurs. A student coughed in quiet expectation.

"Miss Orlov?" Galen called again, with a calculated trace of impatience. *What do you see there?* he wondered. What creatures roam your fantasy? Another coyote or something more fantasy than fact?

Orlov turned her head slowly from the window, the light catching in the bright burgundy of her hair. Her gaze lingered, then followed reluctantly, and she blinked sunlight and daydreams from her eyes. Yet no trace of yesterday's encounter remained in her mien. It had become a surreal memory, not quite to be believed.

"Have you ever seen a solar eclipse, Professor?" she asked, as if her mind still wandered some sun-dappled hinterland.

The class responded with chuckles and snickers, but Galen was taken aback, not so much by her question as by the sharp tang of memory it invoked. Black moon disk, pale, blue fire.

"As a matter of fact, I have," he answered boldly, yielding to the temptation to impress his class with something beyond theories of commerce. A momentary diversion wouldn't hurt if it would keep Orlov's attention *here*. "In June of 1918, the path of totality crossed the United States from Washington state to Florida. The partial phase was visible throughout the country." His gaze drifted to the ceiling to calculate time passed. "But then, all of you—" He waved his arm to include the rest of the class. "—were mere babes-in-arms, I suppose."

Orlov nodded, then announced, "I was born in its shadow. My mother traveled to Denver so that would be so."

Galen backed away from the intimacy of that statement, his hands gripping the shield of his lectern. Such personal topics might threaten his scrupulous reputation. Yet like a bright pebble found on an unknown trail, he couldn't resist picking it up and tucking it away in a hidden pocket in his mind.

"Interesting. But what does it have to do with economics or John Keynes?" Galen asked, seeking to coax her attention once again to the here and now. Orlov winced as if she had sampled something distasteful.

"Keynes corrupts the world with false premises," she answered with unusual vehemence. "He is as much a threat as Communism or the Nazis."

Ah, the challenge, he thought, brushing back the sand-colored hair falling across his forehead. "Really, now." He raised one bushy eyebrow to regard his student with bemused skepticism.

At the edge of his vision, Galen noted most of the class settling back as if to enjoy the show. Only a handful shifted forward, eager for battle. *Vultures,* he thought. He, himself, leaned back against the wall and folded his arms. He dared to hold Orlov's gaze, to pin it here, in this room, at this time. "Rather harsh judgment from a freshman. On what do you base this accusation?"

"'Fair is foul and foul is fair; for foul is useful and fair is not,'" she quoted as if the words themselves tasted bitter. "Keynes wrote that in 1930, when people crushed by the Depression were desperate and vulnerable. It tempts the poor and the broken to set aside their values and moral judgment in the name of survival, to 'make gods of avarice, usury and precaution for a little while longer.' But who is to say how much is enough?"

Galen shuddered. *Who is to say, indeed?* What price security? How much wealth could prevail against the vagaries of commerce? How much money would ensure his world would never again collapse as it had in '29? More, and a little more, and just a little more. An exponential curve that approached but would never equal that magical, ethereal quantity of *enough*. Could any amount scrub the stain from his memory as October rains had washed Edward's blood from the sidewalk?

But to Orlov he said, "Ah, but we're talking economics, not philosophy. The Depression is over, or nearly so, and I don't see society wallowing in depravity and greed."

"It's not over yet, Professor. The market will crash once more, and far worse will follow. The pattern is set and woven— it's too late to stop it." Her gaze wandered again toward the window. "Already, it's too late."

Galen leaned forward against the lectern as if he could physically catch her thoughts and hold them prisoner. *Another pebble in the trail,* he thought. But this one was soft, crumbling before he could quite grasp it.

"What could be worse than economic collapse and upheaval?" Galen challenged in response, thinking of breadlines and tent cities and…He shuddered. *Despair. Edward's despair, too much to endure.*

With a sigh, Orlov turned to meet his gaze with unflinching certitude. "War with Germany. The whole world at war," she said aloud. Her hand stroked the air half an inch above her desk. "The Nazis spread their evil across Europe. They will do unspeakable things."

Students stirred uneasily. Were they embarrassed by her rambling or discomfited by the images evoked?

"The entire world on fire," Orlov continued, speaking so quietly, Galen was not certain he heard the words or merely read them from her lips. She squeezed tight her eyes and clutched the edges of her desk. An instant's flash of light and heat startled Galen, but in the next moment, it was gone and forgotten. Orlov hugged herself, holding some dark memory.

A student to Galen's left snorted derisively, reminding Galen that he and Orlov were not alone in the room.

Galen turned on the young man. "And your opinion, Mr. Johnson?"

"We would never go to war; we have enough problems already."

"Ah, but economically speaking, would war be such a bad thing?" Galen spread his arms out wide, an invitation to the entire class. "Even among the ancient Greeks, war was a tool to boost a failing economy."

His challenge went unanswered; the class merely stared back at him, empty of thought. A student in the second row surreptitiously flipped through his textbook. Johnson began a statement that had the sound of mimicry rather than original thought.

Galen slapped the lectern with the flat of his hand, startling even Orlov to attention. "The answer's not in your text! Nor will you find it in your father's rhetoric, Mr. Johnson. You must seek it for yourselves. Think! Knowledge isn't some elixir poured out for your consumption." He hefted his own text and wagged it in the air.

"This is not knowledge! This is nothing more than fact and theorem—beads and baubles. Take them up, handle them. Hold them up to the light and examine their flaws. Then string them on threads of logic and experience. *That* is knowledge! Not the facts themselves, but what you do with them." He paused, breathless, and only then realized he was ranting. Setting down the book, he took a slow, deep breath to settle himself. Students stared at him as if he'd gone quite mad, but over by the window, Orlov nodded as if in approval and let slip a smile. *You have potential.*

His outburst released some hidden gate, releasing a debate. Slow and cautious at first, it gathered momentum. Galen glanced aside in time to see Orlov's attention flutter out the window once more. *Follow me,* it beckoned, and his mind's inner voice took up the chant. *Follow me. Follow—*

The tolling of the tower bells startled him. Whatever else the voice whispered was lost in the slamming of textbooks and scrape of chairs, the chatter of students scurrying to escape.

He imagined them chatting about his uncharacteristic outburst, his duel with Orlov. What would the dean think should he find out? He couldn't understand their babble, but a random word, a shred of phrase, indicated the discussion continued. He smiled; perhaps he'd done something right after all.

Shrugging the class from his mind, he turned to erase his notes from the blackboard, still wondering what had gotten into him to make him spout off so. This was only his second year teaching. He shouldn't take such chances, risking the security of his faculty position. The thought chilled him and caused his arm to hesitate in mid-swipe.

A small sound, a feeling of *presence*, caught his notice. He turned into Orlov's patient gaze. Her eyes always startled him, intense green flecked with blue and brown and ancient gold. The burning red of her hair might catch the attention, but the eyes held it.

Galen coughed away a catch in his throat. Orlov usually slipped in and out of the room unnoticed, as if she preferred as much as he to maintain a distance. Now she stood scarcely five feet away, with only the lectern between them.

Galen took a step back.

"A touch of spring fever today, Miss Orlov?" He gazed wistfully out at the campus quad. A haze of green hovered, snagged in empty branches, and a blush of pink. *It's coming.* "I can't say that I blame you." *Be ready.*

"Professor, do you have a minute?"

Galen raised his eyebrows and cocked his head. *What pebble are you bringing this time?* "Is it about that question you missed on the midterm exam?" She'd had perfect scores all semester, and to miss such an easy question— "You should've known it was Sismondi." A thought strayed across his mind. "Did you miss it on purpose?"

She regarded him as if he'd been the one to miss something. "Someday you'll need it," Orlov replied. Half a smile pinched the corner of her mouth, as cryptic as her words.

"Then yesterday—"

Orlov shook her head. "I owe you thanks for that, but no— though it did confirm my choice. I must ask something of you."

Galen felt the briefest surge of panic. Did she think yesterday's small deed marked a change in attitude? He stroked his fingers through his hair and frowned. *Don't do this. Not again,* he thought, as if she might read his mind. *You know I don't get involved in students' problems.*

"I need talk to you before I leave."

Galen's frown twisted in confusion and consternation. "Leave?" he asked, wondering what he'd missed. The look on her face confirmed her words.

"Aah," he said, shifting his weight from right foot to left. Stalling. "I have a faculty meeting, and I'm already late." *I owe you nothing. My job is to teach, no more or less.*

She traced a finger along the edge of the lectern. A twitch at the corner of her mouth threatened to shatter a fragile composure. His own resolve turned to ash. That sense of anticipation again fluttered in his gut. *Something's coming.*

"I have office hours this afternoon."

But Orlov shook her head. "I'll be gone by then." She hesitated, eyeing the students filing in for the next class. "It's something personal."

Another pebble. How could he leave it be? *Don't lose her.* A deep and deliberate sigh released his resolve. He gathered up his own books and notes, then made a show of consulting his watch. "Ten o'clock, then." He caught several glances cast his way, his lowered voice attracting the very attention he sought to avoid. "I can give you five minutes."

She nodded with a grateful sigh and moved toward the door. Galen followed. Harry Tucker stood in the doorway, leaning against the jamb and obviously enjoying the scene. Galen winced, wondering how much the teaching assistant had witnessed and what he would think of "something personal."

Harry's gaze flicked over Orlov as she passed, and he winked at Galen.

"Nice," he said from the corner of his mouth, in a voice meant only for Galen.

"Forget it, Harry," Galen cut in. "You know me better than that." The feeling he'd made a mistake unwound from his stomach to trickle along his spine.

"Yeah, but I keep hoping," Harry responded with a sly grin. Harry had the looks and money—and the reputation—that attracted women. Black, wavy hair slicked back and a pencil-thin mustache, almost a Clark Gable look-alike. Not like Galen, whose features were hewn rugged and blunt, a sculpture unfinished. The line of his bushy brows slanted to the left, his mouth lifting toward it, skewing his aspect. Thick, brown hair refused to stay groomed. Hardly professorial.

Galen pushed past Harry, hoping his friend would leave well enough alone, but Harry kept pace with him down the hallway.

"Don't tell me the great master of ethics and honor is interested in—"

"Not interested so much as intrigued, Harry." Galen glanced ahead. Orlov had already vanished into the tide of passing students. "She's the best student I have. She managed to explain Ricardo's Labor Theory so even that twit, Johnson, could understand it. She's an enigma, Harry."

"And a pretty one, at that. So tell me about her."

"There's nothing to tell."

Harry gazed down the hall, squinting as if peering at some memory. "She's the one—Last fall, she claimed Sullivan tried to get her between the sheets."

"Not in such crass words," Galen said in sharp reproach. "The women's dean took care of it." Much to his own relief.

Harry nodded. "Swept it under the rug, if you ask me." He stopped abruptly. "She asked you for help, didn't she?"

Galen considered the comment. Had he gotten involved, would the outcome have been different? "A second year assistant against a tenured professor? Professional suicide, if you ask me. I couldn't take the risk." An icy shudder trickled down his spine. He'd been right not to get involved. Hadn't he?

"No, I suppose not," Harry replied, seeming disappointed.

"I had to turn her down," Galen argued. "You know I don't get involved in students' personal problems. Not then, not now." *But maybe I should,* he thought. He recalled the look of betrayal on Orlov's face when he'd refused to intervene, afraid for his own security. The incident had set a distance between them he'd found safe and comfortable—until now.

"Now she says she's leaving, though." Galen added.

"Ah, intriguing. The lure of mystery!"

Galen waved him off. "Don't you have a class or something, Harry?" He strode down the hall intent on outdistancing both Harry and the whole incident.

~ * ~

At ten o'clock, Orlov waited outside his office. Galen feigned mild surprise, as if he'd forgotten. As if he hadn't been distracted throughout the meeting, wondering what could possibly be *something personal*. Female students, more interested in husbands than degrees, often pursued unmarried professors. Vulnerable to gossip and scandal, Galen nurtured a distinct emotional distance, avoiding anything that might threaten the tenuous security of his position.

Unlocking the door, he ushered Orlov into the office, glancing around the small room, trying to assess it in her eyes. This was his sanctuary, a retreat from the empty chatter, the casual chaos. The dreams that would never come true. Too small to be cozy and too crowded to ever be considered neat, there was a precision to the marching rows of books, the stacks of papers. Galen knew the exact location of every piece of paper, each volume.

He cleared a chair of exam papers, hefting them to take their measure in minutes spent grading rather than pounds. Weighing the noise in the hall against the propriety of having a female student in his office, he used the exams to prop the door ajar and gestured for Orlov to sit.

As he rounded his desk to take his own seat, however, the papers slid out in a wide fan, and the door swung closed anyway. He glanced at Orlov as if it was her doing. She sat straight-backed and rigid on the edge of the chair, hugging a folder against her middle, so taut she almost trembled.

His own hard oak chair creaked as he leaned back and laced his fingers across his stomach. He studied her face. He'd never had the courage to ask for her first name, nor had she ever offered. The student rolls listed her only as G. M. Orlov. Privately, he thought of her as GeM, but he would never voice such familiarity. "So what is so important, Miss Orlov?"

She started, the folder slipping forward in uncertain offering. She caught it, held it captive in her lap, and bit at her lower lip as if reconsidering her purpose.

"Do you know there's going to be a total eclipse in Peru next month? Wonderful, mystical things happen during eclipses. Things of power and enchantment."

"That's hardly a scientific observation." Yet he could almost agree. He remembered standing in the farmyard as the sun abruptly disappeared. The black hole hovering in the sky tugged at his very soul, a ring of blue fire igniting a passion for astronomy, first as a hobby later as a college major. It had taken worldwide depression, economic collapse, and a bleak Tuesday to quench that enchantment. It'd taken his brother's blood spilled on the sidewalk.

He shook the memory from his shoulders.

"This isn't what you wanted to talk about, is it?" he asked, irritated that a trivial question could dredge up such unwanted memories. Eight years later, shouldn't he be free?

Orlov took a deep breath, addressing a task she'd rather avoid, had been avoiding for some time perhaps. "It's about the final exam," she said obliquely, choosing now to approach the problem from yet another angle. She held out the folder. "Since I won't be here, I was hoping you'd accept this instead." When he didn't reach for it, she set it on the edge of his desk.

"You mentioned leaving," he responded, hoping he'd misunderstood. "I thought you meant only—" A knot formed in his throat, choking off the next word. "Permanently?" He felt more than a little concern, even a strong sense of empathy. Eight years ago, he'd faced his favorite teacher with much the same pronouncement.

She could only nod, and Galen noticed now how the corners of her mouth twitched, battling against a frown. He thought that had she tried to speak, she would have shattered into a thousand pieces, each one a silver tear.

"When?"

"Today." She barely managed the word. A deep breath, then, "This afternoon. Now." Her gaze dropped into her lap and tangled in her fingers as they twisted restively.

"What is it?" He leaned forward, one hand extended across the desk. He wanted to call her by name, but had none. Orlov was too impersonal, G.M. a corporation. He dared not call her GeM, could not imagine voicing that private name aloud.

"You're not, um—?" There was generally one reason female students left school so abruptly, though he could not imagine Orlov in such a condition.

"No!" She shook her head, by her expression greatly disappointed that he would think such of her.

"A problem with money, then?" he asked. "That's common enough, these days. It happened to me, you know." He leaned back into lecture pose. "When Wall Street crashed, it took my family's fortune with it. We lost everything." Galen paused in his telling, tasting bitter memories. No single cause, but a series of events, tumbling like dominos.

"I dropped out of Cornell but eventually finished school here." He had abandoned astronomy for economics, desperate to understand what had happened to his family, to protect them and make sure it never happened again. He'd chosen teaching to help others avoid the same fate. Galen continued, feeling quite smug that he could so easily advise her. "I succeeded. You can, too, if you want it badly enough. There are scholarships and jobs. I understand there's a new work program for students, the National Youth Administration. You could—"

"No, it's not money," Orlov imposed. "It's a family matter." Once more, her gaze focused on some undefined realm.

Memories whispered of despair and conflict. The ring of the telephone, his brother's voice. "I'm sorry," Edward had said, and "I've let you down." That'd been Edward's final message, that and "Good-bye." Galen hadn't understood, not until it was too late to tell him it wasn't his fault.

"I hope no one has died," he said to Orlov.

Orlov pressed her lips in a flat, thin line. "It's not something easily explained, not here or now, at least. I have an obligation to fulfill."

Galen started to comb his fingers through his hair. He caught the gesture and brought his hand down, held it with the other on his desk. He sensed he was about to let her down again. Something important eluded his grasp, pebbles all turned to sand.

I don't get involved with students' personal lives. Once before he had told her that. Why was it this time, the words once glibly spoken now clogged his throat and refused to come forth? As much as he worked diligently to keep himself aloof and separate, at this moment he wished otherwise.

"What can I do?" he asked finally. His throat tightened around the words, reluctant to let them loose.

A smile flickered and took hold, Orlov's expression one of relief, as if he'd made an offer she'd hoped for but couldn't bring herself to request. Her eyes brightened with expectation.

"I have a journey to complete." Her tone suggested something beyond mere geography. "It requires an escort, a guardian. Someone I can trust."

Galen pushed back in his chair, tilting it against the wall behind him. *What is she asking? Certainly not—* "Surely, you have family. A brother or cousin, perhaps. A close friend?"

She shook her head. "Only aunts and sisters," she said, and then, "It's a long way to Peru."

Galen felt his brow pucker in confusion. What were they talking about now? Her journey? The eclipse? Were the two connected somehow?

The tremor he'd felt earlier returned, a quivering sense of anticipation, a mouse trembling in darkness. He held himself still, so perfectly still, the cat waiting to pounce. But his prey eluded him, slipping back to whatever nether regions it had come from. He let out his breath slowly, so Orlov wouldn't know he'd been holding it.

But she watched him with a curious half smile, as if she did know, and more than he. As if aware of his thoughts and more important, where they would lead him.

"Dreams are such fragile things, Professor," she said. "Too often people throw them away when they break, thinking they cannot be mended. You had dreams once. Did you keep the pieces? Where did they go?"

Down the gutter with Edward's blood, Galen thought bleakly. Out in the trash with a box of certificates suddenly worth less than the match that reduced them to ashes. He sat there, trapped by his own history.

A sharp tap startled him. A woman opened the door but did not enter. Backlit by the hallway lights, Galen could barely make out her features. Older than Orlov, yet apparently related, though she was tall and thin, brown-haired and severe of face. The woman ignored him and spoke directly to Orlov. "Here you are. It's time to go. We have a long journey ahead of us." Then her gaze raked over Galen and she presented him a flat, sour frown. He wondered what he'd done to earn such scorn.

Orlov appeared about to protest, but a subtle change trickled down her face, across her shoulders. Whatever she'd wanted to ask of him dissolved into dust and drifted away. She stood, gathering herself like so many shards.

Galen stood also.

"I hope we meet again some place," she said with that same quirky smile that hinted at secrets. She walked out the door, pulling it shut behind her.

Galen sat abruptly, suddenly released from an unseen tether.

She'd just left a handful of pebbles, but he had no idea where they might lead. He moved to brush his hands across his desk to scatter those pebbles into oblivion, but Orlov's report sat squarely in the center. And that was odd because he was certain she'd taken it with her. He stared at its cover. "Economics in the Land of the Inca," the title read. There was more to this than a simple grade, he thought. She had come to ask him something. Why had she changed her mind?

Perplexed, he flicked through the pages, and an envelope fell out. Within, he found a sheet of blue paper and a crudely drawn map. The paper was a travel voucher. Grace Lines USS Santa Inez, departing New York May 14, destination, port of Callao, Peru, arriving May 27.

Galen's first thought was that Orlov had accidentally left the envelope in the folder—hadn't she mentioned a journey? He hurried out into the hallway. Two floors below, a door closed, the echoing *click-thunk* only accenting the emptiness.

Should he chase after her? Find a student to deliver the envelope to her dorm—and how would that look? He glanced again at the blue paper, seeking an answer to the dilemma, and finding further cause for concern instead. The voucher read:

Passenger name: Galen S. Williams.

He shook his head and brushed at his hair, as if that would clear his sight. He read the name again, and it was indeed his own. Galen's hand began to shake, and he clenched the voucher tight to make it stop, crumpling the flimsy paper. It had to be a mistake; he couldn't accept this. But that maddening inner voice whispered promises of adventure and wonder.

He paced across his office to the window, one hand raking his hair to scratch at a sudden itch. Looking out upon the campus quad, he saw the two women hurrying toward South University and a waiting taxi. Orlov paused to turn and stare directly at his window, as if she expected him to be watching. Her hand raised in a short wave. It was a challenge, a "guess-what-I'm-up-to" lure. A pebble of inordinate color.

Teachers didn't accept gifts from students. They certainly didn't journey halfway around the world with them. If someone found out, it could jeopardize his reputation, his security. And security was the most important thing in his life.

He stared after the taxi as it drove off then looked down at the paper in his hand. He might not be able to return it, but he didn't have to use it. The thought of leaving now, near the semester's end, was ridiculous, anyway. The Dean would never grant him leave of absence—and second-year teachers didn't dare ask for one, anyway.

Yet his thoughts kept turning to the 1918 eclipse. He remembered watching, but could not recall the event itself. No image sustained the dream that had once shaped his future.

Like someone waking, momentarily disoriented, he gazed at the books on his shelves, the sum total of his existence, and found they lacked meaning. He circled the room, finding even the smell of it loathsome. How did he get here? Where had the dream gone and was it too late to follow?

Yet he had papers to grade, classes to teach, final exams to prepare. He had obligations. How dare Orlov tempt him with dead and broken dreams? How dare she open old wounds?

With a sigh, he crushed the voucher in his hand and dropped it into the trash.

Wednesday, May 12

SESHA ORLOV

Sesha Orlov felt the early morning chill as she entered the canyon. The sun still loitered behind the ridge, and shadow painted the steep rock walls and puddled among the boulders of its floor. Mist hovered over the creek tumbling through the narrow gorge.

The narrow trail dodged a pinion pine to bump up against a boulder the size of a large shed. The angular rock jutted out over the creek like the bow of a ship, a single juniper captaining its prow. Sesha climbed around the boulder's edge and along its spine to stand beside the spindly, twisted trunk. The creek cut through a narrow cleft, stumbling down a staircase of broken rock. She gazed at the turbid water, heavy with snowmelt from the Chuska Mountains, and surveyed the patterns of foam and wave.

A branch stretched out over the creek, only waist high—it had seemed much higher when she was eight. She had hung a rope from that branch and swung out over the chasm—great fun until the limb cracked, almost plunging her into the creek. Gil had tried to heal it, her clumsy effort leaving it bent with an arthritic knuckle. As solemnly as only a seven-year-old could be, Gil had then informed Sesha she shouldn't be doing such crazy stunts. Gazing down at the rocks and water below, Sesha shuddered at what might have happened. They had vowed never to tell anyone else about the incident, just one of many secrets they shared.

Another waited above, just above the wide talus slope that skirted the canyon's cliffs. The wide, narrow niche sheltered beneath a cap of obdurate sandstone couldn't be seen from below. No trail led beyond this point, only narrow tracks carved by deer and bighorn sheep across the broken rock.

Sesha would wait for Gil there, in that secret place only the two of them knew.

GIL

After the long flight to Albuquerque and the longer drive west to the family ranch, Gil was tempted to sleep in. An unsettling mix of anticipation and anxiety awakened her early, scattering the remnants of a worrisome dream she was all too eager to abandon.

Even at this pre-dawn hour, the sparrow-chattering of aunts and sisters filled the air as they shouted from one room to one another, from upstairs to down. Discussion bordered on argument and discourse came close to bickering. Their tension threaded through the house, a cat's cradle of wants and needs and wills.

"Where's Sesha," Gil asked, missing the one face she longed most to see. Older than Gil by scarcely ten months, Sesha was the closest of her sisters. *Almost a twin.* That thought oddly called to mind the Other—that enigmatic presence tethered to her soul like Earth and Moon.

"She said you'd know where to meet," Aunt Ada responded, waving her wooden spoon in no particular direction. Gil found her favorite horse already saddled and waiting, and so she fled the conflict and chaos for the deep quiet of the shadowed canyon behind the ranch.

Petra would be in a high dither when she discovered Gil had left, but she had her own preparations to make, of a different nature than packing clothes and collecting equipment. More than an escape from the chaos or a trek into childhood nostalgia, it had the feel of ceremony and ritual, of arrangements no less essential than schedules and passports.

So different from Chicago, New Mexico seemed a different world. The Depression had hardly touched this area, perhaps because there was little here it could harm. No economic folly could diminish the mountains or stain the desert's stark colors. The land endured, unchanging, and so did its people.

Even time kept a different pace here. Gil slowed to match that pace, as if she could in turn slow time itself. She drew a deep breath and stopped altogether.

Here where the trail became too steep and rocky for horses, Sesha's little roan was tethered to a manzanita bush, eyeing Gil quietly while munching on the woody branches. Gil dismounted and tied her horse beside the other. Sesha would be waiting fur-

24

ther up the canyon, but Gil chose to sit for a moment to catch her breath and her mental bearings.

From this vantage point, her family home looked like a pile of blocks tumbled from the canyon's mouth, the brown adobe in harmony with the surrounding rock and trees. A thin, gray haze marked the road south to Gallup where someone had just recently passed, the dust not yet settled.

"I'm not ready yet!" she shouted at the unhearing sky and the creek rushing by, quick as time, itself. "It's too soon."

But the travels of the sun and the paths of history would not wait for her. The course of events seldom waited upon convenience. Next year's eclipse would be in the south Atlantic, Antarctica the year after that, and not until 1940 would another cross a place of power. Besides, this eclipse would occur on her birthday, perhaps completing something left unfinished. *It must be now, before it's too late.*

She was all too aware of the steady progression, the uncurling of pathways that would shape the next hundred years. So many were already beyond her help, their cries of anguish a sharp pang in her soul.

Images, unbidden and vivid, haunted her soul, the temptation to alter them a maddening itch. One hand rose, unbidden, in her longing to touch them, and in that touching, to mold and shape them to her desires. But her fingers merely drifted through them as if she would grasp smoke.

Something small, a ground squirrel perhaps, rustled in the rabbit brush to her right, and a gray pinion jay berated her intrusion from the branches overhead. Far off, a coyote's thin wail reminded her of the incident in Chicago. She shivered with a sudden chill and shut the images from her mind.

The vibrant red and gold of a New Mexico dawn bled into the rock as the sun crawled out from behind the distant mountains. It painted the cliffs above Gil with golden fire, one of those intense dawns where even the air glowed, as if the lingering haze of the latest Oklahoma dust storm had caught fire.

Like the Vision.

She turned away, but too late.

No! Gil pleaded and braced herself against the rock as the Vision took its cue from the sun. "No, no, no…" she continued in determined whimpers. A futile mantra. The Vision enveloped her, red and black rose blooming on the horizon. The air itself burned, sweeping over her. Her lungs turned to ash even as her skin melted. Her mind screamed with two and a half billion voices as the firestorm engulfed the planet. Not a soul was spared.

SESHA

Silence slid down the canyon, utter calm and peace. No birds rustled in the trees, no lizards skittered across the warming rock, no insects buzzed among the yucca and serviceberry. Overhead, the sky—as blue as her grandmother's turquoise—was barren of cloud. Even the wind fell to stillness, Time holding its breath, waiting for the land to catch up to some predetermined benchmark. Sesha held hers in an effort to hear even the scrape of a snake gliding across the sandstone rock.

Time. According to Aunt Faye, "Sesha" was a Hindu word for time. It set her apart, for her name alone was not among the eight races represented by her grandparents, chosen to include that culture in their great mission. Their lives had been carefully planned, not a single opportunity lost. Even their names had been selected for the power they could invoke.

If she was named for the element of Time, it seemed only proper she should have some control over it. Yet she could no more slow time than she could fly.

Aunt Faye had discovered the Ritual, but Sesha had chosen the location and planned the journey. She believed in it, knew instinctively that it would succeed and had convinced her sisters it was their only hope. In two weeks, they would be in Peru, trekking deep into the Andes.

Why then did she feel such apprehension and misgiving? What detail was she missing?

She brushed at some dirt on her old dungarees and rubbed her arms against the chill of the shadowed air. Just inches from her feet, the sun warmed the rock so that it glowed with color. At her back, the rear wall of the niche was a smooth panel six feet high and thirty wide, covered with red and black handprints of all sizes. The prints overlapped, generations touching one upon another. In joyful profusion, they celebrated life, statements of identity more profound than any memorial erected by civilized man. *I am here; I am alive!* each print proclaimed. *Only I could make this print, this size, this shape. This is me!*

Sesha still wondered how Gil had found the site. She was summoned, Gil had explained, by the memories left behind. Sesha and Gil had often climbed up here to match their own hands against those preserved here for a thousand years and more, seeking one that fit. For these brief minutes at the edge of dawn, light touched the artwork. The handprints of a people long departed appeared to come alive, glowing with ancient power. Gil would press her hand against one, summoning the essence of the person who'd made it, the touch of skin against pigment connecting her across the barrier of time. She would learn their names and hear their voices and would share their memories with Sesha, singing old songs that only the stones remembered. Another secret shared.

The sight of those prints never failed to make Sesha smile. She had not been up here in a long time, too concerned with the business of growing up and planning the future and life in general. She was dismayed to find her hand now larger than any of the prints. The Ancient Ones had been a small people.

The rustle of loose gravel summoned Sesha's attention back to the present. Red hair appeared beyond the lip of the niche as her sister came around the last of the narrow switchbacks, dressed in a green plaid shirt and jeans. She reached the ledge and crawled in to sit beside Sesha, shoulder almost touching her own, feet braced to keep from sliding forward. She was breathing heavily.

"College life must be making you soft," Sesha remarked with affectionate reproach, met by a sour frown.

A dozen "remember-whens" sat poised on Sesha's tongue. The future was a dark hole consuming everything, even their past. After the ritual, nothing would be the same.

"Remember when you tried to put your own hand print there?" Sesha asked, offering her the water canteen.

Her sister smiled tightly in response, her head tilted back, eyes closed against the bright glare. She took a long drink before answering.

"I used red paint from the tool shed. We were twelve."

"When I found out, I made you scrub it off and scolded you for a week." Sesha picked at one of the tiny flecks of red paint yet remaining. "I told you it wasn't right to add your print to theirs. It didn't belong here. I promised never to tell anyone."

Green eyes measured Sesha's face. "Is this a test?"

"No! Not at all," Sesha responded in surprise. "Just a reminder. We've always shared secrets. If you need to talk, I'm here."

Her sister stared into the golden haze spilling down the canyon. "Talk about what?"

"Whatever's bothering you. Petra said you barely spoke three words the entire trip home. But then I don't blame you." She ended with a short laugh. Petra was hardly the most sympathetic ear in the family. Of all the sisters, Sesha alone could read Gil's mood and draw out her confidence. That was the real purpose that had drawn her here. Yet now, this woman might have been a stranger. Had college changed her so much?

Sesha watched her toss a pebble down the slope. It dislodged more stones, gathering followers in its headlong tumble, finally bouncing high over the edge and into the creek, leaving the slope forever changed.

"Are you certain this ritual is necessary?"

Sesha hesitated, selecting her words like fruit at the market. "You were born in the shadow of a total eclipse. There was power in that, power conceived and nurtured. To stand in that shadow again will release what was created that day. The power that will defeat the Vision."

"The power I now lack." Again, the sour frown. "How can you be so certain it will work?"

"It's in the ancient records Aunt Faye found. Trust me, Gil. This will work. Whatever power you need, you will have."

"Power," the other whispered, running the tip of her tongue along her lips as if tasting something sweet. And then, "What if something goes wrong? What if someone interferes?"

Sesha squeezed her sister's hand. "We'll be with you. You won't be alone."

She responded with a long, hard gaze. "Will you? Can you honestly promise you'll be there with *me*?"

"Of course. The family has its differences, but this transcends all that."

"I wish I could believe that," her sister said softly. She closed her eyes and there was a catch in her breath like a wistful sigh.

Sesha clutched her sister's hand and insisted, "We'll be there, Gil. All of us."

The other woman shifted her gaze to the far horizon, her

mouth pressed into a flat line, and Sesha could not read her face. "Yes, all of us," she whispered, then stood abruptly, brushing the dirt from her pants. "Come on. We'd better get back before Petra sends someone to find us. You wouldn't want anyone else to find our secret, would you?" Something pointed and sarcastic in the way she spoke made Sesha wince. She started down at a pace that seemed not to care whether Sesha kept up or not.

"So how did it go with the professor?" Sesha called as she scampered after.

"Which one?"

"What's-his-name? Williams? Did you ask him? Is he coming with us?"

"Ah." Her sister stopped to gaze at the horizon. "I don't know yet."

"But you—" A rock came loose as Sesha stepped on it. It tumbled down the slope, accompanied by a scattering of pebbles and dirt.

Sesha went with it. A single yelp announced her plight. There nothing to grab hold of on the barren slope but winter-dried grasses and tender spring shoots. If she tried to stop, she would only end up tumbling as helpless as a rock. Her only hope was to stay on her feet, controlling her slide like a skier. She let herself go, skipping across the loose debris. One hand trailed behind like a rudder, the other flailed for balance. Except for that brief, initial yelp, she made no sound—she was too busy to give voice to her terror.

Preceding her like a herald, the dislodged rock bounced over the abrupt edge of the lower canyon, falling into the stream below with a deep *plunk* Sesha could hear even above the water's tumult and her own mad scrambling.

Her headlong rush brought her to the massive boulder and its lone juniper. She flung herself toward the trunk of the old juniper but missed. The low branch caught her across the middle, and she hung over the creek, the limb secure under her arms. She weighed much more than when she was eight. The ancient wood creaked and sagged beneath her weight. Spray from the tumbling water leapt at her dangling feet.

With her back to the cliff, Sesha couldn't see her sister coming. She seemed to be taking her time. "Help me, Gil! I'm slipping!"

Footsteps crossed the rock and stopped at the boulder's edge. Sesha kicked her feet behind her, seeking a foothold.

"Gil! Help me!"

Her sister did not answer.

"Gil!"

"I'm not Gilaishling."

The simple words struck like a shard of ice. Sesha slipped. Catching the branch by her hands, she swung around to face the cliff. Her feet still could not gain a secure hold on the smooth, spray-slicked surface. The branch creaked, a sharp snap. Below, the turgid water gurgled in anticipation. Her hands were slipping, the shaggy bark shredding beneath her grasp. Again, the branch uttered another anguished *crack!*

"What do you mean? Of course you are." Sesha tried to swing hand over hand toward the tree's trunk. It only made the limb crack more.

A slow smile carved a wicked arc across her sister's face. "My name is Gemella," she said simply. "It means *twin*."

"Gemella?" Sesha repeated, confused and desperate. The woman continued to stare at her as Sesha struggled.

"You can't tell the difference, can you? You never could."

She turned and walked away.

GIL

The Vision left Gil gasping in the cool morning air. She was both sweating and shivering, trembling. Benumbed lips still shaped her desperate denial. "No." She had fallen, bruising her shoulder on the hard ground, but her fingers curved as if still clutching at the rock.

What was this catastrophe the Vision foretold? Surely, no such power existed on Earth, yet she was convinced that somewhere, someone contemplated it, granting it the realm of possibility with the mere suggestion of a thought. Somewhere, a scientist scribbled symbols and formulae more potent than any wizard's arcane conjuring. How could she stop it if she didn't even know what it was?

And was she meant to? There were those who thought her great grandmother Tuawta's Vision was a warning, as in ancient times, to prepare for an ending as inevitable as the sunset. According to Hopi legend, the gods had destroyed the world three times before, whenever men had become too evil and twisted. Each time, the True People had been warned so they could hide inside the Earth and survive.

But this time mankind was creating its own destruction; there would be no sanctuary for the innocent. The Vision was a mandate. Her purpose was not to fulfill the images of the Vision, but to defeat them. Of that she was certain.

Because of her Visions the tribal elders had banished Tuawta. But instead of stopping her mission, they had freed her to fulfill it. With her Basque husband, she had traveled to the south and to the east, to north and west, discovering others who had similarly been summoned. Her travels had exposed her to a variety of cultures and beliefs and secrets. She had become remarkably well-educated for a fugitive.

"Gil!"

The sound of her name, distant but clear, interrupted Gil's meandering thoughts.

"Gil, help me!" Sesha's voice, full of desperation and terror.

Images flashed across her mind, maddeningly vague. Sesha slipping. Sesha falling. Water and rocks.

"No!" she cried out in protest. *Not Sesha*, she thought. *Please don't take Sesha.*

Gil dashed recklessly up the trail. The steep incline soon forced her to a hurried walk. She held her hand against a sharp stitch in her side.

She shook her head to clear the images that played in her mind, denying their attempt to become reality. Reaching the massive boulder, she clambered up along its side and onto its top. Sesha hung from a branch of the ancient juniper, suspended over the turbulent water. Her grip was slipping, and the branch she clung to had already cracked. Her perspective shifted, an abrupt juxtaposition of time. Had she not healed that branch all those years ago, it wouldn't be here today.

Sesha was too far from the cliff. Even with a foothold on the rock, she had no leverage to push against to reach safety. Gil climbed into the tree. She shinnied out along a thick limb above and just in front of Sesha and reached for her.

"Grab my hand!" she yelled.

Sesha glanced up at her. The look of mistrust and terror she cast almost shook Gil from her perch.

"Sesha, grab my hand!"

Sesha shook her head. "I can't!"

One hand slipped from the branch. Gil lurched forward to grab her sister's wrist.

"I've got you. Let go of the branch."

Sesha glanced up once more. Her mouth tightened into a grimace of sheer determination.

"I've got you! I won't let you fall!"

Sesha let go. Gil swung her up and forward, using her own weight to counterbalance, until Sesha could set her feet on the rock, then pushed her forward. Gil climbed quickly back down the tree while Sesha knelt at the juniper's base.

"Sesha, are you all right?"

"That wasn't funny, Gil! How could you just walk away like that?" Sesha screamed. She turned on Gil, hitting at her with hysterical blindness. Gil was too surprised to do little more than raise her hands against the blows.

"Sesha, what are you talking about? I would never let you fall. I wasn't here." She grabbed her sister's wrists and held them. "Sesha! Sesha, look at me."

Sesha blinked twice, then peered closely at Gil's face. Her gaze flicked from one detail to another, then dropped to Gil's pink shirt. She trembled. "You changed your shirt."

"It wasn't me," Gil assured her.

"Then who else could it be?"

Gil knew. *The Other.* She had never before considered that that *presence* might be a real person. Each time she had sought its source, she'd been turned aside or distracted, or found only an empty space. After a time, she had decided it was but an echo of her own self.

Her gaze scoured the canyon as if she might snag a glimpse of that elusive alter-self. But there were side trails and rocks and gullies, and by now the Other was long gone. Yet she had truly been here. Gil sensed the lingering trace of her presence. More than Sesha's near brush with death, this shook her, spasms running down her back. Knees suddenly gone to water, she sat abruptly. Sesha collapsed with her.

"Tell me you were up at the niche," Sesha demanded.

Gil shook her head. "I never made it there. I was still in the lower canyon when I heard you scream. I came as fast as I could."

"She said her name was Gemella. I thought you were joking." Sesha trembled so, she could barely speak, yet her words spilled in a torrent. "She looks just like you. Identical. She said I couldn't tell the difference, that I never could." Gil stared up toward the niche sheltering the petroglyph panel as the implications drifted into place.

The Other had come here, a place Gil and Sesha kept secret between them.

"Who is she, Gil? What does she know?" Sesha asked, echoing Gil's thoughts. "How often has she done this before?" Gil watched the memories passing in her sister's eyes. Sesha shook her head, her voice a husky whisper. "So many times you asked strange questions or forgot some detail or task, or seemed distant, indifferent. And times it seemed you were two places at once."

Gil's sense of self trembled on the verge of dissolution. The Other—this Gemella—could take her place at will. Had apparently done so in the past, and who would know when or how often? Which of Sesha's memories did she share, and which were now suspect? What did this Gemella know of her life, and she not a whit of the other's?

"All those times, Gil, it wasn't you."

GALEN

"So what do I do?" Galen asked as if addressing the card catalog in front of him. He consulted the rumpled piece of paper set atop the case as his fingers flicked through the entries, then glanced over his shoulder to see if Harry was listening.

Stretched out casually at the table behind him, Harry leafed through Orlov's research paper. A graduate student and teaching assistant, Harry was assigned to one of the senior professors. But he'd attached himself instead to Galen, and because his family had money, the dean did not overtly object. They were almost the same age, for Harry was one of those perpetual students who collected degrees the way others might collect rare coins. As long as his family contributed to the University, that was fine.

"Burn it," Harry advised with a shrug.

Galen glanced at the voucher on the table, crumpled and stained, poised to rise up like a serpent to strike at him. His fingers twitched as if to strike a match. "It's worth money. It would be like burning a wad of bills."

The dilemma had haunted him the rest of the day. He'd suffered through classes with the same distraction that afflicted his students. In the evening, he'd prowled his room restlessly, glaring at a stack of quizzes, unable to sit down to grade them. Around midnight he had returned to Rosenwald Hall, accosting the night janitor and pawing through collected trash to retrieve the voucher and the map that accompanied it.

"Give it back, then."

Galen wiped his hand on his pants leg as if that might erase the temptation. "I can't. She's already left."

"Cash it in. Sell it. It's probably worth—oh, four hundred dollars. You could use the extra dough."

Galen imagined his friend's voice taking on the subtle hiss of a serpent's tongue. He shook his head. "I thought about it. But what if someone questions where I got the money? How do I explain that a female student just dropped it in my lap?" *In lieu of a final exam.*

Why couldn't she have left an apple like everyone else?

Besides, cashing it in felt *wrong*. The ticket was an invitation to join her, if he so chose. To use the ticket for his own gain seemed a betrayal, both of her trust and his own sense of honor.

He couldn't explain that to Harry, though. His friend had a habit of leaving honor behind as other people left umbrellas. Harry was always doing things he shouldn't. And with his swift grin and his family's money, he usually got away with it.

"I really don't understand the problem." Harry dug into a pants pocket and pulled out his pocketknife. Opening it, he began to pare his fingernails.

"No, I don't suppose you would."

Galen jotted a note on the paper, then slammed the card file shut. He swept up the ticket and papers and strode toward the stairway. The sharp clang of his steps on the metal stairs leading to the basement was somehow satisfying. Harry's footsteps followed like an echo.

Of course Harry didn't see the problem. Why had he confided in the man in the first place?

Galen often worried that Harry's reputation might damage his own. But he could never bring himself to end their friendship.

Harry embodied something missing in himself, a spark of daring and mischief. A small part of him clung to that, rebelling against the strictures of his own life, against the compulsion to play it safe. Galen acted as Harry's conscience; Harry was his tempter. They balanced one another.

Perhaps he wanted the answer he knew Harry would give.

"So the upright, proper Galen S. Williams has a moral dilemma to solve. This girl's really gotten under your skin."

Galen frowned. "She's a student. I don't—"

"I know; you don't get involved with students. But she has a hold on you. Admit it." Galen only shook his head. He turned abruptly to backpedal down the barren hallway.

"Why are you here, Harry? Your family's still rich; you could do anything you want. Why do you stay in college?"

His friend shrugged and tossed off a spare grin. "I like the coeds. Besides, I was bored with parties and polo." Then he turned serious. "I don't know. The world is changing so fast, and faster every day, like a car without brakes, and the road is full of rocks and potholes. Some would say I'm hiding from it, but maybe I'm simply trying to find a way to survive."

Galen was silent for a moment, respectful of this rare glimpse into Harry's deeper side, so at odds with what Galen, himself, was thinking. "Do you know what my first thought was this morning? 'I hate economics. I hate teaching. I hate my life!' So how did I come to this? What am I doing here?"

Harry made a sound and gesture like a diving plane. "Crashed and burned at twenty-seven. What a waste!"

Galen turned and ducked into the archives vault. Bare bulbs cast a harsh, forlorn light divided by cold, stark shadow as he ventured into the stacks. Water dripped in some far off corner, and the air smelled of mildew and dust.

Harry stopped in the doorway. "What *are* we doing here?"

"Looking for this." Galen pulled a volume of bound journals from a shelf and wagged it in front of him as he headed toward a scarred, rickety table that seemed to have been simply abandoned rather than placed for anyone's convenience. He dropped the research paper and ticket onto the table beside the volume, then laid out the map on the table, trying to smooth out the wrinkles. "This map was attached to the ticket, along with an itinerary. There's a note in the margin—see, right there—referring to a monograph published in 1928."

"Archeology?" Harry said with raised brow, peering over Galen's shoulder. "You're actually poking your head outside of your discipline? This *is* a novelty. What's the big deal?"

Galen flipped back and forth through the pages. "Some place called Killichaka. Here it is!"

He stared at the page, but the words were like cryptic runes, meaningless secrets awaiting his touch to set them free. His fingers hovered half an inch above the page. The lines of the map became a web, luring him into some hidden trap. He set his hands against the table on either side of the book, leaning on them to anchor himself in the here and now.

She's still dropping pebbles, he thought as the far-away voice whispered again and his blood trembled in his veins. *Something's waiting.* He closed his eyes and took a deep, slow breath, swaying as if he would tumble into that map like Alice down the rabbit hole.

The table shifted, its legs creaking and scratching against the bare concrete floor. When he looked up, Harry had hitched one leg up and sat fingering his knife, running his fingernail along a crack in the ivory casing. According to Harry, the knife had saved his grandfather's life during the Civil War, deflecting a Confederate sniper's bullet. Harry also claimed traces of that same Reb's blood still remained deep in the hinge. *Can't ever get all the blood out. It stains forever.*

"I don't get it," Harry said. "I mean, if this is really a bribe, why Peru?" His face screwed into an expression of *who would want to go there?* "Why not Paris or London? Some place with class."

Galen turned to his friend. "It's not the place, Harry, it's the event. There's an eclipse next month on the eighth."

"Aah," Harry said, as if that explained it all, and then, "But why this Killi place? Why not Lima?" He cocked his head as if, at a different angle, the map might make more sense.

"You're supposed to be a research assistant. Why don't you see what you can dig up?"

Harry shrugged noncommittally. "An eclipse is just a shadow. I saw one once, a nick in the sun no one could look at anyway. So what's the big deal?"

"It's more than that, Harry. A total eclipse is nothing like a partial. There are shadow bands and Bailey's Beads, the Diamond

Ring effect and solar flares. It gets dark in the middle of the day, and the stars come out. Suddenly, there's a hole in the sky where the sun should be. It's almost mystical."

"Mystical?" Harry raised his hands in mock horror. "You're getting too deep for me, my friend."

"The one in 1918 changed my whole life." Galen tried to force the memory, but the image was like a black paper cutout pasted on a blue background. *How could I have forgotten?* Galen wondered. *What happened to the dream?*

"In '25, in January, one crossed the Great Lakes region. I was fifteen, and I took a bus to Detroit and tried to hitchhike upstate. It was cloudy, though, and there was nothing to see."

"You hitchhiked?" Harry asked incredulously. "*You?*" He began to laugh, shaking his head in disbelief.

"And you can bet I caught it but good when I got home. My father would've flayed me alive if not for Edward." He still choked as he said the name. Edward had always protected him; only once had he let Galen down. "After that, I never wanted to wander off anywhere again." Galen glared at his friend.

"Sorry," Harry said as his laughter sputtered to a stop. "I just can't imagine you doing anything so—so *reckless*. There's hope for you yet!"

"That's what Orlov said," Galen murmured to himself. Louder, avoiding that line of thought, he went on. "What about the eclipse in '32? The path crossed New England—Boston was right on the edge. Surely you saw that one."

Harry considered, then shook his head. "No, not that I remember. I could have been abroad that year."

Galen paused as his thoughts rolled over, a new one surfacing. "I would've graduated from Cornell that spring." He spoke in soft wonder, as if the thought had never occurred to him before. "I would've been an astronomer." Instead, he had spent the day puttering around in his parent's basement, hiding from even the partial event. Hiding from broken dreams.

"So why aren't you?" Harry asked. "What happened?"

"The Depression happened," Galen responded with an angry shrug, as if the answer should be obvious, the one answer for all such questions. The Depression had stampeded across the country like a wild beast, crushing spirits and trampling dreams, oblivious to the damage wreaked. "I had to move back home and wait on tables to finish college. That's why I changed majors. I wanted to understand what had happened and why."

Yet he felt the true answer still eluded him. How could he have given up so easily? Could he dare that particular dream again? Was it too late to reclaim it? Or would he spend the rest of his life thinking *I could have been...?* He closed his eyes briefly, unwilling to face the possibilities.

"Galen, you can't blame the Depression for everything."

"That's easy for you to say. Your family didn't go down in the crash; it survived intact. Some families had all the luck."

Harry traced circles on the table with his finger. "It's time to stop regretting the past and do something about the future. Do you want to go or not?"

"Go?" Galen blinked his thoughts back to the present. "I guess so. Yes, I do. I really do. I just don't know how. How do I get to New York in two days? How do I abandon my classes?" He paused for a deep breath. "How do I get away with it?"

"We're three weeks from the end of term. Get some graduate student to take over. They can even administer the final exams; you just have to prepare them. Better yet, use last year's."

"What about the dean? He'll never let me go."

"Tell him you're going to do research on how the Depression has affected the economy of Peru. You might even get a paper published if you play it right. Think of it as a shortcut to your precious security."

Galen shook his head. "The dean won't approve. What if he asks where I got the funding? He knows I can't afford a bus to New York, let alone a ship to Peru."

"Tell him before he asks." Harry stood and paced a circle around the table. He picked up Orlov's essay and balanced it on his fingertips, serving it as a gourmet meal. "You know what this is? It's a grant proposal. From the Orlov Institute for, uh, Economic Research."

"I can't say that!" Galen almost shouted.

"Why not?" Who's to say it isn't? That's what it looks like to me. Yes, a research grant." He held up the paper as if he could read those very words on the cover. "Quote a few lines of Sismondi to him. He loves that stuff."

"Do you really think that would work?"

Harry flipped his knife so that it thunked into the battered tabletop. "I'll bet Granddad's folding knife on it."

"Harry!" Galen wrenched the knife free, rubbing a finger across the hole as if that would heal it, as if one more scar mattered. Closing the blade, he fingered the cracked casing.

Harry stood and grabbed up the documents. "Or I could just burn this for you. Problem solved." Pulling out his cigarette lighter, he flicked open the lid and struck up a flame.

The speed with which Galen snatched the papers from Harry's hand surprised even him. He shrugged, feigning nonchalance.

"I guess I'm going to Peru."

GIL

The mandala hung on the wall behind the fire pit in the kiva-styled great room. Thick, royal blue wool spiraled from an off-center hole where a rainbow of threads poured out. Woven into the blue like bright stars, symbols of power and faith hung in tranquil harmony, nothing more natural than that they merge into one central creed. Among the objects on the mantle below, a fat jade Buddha with outstretched arms contemplated the figure on the crucifix it faced, and an African tribal mask grinned at a dancing Kachina.

The hole at its center is for you to fill, with whatever it is that you are. That was her mother's message. She had started weaving the mandala, patterned after the eclipse witnessed at Gil's birth, when Gil was two. She had died a year later when it was finished. Gil's only memories off her were pale, sad, and empty, a fragile woman of weak health. Aunt Mercedes, who had raised Gil and her sisters after that, often said Amani had poured out all of herself in Gil's birth.

Gil gazed now at that empty space, longing to fall into it. Fall in and hide. Take refuge in that darkened void.

Her sisters entered, and she turned to them. Her gaze wandered among the familiar faces, smiling at their diversity. *Only in America,* Aunt Ada was fond of saying, whenever someone told the story of their clan, of how they'd gathered from the four directions. Only in America was such a blending of races and cultures possible. Petra, brown-haired and blue-eyed like Aunt Vera, favored their Russian great-grandfather, while Sesha clearly took after his Chinese wife. Tall, thin Maji was dark and curly haired;

Evita olive skinned, brown-eyed. Gil's own red hair melded with ruddy skin and almond-shaped eyes, a servant to the world.

"Where's Sumala?" she asked, mentally taking roll.

"Here," came a breathless voice from the doorway. Sumala set her Gladstone bag down by the door and paused to brush back a strand of her straight black hair. Sumala, it was said, most resembled Tuawta, their Hopi great-grandmother. "Juan's youngest fell off a fence and broke his arm." She bit at her lip, and Gil knew she worried over leaving her patients behind. She was the only doctor for twenty miles.

"And here comes Lena!" Maji called from near the window, her words confirmed by the slamming of a car door.

Gil hurried to greet her third-oldest sister with a hug, and then another. Lena, blonde and plump, had been particularly close to Aunt Faye, and shadows of grief still clouded her presence. Gil's hand brushed lightly across Lena's belly.

"Another boy," she whispered so that the others would not hear. "Strong and healthy. His name is Gabriel."

"But I'm not—" Lena started, then her eyes went wide. Gil cut her off with a wink, then surrendered her to a flurry of hugs and queries about her husband and children and the weather in Colorado.

With Lena's arrival, the family was complete. In the last ten years, they had scattered across the country—Maji to Los Angeles, Lena to Colorado, Sesha and Evita to Taos. Only a month ago, they had gathered for Aunt Faye's funeral. Now they returned once more for the sake of the Vision. For Gil.

The sisters returned to the great room and settled there. Gil sat with Lena on one of the leather couches, Sesha and Maji on the other. Evita chose the wide ledge that ran around the perimeter of the circular room, but Sumala took the floor just to Gil's right.

"Now that we're all here, it's time to review our plans," Petra announced. She alone remained standing, near the wall to the left of the fireplace. *A leader's position*, Gil thought. *She's still taking charge.* Petra—the oldest, the controller, the overachiever. She stood swaybacked so that head preceded body, thoughts always a step ahead of action. Gil swallowed her resentment and listened to muted groans and sighs and rustlings as each woman physically shifted position to face the topic. *Leave it to Petra to spoil the mood.*

"Never mind plans," Maji said bluntly. "What about this Ge-mella woman who attacked Sesha this morning? Who is she?"

"She didn't attack—" Sesha started to explain.

"Gemella means 'twin,'" Petra cut in, her mouth twisted into a persimmon frown so much like Aunt Vera. She nodded pointed-ly toward Gil. The others reacted in varying degrees of surprise and denial, but for Gil, it was a moment of *ah-ha*, a missing piece of self *snicking* into place. As Petra related the story of Gil's birth and the unexpected twin, Gil's gaze raked across her sisters' faces, wondering who might already know. She saw only the same sense of betrayal she felt herself.

From the tempest of emotions a single question emerged, ex-pressed in a chorus of voices.

"What happened to the second baby?"

"No one knew how it would affect the Mission," Petra con-tinued, raising her voice to be heard. "There's nothing in the an-cient lore about twins. It'd never happened before. Our aunts didn't know what else to do, so they decided to get rid of her. Aunt Vera was supposed to take care of it."

"But she kept her instead?"

Petra responded with a single nod, and Gil sensed she knew more than she was willing to tell. Yet it explained much. Though Aunt Vera lived only three miles from the ranch, it might as well have been a thousand. She rarely visited outside of holidays and family celebrations and never, so far as Gil knew, had anyone traveled to her house. Scandal veiled her presence, something the other aunts refused to speak of.

Then an idea snapped silently in Gil's mind. In both wonder and anger, she stood to face her oldest sister.

"You were there, weren't you? When I was born, you were there. You've known about Gemella all this time." Petra stared at her for so long, Gil thought she would refuse to answer.

"I was only sixteen. I wasn't part of the decision." Pinned against the wall by their collective outrage, Petra lashed back. "They made me promise! They said terrible things might happen if you ever found out—that the mission would fail and the Vision succeed." For a moment, Petra revealed her own anguish, and for that moment, Gil could forgive her.

"You should've told me."

Gil's sense of the Other had always confused and troubled

41

her. A simple word could've allayed so much needless anguish and fear. Curious, she thought, how now that she had a name for that ever-present entity, she still persisted in calling it the Other. Denying the truth, she wondered, avoiding its import?

But her sisters had other concerns. A chorus of question and conjecture followed.

"So now what?" one asked, and another, "Why show up now? What does she want?"

"It must have something to do with the Ritual."

"But she's not the seventh."

"She wants to be," Sesha said abruptly. "She wants to take Gil's place and steal her power."

Gil pursed her lips and shook her head to caution Sesha. They should never have mentioned the incident, she realized now. There were enough problems, and as a group, they were still too fragmented. The Vision bound them so tightly, in all other directions they pulled apart. This revelation was bound to cause strain. Gil felt their unease penetrate to her core as she gauged the barometer of rising tension.

"It'll be all right," Maji stated, just as the barometer indicated inevitable storm. The middle sister, Maji was the ultimate diplomat. Her matter-of-fact voice spread like oil over the turbulence. "Even if Aunt Vera knows our plans, she doesn't have the map. In two weeks, we'll be in Peru, and there's nothing she can do to stop us."

"*If* we can get there. We have to be in New York by Friday."

Petra stepped in, trying to regain control. "We'll get there. In the meantime, we have to be prepared. We need to arrange for supplies and transportation. And papers. Peru is a military state; the right documents will make things go easier; their absence could make them impossible. We'll need more maps, too, and a guide."

We need more time, Gil silently added. Everything was happening too fast. She picked up one of Evita's geodes from the collection on the table in front of her. Energy lurked in the dark, smoky quartz lining the cavity, dormant and inert.

Aunt Faye had found reference to the Ritual only last winter, and they had wasted weeks in argument. Now events were gaining momentum, sweeping the family along with little time to prepare. Since Faye's death, they were fumbling in the dark. It was too easy to trip over unforeseen obstacles. In the dark, monsters prowl and traps abide. She fingered the points of the crystals, but she could not awaken their light.

"…could Aunt Vera have killed Faye?" Evita was saying. Gil realized the conversation had drifted and frowned at her own lack of attention.

Sumala spoke up, the coarse grit of guilt in her voice. "There's no proof anyone killed her; Aunt Faye was ill and in great pain. The overdose of laudanum could have been an accident or even suicide." She held her gaze in her hands. "I should have seen how ill she was."

"It wasn't your fault, either," Gil said, touching Sumala's shoulder. "She kept her condition to herself."

"If only you had been here," Lena said quietly, and Gil was surprised at the bitterness she tasted in those words.

"Gil was at school," Sesha said in her defense. "By the time we found out, it was too late for anyone to do anything." Lena's glance sliced toward Sesha like a sharpened blade. After a moment, it dropped away, and she said nothing more, though her fingers played upon her knee and the corners of her mouth twitched, fighting a frown. She glanced up only once, with a look of sharp reproach. *You're supposed to help people.*

And that, of course, was why they were making this journey. According to the folklore, the seventh daughter of a seventh daughter should see the future clearly and have power over life and nature. She should be able to heal both mind and body. But Gil's abilities were weak and limited.

Holding up her right hand, she studied the lines and curves of it, the color and texture. There should be power there, and there was not. Her weakness threatened her purpose. So it came to this journey and this ritual. If it failed—

No! She rubbed her hand against her thigh, erasing the doubt. She could not allow herself to think of such consequences. The Vision haunted her, making her head pound and her skin burn. It weakened her, as if in contemplating it, she gave it power, reinforced its reality.

"But what of Gemella?" Maji asked, steering the conversation back to present matters. "What if she follows us to Peru?" A flurry of conjecture mixed with denial followed.

What of Gemella? The revelation of her twin's existence was a complex and tangled knot, potentially reweaving the patterns of the future. Was Gemella the cause of Gil's weakness? If so, could she also be the solution?

"Let Gemella come," Gil said abruptly, and the others stared at her as if she'd uttered heresy. "Perhaps there's a purpose to it, a way to reconcile what was done to her."

"Reconcile?" Lena responded with a snort. "You might as well build a bridge to the moon!"

Gil smiled. "But in Quechuan, *Killichaka* means 'Bridge to the Moon.'"

Their unspoken response was chill enough to make Gil shiver. Petra, in particular, kept an uncomfortable silence and would not meet Gil's gaze.

Aunt Mercedes entered then, plump and matronly and waving a spoon. "Enough talk. Supper's ready," she announced, and Gil wondered how long she'd stood at the doorway, listening.

Some invisible string severed, all the beads of tension went skittering across the floor and were gone. The sisters rose from their seats and flocked to the dining room, all chattering at once.

"I still don't understand why we can't fly to Peru," Maji said with a trace of petulance. "We'd have more time to prepare instead of being stuck on a ship for two weeks."

"There's seven of us," Petra explained with a *we've been over this before* sigh. "Airfare is three times the price of ship's passage."

"Besides, Maji, think of how romantic a sea cruise is," Sesha added, tossing the remark over her shoulder. "The sea, the moon." Evita and Lena together crooned a suggestive, "Ooh."

"But a plane is so much more—oh, adventurous."

"So much more *dangerous*."

"Exactly!" Maji cried with an eager sparkle in her eye.

"Exactly why we *won't* fly," Petra stated with a tone of finality as they settled down to a meal of fry bread with rice and beans. Aunt Mercedes left them to their plans.

"And what about a guardian," Maji asked. "Doesn't the lore mention a guardian?"

"Uncle Jim's too old; Lena's Frank can't leave the farm."

"What about Lorenzo? He's paying most of our expenses." Lorenzo Hubbell managed a string of trading posts in the Indian lands to the west, dominating the region like a royal sovereign. Without his aid, the venture would have foundered before it began.

Petra shook her head. "I already asked. He won't go."

Gil glared at her oldest sister. "It wasn't your place to ask," she said quietly. "That choice is mine. A guardian is defined not merely by what he can do but for what he would gain." *Someone with potential, willing to take the risk to discover it.* Petra opened her mouth to retort, but Gil's gaze dissuaded her.

"But who, then?" Maji repeated.

Gil shrugged and let the question go unanswered. The conversation drifted to other subjects—Lena's children, Maji's latest madcap idea, Aunt Ada's fling with a banker from Santa Fe. Gil picked up the thread and wove herself back into the group.

Mercedes bustled back into the room. "Lorenzo's here!" she announced with a red-faced giggle. "I mean, Mr. Hubbell."

The trader from Oraibi followed behind her, his bulk filling the doorway. Gil wondered what fanciful compliment Lorenzo had paid her aunt. His courtly attitude toward women was old-fashioned but nonetheless endearing.

The sisters rearranged themselves to accommodate his presence. Lorenzo took a seat and helped finish off the remainder of the meal. Mercedes brought fresh coffee and fruit-filled empanadas.

Lorenzo's father, J. L. Hubbell, had long supported Gil's family and their mission, even providing the land for the small ranch the clan considered home. After his death in 1930, Lorenzo had inherited that responsibility along with the trading posts. When they'd started planning this journey, Lorenzo had come forward when every other resource turned them down. How he had found out about their need was a mystery.

"Everything is set, ladies. You leave tomorrow," he announced with a self-satisfied grin. "I've hired a pilot who assures me he'll get you to New York in time to board the *Santa Inez* on Friday. You'll arrive in Lima on the twenty-seventh."

"I do wish you would reconsider accompanying us," Petra said with a coy smile that was embarrassing for a woman her age. "We could certainly use your skills and influence." She glanced at Gil, daring her to object.

"As much as I would enjoy the company of such beauty and virtue, you know I can't leave the trading posts untended," he said with a gracious smile. Which, of course, was a lie. Lorenzo had been known to disappear for as much as six months, then reappear just as mysteriously. "Besides, I have other business to attend to." Lorenzo caught Gil's gaze with a deft wink, hinting that a secret lurked between them. "I'm sure you'll find someone else to escort you."

Lorenzo shifted his considerable bulk to pull an envelope from the inner pocket of his jacket. "However, I would not leave you without resources. I have letters from the Peruvian ambassador, himself, guaranteeing safe passage and assistance from the local authorities should you need it." He offered the packet to Gil. "Here's names and addresses of people my father knew. You should have no trouble."

Gil nodded appreciably. Lorenzo's father had been an international figure; his influence might still cut through the tangled politics of President Benavides' regime.

"We'll never be able to repay you," Petra responded, and Lorenzo expressed offense that she would suggest such a thing.

"My dear lady, you have an important mission. The honor of serving your family is more payment than I deserve."

Gil wouldn't have been surprised if Lorenzo had then kissed Petra's hand. Such was his personality, as sincere as it was overblown. Some of Gil's sisters giggled and squirmed at such flattery, and Aunt Mercedes appeared about to swoon.

"But we still need a guardian," Petra insisted. "You wouldn't want us wandering such an uncivilized region alone, would you?" Gil frowned at her sister's obvious and futile attempt to manipulate the man.

"We'll have one," she interjected before Lorenzo could respond. "Trust me. He'll be there when we need him."

Friday, May 14

GALEN

Galen didn't go to Peru.

"Economists don't do field work," the dean had responded with a sharp laugh when Galen requested leave. When Galen quoted Sismondi, the old man only scowled.

"You're still hanging around Tucker, aren't you? You're a fool if you think I'll fall for that line twice." *Tucker has money; you don't.* That was the implication. The matter was closed, the dean making it clear any further proposals would not be tolerated. Galen backed off and said no more.

Perhaps it was just as well, he reflected now. Orlov had only provided passage from New York to Peru; he would've had to get to New York on his own. He couldn't imagine scraping together enough money for a train or bus, not in two days.

He had spent those days anticipating some kind of miracle, but it never happened. He pretended it didn't matter, but kept hoping something would change. *Something.* Anything.

Now that it was too late, he could imagine himself storming into the dean's office and yelling, "I quit!" It was safe to imagine and regret. He stared at the date on the calendar as if sheer will could transport him instantly to New York harbor. He envisioned the ship slipping from its moorings, sliding gracefully, irretrievably, from the reach of his dreams.

The sound of students impatiently fidgeting startled him. He coughed quietly, trying futilely to remember what he had been saying, and finally gave up with a short sigh.

"Class dismissed," he announced. "I know it's early, but I have, um, something to take care of."

His students were only too happy to oblige. He listened to the clamor of their going as he gathered and shuffled his notes, but dared not look up to face them. He hurried to his office and then simply sat there, staring at a map of Peru pinned on the wall—how or when it got there, he wasn't entirely certain.

"Tsk, tsk. What would the dean say?"

Galen started, snapping his gaze back from wherever it had wandered as Harry entered the room. "At this moment, I hardly care," Galen responded, more irritated with his own lapse in discipline than with Harry for catching him at it.

"I just stopped by to give you this," Harry said, holding out the ivory-handled pocketknife. "I guess you win the bet," he added with a touch of bitter disgust.

Galen stared at the offered prize, reluctant to accept it. Somehow, he wasn't quite prepared to give up yet, and taking the knife would mean admitting that he truly wasn't going.

"You could've gone, you know," Harry said quietly as he set the knife on Galen's desk, next to the useless voucher. Why had he kept that flimsy piece of paper? Why did he punish himself with its presence, a constant reminder of a dream held just beyond reach?

"Why should you care?" Galen responded sharply to hide his own disappointment.

"We're too much alike, you and I. I'm the third son; you're the fourth. Do you know that in medieval times, we would've been shipped off to a monastery? Face it, Galen, we're spare parts. Our future is our own. If you'd wanted it enough, you would've found a way to go. So why didn't you?"

"There's a little question of money and my job." He wondered if his expression was as bitter and empty as his mood.

"Pfft!" Harry spit with true ire. "The dean wouldn't fire you. Besides, there're always other jobs. As for the money, if it's worth doing, it's worth a little sacrifice."

"That's easy for you to say. You've never needed money you didn't have."

"Dam't, Galen, it's not about the money!" Harry hit the desk with such force, both Galen and the knife jumped. The ticket fluttered, drifting toward the edge of the desk. "I could've loaned you the money." Galen had never seen the man so impassioned and could not understand his anger.

"It's a little late to offer."

Harry nodded, swallowing too large a retort. "Maybe. Truth is, my friend, you built a shell out of cynicism and bitterness and walled yourself off from life. You think you're safe and secure. But Orlov threatens that perception, and you're afraid of where it will lead. How much longer are you going to hide behind the excuse of Edward's death?"

"What's that supposed to mean?" Galen responded, angry that this assistant, this *student* would dare talk to him so directly. Angry because Harry was cutting too close to the bone.

"Why did you really give up on becoming an astronomer?"

"You know why. My brother lost all our money. Edward still haunts me. He follows me like a shadow, guilty about ruining my dream."

"He haunts you because you let go of the dream he wanted you to have. Edward jumped from that window because he thought he'd taken something from you, but he was wrong. He didn't ruin it—you did. You quit. *You* abandoned your dream when you changed majors. Now you're doing it again. Edward's memory won't leave you in peace until you do something about it. If you really want something, you go after it—you take the risk."

Galen set his mouth in a flat, tight line. "Dreams don't matter," he said, turning his back to Harry to rifle through a stack of papers, pretending he was too busy to continue the conversation. *Only money and security matter. Hard, physical things you can touch and hold and keep.* Dreams were too insubstantial to have value, too delicate to grasp.

He wasn't aware of Harry leaving, only that he was now absent. For a long time, Galen stared at the window, wishing he could blink and transform it into a porthole. Maybe Harry was right. Galen still hadn't learned to hold on to his dreams. For a second time, he'd let one slip from his grasp. Finally, he sighed and brought his thoughts back to the here and now. He looked for the ticket, intending finally to dispose of it—and his dreams along with it. But it was gone.

Only Harry's knife remained.

Part Two

A Quarter Moon Waxing

MOONRISE: 12:39 a.m. EST ~ MOONSET: 1:16 p.m. EST
SUNRISE: 5:40 a.m. EST ~ SUNSET: 6:54 p.m. EST
Tuesday, May 18

GIL

The first days aboard the Santa Inez had been full of new sights and circumstances, of blundering around the ship and its unfamiliar customs and schedules. Novelty soon settled into routine, however, and the days became long and empty. The sisters drifted each to her own harbor of interest, meeting only for meals or Petra's wearisome planning sessions.

Lena kept to her cabin claiming seasickness while Maji mingled with the group of astronomers and radio crew from the Hayden Planetarium expedition. She had become particularly attached to Owen Stephens, an artist commissioned to paint the up-coming eclipse. Photography, he explained, could not accurately capture the delicate colors of the corona.

At her first opportunity, Gil had sought out Professor Williams, but he was not on board. Disappointed, she roamed the decks restlessly. She had not realized how much she had been counting on his presence until she felt the void of his absence. She had been so certain he would come, she could not imagine any other possibility. Shadow bands shifted across the future's landscape, obscuring its forms and patterns.

Now that they were finally on their way, however, she was eager to get on with the mission. She stood by the railing near the bow and watched the hazy smudge of the horizon where blue met blue, hugging herself to contain the energy roiling just beneath the surface. How was she ever going to endure this prison for ten more days?

A lone Beluga whale ran escort some distance to port, a pale form cleaving the waves. Something else followed, a shadow on the water riding the ship's wake. The subtle presence flavored the salt spray with acrid smoke and added a discordant note to the song of the wind. *I know this thing.*

Gil hadn't allowed herself to think about the coyote's attack. Now from a week's distance, it seemed safe to examine the incident. She could almost convince herself that it hadn't truly hap-

52

pened the way she remembered it. The coyote, she decided, had been real enough, but whether it was merely a hapless creature lost in the wilderness of the city or a manifestation of some unknown power, she was no longer certain. Nor could she imagine who might have summoned it.

Gemella? The name still felt awkward in her mind. But the flavor was wrong. She knew the taste of the Other's presence as surely and as intimately as her own. No, this was a new entity, a peril no one had foreseen. Even now, she felt its lure.

Gil leaned against the railing, seeking its source. She studied the intricate brocade of the ocean's surface, layered wave upon wave, crest crossing crest, ebb and billow, each with its own source and destination, washed back and forth at the whim of wind and tide, an intricate weaving of events large and small. How like life that seemed. The rhythm settled within her, inviting her to merge with the pattern, to float and—

"Careful, Miss." A steward pulled her back from the rail. Gil blinked and gasped as the spell ebbed from her bones.

"I beg pardon, but you were about to take a dip in the briny. The captain takes a dim view of such antics."

Gil muttered thanks with a weak smile and then began to tremble. The steward settled her in a deck chair and offered a blanket, then tipped his cap and continued on. He kept glancing back.

Gil clutched at the arms of the chair and huddled beneath the blanket, her eyes closed tight until the shivers subsided. She shuddered, unable to imagine what that malign entity wanted of her. Though still diffuse and inchoate, it threatened the very *self* of her existence, the autonomy of her will.

I'll have to be better prepared next time, she thought, and realized that *yes,* there would be a next time. The entity awaited another opportunity. It would be stronger, more focused. That revelation chilled her even more than the wind blowing off the bow.

Professor Williams, where are you?

GALEN

Galen sat staring at curtains tightly drawn against the dark of the night, thinking about Orlov and the eclipse. There had been a time when he had craved that dark and shunned the star-obscuring lights. But that was before October 29, 1929, when it seemed that same dark sky fell upon him, smothering his life and dreams. If it hadn't been for the Depression, he might've been part of any number of expeditions headed to Peru.

Memories played upon the backdrop of the drapes. When Galen's father and uncle sold their family farm in 1914, speculating on the stock market had proven a shrewd strategy. The two families had moved to Chicago, not yet wealthy, but on the way. Edward, the oldest brother, took over the family's business affairs and continued the same strategy. He had used profits to make private loans to foreign countries still paying war debts—a lucrative investment, since the government kept raising the interest rates in a futile attempt to discourage the loans. Unknown to the family, Edward was also using Galen's college money and the family savings to invest on margin—buying stock for ten percent cash, borrowing the balance, using the stock itself as collateral. He'd done all the right things at the worst possible time. The Germans defaulted, the market crashed, and the banks closed, leaving them with enormous debts owed on worthless stock. Soon everything but their house was gone and his mother was sewing dresses from flour sacks. Edward had called Galen to tell him he'd have to abandon his dreams, to beg forgiveness that Galen, in stunned denial, couldn't give.

By the time Galen had returned home for Edward's funeral, the fading stain on the sidewalk seemed more a shadow than a man's life. Now Galen kept the lights on to hold that shadow at bay. The memory of that last call still echoed in his hearing.

I should've known. I should've been able to stop him.

He veered sharply from such thoughts and the curtained window only to be confronted by Orlov's paper on his desk.

What was he to do with it? What did she expect of him? Evidently done in a hurry, the writing was far from her usual level of work. The report wandered from its stated premise like a butterfly, flitting from one evocative subject to another toward some alternate purpose. Was she trying to tell him something, and he simply wasn't getting the message?

The pounding of a fist on the door intruded sharply. Galen dared to peek through the curtains and saw Harry Tucker's Packard parked at the curb. Moving to the door, Galen hesitated, one hand resting on the glass knob. While he denied students—even teaching assistants—access to his personal life, Harry had become an exception. In some strange twist, he often behaved more as Galen's mentor than assistant.

"Come on; we'll be late!" Harry announced as soon as Galen opened the door.

"Late for what?" Galen frowned, wondering if he'd forgotten some department function.

"The movies! *The Good Earth* is opening tonight at the Bijou, and we still have to pick up the girls."

"Girls?" Galen repeated, his frown tightening.

"I met Mitzi at the beach, and she's bringing a friend."

Galen shook his head, frowning at Harry's irresponsible ethics. "It's a school night, Harry. I have work to do." He gestured across the small room where stacks of papers competed with personal possessions for available space. Galen lived simply—some would say miserly—turning over most of his meager wages to his family. "Which reminds me, shouldn't you be working on that research project for Professor Stigler?"

Harry waved off the task. "It can wait. By next week, he'll change his mind, anyway. But tonight, I'm assigning you a research project of your own. Her name is Wanda."

"Harry, I don't want to go anywhere tonight."

"You know, ever since that Orlov thing, you've become positively severe, not to mention possessed. I mean, look at this place." He, too, gestured at the clutter, shifting Galen's focus to the maps and star charts pinned to the walls and the astronomy books, still dusty, retrieved from his parents' basement. *Where did it all come from?* he asked himself, as if it had appeared in this moment instead of slowly encroaching, one layer of his life lapping over the other.

"There's more astronomy than economics here. People are tired of hearing about eclipses and Peru; they're avoiding you. But I won't be so easily dissuaded, my pal. I'm on a mission to save you from your own drear self." Galen forced a smile at Harry's cavalier gesture. Against his better judgment, he allowed Harry to usher him from the room.

MOONRISE: 2:59 p.m. EST ~ MOONSET: 3:00 a.m. EST
SUNRISE: 5:44 a.m. EST ~ SUNSET: 6:33 p.m. EST
Thursday, May 20

SESHA

"I am Water, free-flowing, pure," Maji intoned, reading from a scrap of paper. Sesha imagined her sister breaking into dance and tried not to giggle.

"Frozen in crystalline perfection, diaphanous as a cloud, vast as the ocean. I give life and sustenance. I come from the North, Masichu'a, the gray-horned lizard. I am—"

"You can't give life," Evita interrupted peevishly. "I'm Life."

"Besides, it's too long," Petra added.

"But we have seven minutes. That's a minute apiece."

"Oh!" Maji yelped. "Oh, no! According to Mr. Stephens, it's seven minutes only at the center of the path—in the middle of the Pacific. We'll be lucky to get three and a half."

"See?" Petra stated smugly. "This is why we need to plan ahead. She turned to the third youngest sister. "And Evita, you're representing Life. You need to be more—well—lively."

"Couldn't you be more poetic, like Maji's," Lena suggested.

"Maji's a poet; I'm not. The idea of writing our own lines for the ritual is to express who we are."

"The words aren't that important," Gil announced. "They merely focus your thoughts and keep you from being distracted."

"So why do we need to rehearse?" Lena cut in. "We have no idea what will happen when the eclipse starts."

"It's important to have a ritual prepared. We won't have time to improvise." Petra's annoyance was plain.

Since the astronomers had commandeered the ship's library, the sisters had taken over a corner of the ship's vast dining hall. They were alone, except for a half dozen waiters setting tables for lunch, passing surreptitious glances, impatient for the women to be gone so their work could be completed.

"All the planning in the world won't do us any good if we can't find the place," Sumala pointed out. She had drifted over to the haphazard collection of maps, books, and pamphlets piled upon one of the tables. "How are we supposed to get from Cerro de

Pasco to Killichaka when it's not even on any of the maps?"

The others were only too happy to follow. Petra made a great show of exasperation before joining them. Sesha chose to ignore her. She picked up a book and riffled its pages. In the little time they'd had in New York before the *Santa Inez* set sail, she had raided as many libraries and bookstores as she could, collecting whatever might be useful. *A thin collection, indeed,* she now decided.

"This map shows only geographic sites like mountains and rivers," Evita observed. "This one has cities and towns. How are we supposed to match them?"

"They don't even show that town—what's it called? Angoltuto?" Lena noted, then added, "These names! Huanuco, Yanahuanca, Cajatambo. *Pachacamac.* Inca names are horrid"

"Quechuan," Sesha explained. "The natives are Quechuan. Inca was the title of their king." They would need a translator, she decided.

"*Pachacamac?*" Gil repeated, seeking out the site on the map. "Isn't that the ancient sea god?"

Maji flipped through one of the travel books. "Here it is: Pachacamac—ancient god who ruled the sea and caused earthquakes as punishment for misdeeds. The temple ruins are just south of Lima—an oracle of some kind, older than the Inca Empire. Here." She tapped at a spot on the map.

Gil stared as if seeing within the small black dot the actual place. Her lips moved, silently testing the word. Sesha could guess what Gil was thinking. Apparently, so did Evita, who spoke up before Sesha had a chance.

"We don't have time to go there!"

"But look, it's so close," Gil argued. We could go and come back in less than a day."

"Why?" Lena argued petulantly. She still seemed pale, though the seas were calmer now that they had entered the Caribbean.

"It's important," was all Gil said, but her face held a determined mien that said, *There are things I know that you can't comprehend.*

"But *why?*" repeated Lena scornfully. "Will Pachacamac rain down disaster upon us? Will he punish us for invading his privacy?"

"Is that any harder to believe than that I'm going to save the Earth from the fires of Hell?" Gil swayed with the motion on the ship, reaching toward Sesha for support.

Sesha tensed, anticipating the vivid images of the Vision. They had all had glimpses of the Vision, blessedly short but almost intolerable in intensity. How it must torture Gil, to endure the unbuffered whole. Sesha noted the same look of apprehension on the faces of her sisters, mixed with differing shades of relief and resentment. They didn't have to bear that awful burden, but neither could they share Gil's achievements. This trip was for her benefit, not theirs.

"Some of us could go," Sesha suggested, expecting to be among them.

Maji eagerly seconded the suggestion. "Sesha's right. It won't take all seven of us to make arrangements."

"It's not safe," Gil said, too quickly. "Apart, we're vulnerable. We should stay together." *Where I can protect you.* Sesha could read the thought from her sister's expression. Something was troubling Gil. *Gemella?*

Petra, however, disagreed. "Maji has a point. Sumala and I will go with Gil to Pachacamac." She nodded, as if listening to other thoughts in her head. "Yes," she murmured softly, her mouth in a tight half-smile. "That will work out well, I think." And louder, "Sesha, you can handle the arrangements."

From the disappointed look on Maji's face, she hadn't envisioned this split any more than Sesha had. Sumala also was frowning. Sesha wondered why Petra was willing to leave; it wasn't like her to delegate authority. *She's playing mother hen again. Doesn't want to let Gil out of her sight.*

"I should go with Gil," Sesha stated, thinking about the encounter with Gemella. "What if—" A look from Gil glanced off her like a warning shot. She let her words lapse into silence, though the thought persisted. *What if Gemella follows us? What if she tries to take Gil's place again?*

"You're the organizer, the *expert*," Petra argued back with pointed sarcasm. "You'll be more useful in Lima."

We're rushing into this too fast. Sesha recalled the panic and helplessness as she slid down the hillside toward the creek. *Only now, I'm blind and can't see the cliff.* Sesha shuddered. The metaphor was still too fresh. The image of Gil's twin watching her as she hung from the branch made Sesha tremble.

There had to be some way to tell the two sisters apart. Something Gemella wouldn't know and couldn't duplicate. She focused on the dilemma and let the discussion flow around and away from her.

MOONRISE: 3:03 p.m. CST ~ MOONSET: 2:11 a.m. CST
SUNRISE: 4:23 a.m. CST ~ SUNSET: 7:13 p.m. CST
Monday, May 24

GALEN

Galen's life had settled back into dull routine, and the only reminder of the ripple Orlov had caused was a single star map still pinned to the wall of his office. He felt restless, so he abandoned the shield of his lectern, pacing the room with a rare and fierce energy. Whispers echoed in his memory. *Something's coming.* He ignored their siren's lure. *No more,* he thought. *No more broken dreams or empty promises.*

Classes over, he walked. Without quite meaning to, he found himself at the cemetery where his brother Edward was buried, standing over the grave and staring blankly at the stone, at the date of Edward's death. Its shadow stretched across the grave towards him, but he stayed beyond its reach.

"It wasn't your fault," he told the silent granite marker. "None of it. Harry's right; I'm the one who gave up. I abandoned the dream. Is that truly why you haunt me?" He shivered suddenly and looked up. It was late afternoon. A bloated, almost full moon lifted itself above the tree tops, and the gravestones cast shadow stripes across the lawn waiting to trip him up. He walked briskly, carefully avoiding stepping on either graves or shadows.

It was almost six as he neared his apartment. Shadows consumed the street as the sun neared the horizon. A figure jumped from behind a bush. Galen yelped and would've fled if not in the same instant, he hadn't recognized Harry's silhouette.

"Shh!" Harry commanded, "Quick, into the car."

"What?" was all Galen could stammer as Harry hustled him toward the Packard across the street.

"Hurry, or you'll be late."

"Late for what? Harry, I'm not up to another night on—"

"No, no! Not a date. The Sleeper to Miami leaves in less than an hour. You'll arrive at five thirty—just in time to catch the flight to Lima at seven."

"Lima?" Galen groaned. "Harry, what have you done?"

Harry merely grinned. "I took the liberty of packing your

60

bags. They're already in the car."

"Harry!" Galen stopped abruptly in the middle of the street. "What have you done?"

"I cashed in your boat ticket and put it towards the airline fare instead. You are going to Peru to see your blessed eclipse, my friend. The way I figure it, you should get there just in time to meet Orlov at the dock."

"But what about the dean? He'd never—"

"Don't worry about that," Harry assured him, pushing Galen into the passenger seat. Glancing up the street, he hurried around to jump into the driver's seat. "I've taken care of everything. The dean will never know you're gone."

Galen curbed a sense of misgiving and didn't press for details. He suspected he didn't want to know. Harry pulled away still checking the rear view mirror, and that was cause enough for concern. Harry wasn't one to ever look back.

Harry's normal driving was bad; when he was in a hurry, it was death-defying. Galen kept pressing his foot against a brake that wasn't there. He steeled himself not to react, telling himself that yes, Harry saw the cab swing into his lane, the red light ahead, and a half dozen other close calls.

As the airport tower came into view Galen realized this was no prank. The incredulous reality wormed its way into his thoughts. The flutter of anticipation returned.

Something's coming.

"But Harry, airfare must be at least twice as much!"

"So pay me back later."

"With what?" Galen screeched. "I'll probably be out of a job. Harry, why are you doing this?"

Harry frowned for a moment, his hands flexing on the steering wheel. "Do you know the real reason why I stay in school? I tell myself it's to annoy my parents, but the sad fact is, I can't do anything else. I mean, I could go anywhere, do anything. But I've never *wanted* to. You, on the other hand, have this chance. Take it, pal. For once in your life risk something, follow that dream! I expect you to come back a changed man. Shake off that ghost once and for all. Just don't make it an annual event." Harry paused as if struck by a sudden panic, swerving around a corner. "You're not *planning* on doing this every year, are you?"

Galen laughed. "I wasn't planning on it *this* year!" He gripped the edge of the seat as Harry dodged a truck. "Harry, what's really going on?"

"Nothing. As I said, it's all under control." There was an edge of untruth to his voice.

"Harry?" Galen used his deepest professorial voice.

"It's nothing!" Harry protested. "That student, Orlov, has been missing for two weeks. You're the last one seen with her."

"She went to Peru."

"*I* know that, but the police don't. Apparently she forgot to tell anyone else. So go to Peru, bring her back, and you're in the clear, free and easy."

"But if I take off now, that'll just make me look guilty! I should stay here and prove my innocence."

"And how much can you prove from a jail cell? The cops were at your place waiting to arrest you."

"Harry!"

"Take it easy. I said I would handle things. They won't even know you've left town." Again, Galen shuddered.

At the airport, Harry handed him a duffel bag and valise and hustled him through the terminal and out onto the tarmac. "Your ticket and your passport, Sir," he said presenting the thin paper with mock formality, then stuffed the document and an envelope into Galen's jacket pocket.

"Harry, I—"

"Don't say it. You need a little adventure in your life. Everyone should have at least one dream fulfilled. I have no dreams, so let me trade on yours. Just let me believe you're going after the girl, not the bloody eclipse." He stuffed his hands into his pockets so that Galen couldn't return the ticket, and watched the toe of his shoe scuff the tarmac. "The Depression ruined too many lives and broke too many dreams. My family was lucky—old money. So maybe we have an obligation to the rest. If I can help just one person reclaim his dreams—"

"Why, Harry," Galen cut in. "You're a romantic at heart."

Harry appeared angry. "Maybe. But if you tell anyone—" He couldn't hold the threat. One of his infamous grins shattered the attempt. "Who would believe you anyway? Now go, will you!" He clapped Galen on the shoulder, just hard enough to propel him toward the waiting plane.

As Galen climbed the stairs into the plane, a popular song

spooled through his mind—"You Can't Stop Me From Dreaming."

Part Three

In the Fullness of the Moon

Tuesday, May 25

GALEN

The sun smudged a foggy horizon. It painted streaks of gold and rose across the placid sea and set aglow Miami's verdant green. The landscape bloomed in colors and forms he'd never known while the heavy smell of salt water stung his nose. *Miami! I'm in Miami, and I'm headed for Peru.* The idea still made him giddy.

The flight from Chicago, swathed in darkness, had seemed more dream than reality. Too tense to sleep, he'd stared out the window at nothing at all. Miami had been but a swathe of lights and the abrupt, empty dark of the ocean. With two hours between flights, he paced through the airport, unable to settle for more than a few minutes. Did he have everything he'd need? Had Harry forgotten anything? The duffel bag's lumpy bulk, slung from his left shoulder, barely reassured him.

Galen hadn't expected a clipper ship, hadn't even considered it. The plane bobbing gently with the swell at the end of the pier only increased his trepidation, reinforcing the fact that this would be a long flight, mostly over water. As Galen approached, a twinge of panic caused him to clutch tight the ticket in his right hand, as if someone might snatch it away, deny him passage. Name him a fool. Even worse, he expected some steely-jawed detective to appear with handcuffs and an arrest warrant.

He paused at the foot of the gangplank, still seeking tangible proof this was no illusion. His fingers clenched the handle of his valise, the only reality he could acknowledge at the moment. He boarded the plane quickly, before his misgivings could catch up to him.

Settling into his seat, he watched out the window as the Sikorsky Flying Boat taxied across the harbor. Sluggishly, the silver plane pulled itself into the sky, as if straining against the strands of doubt that tethered Galen to the ground. Airborne at last, he remembered to breathe and released his grip on the armrest.

Banking south, Galen caught the full moon sitting on the western horizon, a bloated disk still colored by the sun's rising. It cast a gold-hued path across the water and the unvoiced whisper echoed in Galen's thoughts.

Follow me.

I'm on my way, Galen responded to that voice not quite his own. He released a long, slow sigh, and with it, his apprehension. He felt an incredible and giddy lightness. This would be an adventure, something he could tell his children about, and his grandchildren.

From the air, the boats appeared anchored in mid-air, so crystalline the water. Further out, swirling patterns of aqua and blue—incredible blue—marked shoals and deeps, dotted with patches of land in green and white and brown. Maps of Florida, Galen decided, should never be drawn with a pen, but a smudge of chalk instead, for there was no distinct border between land and sea, only a gradual yielding, one into the other.

When he tired of gazing at the awesome view, Galen pulled the passport and envelope from his pocket, then hauled the valise onto his lap to see what Harry had packed. The envelope contained a wad of bills—at least a thousand dollars. Galen hurriedly stuffed the money deep into the case. He would pay back every penny, even if it took the rest of his life.

In the valise he found a Spanish phrasebook and a copy of Henry Franck's *Vagabonding Down the Andes*, published in 1917. A note in Harry's hand assured him it was as up-to-date as any recent travel guide—apparently little changed in Peru. How much could he learn about his exotic destination during the two-day flight to Lima? How much Spanish could he master? *Not nearly enough,* he realized, but perhaps he could get by, at least until he caught up with Orlov.

Thinking of Orlov brought to mind her research paper. Yes, Harry had packed that, too, along with the map and the monograph, torn from the bound journal. Galen shook his head. What else had Harry done that Galen would regret when he returned?

First he studied the map, a hand-copied, crude combination of contour lines and pictographs—a coded shorthand decipherable only by the man who had drawn it. The thin line of a trail passed a long, narrow lake, then turned west between jagged lines that must be mountains. It ended at a precise grid of squares and lines depicting, perhaps, ruins. Galen assumed the small X's were mine adits. Close-set, nested V's intruded from the right, separating the ruins from a fan-like scribble. He folded it and tucked it in his jacket's inside pocket and then took up the monograph.

Galen read through the article carefully, hoping to find some clue to the mystery of Orlov. The obscure, self-published paper described ruins found in the high Andes north and west of Cerro de Pasco. According to the author, Killichaka was a small settlement where the Mochica mined gold and silver. He assigned the site to the Mochica civilization, which flourished five hundred years before Manco Capac and his sister founded Cuzco and the Empire of the Inca. The Moche had built the pyramids of the Sun and Moon, but nothing this far south, so that in itself was controversial. The archeologist had spent some time exploring and documenting this site before stumbling upon a hidden temple.

"Though blood stained, I do not believe it was a site for human sacrifice," the author had written. "The Moche were far advanced in the arts of medicine and healing, even surgery. Their ceremonies celebrated life, and their power remains to tell the story, if one can only hear. The crystal altar resonates with power; one feels it penetrate even the bones.

"Images permeate one's dreams, and the wind whispers secrets among the stones. The blood, I believe, is a sign of betrayal and has something to do with why the site was abandoned. Local natives still regard it as *huaca*, a place of power and magic. Few will even acknowledge its existence."

Galen understood why the author had self-published the piece. No respectable journal would have printed such an unsubstantiated, subjective piece. Harry had also included several rebuttals printed in various journals that sharply criticized his conclusions. The kinder of them attributed the entire episode to a case of *soroche*—altitude sickness. Hallucinations, it concluded rather snidely, were often a symptom of cerebral edema. Galen gathered that this piece had severely compromised the man's professional reputation, edging him toward the status of trophy hunter and adventurer, existing on the fringes of true archeology. *And what will this trip do to my own status?* he pondered, and shuddered at the possibilities.

Galen let the pages fall into his lap, staring out the window. Clouds floated in bunches below him, casting shadows on the smoky blue sea. Ocean merged with sky in a blurred smudge of horizon, and for a moment, Galen couldn't tell which was which.

For all he knew, the plane could be upside down. His hands clutched the armrests.

What am I doing here?

GIL

The sun left the sky into the moon's keeping. Rising from the eastern horizon, it threaded between layers of clouds before emerging full and yellow. The wind off the bow blew Gil's skirt in long, fluttering folds and tangled her hair, sweeping it away from her face. It blew away even her thoughts, so she couldn't focus on any one image long enough for it to haunt her. She closed her eyes and savored the emptiness.

She surrendered all sense of time, so she had no idea how long she'd stood there before she became aware of a presence beside her. Opening her eyes, she found Sesha watching the long, blue waves of the Caribbean.

"You looked so calm, I didn't want to disturb you," Sesha said when Gil shifted her position.

"I don't think I'll have many such moments in the future," Gil responded with a smile. The bow section was deserted, though a half dozen astronomers occupied the foredeck just below, checking out their equipment.

"I should warn you, I've been sent to collect you for another meeting, but the others are tired of Petra and her unending planning sessions. We're staging an informal strike."

Gil nodded. This morning's meeting had broken up with a feeling of dissatisfaction when the Maitre-D' had politely but firmly insisted they leave. Nothing had been resolved except that Petra, as usual, would have her way.

"I wanted to give you this." Sesha held out a small package wrapped in colored paper. "It's your birthday present."

"But my birthday isn't for two more weeks." *The same day as the eclipse.* Sesha had used that coincidence as part of the argument for her plan.

Coincidence or destiny? Gil wondered. She held up her hand to push the present away. "Sesha, you should wait—"

"I was going to, but now it's important." She pressed the package back into Gil's grasp.

Studying her sister askance, Gil tore the paper from a small white box. Inside, she found a pendant on a silver chain, fashioned to resemble her mother's mandala. One small silver ring within another, bound off-center by thin turquoise spokes, a dark purple crystal at its heart.

"I had it made special," Sesha said. "A silversmith at Acoma Pueblo helped me. He says the silver is for healing, the turquoise for wisdom, and the crystal for insight."

"It's beautiful, Sesha." Gil held it up to study the intricate work as Sesha fastened the chain around Gil's neck.

"You'll have to keep it hidden for now," Sesha cautioned. Gil saw how her sister's thoughts turned.

"You're thinking Gemella might follow us to Peru."

With a self-conscious shrug, Sesha suggested, "Why else would she reveal herself now?"

Gil nodded slowly, absently, seeking the touch of the Other. *Not here. Not even close.* That absence troubled her.

"I keep thinking about what happened in the canyon," Sesha said with a pained wince, watching Gil closely, even now suspecting Gil's identity. That was the cruelty of Gemella's deception, wedging a shadow of doubt and suspicion between them. From now on, whenever they met, Gil would see the flicker of a question in Sesha's eyes. *Is that really you?*

"This will be a sign between us that no one else knows," Sesha suggested, tapping the pendant. Again, Gil tracked her line of thought. Hidden and unknown, her twin could not steal or copy it.

"It seems a shame to hide it; it really is beautiful, Sesha." Reluctantly, she slipped the pendant inside her blouse, feeling the cold metal slide down her skin. "But how do you know whether I'm Gil or Gemella even now?" She stared at her sister with a hard and narrow frown that made Sesha's confidence wither—a cruel but necessary jest. She managed to hold the look for all of five seconds before a smile leaked from the corners of her mouth. She began to giggle.

"Obviously, she's had more practice being you," Sesha observed with mock scorn. "But seriously, how do I know you're the real Gilaishling?"

Gil's expression soured briefly at the sound of her full name. She stared levelly at Sesha, hurt by the question, but understanding the need of it.

"What can I say? That I hate being called Gilaishling? That I broke my arm in the sixth grade, or you used to have a crush on Bobby Whitehorse. Gemella must know that as well as I. But she's not aboard. I would know." Gil wrapped her arms about her, chilled. *I would know, wouldn't I?* She'd been so close in the canyon, missing her twin by mere minutes, and yet unaware of her presence. The thought of such an encounter made her tremble. It was too soon, she kept telling herself. She was still getting used to the idea. But then, when would be the right time?

"Sesha, there's something else you should know. Gemella isn't the only one we need to watch out for," she said, and described the incident with the coyote. "Something is stalking me—us, perhaps—and I don't know what it is yet or what it can do, much less how to deal with it. I don't even know what it wants." She began to realize just how limited her experience and understanding was. "I don't know enough about the world and its risks."

"Petra didn't want you to waste your power, and Aunt Mercedes always panicked if you so much as scraped a knee. We all protected you. We thought it was for the best."

Though the memories invoked a wan smile, Gil shook her head. "It was a mistake." *A mistake that cost Aunt Faye her life,* she now realized.

What else might wait ahead for which she was unprepared?

Wednesday, May 26

GALEN

The full moon rose blood red over the Andes. Galen shivered and drew the curtains. He didn't open them again until the Douglas DC2 he'd boarded in Guayquil touched down at the Lima airport. He tucked his phrase book back into his jacket pocket, along with the map. The flight had hopped from one city to the next down the South American coast, a narrow band of desert between the formidable wall of the Andes and the endless expanse of the Pacific Ocean. He'd managed to confine his doubts and fears below the horizon of his thoughts, but now, as he disembarked into the noise and confusion of Lima Aeroporto, they boiled over like an afternoon thunderstorm.

It was seven-thirty at night, and the sun had already set. A sodden blanket of fog trapped the heat of the day and smothered Galen as he emerged from the plane. He was south of the equator now. Weather, seasons, everything was reversed.

He let the crowd of passengers lead him across the tarmac and into the crude shed of the terminal, grateful that others at least knew the way. Once through customs, he faced a throng of colorfully dressed people waiting like a wall to be breached.

With a deep breath for courage, he ventured forward. Surely, these people weren't all here to meet passengers, Galen thought, but of course they were, whether they were family and friends or vendors selling goods and services.

"Taxi, *Señor?*"

Galen frowned at the small man who had boldly approached before he'd crossed half the distance to the crowd.

"No," he managed to stammer. "Uh, *gracias.*" He craned his neck, seeking some sign that would point the way. Where to go first? He had been so focused on plans for finding Orlov, he'd given no thought to what to do once he'd arrived.

A hotel. Last night, in Cristobal, he'd slept in the airport, afraid thatif he left, he wouldn't be able to find his way back in time for the 4:30 a.m. departure that began the second leg of his flight. The thought of a soft bed and clean sheets became a desperate craving.

He was on the fringe of the crowd now, engulfed in a tumult of Spanish. Rank odors assaulted him, clung to him beneath the weight of the damp air. He had the uneasy feeling someone watched him, that someone, some*thing* hovered nearby. A sense of menace pricked the back of his neck.

"Do you know where you are going, *Señor*?" The man blocking his path was uniformed, appearing both official and efficient. Galen hesitated, but since this was a military state, decided it would be prudent to cooperate.

"Gran Hotel Bolivar?" he responded, picking the first name he could recall from the travel guide.

The man swept up his duffel bag. "Follow me, *Señor*."

"No, wait!" Galen yelled, his own voice lost in the noise of the crowd. Tightening his grip on the valise, he waded into the thick of the crowd, struggling to keep up, fearing he'd seen the last of his bag. People jostled him, nudging him back and forth. Hands plucked at his clothes. Again, he felt watched, followed, but he dared not take his gaze from the peaked cap slicing steadily through the tide of dark-haired heads. The man deposited Galen's bag at the curb and whistled up a taxi. He then held out his hand expectantly. Galen frowned, wondering if it was proper for such a person to expect a tip. He fumbled for the coins in his pocket and offered them with an uncertain shrug. The man looked disappointed, but Galen had no more change, only Harry's pocketknife. His fingers brushed against the worn ivory handle, the touch of something familiar a small, warm comfort.

The air in the cab was oppressive, but when he rolled down the window, the smell of urine and garbage stewing in the desert sun was far worse. The city seemed dirty and shabby, a small town forced into a larger role, built where no city should be. Without sufficient rain to wash away the filth, it festered in its own garbage. As they drove down the narrow streets, Galen peered upward through the window at row houses with dark, Moorish-styled balconies jutting out over the narrow street and felt as if he were shrinking into himself. This was a foreign culture, utterly alien to him. His driver said something in Spanish and glared at him suspiciously when he did not respond. And still, the sense of someone watching followed like a persistent shadow. He twisted about to peer through the back window, but could see nothing of consequence—not that he'd know it if he did. Perhaps it was merely his own conscience, he thought, telling him this was all a big mistake.

By the time he reached the hotel, his sense of adventure was crumbling around the edges, his self esteem deflating. At least the desk clerk spoke some English. When Galen tried to explain he needed to meet the *Santa Inez* when it docked in the morning, the short, balding man nodded vigorously.

"*Sí*. Callao."

"Callao?" Galen responded in dismay. "I thought it docked here, in Lima."

"No, *Señor*. Callao is the port. You can take a taxi. It is not far." The man spoke carefully, smiling broadly as if proud of his memorized phrases. "Do you wish to be awakened?"

Galen nodded numbly as the feeling of plans unraveling stirred in the pit of his stomach like a restless beast. The clerk grudgingly accepted Galen's U.S. dollars, as had the cab driver, and even exchanged a twenty for a wad of Peruvian *soles* thick enough, Galen thought, to choke a horse.

Wearily, he followed the bellboy through a pair of stained glass doors into a circular hall and up a magnificently carved staircase, their footsteps hushed by thick, embroidered carpeting. The climb felt like a mountain and left him feeling slightly winded. He wasn't ready for mountains just yet.

Alone in his room, he sat on the bed in a morose fog. The list of house rules tacked on the door was in Spanish; likewise the hotel directory. A painting of steel-clad conquistadors on horseback confronting proud natives in feathers and gold hung on the wall. A copy of *Sacro Biblio* sat on the table.

What have I gotten myself into? he wondered. *I don't belong here.* With a sigh, he stood and peeled off his sweat-soaked shirt like a second skin, then entered the small bathroom. Automatically, he reached for the light switch, and then turned on the tap. He watched the water swirl in the basin and smiled. Right was still cold and left was still hot—in spite of the "C" on the handle. Even the light switch had worked the same as at home, he now realized. *This isn't some alien planet on the far side of the universe,* he thought. His apprehensions dropped away like a sigh. Tomorrow, he would meet Orlov at the dock. Everything would work out.

Thursday, May 27

GALEN

"What do you mean, they're already gone? The ship was due today." Yet it was undeniably here, towering over him, its shadow a welcome relief against the equatorial sun. Only a dozen or so crewmen were in sight.

The short, stocky man at the bottom of the gangplank shrugged. "*Si, Señor.* We dock this morning, five o'clock. The passengers have all departed. What can I say?" He turned to a pair of crewmen carrying a crate labeled "Fragile. Astronomical equipment" and shouted in Spanish. Galen plucked at his sleeve.

"You're sure *all* the passengers have left?"

The man drew himself up with a click of his heels as if that would increase his stature and affected a short, stiff bow. "I am chief steward of Forward B Deck. Of course I am sure."

"But where did they go?" Galen rubbed his hand across his forehead and through his hair. Scarcely eight-thirty, yet the sun had already burned off last night's fog. The muggy heat was becoming unbearable. The noise of the docks shattered his thoughts into shards of glass. Orlov was supposed to be here. He was supposed to greet her with a casual "Hi, there! Here I am!" and she would all but swoon with gratitude. And then—

Beyond that, the scene lost focus. He realized just how foolish and naïve this whole trip was. Leave it to Harry to miss such an important detail. Of course, Harry didn't plan for such things. Harry never planned ahead at all. He was the impulsive, learn-as-you-go type.

Again the steward shrugged, and then started flipping through the pages on his clipboard. "What person are you looking for?"

"Orlov. G. M. Orlov."

"Orlov. Ah, here they are. All I can tell you is that most of their luggage was delivered to Desamparacos. That is the train station. Perhaps you will find them there."

Galen turned from him, then turned again, like a compass

needle seeking a new direction. *They?* he wondered briefly. Of course, Orlov would not be traveling alone. But how to catch them now?

He pulled the packet Orlov had left him from the inside pocket of his jacket and unfolded the blue paper.

Arrive Lima, May 27.

Cerro de Pasco, May 28.

He tapped the steward's shoulder even as the man was turning away. "How do I get to Cerro de Pasco?"

"The train, of course," the steward replied, evidently out of patience. He tapped on his clipboard as if to remind Galen that some people had work to do. "I believe it leaves every morning at seven-forty."

Galen looked at his watch, though he knew it was well past that. He blew out his breath in a prolonged sigh, combing his fingers back through his hair. Catching the motion, he stuffed his hands into his pockets and pressed his elbows close to his ribs. The prospect of wandering around Peru, always one day behind, of trying to communicate with strangers whose English, if any, was almost as unintelligible as their Spanish, momentarily brought him to a complete paralysis of thought.

But what else was he to do? He leaned forward until he fell into a step, forcing himself into action.

Harry, what have you gotten me into?

GIL

Oh, but there is power here. Gil could feel its quiet ebb and flow, the gentle, slow rhythm of deep sleep. She stood at the base of a misshapen mound, eyes closed, inhaling the heated air as if it were the essence of Pachacamac, itself.

"There's certainly not much to see here." Petra's loud voice broke the spell of Gil's meditation. She wanted to *shush* her sister before she could awaken the slumbering power, but that, of course, was absurd. No one in a thousand years or more had disturbed what waited here—if such power were not itself mere fantasy. Gil was never sure if things she sensed were true phenomenon or false imaginings, conjured from desire. And right now, she wanted Pachacamac to be real, a greater power on her side, protecting her on this journey. She needed some kind of affirmation that what they were doing would succeed.

But Petra was right. There wasn't much to see. Except for a certain pattern imposed on the scene, the abandoned site might be nothing more than barren hills. The occasional scar of a stone wall was the only sign of human workmanship. Once the largest city in Peru, the ruins of Pachacamac appeared more like sand castles washed by the tide, melting beneath the desert sun. They clustered around the massive ruin of the Temple of the Sun that crowned the low hill. Even unexcavated, she could identify the massive bulk of the pyramid beneath its five-hundred-year mantle of sand and neglect.

While the others checked into the Gran Hotel Bolivar, Petra had borrowed a car—an ancient and wheezing Tin Lizzy—from one of Lorenzo's contacts. She, Gil, and Sumala had taken the coastal road south.

"Was this really necessary?"

Sumala's words echoed her own thoughts. Gil wondered just what had brought her here. A whim? Some exotic idea of asking a long vanquished deity permission to trespass in his territory? What had she expected besides sand and buried stone?

Now that she stood among these empty ruins, she found the idea absurd. If power slumbered here, it must deign her too insignificant to respond to her summoning. She could never admit such folly, though—not to Petra. She adopted a distant air and focused on the fog bank lurking just off shore as if gazing at scenes invisible to other eyes. What she was really thinking was how cool that fog might feel if it rolled ashore. Then again, it might only increase the humidity, turning the valley into a giant sweat lodge.

"Don't you feel it?" she responded cryptically, stretching her arms out and spreading her fingers to stroke the fine weft of the air.

"I feel like I'm melting," Sumala said, pulling at her shirt where it was sticking to her skin. "Only fools would come out here in this heat. In fact, we should probably head back soon, if we're to get back to Lima before nightfall." She frowned at the surrounding dunes with the eye of someone accustomed to the capricious ways of the desert. Gil saw as Sumala did the blur of dirty cloud to the south. Its sinister form made her shiver, in spite of the heat and beyond the threat of a normal storm.

She took a swig from the canteen hung from her belt, but the water was warm and tasted of metal and grit. It only made her more thirsty. The thought of an iced drink in the cool, dim refuge of some *taberna* became an all-consuming desire.

But something remained undone here, and she couldn't leave just yet. She hadn't come here just to stand among empty ruins. There was more here than neglected mounds of earth, nature contriving to conceal the true structures beneath.

"Just give me a few more minutes. I'll meet you at the car." She turned and strode forward before Petra could object. Once she was out of their sight, she paused and waited until she heard them moving off toward the car parked beside the road just a hundred yards distant.

Gil climbed the low hill, and then the steep slope of the temple itself, a feat more difficult than it appeared. With each step forward, she slid half a step back, feet sinking into the heated sand. The humidity and heat weighed her down in a smothering embrace. She clawed for purchase at the heavy air. When she finally reached the top, she could only sit and gasp.

After a time, she stood to seek her bearings. This foreign land disoriented and confused her. Passing south of the equator had turned everything around. Imitating her great grandmother's rituals, she faced each of the four directions. Twenty miles east, the Andes rose in an abrupt and solemn wall, tantalizing snowfields too bright in the lowering sun. Opposite and closer to hand, the flat, gray line of the Pacific faded into offshore fog. In between, the desolation of the coastal desert stretched north and south, habitable only in verdant canyons where rivers sliced through mountain barriers. Sand dunes swept relentlessly across the landscape, scornful of man's ephemeral efforts. Lima, only nineteen miles away, seemed an illusion.

"I am here," she whispered, unable to think of anything more significant. On an impulse, she stooped and brushed away the sand and dirt to reveal a stone surface. With water from her canteen, she made a mud paste and smeared it on her hand. She pressed it against the stone, a crude mark compared to those back home. It wouldn't last. Even now, as the mud dried, it faded to the color of the stone.

Remember that, she told herself. *Someday, you'll be gone, and the world will never know you were here.*

But while the print remained, she knew she existed and had a place in the world. That made her smile again. She had a place and a purpose. That purpose would leave its own mark, for good or ill, as indelible as the work of the wind, and as invisible.

"I am here!" She shouted now, raising her gaze to the gray-green line of the ocean, the realm of Pachacamac. She didn't really expect an answer, yet felt a stirring of power, as if a dream shifted and a sleeper sighed.

The wind circled her, plucking at her skirt and fingering her hair. Sand blowing across the dunes whispered in myriad voices. Again she felt the deep, slow turning of power. *For good or ill?* she wondered, and immediately, the memory of the coyote in Chicago—and the entity that had willed that attack—came to mind.

It was here now, as if her thoughts had summoned it, a presence elusive as shadow, insubstantial as the whisper of the sand sliding over the dunes. It could find no creature in this wasteland to do its bidding, save the wind. Even so, it assailed her with the taste of dust. She scarcely dared to breathe, lest she inhale the taint of its essence.

"Who are you?" Gil whispered.

Sand slid across the face of the dunes, hissing.

"Who are you?" she demanded out loud.

But the presence had no voice but the wind's. The dormant power here held it in check, and Gil felt secure atop the pyramid. It could not surmount the walls, but circled the ruined temple in eddies and whirlwinds.

"What do you want?" she asked, but heard only laughter as the wind rose abruptly, a beast unleashed. A thick, dark cloud reduced the sun's glare to a pale circle, casting the pyramid into shadow.

"Gilaishling!" Petra called from somewhere below, her voice carrying a sense of desperation, as if she'd been calling for some time. "We need to leave *now!*" The car's horn brayed.

Gil glanced around as if she'd been somewhere else and only just returned. The storm from the south was almost upon them, and a sense of urgency unfurled from the pit of her stomach. She hurried down the steep slope of the temple, sliding more than running, each stride lengthening until she could no longer keep up with her own momentum. She fell and rolled to the bottom.

Scrambling to her feet, Gil futilely brushed at the sand on her clothes. The bulk of the temple sheltered her from the wind now, but she couldn't see more than fifty feet.

"Petra!" she called out, and started forward.

"Gilaishling!" Sumala added her voice to Petra's, but the rising dust obscured them from sight. One of them kept sounding the car's horn. The wind caught the sound and shredded it, tossing it to the four corners. Gil lost all sense of direction as she blundered through the ruined city. Sand grains pricked exposed skin like needles, and the thick dust scratched her throat as she gasped for a clear breath. She stood still and closed her eyes, seeking with other senses for their essence. Still the wind hounded and herded her, skewing her path. In its voice, she heard wicked laughter.

She stumbled and fell and was tempted to just stay there and let Petra find her. But the sand drifted against her, threatening to make her the anchor of a new dune. She closed her eyes and tried to vanquish the wind, but such power was beyond her. *I should be able to control this,* she thought. *I should have that power.*

As if in response, a fresh wind stirred, smelling incongruously of salt and kelp. The blowing sand cleared, revealing the car on her left. She had almost walked past it. Petra stood in the lee between open doors, beckoning for her to hurry. As Gil ran the wind and sand closed in again. She lunged forward, diving past Petra into the back seat. Sumala gunned the engine even as Petra climbed in and slammed the door. The wind chased after them.

Gil sat rigid, hands clutching the edge of the seat and eyes closed. *I'm not ready for this,* she thought. *I don't know how to handle it.* What did she know, really? Petra and the clan had kept her sheltered and isolated. She wondered what other perils waited for which she had no experience. The prospect made her tremble, and she hugged her knees to her chest, curling into as small an intrusion upon the universe as she could manage.

Gradually, her trembling ceased and she relaxed. When Gil looked up, Petra was watching her over the back of the front seat with a sour frown, as if the storm was Gil's own doing.

She wasn't sure which was worse—the threat of this strange and unnamed entity or Petra's scorn.

~ * ~

"We have to stop! I can't see the road anymore," Sumala announced. She was leaning forward, peering through the windshield into veils of blowing sand. Her grip on the steering wheel was as tight as the set of her jaw.

"If we stop here, the sand will bury us," Petra argued, and though her voice was calm, an anxious tone edged its timbre.

"If we keep going, we could lose the road altogether. I'm not even sure we're on it now."

"Keep going," Gil said from the back seat. "Another quarter mile. There's an abandoned *taberna* on the left."

"Are you sure?" Petra asked with undisguised skepticism.

"Of course I am," Gil countered hotly, though she herself had doubts. She'd seen one on the trip down and perhaps she was merely guessing—hoping—that it was ahead. But she felt its solid bulk through the tenuous fabric of the sand as surely as she sensed the road beneath them. She shifted forward to place a hand on Sumala's shoulder, guiding her.

It seemed they hardly moved at all. The sand enveloped them, obscuring any reference points. The mysterious presence was gone from the storm, but nature, itself, now conspired against them. The headlight beams reflected back from a thousand grains of dancing sand. What little light penetrated the murk of the storm was fading as the sun, unseen, settled for the night.

At last, Gil told Sumala to pull off the road, though there was no sign of a building. In a supreme act of trust, Sumala turned the wheel. For a long time, Gil held her breath as the car ground through loose sand. It was some time before they realized the headlights were reflecting off a solid, white surface. Sumala stopped only inches from the building. Gil felt as relieved as her sisters.

They parked on the lee side of the building and found their way inside. The floor was littered with debris and the leavings of small animals. Faded, torn posters still clung to crumbling plaster, and a crude wooden counter ran the length of one wall, thick with gritty dust.

"I suppose we're stuck here for the night," Sumala observed, eyeing a dark corner where something small scratched and burrowed in a drift of debris.

"We'll miss the morning train," Petra added.

Gil closed her eyes and listened to the song of the wind. She touched the air like a musician stroking harp strings. "The storm will end soon. If the road isn't too drifted over, we might make it yet."

MOONRISE: 8:47 p.m. EST ~ MOONSET: 8:55 a.m. EST
SUNRISE: 6:13 a.m. EST ~ SUNSET: 5:49 p.m. EST
Friday, May 28

GALEN

The train was crowded and hot and smelly. Reading about primitive conditions and native customs was no preparation for experiencing them. Galen had almost gagged when he'd first realized that the gray and white splotches on the floor had more to do with poultry than a sloppy painter. He kept his attention focused beyond the window, but that, too, was smeared. Perhaps it was for the best, he decided, for the view was equally unsettling. The rickety train wheezed its way through switchbacks up a nearly vertical cliff in a canyon too narrow to echo back the train's own whistle. The railroad had been constructed in the late nineteenth century, and Galen thought that the train, itself, must be at least twice that old, if not in actual years, then in wear and tear. Flakes of paint in inaccessible corners attested to past elegance, but the overall finish was the dark, oily varnish of human touch.

Galen had been more or less forced into his seat by the crush of the crowd and trapped there against the window by the woman claiming the aisle seat, defeating his plan to wander the aisles looking for Orlov. She was amply built, dressed in layers of bright Peruvian woolens and wearing three hats. An infant nestled in a colorful *lliclla* against her bosom, and a large bag full of packages crouched on the floor between her feet. The baby never made a sound.

The train lurched to a stop at the end of one switchback, then jolted into reverse to struggle up the next. But the top of the cliff revealed another valley, and beyond that, yet another climb. He'd lost count of the tunnels somewhere in the twenties; the guidebook said there were sixty-five of them—and sixty-one bridges.

The relatively swift ascent allowed no chance to adjust to the change in altitude. His chest hurt with the effort to breathe what little air circulated through the ramshackle car. He tried to open the window, desperate for even a single breath of clean, fresh air, but it was jammed shut. He couldn't manage the right leverage to force it. His head pounded, and his eyesight blurred from dizziness, symptoms of altitude sickness according to the guidebook. So, too, was the nausea clutching at his stomach with an ever-tightening grip. Something he'd eaten the day before was not agreeing with him. His stomach churned and gurgled and otherwise threatened eruption. He'd managed to keep from vomiting, but from the odors wafting through the air, others had not. Perhaps he was fortunate he'd not had time for breakfast.

His seat companion took up all of her seat and half of his. He couldn't even shrug out of his jacket. He'd managed to stuff his duffel bag under the seat, hooking the strap around his ankle to keep it from being stolen, but the valise he kept in his lap, hugging it to his chest. His shoulders ached from their hunched posture. When he tried to shift sideways, the woman smiled a broad, broken-toothed smile. She spoke in a language that sounded like Spanish diced and blended with something both more guttural and fluid. He could only nod and smile back.

Two children stood next to her in the aisle, clinging to their mother's skirts. As the train lurched and rocked, they scrambled to keep their balance. There was little chance of their falling—the aisle was too crowded—but he wondered how they could breathe in the midst of all those bodies so much taller than they.

The younger child, a girl perhaps three or four years old, thin and bedraggled, wore a dress stained and patched, but her hair had been washed and neatly combed. Her large, dark eyes captured and beguiled him; his gaze kept returning to them. Finally and with a resigned sigh, he pushed his valise down between his feet and motioned that she could sit on his lap. She looked to her mother, who in turn looked Galen up and down and through, then nodded slowly. With a shy smile, the girl climbed over her mother's knees and onto Galen's lap. Her brother glared at him, but Galen had only one lap to spare.

He soon regretted the offer. Even the girl's slight weight became a burden, and her presence only added to the heat pooling around him like thick syrup. He tried to shift her weight, but she held herself rigid, leaning away from him. The silence between them was as thick as the heat.

"What's your name?" Galen asked finally. What had the Spanish phrase book said? "*¿Comma see ama?*" The little girl stared at him blankly. He twisted around to slide the book from his jacket pocket.

"Ah, here it is. *¿Cómo se llama?*"

She glanced again at her mother, who spoke briefly. Apparently his phrase-book Spanish was equally difficult for them.

Finally the girl answered in a shy murmur. "Eisabel."

"Ees-bel?" Galen parroted. It took four more attempts before he came close enough to elicit a nod. *Ay-ee-sa-bel.* He thought perhaps she'd merely given up. He wasn't even sure it was her name. For all he knew, it could have meant "mind your own business."

Galen persisted, though. If he was going to survive in this country until he caught up with Orlov, he reasoned, he needed all the practice he could get.

He turned to the little boy. "*¿Cómo se llama?*"

"Pedro," the boy answered proudly, eager to show he understood the American better than the others.

"And *¿cómo se llama*, uh—" He nodded at the girl's mother. Eisabel only looked puzzled. "*¿Cómo se llama yo mama?*"

"*Se llama Mama*," she answered solemnly.

He gave up on any further conversation and turned back to the window.

The worst of the trip was the Galera Tunnel at Ticlio, dark and airless. Galen felt as if he had personally hauled the train up every one of the 13,000 feet they had climbed. He squirmed beneath Eisabel's weight, aching for a breath. After that came a blessed descent, and the pain in his chest eased somewhat.

Eisabel seemed to lose her temerity. Too young to comprehend that Galen could not understand her, she chattered amiably, pointing out the window or making gestures as enigmatic as the language. Galen could only nod and mumble, charmed by the clear, dark magic of her eyes, as if the translation of her words lurked in those depths.

Finally, the train lurched to a stop and people scrambled to get off. A panic seized Galen.

"La Oroya?" he asked of Eisabel's mother. She was too busy gathering her belongings and children to answer.

"La Oroya?" Galen shouted into the crowd, but no one paid him any mind. From La Oroya, this train continued south to Cuzco. He needed to switch to the northbound train to reach Cerro De Pasco. He repeated his request, and still people ignored him.

Little Eisabel tugged at his sleeve, and he looked up to see Mama motioning for him to move, her prodigious bulk holding back the tide of passengers surging toward the exit.

As he disentangled his foot from the strap of his duffel bag and stumbled into the aisle, he wondered if his own queries had been misinterpreted, and all these people were getting off the train because of him.

He stood on the platform, lost among the passengers. A horde of women in trilby hats sold knit goods and food. The blend of odors was both mouthwatering and nauseating. He rubbed at his empty stomach, swaying dizzily. He'd not had anything to eat since dinner last night—a strange and spicy concoction of meat and potatoes he'd bought from a street vendor and a bottle of Inca Cola. Foolishly, he'd expected a dining car like on American trains.

"Cerro de Pasco?" he called out, but no one answered. "¿El tren Cerro de Pasco?" he asked of a uniformed attendant after consulting his phrase book again. The man stared past him as if he were a statue.

Galen searched among the passengers milling about the platform, seeking a familiar flash of red hair. His height gave him an advantage. Craning his neck, he peered at the farthest edges on the crowd, but could not spot his quarry. Turning, he bumped against a short, dark-haired woman.

"Excuse me," he said automatically, nodding as if he were tipping his hat.

"It's quite all right," she responded in the first unaccented English he'd heard since arriving in Peru. She smiled and he was taken by the bright flash of her eyes, dark and liquid in a round face that seemed vaguely oriental.

"Come on, Sesha!" someone called, and she turned toward a group of women clustered in the middle of the platform.

Galen felt a tug at his sleeve. Eisabel stood by him, pointing toward her mother, who was talking to one of the vendors. When he glanced back, the woman named Sesha and her companions had merged into the colorful mosaic of the crowd.

Eisabel tugged again at his sleeve, and with a sigh, Galen let her lead him across the platform. The vendor pushed a cup of hot tea into his hands. He tried to refuse, but she insisted, making drinking gestures, and Eisabel and her mother also urged him to drink. Then the vendor rubbed her fingers together, mumbling something about *soles*. He pulled out the wad he'd received at the hotel, an incredible amount, he thought, for twenty dollars. The peasant woman's eyes went wide, and she snatched a bill quickly from the selection Galen offered. As he tucked the rest back into his money belt, he was aware of Mama watching closely as well. He suspected he'd overpaid, though by his rough calculation, it was less than a nickel.

But no matter, it was worth it. As he drank the tea, a warm numbness spread outward from his stomach, easing his headache and stifling the dizziness with a pleasant buzz.

The vendor, all gap-toothed smiles and nods and cheerful prattle, poured more tea. She and Mama started to argue about something, and the vendor then offered him a handful of fruit and potatoes. Galen looked to Mama for help, but she merely urged him to accept, launching into a spate of rapid Spanish, and pointing at the *soles* he had given the woman. Galen realized she was insisting he got his money's worth.

With Harry's pocketknife, Galen cut up the fruit and shared it with Eisabel and Pedro while Mama wandered off, presumably to nurse the baby. They stood there, juice running down their chins and Eisabel's dark eyes bright with mischief and little girl giggles.

Galen heard someone shouting. The only words he could understand were "Cerro de Pasco."

"*¿El tren Cerro de Pasco?*" he asked of Pedro.

The boy merely nodded and said, "*Sí, Cerro de Pasco.*" Mama reappeared.

"*¡Apúrense!*" she called out, and the little family herded him across the platform and into a crowd rushing to board a second train. The crush of passengers pushed him into yet another window seat, and Mama settled herself next to him, cradling the still silent baby. Eisabel climbed once again into his lap, as if from long established custom.

Even more people boarded, crowding the aisle and hanging out the doors, even standing on the couplings between cars. The train pulled out of town, past slag heaps and mine tailings, and onto a hilly plain, so barren and featureless, some giant might have swept it with a broom. The Junin Plain was a desolate place where even the air tasted metallic. The La Oroya smelters had turned it into a toxic wasteland—dead trees, dead cattle, dead hope in the eyes of the people. The Peruvian government had ordered the miners to add a filtering system in 1925. Twelve years later, it was still incomplete. The land was a ruin, yet the Cerro de Pasco Mining Corporation—owned by American interests—was buying it up like a vulture picking at a carcass. What could be the profit in that, Galen wondered.

He stared morosely out the window as the passing scene faded into a murky dusk. Clouds clotted the sky, bringing a premature evening. Lake Junin passed somewhere to the left. Eisabel leaned closer to him, finally hiding her face in his jacket as if the darkness beyond the window terrified her more than this helpless and foreign stranger. She settled against his shoulder and fell asleep. Her mother prattled something at him in her language full of stops and clicks and harsh, explosive sounds. He could only shrug and smile thinly.

Galen had started to nod off when a single voice tugged at his ear, filling an abrupt lull in the constant chatter of foreign tongues.

Someone was speaking English, and the familiar timbre and tone snagged his attention. Unable to stand without disturbing the sleeping Eisabel, Galen craned his neck trying to pinpoint the source.

"Miss Orlov!" he called out, hoping to be heard above the renewed din. A sliver of head turned, seeking the source of the voice.

"Miss Orlov, over here!" Galen waved, but could not catch her glance. Strange, he thought, that he had not noticed her before, either on the train or the platform in La Oroya, or that she had not seen him. No matter. When the train stopped, he'd be able to catch her.

An eternity and a half later, the train pulled into Cerro de Pasco. The passengers in the doorways tumbled forth, followed by the rest. Galen tried to track the red-haired woman as she moved toward the exit.

Eisabel continued to sleep in Galen's lap, and when he tried to stand, he discovered his arm had gone numb. Mama chattered urgently and made complex gestures, but he could understand neither. He managed to clutch the handle of his valise with one hand and, once Mama had moved out into the aisle, retrieve his duffel bag, all without disturbing the sleeping child. Pedro tugged at the bag's strap until Galen gave it up. Proudly, the boy shouldered it, though it seemed almost as big as he.

Through the window, Galen saw the woman crossing the

platform, but what he'd taken for red hair was but a scarf. He pounded on the window anyway and called her name, but she gave no indication of hearing. Hoisting Eisabel, he struggled along the narrow aisle.

Galen paused on the platform to catch his breath and his bearings. Neither came easily. He scanned the faces coming and going. Orlov had disappeared, swallowed up by the darkness hung like a blanket beyond the flare of lights whose brightness served to hinder sight as much as aid it.

"Miss Orlov, where are you?" he called out.

Eisabel's mother headed off as if confident he would follow. So did Pedro, along with Galen's duffel bag.

"No, wait!" he called out in protest. "I don't want to go with you." What he wanted most was a warm meal. And a hot bath. And a soft bed. He couldn't decide which he wanted most.

"Hey, Pedro, I'll trade your sister for my bag!" But if they heard him, they paid him no heed. Burdened with the sleeping child, he had no choice but to follow. He decided he would carry the little girl home; surely if they were walking, it couldn't be too far. Since they had taken care of him on the train, he could do no less. Then he would return to the station and track down the elusive Miss Orlov.

The city's sporadic lighting cast long shadows across the unpaved streets as the little group skirted open pits and long trenches. He could scarcely see where they led him and, if not for Pedro's guidance, would've fallen in a ditch on more than one occasion. The day's heat had drained away and Galen was soon shivering in spite of his exertion.

Beyond the edge of town, they climbed a small hill past tailing mounds and refuse heaps. At first, it felt good to stretch his legs after the confinement of the train, but all too soon, he tired. Inhaling the thin air in quick, convulsive gasps, each breath became a major undertaking, and he could spare none to call out a protest. The muscles in his legs quivered and ached as he labored under Eisabel's slight weight. *Foolishness,* his mind insisted, yet he kept doggedly on. Mama had outdistanced him, but Pedro kept pace, just far enough ahead that Galen held a hope of retrieving his duffel bag. Somehow that kept him going, one step and then another.

When the path leveled out, he paused and turned to look back on a constellation of lights that seemed no more a town than the stars overhead—and equally, unreachably distant. How would he ever find his way back? He felt isolated and vulnerable and glanced suspiciously at the pack of shadows gathered around him.

But what was he to do? Drop the sleeping child in the dirt, grab his bag and run? Somehow, he couldn't envision it—or rather, he could, and it looked so comical and cowardly, he refused to consider it.

Mama stopped at last at a mud hut with a thatched roof that grew up out of the dark as if born of the gloom. She gestured for him to wait while she went inside. Eisabel suddenly and conveniently awoke and wiggled out of his arms. She giggled shyly, and Galen wondered if she'd really been asleep at all. He waited uneasily, uncertain of what to expect. Had they lured him here, the unsuspecting tourist? The wind blew cold through the fabric of his jacket, and he hugged himself for warmth.

Mama emerged from the hut with a pottery cup and ceramic bottle. She poured a dark liquid into the cup and offered it to Galen.

"Thanks," he said, taking the cup and raising it as in a toast. "Uh, *gracias.*" The cup was filthy, but Galen didn't want to insult the woman by refusing it. Perhaps only a sip would satisfy her need for hospitality. He swirled the dark contents and turned the cup, looking for the cleanest part of the rim. As he raised the cup to drink, however, Mama erupted into a spate of gestures and words. Holding his hand as one might teach a child, she tipped the cup to pour out a few drops on the ground.

"*Ch'ura,*" she said. "*Por Pachamama.*" Galen remembered a trivial item in the guidebook. Pachamama was the Earth Mother. If this little ritual honored her, it must be in thanksgiving for a safe journey; certainly this impoverished family didn't travel often.

"*Por Pachamama,*" he repeated carefully and then, at Mama's urging, bravely smiled and sipped from the cup.

He'd had Scotch whiskey and bourbon and once on a dare, pure grain alcohol—nothing compared to the breath-stealing fire that slid down his throat, igniting skyrockets in his stomach. His sinuses steamed, melting his eyes into puddles of tears.

"Wha—" he gasped and discovered he had no voice.

"Pisco," Mama answered with a proud smile, pouring herself a cup and repeating the offering to Pachamama. She urged Galen to drink more. Galen shrugged, thinking at least the alcohol might kill any germs. The fire in his stomach banked down to a warm glow that spread along his arms and legs, easing the aches of the journey and warming the chills that had settled upon him. Even his hunger abated. He drained the cup. In return, he offered her the potatoes the vendor in La Oroyo had given him. He certainly had little use for them.

Mama nodded. She and the children herded him toward the hut. He tried to protest, to tell them he had to leave, to return to the city and find a hotel. He fumbled with the phrase book, but it was too dark to read.

Eisabel tugged at the sleeve of his jacket and her wide, dark eyes lured his heart. As the heat of the pisco soaked through his muscles, he found himself incredibly tired. He wanted to melt into a corner and sleep.

This family was inviting him into their home, but if this was their house, they certainly had little to spare.

How much is enough? Orlov's question echoed back to him. Food to eat, clothes to wear, a warm, dry place to sleep. This woman had little, and yet enough to spare for a lost and inept stranger. To refuse their hospitality, such as it was, might only insult them, steal from them the precious gem of dignity. So he stumbled after the little girl and bent to enter through a low door covered with a woolen blanket.

He found himself in a kitchen of sorts. A cook pot hung in one corner, and Pedro was already kindling a fire beneath it. Smoke exited through a hole in the roof, but not before filling the room with its acrid sting. Galen almost wished he'd taken up cigarettes, for then he might be accustomed to the dry burn in his throat. A small, crude table occupied the center of a packed earth floor blackened with droppings and grease. Boxes and bags and indefinable lumps hugged the walls. Something—several somethings—rustled and chittered in the shadows.

Mama disappeared with the baby through a blanketed doorway at the back of the room. Eisabel sat Galen down on a wooden stool, then turned her attention to the cook pot, filling it with items from the boxes in the corner and water ladled from a large, cracked jug and Galen's own potatoes.

Pedro poured him another drink.

Saturday, May 29

GALEN

Someone was playing a set of pipes. The breathy trill, deep and hollow, pierced the stuffed cotton of Galen's head, setting off a bass drum where his skull should be. He shifted position and his bedding rustled thunderously.

An unremembered dream left a taste of anxiety, so that when he opened his eyes to darkness, he panicked, unsure of where he was. He thrashed about in a tangle of thick, woolen blankets until he had freed his head and managed to sit up. The air was chill and smelled of old grease and stale smoke. A faint and fetid odor reminded him of his early childhood on a Kansas farm. Pale, dusty light revealed the crude mud walls of Mama's kitchen. He was huddled in one corner on a thick mat of dried grass.

As he wrestled free of the blankets, an empty plate clattered across the floor. He couldn't remember eating, but did remember a second drink of pisco and trying to refuse a third. He remembered standing and turning to leave. And that was all.

The hut was deathly still. Mama and her family were gone.

So was his duffel bag.

Frantically, Galen groped among the blankets for the valise but found only packed earth and dry grass. He slapped his pockets. His wallet and passport, Harry's money, even Harry's knife— all were gone. Ironically, he felt more concern over the knife than the money.

He strode toward the inner room. Pulling aside the blanket, a feculent stench overwhelmed him. Morbid dread quelled his anger. A whisper sighed upon his ear, echoing a forgotten dream. Clenching his teeth, swallowing hard to quell his heaving stomach, he entered.

The only sound in the dim room was the buzz of insects, but in that silence, he heard something move. Again he thought of his parents' farm. He knew this odor. It evoked shudders of horror and apprehension and visions of blood.

"No," he whispered. Dream images, overexposed in daylight,

nudged for attention, but his rational mind refused to bring them into focus. Dread shivered in every limb and quickened his breath to shallow, reluctant gasps. At first, he could make out only faint glimmers in the dark. A pair of shining eyes stared at him, unblinking. As his sight adjusted to the gloom, a face formed around those eyes, a wide, dark smile. And still the eyes did not blink.

He did, and with each blink, more became clear. Mama sat straight legged on a crude bed, back against the far wall. What Galen had taken for a smile was a gaping slash across her throat. The baby lay across her lap like a sacrifice. Pedro sat beside his mother, head bowed as if contemplating the fist-sized object cupped in his hands, dark red and shiny wet.

"Lord, no," Galen prayed. Stepping forward, he swung his hand to sweep away the cobwebs of nightmare. His foot nudged something soft.

Eisabel lay prone on the floor, one arm reaching toward where he had slept. Galen sank to his knees and gathered her into his arms, praying she still lived. Eisabel gazed at his face with those eyes that had so captured him, beguiling him still. She touched his chest with a bloodied hand.

"*Sálvenos,*" she whispered, a long sigh that seemed to deflate her small body. She slipped from his embrace like melting wax and rolled onto the floor. A single beam of dusty light illumined the cracked ivory haft protruding from her back.

Heartbeat like a bass drum, Galen scuttled backward, then turned and crawled to the doorway. Clutching at the blanket that covered it, he staggered to his feet. It tore free and fell upon him. He fought to escape its dusty embrace, gasping in horror and panic. How could he have slept through such slaughter? How could he not have heard?

Yet, when he blinked, dream fragments replayed themselves behind his eyes—a robed figure, face hidden in hooded shadow. The gleam of bright metal. Screams and pleas and unanswered prayers. And he, bound helpless, unable to respond.

"Why?" he cried out now, for it was the only word he could find. The cry engulfed his universe and swallowed it whole.

A gust of wind entered the empty house, and Galen watched it swirl the dust, keening a mournful dirge. Lurching through the outer doorway, he stumbled into the embrace of harsh sunlight. He spun around to stare at the hut, hoping it might vanish into the haze of nightmare. His head took a moment longer to catch up. Dizzy, he fell to his knees. With violent convulsions, he wretched as if he could empty himself of the vile images, continuing long after his stomach was empty and only green bile seared his throat.

He sat in the dirt, head hung between his knees, letting his mind clear. The heat of the sun soaked the chill from his bones, but it could not thaw the horror that held him motionless.

Reason seeped through the muddled sludge of his thoughts, and he began to consider his situation. Stranded in a foreign country, an alien culture, he couldn't even speak the language. He had nothing—absolutely nothing—and didn't know a soul for four thousand miles.

And now, he would be suspected of murder.

That fearsome thought brought him to his feet at last. Shading his eyes, he peered around. The hut stood alone on the shoulder of a low hill. Cerro de Pasco descended down the slope to the open pits of its mines. To the west and east, far across the flat and barren altiplano, mountain ranges erupted abruptly, as if this land knew no compromise between horizontal and vertical.

Nearby, a man in a bright poncho and wide-brimmed hat sat beneath a leafless tree festooned with bright blue flowers. Seed pods stirring in the breeze produced a thin, sweet sound to accompany the man's pipes, a set of hollow reeds bound with brightly colored thread, the longest almost two feet in length. He nodded at Galen, but continued to play. The forlorn, haunting melody echoed Galen's dreams. It hovered in the air like the hooded figure. Galen shuddered, shattering the ominous image before he could remember more.

Galen looked down at his shirt. A reddish brown handprint, much larger than Eisabel's tiny hand, stained the fabric above his left breast. Swiping at it, his hand felt tainted by the touch. He stared at his hands, then wiped them one against the other. With a violent shudder, he repressed an impulse to tear the shirt from his back and hurl it away. First Edward, now this. Would blood forever haunt him?

He should never have come to Peru, never looked into Eisabel's beguiling eyes or offered to hold her in his lap. He should've dumped her at the train station and sought out Orlov.

Orlov!

So abrupt was the surge of hope, he shouted her name out loud. Orlov would help; she would know what to do. Everything would be all right. He had only to find her.

If she's still here.

He had no idea where she might be headed from here, but surely, she couldn't have left by now—whenever *now* was. Though frost still lingered in shadows, the sun had climbed perhaps half way toward noon.

Despair thawed in the heat of fresh panic, freeing him at last to move. He stood, swaying dizzily, and stared at Eisabel's hut. He should go back for the knife, he thought. Harry's knife. It was the one item that incriminated him. But he could not contemplate entering that hut once more. He tried, a single step, but his feet refused another. Malign shadow lingered. He might yet become its victim, if it did not own him already. He reached inside his shirt to rub and scratch his chest where the bloody handprint had soaked through his shirt. Like centaur's blood, it seemed to burn and poison his skin.

Guilt added to the mix of emotions churning in his stomach, but he could not let that deter him any longer. He had to find Orlov before she moved on. He had to get away from here before anyone found out what had happened. Turning away, he saw the pipe player still sitting under the tree, watching him with an empty, impassive stare.

With a shrug to square his shoulders, Galen ran his fingers through the tangles of his hair. He buttoned his jacket to conceal the bloodied shirt and brushed down his clothes, then strode off as if he had nothing to hide.

~ * ~

Galen's feet seemed to remember the way better than he, and he soon found the train station. From there, he wandered toward the center of town, a small plaza with a tiled fountain at its center. A church on one end of the plaza confronted a small hotel or inn on the other. It seemed as likely a place as any to begin. The sun had baked away the effects of the pisco, but his head still pounded from the altitude, and now he felt hungry, his stomach churning. Lightheaded, he staggered as he entered the inn.

The lobby was also a restaurant, and the smell of cooking food distracted Galen as he approached the wooden plank that served as a counter. His mind relegated the morning's events to oblivion for now. In the interest of survival, the horror had numbed down to a small, distant voice still crying out *why?*

The man behind the counter hunched over an accounting ledger, and judging from his furrowed brow, wasn't making much progress. He looked up as Galen approached and offered a disgusted frown. Galen realized just what a mess he must appear, his clothes dirty and disheveled, hair tousled. Combing fingers through his hair, he endeavored to display some sense of dignity.

"Excuse me, Sir. I'm looking for a woman, a—uh, a friend of mine. She has…"

The clerk only peered at him with a blank, disinterested stare.

"Do you speak English?"

The man returned to tallying up figures in the ledger. Galen sighed and tried to remember Spanish, any Spanish.

"I'm looking for a *Señorita. Señorita?*"

The clerk glanced up.

"*Señorita.* Ah, American. *¿Americana Señorita?* This tall." Galen held up a hand to indicate Orlov's height. The clerk lost interest. Galen went back to "*Americana Señorita,*" then touched his hair. "*Rojo. Rojo, ah, cabeza?*"

"Aah," the clerk responded with a sly smile. He babbled something in Spanish, tipping his chin toward the door. Galen frowned, unable to understand a single word. Muttering "Gracias," he wandered out the door. He stood there squinting in the bright light, hands in pockets. What now? For all he knew, the man had told him where to go for a bath. At least he hadn't heard any word that sounded like police.

He wandered into the plaza, toward the small church at the far end. After perhaps a hundred feet, he stopped and turned back, as if the spicy aroma of food were a tether and he had reached its end.

But he had no money. He doubted they would give him a meal on credit. Perhaps he could offer to balance their books in exchange for a meal—but how could he negotiate such a deal when he couldn't speak the language? He was staring at the inn with such single-minded intensity that the two figures emerging from his right had crossed half the span of his vision before registering on his awareness.

"Miss Orlov!" he called with a start, and hurried toward the red-haired woman. "It's me. Professor Williams."

The women stopped to regard him as he approached. Orlov's expression was expectant but blank.

"Professor Williams, yes," her companion responded. "I've heard much about you. Economics, was it not?" She glanced at Orlov as if that were a cue. Face half in shadow, she resembled the woman who had interrupted their conversation in Chicago.

Galen expected an introduction. Perhaps Orlov thought they had already met.

"Yes, Professor," Orlov responded instead with a slight emphasis on his title and a cool smile, "I simply didn't expect to see you here."

Galen stopped about five feet away. "I'm sorry to have missed the boat. I tried to meet you at the docks, but you had already left the ship."

Orlov blinked, a sense of confusion plain on her face.

"You did invite me here," Galen stated. "I mean, the ticket, the map? You said you needed me." The sun's heat turned thoughts to mush. He reeled beneath its weight. He had the odd feeling he was babbling, saying too much. "At any rate, I've finally caught up, and I have quite a story to tell."

"I can see that," Orlov responded, her gaze passing down his right side and up the left. She nodded toward his chest. "Did you cut yourself shaving?"

Galen felt his brows pucker into a frown, finding the question absurd. He hadn't shaved at all; his beard itched. But her gaze was pinned on where the bloody prints—Eisabel's and the other—showed past the edge of his jacket.

"I, uh. Yeah, something like that," he admitted. His hands itched, and he swiped them across the tweed of his jacket. He desperately wanted to blurt out the whole story, but now was neither the time nor place. Too many people milled about the plaza, and though probably none of them understood English, he felt exposed and vulnerable. He desperately wanted a dark quiet corner in which to hide while he sorted out this mess.

"Do you suppose we could—" Galen gestured vaguely in the direction of the inn. He felt himself swaying. "Breakfast?"

"I've already eaten," Orlov responded, glancing pointedly at the height of the sun. She looked him over with a critical eye. "You look as if you could use some, though. You seem to have had a rough night."

"Indeed. I was—" Galen hesitated. It seemed so ridiculous and foolish. "I was robbed." It was difficult to admit his folly. "They took my money, my baggage, everything." His tongue clogged his mouth and his throat tightened, refusing to allow more than that to pass. He swallowed hard and pulled his dignity to full height.

"Miss Orlov, I would appreciate a small loan—something to eat." He raised his hand to brush back his hair, but halted the gesture. He stared at the smear of dried blood on his palm. The skin beneath the stain on his shirt still itched. "Some place to bathe?"

"But of course," Orlov responded with a sudden and sly smile. Taking him by the arm, she gestured toward the inn. "But please, call me Miriam."

Galen stopped abruptly, shrugging out of her grip to study her face. "Miriam? But your initials—"

"G. M.? Did I never tell you that my middle name is Miriam? To be honest, I detest my first name. Here, in this place, Miriam seems much more appropriate. It means bitter, you know. Here, I am Miriam, and it suits me just fine."

Indeed, her smile held a touch of bitterness. Galen nodded, pretending to understand.

"Miriam," the other woman said, rather pointedly, "We should be—"

"See to it yourself. Meet me in the *tambo*." Miriam's tone was harsh and seemed to flay the woman's spirit, who nodded once and turned away. Miriam guided Galen towards the inn.

The temperature inside was only slightly cooler, the air stuffy and the light dim. Nevertheless, the weight of the day lifted from him as Galen paused to let his eyes adjust. He was soon seated before a plate of eggs and bread, a bowl of some kind of potato mush, and a mug of tea. The first bite required caution—gruesome images of Eisabel and her family still floated across his sight. He chewed the food slowly and waited to see how his stomach would react. Teased with that morsel, it merely demanded more. The second, third, and fourth bites came in quick succession. He spooned the food into his mouth ravenously, not caring about taste or content or hygiene.

Miriam leaned back in her seat, watching him eat with cool regard. As his hunger subsided, Galen began to feel uncomfortable beneath her gaze. The woman that sat across from him was not the same student who hid in the back of his class. She was self-assured, diffident, detached. There was a brittle edge to her, a touch of ice, even in her smile.

"So tell me your story, Professor Williams," she said when he had slowed his eating enough to talk. He didn't like the way she said "professor," as if chiding him for some unearned pretense.

"Galen. Call me Galen," he said by means of stalling before he began his tale. Miriam eyed him expectantly, waiting. He focused on his plate, relating the story of Mama and her family. "…They were all—" He couldn't bring himself to speak the word. *Dead. They were dead.*

Aloud he said simply, "—gone." He should weep for them, he thought. Someone should mourn them. But the heat seemed to have dried the moisture from his eyes.

"And what will you do now?"

He shrugged. "I don't know." And now that he could think about it without hunger or panic blinding his reason, he really didn't. He had expected Orlov to rescue him, but instead, she seemed put off by his presence. He had no money, no passport. By now, someone surely had found the bodies. He remembered how the flute player had watched him. He could be wanted for murder. A tremor slid down his spine all the way to his toes. He should've gone back for the knife.

"I had the idea this would be a bit of adventure to share with grandchildren someday. How many people travel halfway around the world to watch an eclipse?" Shaking his head ruefully, he added, "I must be crazy."

"Is that why you came? To see an eclipse?"

When Galen looked up to meet Miriam's gaze, he found her smiling, ever so slightly. There was an invitation in that smile he didn't feel prepared to accept. He had the impression he was caught in some game without knowing the rules.

"That's why you invited me, isn't it?"

Miriam's smile flattened. Galen found it disconcerting. The tables were turned here, their roles reversed. She was the teacher now, he the student, dependent on her for guidance to a degree not found in the comfort of a classroom.

And she was enjoying his unease. She rested her chin upon her palm. "Just what did you hope to find?"

He could only shrug at first. "Answers, I guess. You're an enigma, and when you dropped that paper on my desk, I thought you were handing me a clue. I suppose, too, that I'm looking for the pieces of those lost dreams we talked about. You told me to follow my dreams, even the broken ones. I guess I had some notion of putting them back together again."

Her head tilted back in a silent *aaah*. "And where are you going to find these answers and dreams?"

Galen started. "Why, that place on the map, of course. Killichaka. Isn't that where you're headed?"

"Of course," she said, nodding, as if she'd been testing him. "You brought the map with you?"

Galen frowned, then patted his jacket. There, in the inner pocket, he felt the rigid crinkle of paper. Gingerly avoiding revealing or touching the stain over his heart, he pulled out the map, unfolded it and spread it on the table.

"At least they didn't get this." He wondered if the map wasn't what they were after in the first place. He'd read in the guidebook how legends of Inca gold, hidden as news spread of Atahualpa's death at the hands of Pizarro, could still spark bouts of gold fever among the locals.

Miriam's fingers twitched as if she would snatch the map from him. He refolded the paper and returned it to his jacket pocket wondering why she had no map of her own. He made one more ploy for her aid before he'd resort to begging.

"You said you needed a guardian."

Miriam clasped her hands together, then steepled her index fingers and touched them to her lips once, twice, and again.

"A guardian. Yes," she whispered, gazing beyond him. "Someone to stand outside the circle, to witness and to—" Her eyes abruptly refocused on him, and her whole manner shifted to a warmer mien, some development now requiring a new attitude.

"You'll join us, of course. But first, let's get you cleaned up and into proper clothes. Something a little less—ah, conspicuous. You certainly can't go trekking about the Andes dressed like that."

Before she could say more, Miriam's attention was diverted. Galen turned to see her companion headed toward their table. He stood as she approached.

"Galen is going to be joining us," Miriam announced.

The glance the woman tossed at Miriam clearly asked *Is this wise?* even as she extended her hand and a welcome to Galen.

"Welcome, Mr. Williams. I'm Miriam's Aunt Vera."

SESHA

Sesha was positively fierce as she paced the station platform, weaving among people and piles of baggage and freight. Maji scurried to keep pace. They paused at the end to peer down the track that too soon curved out of sight.

"We should never have separated," Sesha muttered. "We should've waited for them in Lima." Her nerves tingled with a sense of *wrong*. Something wasn't right. Even the air here tasted foul, smelled of lighting and sulfur.

When Gil, Sumala, and Petra failed to return from Pachacamac, Lena had insisted on leaving on schedule. *They can catch tomorrow's train,* she had argued. Sesha wasn't so sure.

The train at last arrived, laboring into the station and dragging twilight behind it. Darkness overtook the town with Andean swiftness. Sesha and Maji scattered among the disembarking passengers, trying to look in all directions at once. They pestered the conductor and waited until the last passenger had departed and the train left the station, until the platform was empty except for the two of them still pacing. Gil wasn't there.

"What if something happened?" Sesha fretted. "Why haven't they contacted us?"

"Maybe Gil decided to stay longer at Pachacamac," Maji offered. "You know how she can be. They'll come tomorrow."

Sesha glared at Maji for a moment. "They'd better," she muttered. She strode off the platform, charging toward the center of town. Maji had a hard time keeping up as they dodged groups of miners returning from their shifts and street vendors packing up their wares. No use stopping to barter now. Whatever they lacked, they would make do without.

The four sisters had spent the day collecting supplies— mostly food and clothing. They spent their energy arguing over prices, doling out limited funds and resisting the temptation to be generous to people whose stark poverty made the Depression back home seem like good fortune. Thick alpaca blankets for bedrolls and clothing—woolen shirts, canvas pants and heavy sheepskin coats—were added to the cookware and kerosene lanterns and stoves they had brought with them. Their food supplies were mostly potatoes with some flour, dried meat and rice. The bulkiest items were two heavy canvas tents with their wooden support poles.

Sesha continued to mutter, unable to release the tension that hunched her shoulders and clenched her fists.

"You know what they say about hindsight and the three-legged dog," Maji finally commented as she jogged alongside her, breathing heavily in the thin air of the altiplano.

Sesha slowed, and only then realized that she, too, breathed in short, labored gasps. Weariness caught at her heels, dragging her pace.

"What do they say?"

Maji shrugged. "I don't know. I was hoping you could come up with a good punch line."

Sesha laughed in spite of her ire. The tension eased. Maji had that talent.

Cerro de Pasco was a mining town centered on a huge, open pit. Even its streets were criss-crossed with trenches and collapsed tunnels. She thought the whole town might someday slump into the earth. A well-deserved fate, she decided, for its greed-wrought hardship and pain. In the three hundred years the area had been mined, over half a billion dollars worth of silver had been exported, not to mention gold, copper, zinc, and lead. Yet the people gained little. Poverty seemed to be the main theme of the architecture—crude mud houses and flimsy metal shacks. Refuse heaps and open latrines. And the people just didn't care—or so it seemed from their empty expressions.

Perhaps that was why they drank pisco and chewed coca, Sesha thought, warily eyeing a trio of drunken miners. So far, they accosted the two women only with words, their undoubtedly vulgar intent lost in a slur of incomprehensible Quechuan.

Do you drink to forget? she wondered. *Do you dream in drunken stupor of the Inca's rule, when people knew dignity and order?* Pizarro's greatest crime had not been robbing them of their gold, but of their identity. The tide of so-called civilization had so utterly overwhelmed the people of the Inca that four hundred years later, they remained a people of conquered spirit.

Sesha shivered, feeling anxious and threatened, wary of hidden traps. Evil spread over the town like a layer of dust, as if the rape of the land had spawned something vile.

Get hold of yourself, she chided herself. *Gil's supposed to be the prescient one.* Perhaps it was only the air, foul with the smelter's pollution, and the dry rasp in her throat that she couldn't quite clear.

"Watch out!" Maji cried out, grabbing Sesha's arm, pulling her back from the edge of a trench, pulling her mind back to the here and now. "And they call me scatter-brained," she teased.

A drunken miner snatched at Maji, and she yelped in alarm. Sesha grabbed the man's wrist and twisted, forcing him to his knees, his own besottedness working to her advantage. For good measure, she booted him toward his two companions. The three of them fell in a drunken heap. Laughter issued from shadowed doorways and windows. Perhaps their spirit wasn't quite so defeated after all, merely dormant.

"Sesha!" Maji exclaimed, both surprised and offended by what her sister had done. "Where did you learn that?"

Sesha shrugged. "Oh, some movie I saw," she said, enjoying the irony of using one of Maji's own favorite lines. She leaned forward, hands braced on knees. "Whew! This altitude is hard on the body," she said as if the trembling she felt in her knees was due to exertion more than fright.

"I thought we were safe in pairs," Maji complained, glancing over her shoulder. The street was almost deserted; dinner seemed to be on everyone's mind.

"They were probably too drunk to care."

"What if we have problems on the trail? What about bandits?"

"We'll be safer away from the city." Sesha eyed the crisp lines of the mountains. Above the grime of the city, the mountain peaks, dark silhouettes against a sky of purple and orange, promised refuge and escape from some nameless menace. "Greed and avarice breeds here, corrupting the soul. Up there, they live a much simpler life. They have what they need; there's no temptation to want more."

"Now who's the romantic idealist!" Maji teased.

To dodge further conversation, Sesha veered across the street. Maji had to circle back to catch up. Sesha stopped to watch three mules grazing on alfalfa and green oats in the walled pasture behind the *tambo* where they were staying. She leaned against the stone wall, her fists still clenching and relaxing in spasms of impatience.

The animals had been Sesha's primary purchase and had not come easily. In the last month of harvest before the Andean winter, few were willing to part with their much-needed animals. Only by luck had they come across these three, their owner eager to be rid of them rather than feed them through the winter.

"I still would've preferred llamas," Maji commented, stopping beside her. Sesha held her breath for a moment, refusing to sigh. The choice of mules over llamas had been but a small matter compared to other decisions.

"Llamas can't carry as much or travel as far," Sesha explained. "And you can't ride one."

"But they're so different. So exotic. So utterly, oh, you know, *Peru*. How can we go home and explain we packed in with mules? Everyday, common mules!"

Sesha laughed and shook her head. Maji was the romantic in the group, a little scatter-brained, but smart enough that Sesha often suspected she merely played a part.

"This isn't some Hollywood movie, Maji," she chided her gently. "The mules will serve us just fine." She pushed away from the stone-walled corral. "Come on; I'm starved."

The *tambo* was an inn, a roadhouse. On the main floor, a large, bare-walled room served as eatery and bar, furnished with a long counter of bare planks and a collection of crude tables and chairs, no two alike. The kitchen was in a separate shack adjoining the main building. Rooms were upstairs. The four women shared one room, furnished only with worn mattresses rolled out on a bare floor and lit fitfully by a bare bulb. The bathroom down the hall had a shower, but no hot water.

"Hot water tomorrow," their host had assured them, but it seemed more a wish than a promise, and a well-worn one at that.

Locals crowded the room, but a group of astronomers from the *Santa Inez* occupied one table, discussing the upcoming eclipse, concerned with the possibility of clouds covering the event. Sesha frowned. *It wouldn't dare hide from us*, she thought. Not after all the work, the planning and time. All the hope.

Evita met them in the middle of the room, peering past Sesha's shoulder. "Weren't they on the train" she asked.

Sesha said simply, "No." Any more would cause an eruption of anger and anxiety.

Lena sat at a table in a far corner, talking with a local man. "It's all right," she responded when Evita repeated Sesha's words. "Petra sent a telegram. There was a sandstorm in Pachacamac. They were delayed again in Lima. She says to go on without them."

A frown puckered Sesha's face and a tremor stirred in her stomach. "What kind of delay? Did she say?"

Lena shrugged, then continued as if the matter were settled and of little consequence. "This is Tomás. He speaks some Spanish, but no English. He's headed home to Gashapampa, and he'll take us with him for two thousand *soles*."

"Two thousand? That's all?"

Lena shrugged. "He accepted it. It must be adequate."

A sullen-faced woman brought plates of thick stew and mugs of *chicha*, a local form of weak beer. Sesha poked at a lump of meat. *Cuy?* she wondered, though guinea pigs were usually served roasted whole. As she ate, Sesha studied Tomás. Typically squat and barrel-chested, with a broad, shallow face, his high cheekbones framed almond-shaped eyes. He was dressed like a herder in poncho, scarves, and heavy woolen pants. In his lap he held the peculiar cap called a *chullo*, shaped in a curved point with earflaps. He fingered the cords as if counting off the stitches. The cap was red with zigzagging stripes of dark blue and yellow, his poncho woven in the same distinctive pattern. Peruvians seemed to prefer bright colors, perhaps to contrast the stark vistas of their landscape.

"Do you trust him?" Sesha asked as if she did not.

Again, Lena shrugged. "We don't have much choice. He's the only one willing to take us."

Sesha tried to read the man's well-tanned face as if its scars and deep-etched lines held a hidden message. His eyes watched with curious interest, bright but distant. Not the dazed indifference of coca chewers, she decided, but more like a denial, a silent rebellion. He could've been thirty or maybe fifty, his life written in the code of wrinkles and lines etched in deep brown skin. Reason told her to be wary, but instinct trusted that face. The twist of the mouth, awaiting a reason to laugh, set her at ease.

"Who are your people?" Sesha asked in Spanish. "Where do you live?"

Tomás tilted his chin northeastward. "From past Gashapampa," he answered, his Spanish thickly accented. Sesha and her sisters spoke fluent Spanish, but it was not quite the same as the language of Peru. She had to listen closely and could barely understand one word in three. "I come here for work. The work is not good. The city is not good. Bad things happen here. I will go home now."

"What kind of work? Why?"

"Sesha," Lena interrupted, "I've already asked him all that. His family herds goats and sheep mostly, and grows potatoes and corn. He came here to sell his crops and find extra work during the winter so his son can go to school, but he doesn't like the city. He wants to go home, and he's willing to drop us off on the way. That's all we need to know."

"No, that's not all. We're about to go trekking across the wilderness with him. I want to know more before I trust him."

"Sesha!" Lena came back sharply, as only an older sister could. She didn't often get to be in charge—not with Petra around. "We're perfectly capable of hiring a guide without your advice. We've had enough of that already."

It was a harsh reprimand, reminding Sesha not only that this whole trip was her idea, but also that it was her suggestion the group split up. That had not gone right, though—she should've accompanied Gil to Pachacamac, not Petra. It stirred the anger simmering beneath the surface of her thoughts.

"If Gil needed to go to Pachacamac, there had to be a good reason," she responded hotly. "It was once an important oracle."

"Pachacamac's nothing but a pile of stone. There's nothing there," Evita argued. "We shouldn't have split up." That she agreed only made Sesha more angry.

Tomás shifted his weight, gathering their attention. Mention of Pachacamac seemed to have made him nervous. Any god who used earthquakes to punish those who displeased him would have wide influence in the unstable terrain of the Andes. And he might not understand their words, but could certainly follow the tone. What must he think of their bickering?

Lena turned to the man and dismissed him with instructions to meet them at sunrise at the *tambo*. She spoke carefully, as if to a child.

Tomás nodded as he rose from his seat. He eyed each one of them, making a short little bow and mumbling something in

Quechuan. Sesha waited until he was halfway across the room, then leaned toward the common center of their group.

"What about Gil and Petra and Sumala?" she demanded. "How can you even think of leaving without them?" She felt their hostility, released in Thomas's absence, a wave of heat.

Evita replied, "Petra's instructions said to go on."

"They'll catch up in a day or two," Lena added. "Tomás is leaving tomorrow, whether we go with him or not. We have no choice."

"But that means extra mules and another guide. Where will we find another guide?" Sesha shifted in her chair. The air itself felt toxic.

Lena wiggled like a hen puffing out her feathers. "I've already left a message with the American astronomers and made arrangements for horses."

"But what if something happened to Gil?"

"Petra can take care of Gil, little sister."

"Petra is a fool!" The words spewed forth unbidden.

"Sesha!" Maji exclaimed, visibly shocked by her outburst. Sesha slashed her gaze across Maji, silently chiding her.

Lena leaned forward and spoke with stern authority. "Petra will catch up to us. We have to move on. If we don't find Killichaka in time, there won't be any ritual. This whole trip will be in vain. Do you want to risk that?"

"This whole journey was your idea in the first place," Evita added. There was an unspoken *and it had better work* in her tone. "This whole myth of eclipses and hidden shrines—"

"We shouldn't be talking like this," Maji whispered. For a moment, they were silent, and in that emptiness, an electric tremble spread from Sesha's stomach. Anger boiled for no reason and with no control. But the others continued, unaware.

"We all agreed. It's necessary to defeat the Vision."

"It was still your idea; you're the one with the maps and the research. We're counting on you to find this place." It wasn't true; Aunt Faye had started it, then left it to Sesha to carry out. But she couldn't think of that now. Just as she had slid down the cliff face back home, she felt her emotions sliding now.

"And what good will that do if Gil isn't there?" Sesha countered, pressing against the back of her chair, feeling assaulted by their stares. She glanced to Maji for support, but for once, the middle sister remained silent. If anything, the sharpness of her gaze took the side of the older sisters.

Evita glared at her. "What if we don't find the site?"

"One day won't make that much difference," Sesha countered. "Anyway, we need time to adapt to the altitude."

Lena nodded. "I could agree with that. I just can't seem to get a deep breath."

"We're at twelve thousand feet," Maji responded. "The same altitude as Telluride."

"Feels higher," Lena said, holding her hand to her side as she attempted a deep breath.

"There's something you're not telling us," Sesha said as she studied her sister closely and remembered how Lena had been sick during the voyage. "You're pregnant again, aren't you?"

Lena's hesitation said more than words, and Evita demanded, "How far along?"

"Almost three months now. Gil says it's a boy."

"Lena, how could you!" the other three cried out almost together.

"This isn't my first child," she countered defensively. "We go up the mountain. We watch the eclipse. We come down. It won't affect the baby that much."

Sesha felt a twinge of horror. What if it did? They'd all made sacrifices to be here, but the life of an unborn child? That was too much to risk.

"Besides," Lena continued, her voice bitter. "I didn't have much choice, did I? None of us did."

And that was the core of the tensions between them. None of them really wanted to be here. Their mutual resentment bound them as much as the mission they shared and were committed to. But Sesha saw how they considered the matter separately, each curling their own point of view around that one truth. They were far from unified, even in this.

"We've all sacrificed too much to get here," Evita said, her gaze too pointedly on Sesha. "Sumala abandoned her patients, and Maji had to quit her job. Lena left behind her husband and four kids. What have you given up, Sesha? For you, this is just one big adventure."

"And when this is over, you all go back to your lives and pick up where you left off. But *someone* has to stay with Gil." She shouldn't have said that, Sesha realized, not in those words and not in that tone. Even as the words tumbled from her mouth, she could see their eyes narrow, the set of their mouths tighten. Looks of bitter envy, pain, even fear. She'd always been closest to Gil, and the others had each in their own way resented that.

In the sullen silence Sesha considered what she had said. Never had anyone spoken of it; never had it been discussed. It was simply assumed. She would be Gil's companion, her aide. Run errands, gather information. In some ways, she'd already taken on the role; her plan had led them here.

If she had once thought of it as a great adventure, an excuse to learn anything and everything, it now became a burden. Once this was over, her freedom was gone.

"Maybe Lena should wait here for Gil and the others," Evita suggested.

Lena felled the idea with a sharp wave of her hand. "Not in this city; not alone."

"Sesha and I could go on, and you and Evita could wait," Maji offered. "That makes more sense."

"No!" Lena's denial verged on anger. "We're not going to split up any more than we are. I live in Telluride, remember? I'm probably more fit than any of you. We go on as planned. I won't stay here one minute longer than necessary."

Her words startled Sesha so that she jerked erect, leaning forward. She wasn't the only one who didn't like this place. *Do you feel it, too?* Sesha wondered. *The evil biding here?* She glanced at the others, seeking signs of unease. Maji plucked at a loose thread on her shirt and Evita leaned toward the wall as if wanting something solid at her back. Perhaps nothing more than the dust of the mines and the taint of the smelters' pollution, or the frog in her throat she couldn't clear, but something malign resided here, and it meant them harm.

"We all go together or stay together," Sesha argued.

"Then we go," Lena stated as if that settled the matter. "So let's call it a night. We need to be up well before sunrise to pack our supplies." As the group stood, pushing back their chairs, Lena blocked Sesha's path.

"Are you certain the mules are secure? Perhaps you should check them before we turn in."

Sesha nodded, weary of arguing. The air felt close and still, stifling. The smell of her unfinished stew took on a tainted quality, and she felt vaguely disoriented. *Chicha* wasn't supposed to be that strong.

"I'll go with you," Maji offered.

"No, I can manage. It's only out back. I'll meet you upstairs in a few minutes."

No one objected. She still felt the chill of their anger and resentment. Their words, strung on a thread of tension, had left more unsaid than spoken. Sesha felt the conflict pushing her away. Perhaps she was being overly sensitive, since they seemed to have put the argument behind them, but right now, she simply wanted to be away, even from Maji, who had betrayed her with her silence. She turned, feeling their gazes pushing at her back, urging her away. As desperate to be alone as for a breath of fresh air, she sidled between chairs and tables toward the back entrance that led to the mules' pasture. *It shouldn't be like this,* she thought. *We should be united.* Hadn't Gil urged them to stay together?

She watched the women cross the room, clearly relaxing away from her presence. Lena was chiding Maji about bringing her make-up kit.

"But I need it," Maji responded petulantly. "My face feels naked without make-up." As they mounted the stairs to their second floor rooms, the others continued teasing her about meeting movie stars in the wilderness. Sesha turned away and left through the rear entrance. Once outside, she leaned against the wall of the *tambo* and took a deep breath, but instantly regretted it. The smells of this city were of squalor and decay, not the pure mountain air she craved.

Sesha considered going back and asking Maji to come with her after all, but she wasn't ready to face them just yet, nor to admit to any weakness. She hugged herself as she stepped away from the lighted doorway and into the dark of the pasture. She had picketed the mules close to the *tambo*, but now couldn't find them. She feared they had been stolen, but then heard a faint snuffle and a soft nicker. The mules had simply broken free of their picket and strayed to the far end of the pasture. She found them under a cluster of *eucalipto*. After securing their picket again, she stood between two of them running her hands along their muscled necks, more for her comfort than theirs. Her quivering anger slowly passed, and she found assurance in their warm, massive bulk and complacent dozing.

Rather than risk unseen hazards in the darkened pasture, Sesha decided to climb over the low stone wall to the street and circle around to the front of the *tambo*. At this hour, she thought, it should be safe—it was only around the corner. But she found herself farther from the *tambo* than she had expected. The street was unexpectedly still and dark, a darkness blacker than any night, deep enough to swallow the soul. She glanced about, but saw no one. Still, she shivered with the feeling of a presence. She started back, one hand brushing the stone wall, needing that touch of reality.

An arm reached out of the dark and wrapped around her chest, pinning her own arms to her sides. The edge of a blade pressed against her throat, cutting short her startled yelp. A rough voice whispered Spanish in her ear, its breath a vile mix of stale *pisco* and coca. The stench clogged her nose and mouth as if a rag were pressed against her face. Her attacker pulled her across the street toward the dark maw of an alleyway.

She couldn't fight him, not with the knife against her. Already, she felt the sting of a cut. She clawed at the air, but touched nothing substantial. The darkness grew, a physical thing, ready to engulf her, to swallow her up like a sacrificial victim. It drank of her terror. She wanted to scream, but the darkness stole her breath.

"Hey!" A voice shouted from somewhere behind her. "What's going on here?" Footsteps approached, and a lantern's beam stabbed at the darkness.

The knife blade dropped away. The arm let her go. She fell to her knees without its support. Shadow melted into the ground and the man fled, poncho flapping like wings.

"It's okay. You're safe now." English words, an American voice. Hands helped her to her feet, and she turned to face a man in his late twenties, tall and lean. He seemed familiar, perhaps one of the astronomers.

"Do I know you?"

"No," he said hastily, and turned his face away from the lantern's glare. "You shouldn't be out here by yourself, you know," he added. She pressed one finger to her throat and felt the slow ooze of her blood. A low hiss filled her mind, and she swayed.

"I just—My room—" She waved toward the *tambo* across the

street and realized she was shaking. "My sisters." She couldn't seem to find more words or to string them together coherently. Numb, still bound by shadow, she shivered and closed her eyes. When she opened them again, her rescuer had walked her across the street, and she had no memory of it. Maji stood in the doorway.

"Sesha, what happened? I heard you scream."

The stranger delivered Sesha into her care, and then melted into the dark before she could find words to thank him. Maji hugged her, kept one arm around her as she shepherded her toward the stairs. Evita and Lena waited in the hall.

"Are you all right?" Evita whispered, and her voice was tight and anxious. "What happened?"

Sesha shook her head, unable to speak of it. The attack took on a surreal quality, and she was certain the intent was more than rape or theft. She remembered Gil's story of the coyote in Chicago.

What would happen, she thought, if one of them were killed, if there weren't the seven? Would the Ritual fail? Would it all be for nothing? She trembled. Maji fetched an alpaca blanket and draped it around her. The others huddled close, their presence warding the night, their previous strife forgotten.

Someone didn't want them to succeed. Gemella? Shesha shivered again, not willing to believe her own sister, however estranged, could do such a thing.

GIL

Gil paced the short distance from bed to dresser to the corner and back again, her hands alternately clenching and relaxing. She turned and stared at the hotel room door. She gripped her crossed arms as if to hold herself prisoner, to keep herself still.

Sumala watched from the chair by the window. A flock of assorted noises and odors intruded through the open window, but so did a welcome breeze. As the thin curtains furled slowly in its wake, shadows drifted across Sumala's face like passing thoughts.

"Relax, Gil. We'll catch up to them."

Gil only shook her head with frustration. She glanced at the closed door and resumed her restless pacing.

"We should never have split up. Petra should never have told them to go on without us. "

"It means losing a whole day. Finding Killichaka might be more difficult than we think. Petra's plan makes sense."

Gil frowned. Her skin itched with a sense of wrongness. What was Petra up to? To take control was one thing, a necessity, in fact, with so many minds at odds with one another. But it was another matter entirely to make such decisions without even mentioning it. Petra kept her thoughts closed, and that bothered Gil. What was she hiding?

"Where is she, anyway? Shouldn't she be back by now?"

Sumala shrugged. "She's trying to send a telegram to Lena."

"Are you sure she's well enough to travel tomorrow?" Sand-drifted roads had delayed their return from *Pachacamac*, and then Petra had become ill. Something she ate, Sumala said. Consulting a local *bruja*, she had treated her sister with herbs and tea. Gil chafed at the delays. Like dominoes, their carefully timed plans were tumbling into chaos.

Sumala shifted forward. "Gil, fretting about it won't help. Everything will work out. You'll see." As if she were the prescient one—she laughed at the irony.

Gil was forced to smile in return. She reluctantly nodded, then bit at her lower lip, worried not so much for herself as for the others. She felt responsible, the reason they were here.

She stopped pacing suddenly, and in the unexpected silence that created, she heard a scratching at the door.

"What if—" Sumala started, but Gil cut her off with a wave of her hand. When the noise repeated, she and Gil exchanged puzzled glances.

"It's just Petra," Sumala suggested with a shrug.

"I would know if it were."

"Mice, then. Or rats?"

But Gil couldn't dismiss it so easily. Alerted now, she sensed the presence, a touch of mind both discomforting and familiar. It had been there for some time, she realized, niggling at her mind like a persistent tap that eventually gains attention.

Someone was working at the lock on their door. Sumala moved to stand beside Gil. They stared at the door. It was flimsy enough to easily force entrance, yet that someone was trying to pick the lock, and clumsily at that.

"Petra?" Sumala called out, obviously hoping it was only their sister with an ill-fitting key. "Petra, is that you?"

The scratching stopped, but there was no answer. Like a shadow pressed against the wood, Gil sensed dark hunger straining to reach her, though the physical form could not. The essence of its desire oozed between door and jamb, seeping beneath the door to stain the wood floor like mildew. It collected in a puddle of shadow, and Gil stepped away from its loathsome touch.

Someone struck the door with a fist and a muttered curse. Even that careless blow caused the flimsy wood to shiver and bow. Gil stared as if sheer force of will could hold it secure.

She felt Sumala tug at her arm but could not move, held prisoner by the scent of something both ancient and foul. As with the coyote in Chicago, she felt drawn forward.

"Who are you?" she demanded. She focused on the entity beyond the door, barely aware of how Sumala stared at her.

Many are my names.

The response startled Gil, for it came as a whisper in her mind. Its touch was brittle and cold, tasting of dust and ashes. She tried to brush it from her mind.

In this land, this place, call me Supay.

Supay. Her lips shaped the word, though she uttered no sound. It was a name unknown to her. She thought that if she spoke it aloud, it might yield to her. Or was that a trap, luring her into its own power?

The voice wrapped around her thoughts, seeking to bind them. It tempted her with dark power, with images of wealth, and taunted her spirit with sweet promises. She dared not yield. Sumala pulled her aside, and she blinked. The visions burst like empty bubbles, shattering to fine mist. Gil swayed and caught her balance. Her sister pushed at the tall dresser that was the only substantial piece of furniture in the room. Gil moved to help. It was old and heavy, and the stubby legs shrieked as they forced it across the bare wooden floor.

The pounding stopped, but Sumala continued to push. Whoever was on the other side must have realized what they were doing. Something hit the door with a loud BAM! The wood around the lock began to splinter.

A rush of panic clutched at Gil's heart.

"Push harder!"

The door gave way to a second blow. The dresser, just inches away, jolted back as the door jammed against it, bouncing the two women back into the room. A bare arm reached through the narrow opening and clawed at the air. Dodging under its reach, Sumala pushed at the chest once more. It rocked against the door, bringing a cry of pain from the other side.

Gil stared at the arm as it pulled back past the door's edge. In spite of the coyote incident, she hadn't wanted to believe, had refused to believe, that anyone truly meant her harm. Now even her aunt's death became a harsh warning. It signified a threat both to her and to her sisters.

What of Sesha and the others? Are they safe? She touched her chest where the pendant rested warm against her skin, as if that physical contact could bring Sesha closer. *We should never have separated.*

"Hurry," Sumala called, grabbing up Gil's thoughts along with their bags. "Let's get out of here."

"How?"

"The window!" Sumala tossed the bags over the balcony railing to the ground below. They were on the second floor, overlooking a narrow alley.

"What about Petra?" Gil cried out as she joined her.

"Huh?" was Sumala's response, and then, "We'll catch her downstairs." They climbed over the railing. Behind her, Gil heard the sound of splintering wood. The chest fell with a loud crash. Hanging from the balcony's floor, they dropped to the ground, then scurried to press like shadows against the wall.

A dark silhouette appeared against the night sky. Light from the room cast his shadow on the opposite wall. Gil could perceive neither form nor features. But the essence of the entity she could now call Supay was strong.

"He knows we're here," she whispered, and shut her mind against its seeking, cowering beneath the weight of the menace above her. The cold, dark presence threatened to engulf and smother her, to consume the marrow of her bones. How could such evil exist, she wondered, and the world not be aware of it? She shivered, and a whimper escaped her. Sumala put her arm around Gil, holding her still when she'd rather flee.

Above them, a fist struck the dark wood of the railing. Then the essence of Supay withdrew, evaporating like mist. The man who had been its host turned and went back into the room.

"What about Petra?" Gil whispered. At any moment, she

could return, walking into a trap. Was she already a prisoner?

Or a victim?

"You stay here. I'll find her."

"No," Gil insisted. "We stay together."

Sumala collected their bags, and they crept along the wall until they found a back entrance to the hotel. Anxious to find Petra, they hurried through the deserted kitchen, their pace fettered by the fear they would run into their assailant.

They came into the main hall, and Sumala pointed to Petra as she mounted the stairway.

"Petra!" she called, too loudly for Gil's sense of safety. "Over here!"

Petra glanced up the stairway as if wondering how they could be in two places at once, then turned to join them.

"What are you doing down here?" she asked in a stern and disapproving voice. "You were to stay in the room."

Sumala raised a finger to her lips for silence, glancing up the stairway. In overlapping sentences, they described the attack. Gil strained her senses for any hint of trouble. A whiff of evil drifted around a far corner.

"It's there," she whispered. "Down that hall."

Petra eyed her skeptically, then approached the corner and peeked around it.

"There's no one there," she announced in the same tone she'd used to banish monsters under the bed when Gil was a young child. "Is this more nonsense like Pachacamac?"

"This time it was real," Sumala insisted. "Someone was attacking us."

"So now she has you believing in this 'evil presence,' too? I thought you were more enlightened than that."

"I believe that *someone* broke down our door," Sumala countered. "Some*body* chased us out the window. We're not safe here."

"It's still lurking nearby, waiting for another chance," added Gil. She rubbed her arms as if scrubbing away cobwebs.

Petra stared at the two of them, as if by considering the situation, she could claim authority over it. Finally, she nodded.

"I don't believe in evil entities, but the concierge was just telling me there was a man asking after us. A tall American."

"Who?" Gil asked, but Petra only shook her head.

"He didn't leave a name."

Gil held out her hand to feel the flow of events, but the future wavered like something seen through flowing water.

"What should we do now?" Sumala asked. "We can't go back to our room. It's obviously not safe."

"We should leave," Petra decided, but Gil was inclined to stay in that one spot until she had unknotted the question. Petra and Sumala each took her by one arm and led her out of the hotel by the same back entrance. They hurried down the street seeking a safe refuge for what remained of the night. They finally found their way to the train station. It was as good a place as any, and even at this hour, people milled about. The company of strangers provided a certain measure of security.

Gil huddled on a hard wooden bench, knees drawn up and arms wrapped around them. They should never have separated. They were too vulnerable as it were. The vague uneasiness she'd felt before gelled now in the pit of her stomach and wound tight like a watch spring. She would not relax, could not, until they were all together again. The rules were different here, in this place, and if they were to survive, she'd have to learn them. She felt her mouth tighten into a thin, flat line, and a change came over her, a hardening. This place would alter her, and she wasn't sure she liked the prospect of what she might become.

Desamparados, the station was called. The Abandoned.

And that was how Gil felt.

GALEN

Galen carefully set the lantern on the table, and then held out his hand to see if it still trembled. Voices came from the next room. He was halfway through the doorway before he realized they were arguing and perhaps it would be better if he didn't intrude.

"—we can't afford to attract attention. His presence complicates things," Aunt Vera was saying.

"I can make my own choices. Your presence is more complication than his. Without you, I could've joined them, and they'd never know the difference." She fanned the flimsy yellow paper of a telegram. "With Gilaishling delayed, we could've had a two-day head start."

"Don't be so certain. Sesha will be suspicious now—you ensured that back home. You still need guidance, Miriam. You're much too impatient and strong-willed. Someone has to—"

"Don't tell me what I need, old woman." The words might have been a slap in the face, such was the older woman's reaction. Something in her crumpled, and she seemed to shrink like a balloon deflating. Galen decided it might be prudent to leave before he was noticed, but Miriam turned on him suddenly, as if she'd known he was there all along.

"And where have you been?" Her face was flushed with anger, her green eyes aflame. Her abrupt attack startled him so that he stepped back to recover his balance, and then took up the offensive.

"I might ask the same of you. You were gone all afternoon."

"I've been arranging things. There's much to accomplish before we leave tomorrow. However, I'm not the one wanted for murder. You jeopardize us all if you are caught."

Galen could only gape at her, her words making concrete something he'd dared not phrase even in his thoughts. "I didn't do it. I found them, but I didn't do it," he stammered.

"That's not what the police think. You failed to mention the family was dead and a witness saw you leave."

"Would you be willing to help if I had?"

Miriam frowned as if reconsidering her offer. "You still haven't answered my question. Where were you?"

"I went out for only a moment. I needed some fresh air. You weren't here; no one was here." He couldn't speak of the sudden need he'd felt to escape. Left alone in the small house where Miriam and her aunt were guests of unseen hosts, he had felt besieged. The corners were full of restless shadows. The empty silence whispered accusations.

He had intended only to step outside, but then he'd taken one more step, and then another. It was dark, and no one was about, and so a little farther. Not far, no more than a dozen or so yards—perhaps a little more.

"A dangerous risk. What if someone saw you?"

"It was dark. There wasn't anyone around except—"

Miriam arched an eyebrow, both reproving and prodding.

"A woman. Something attacked her—I saw it drag her into an alley. I couldn't just stand by and let her—" He cut off the thought before it could form. *Not like Eisabel.* He couldn't let that

118

happen again.

"*Something*, you say?" Miriam circled him slowly, so Galen had to keep turning to face her. "And this woman?"

"An American, I believe. She's staying at that *tambo* down the street. The others called her Sesha." He pictured her face, round and pale, surrounded by short, black curls, with wide, dark eyes, full of terror and confusion. She had trembled as he guided her across the street, and he had wanted to hold her until that trembling stilled. When her sisters appeared, he'd considered it more prudent to simply leave unseen. Though he had denied knowing her, he had, indeed, recognized the woman he'd bumped into on the platform in La Oroya. How different things might have been if he'd followed after her then.

Miriam repeated the name with a hiss, and then took a deep breath. "And this 'something' that attacked her? Not a man but a *thing?*"

Galen shrugged, still confused by what he'd seen.

"It looked like a man, but I couldn't see it clearly—it kept hidden." Hidden in shadow, wearing darkness like a cloak. More than that, he thought, it *was* shadow, and, when Galen had called out, consumed by shadow. The man part had fled, but the other had simply ceased to be, bleeding into the night and draining into the broken stones of the street. He could still feel the icy touch of its passing, a memory that made him shiver. It reminded him of the dregs of a nightmare after the memory has faded.

Miriam seemed to resolve the matter in her own thoughts, shrugging it off like a shawl. "We'll be leaving in the morning, and you'll be safe. But should you encounter these women again, I suggest you avoid them. You can't trust them."

"She seemed nice enough."

"She's a witch," Miriam responded, so acidly, Galen wondered if she meant it literally. "You've no idea the evil that brood has wrought."

"You know them?"

She would say no more. Instead, she waved a hand at a pile of clothing on a nearby chair. "I managed to find you some decent clothes. You have no idea how difficult it was; you're so much taller than the locals. But we certainly can't have you wandering around in those. They're much too obvious." Her glance passed over Galen's clothes, pausing on his shirt. He had tried to wash away the blood, scrubbing until the fabric all but wore through and his fingers ached. But still he could feel the stain against his skin.

"I appreciate your help. I don't know how I can repay you."

Miriam smiled, a thin and secretive curve. "I'll think of something," she said as she circled behind him. She ran her fingers lightly across his shoulder as if measuring his size. Galen tensed, uncertain just where he stood with this woman. What did she expect of him?

Miriam then turned toward the room she shared with her aunt, pausing at the door. "We have an early start tomorrow. I suggest you get some sleep." She closed the door firmly behind her, leaving him to ponder what might be hidden in her words.

He fingered the sturdy weave of the new clothes. His thoughts kept returning to the woman named Sesha, and the darkness that had attacked her. If it had a face, would it have the eyes of a coyote? He felt a connection with the attack in Chicago, though at this point, he couldn't define it. Was he now destined to forever save women from strange beasts?

He took the clothes Miriam had bought to his own room and tore off his old clothes as if they were infested. The new pants, a sturdy canvas, were a couple inches too short, as were the sleeves of the soft woolen shirt. There was also a thick, woolen coat lined with fleece, a leather hat, wide-brimmed, and sturdy boots.

He took the map from his jacket pocket and unfolded it, spreading it out on his bed to study the meaningless lines and symbols. He traced what must be the trail along a sinuous path to the curious starburst design that represented Killichaka. Miriam had wanted this. He could almost taste her hunger as she'd stared at it, had felt her attitude shift. This was, oddly enough, his key to survival. As long as he possessed this map, he would be secure. He worked loose about four inches of a seam in the lining in the new coat and slid the map inside.

He carried the bloodied shirt, as well as his old pants and jacket, out to the main room and tossed them into the fireplace. Stirring up the banked coals, he watched them burn. The flames set shadows capering on the walls and across the ceiling. They lurked in dark corners but he stayed to make sure every thread was consumed. He poked at the remains until they crumpled to ashes. And still his skin itched as if the bloody print remained.

MOONRISE: 10:27 p.m. EST ~ MOONSET: 10:25 a.m. EST
SUNRISE: 6:14 a.m. EST ~ SUNSET: 5:49 p.m. EST
Sunday, May 30

GALEN

The *colectivo* lurched across a rut, jolting Galen from a light doze and banishing visions born from nightmare. The motion tossed him forward. He groped for something to catch his fall, but nothing was quite where he reached for it. He ended up sitting on the floor of the open-bed truck. The other passengers laughed.

"At least you didn't fall out of the truck," Vera commented as Galen scrambled to his feet. He dropped back onto the wooden plank that served as seating.

"I'm glad I could provide some entertainment," he retorted with a wry smile that quickly faded. The dregs of nightmare taunted him with cruel memories, and his skin still itched where blood had marked him. He held one hand with the other to keep from scratching. He should mourn the little family, he thought, but he knew only Pedro and Eisabel by name. The woman was merely Mama. The infant had no name at all by which to grieve.

In the common manner of travelers, people watched the landscape, gazes empty, mentally elsewhere. But Galen caught furtive glances and open stares. Accusations, he imagined. *Murderer. Coward.*

Galen turned gaze and thoughts away, though there was little to see—wide, flat *puna* and tall, glowering mountains, all gray and brown, autumn on the cusp of winter. Vera's sidelong glance and sour frown blamed him for their plight. Pale and wheezing, she endured with iron-tight mien, managing the altitude better than he.

Someone played pipes. Galen hummed along until he realized it was the same tune the old man had been playing outside Eisabel's house. He stopped abruptly, but his head throbbed in time to the music.

~ * ~

Perched on a hillside, Yanahuanca was a narrow town, small

121

and dirty. Miriam insisted on caution and deposited Galen in an abandoned, mud-walled hut.

"Stay hidden, Professor," she warned in stern, not-to-be-denied tones. "The authorities have no doubt received word from Cerro de Pasco, and you are not easy to overlook. I'll have someone fetch you later."

A former chicken coop, perhaps, with a floor of dirt and guano, the ceiling was too low for Galen's height. He found a crate and sat by the single window where the shadows could not touch him and he could hope for an occasional breeze to cool him and waft away the stench. He watched the passing scene with interest, thoughts retreating to his chosen profession in defense against his current predicament.

Nearby, a group of women plied their fingers on ingeniously simple backstrap looms, while men worked the fields with large digging sticks. Children toiled beside their parents. Poverty didn't keep the Sabbath.

Galen had witnessed so much deprivation in the last seven years, had been so consumed with his own plight, that he'd scarcely considered the barren shabbiness surrounding him until now. As he observed how matter-of-factly they went about their work, he realized that the Great Depression gripping the rest of the world had, indeed, never touched this place. It existed beyond the grasp of modern economics. What he perceived as poverty was a way of life almost as old as the mountains.

Yet the people seemed satisfied. Following customs centuries old, they knew no other way, and in that, they were better off than victims back home who knew what they had lost. What Galen deemed luxuries were beyond their comprehension; what he considered necessity held no meaning. They had enough to survive and needed no more. In their own want, they were generous with strangers.

How much is enough?

Once more, Orlov's words challenged him.

Later, as he and Miriam shared dinner in a shadowed corner of the local *tambo*, he tried to explain his observations.

"It would make an interesting study," he noted. "We could publish a treatise on how primitive societies can exist outside the dominant economic structure." *Harry wasn't so far off,* he thought wryly.

"Whatever for, Professor?" she responded with an accent on his title that made it a mockery.

"You were always more interested in the human elements of economics. Here is the antithesis of Keynes, a society that functions without the 'more is better' machinery."

"Classroom rhetoric is one thing. Living among them is quite another." She made a deliberate show of picking something out of her stew and flicking it to the dirt floor. "Personally, I can't wait to go home."

"Miriam," Vera said with a reproving tone. "You should be more considerate of our hosts."

"Our hosts should have greater respect for habits of cleanliness." She pushed away her plate in disgust.

Galen studied her face, wondering how someone could change so drastically, as if crossing the equator had generated a reversal of character.

"I can't believe your concern was not sincere. Anyone who could lash out at Keynes the way you did—"

"Perhaps you don't know me as well as you think." She leaned forward, her posture accenting the curve of her bosom, her smile a mirthless, teasing thing. "Tell me, Professor, what kind of grade did such pretense earn?"

The way she kept saying "Professor" was growing irksome.

Before he could respond, a new shadow joined the others huddled in their corner. A man stood behind his right shoulder, a mixed-breed *mestizo*—short like the Quechuan, but without the barrel-chested stockiness. Dressed as a horseman, his dark hair was long and unkempt, his face marked with scars. His presence made Galen's back itch.

Miriam spoke to the man in Spanish, a wave of her hand inviting him to join them. He sat down and yelled across the room at the serving woman. She brought a plate of food and a bottle of the local beer. He ignored the utensils on the table and produced a knife from his belt, eating with a certain nonchalance, as if risking the blade's sharp edge was a display of virility. He gestured carelessly with it as he spoke, and Galen watched the blade as a bird watches a snake. The knife appeared well-used but ill-kept. The metal was age-dark, except for the bright, honed edge that gleamed like a wicked smile. The slash and sweep of that smile made Galen shudder.

123

Though he couldn't understand what was said, Galen took an instant dislike to the man, and he felt Carlo's contempt in return. The man's bearing was one of belligerent arrogance, and his dark eyes spoke of avarice and lechery as he listened to whatever Miriam was offering. Could she not see that in him, or did she choose to ignore it?

Vera said nothing, but her tight-lipped frown indicated she did not favor whatever Miriam proposed. She glanced once at Galen, and he was surprised to see a forlorn plea in her eyes, as if expecting him to intervene.

"I forget, you don't speak Spanish, Professor," Miriam said to Galen suddenly. "Carlo, here, and his men will escort us to Killichaka." Miriam paused and added as if an afterthought. "You do know how to ride a horse, don't you? Professor?"

Carlo grinned, a mirthless expression, more challenge than humor. As he spoke, he gestured toward Galen, though his gaze never left Miriam's trim figure in her slacks and green blouse. Miriam replied sharply, and then turned to Galen.

"He can't understand how you could travel with me and not be my husband." She seemed amused at some aspect of the situation and smiled suggestively. Out of habits cultivated in the classroom, Galen pretended to ignore the not-so-subtle hint she tried to plant.

Finished eating, Carlo wiped the blade across his pants leg and returned it to its sheath. He stared at Galen with narrowed eyes, then spoke in Spanish, something that sounded like a challenge. When Galen didn't answer, he laughed. Galen looked to Miriam for a translation, but she seemed disinclined to give one. She only watched, her chin resting in the palm of her hand, an interested, almost feral slant to her gaze.

Vera apparently disliked the man as much as he. "Miriam," she said. "Should we really consider traveling with these men?"

"They suit my purpose. I can handle them," Miriam responded, lifting her chin ever so slightly. She spoke to Carlo in Spanish. He stood and swaggered toward the door.

"I've heard they cannot be trusted," Vera continued. "*Cholos*, they're called, as if that were something disgusting."

"I said I can handle them. You need not worry over my welfare."

"I'm still your aunt, and the woman who raised you—"

"I don't need your advice!" Miriam kept her voice low, yet the intensity was fierce. "Need I remind you of the Vision?"

"No," Vera said, shrinking back as if physically slapped. She glanced at Galen, her expression both plea and warning. Galen shifted in his seat. This seemed to be a family matter, and he wasn't sure he should interfere.

"The Vision?" he asked nevertheless. It seemed a harmless question, but Vera shook her head ever so slightly. She opened her mouth as if to warn him but kept silent. Miriam released a narrow, mirthless smile.

"Perhaps you should have a taste of what this is all about." She reached forward to touch his forehead. Galen blinked.

He stood at the brink of Hell. A wall of fire as tall as the sky bore down on him, the air itself aflame. It ignited and consumed everything in its path. His flesh curled into ash and his bones melted. He could neither scream nor utter protest and shrank into a single kernel of denial. The Earth perished as the vision vanished. Only terror remained, and even that faded. His mind refused to hold any memory of the ordeal.

Miriam watched his reaction with an expression both snide and calculating.

"What was that?" he gasped with a throat burned dry.

"That, Professor, is what will happen if we fail."

Monday, May 31

GIL

Gil leaned against the doorway of the *tambo*, watching the mid-morning events in the small plaza. A tiled fountain splashed crystal clear water at the center, and knots of locals gathered, some buying and selling, others seeming to do no more than gossip. The American astronomers testing their equipment attracted a small crowd.

An artist drew pictures of the children gathered around him, much to their delight. Gil smiled at the giggles as each child recognized its own face rendered in charcoal. She remembered the man from the ship and had met him briefly last night in the *tambo*'s restaurant. Petra, Sumala, and she had just arrived in Cerro de Pasco and were too weary for much socializing. He had passed on a message from Lena, along with their share of supplies and gear.

Lena's group had already left Cerro do Pasco, a telegram from Petra instructing them to go on to Angoltuto. But Petra had claimed she couldn't get a message through.

"We've wasted too much time as it is," Petra stated when Gil had questioned her. She had glared pointedly at Gil, as if the sandstorm and her own illness were Gil's fault. Gil frowned, uneasy about this new development. They should not be separate, beads scattered along a fraying thread.

Gil felt impatient to leave. She did not like this town. Apparently, Sesha had shared her misgivings. Sesha had added a warning at the end of Lena's message, the script cramped and hurried. *Beware of coyotes.* The ink fairly vibrated with Sesha's anxiety and terror. What had happened here?

Gil sensed no such evil, though, as she had at *Pachacamac* and in Lima. If Supay was here, his presence was masked by the general ambience of iniquity and corruption. Perhaps only the polluted air had disturbed her sister. The stench from the smelters and the dust from the mines made her nose sting and her lungs ache for a breath of pure air. How could they destroy so much and accept no liability? Gil sighed. Here was another lesson she would

126

have to teach, when her time came.

A new enthusiasm caught fire as she thought of all she could accomplish, once the Ritual was complete. It would be so simple, she thought, once she took care of the threat of the Vision, to guide mankind toward better ways. The right words in the right ears, a small touch here and there. The temptation of such power was both thrilling and terrifying. What could she accomplish? What harm could be wrought?

She turned her attention back to the artist in the plaza. He seemed an energetic man, dedicated and enthusiastic. He had apparently acclimated better than the rest of his party, though he was older than most. Even now, he was preparing to climb the fifteen thousand-foot peak the group had chosen for its observations. "Going to paint the stars," someone commented. Gil smiled at the literal translation.

Yet she sensed a chill upon him, death hovering close by. A snag in his life's strand, frayed and parted the threads. She'd never experienced such a feeling so clearly, and it troubled her.

She could heal that snag, but Petra would not allow it. They'd argued, and not for the first time. Petra always insisted she save her talents for "people of importance." Gil countered with, "Who am I to pass such judgment?" But Petra's will still held sway, and the debate always came to an impasse.

She could do it now, and Petra would never know. She and Sumala had left to find the man with the horses Lena had hired.

A brief touch and she could dissolve the clot that would spark this man's death. She needed only an acceptable excuse for such contact, a prospect that made her hesitate. Perhaps she could trip against him or pretend to swoon. Or merely shake his hand.

Gil glanced around the plaza to make sure Petra was not yet returning. She had been warned not to leave the *tambo* alone, but among the crowd of Americans, surely she would be safe. She stepped from the shadowed doorway into harsh sunlight.

She hadn't gone more than twenty feet when she halted. In spite of the heat, she shivered.

Stronger even than at *Pachacamac*, the taint of evil soured the air, polluting it like soot, so that its touch dirtied her. Breathing shallowly, her lungs refusing such contamination, she turned slowly, seeking its source. People clustered near by spoke in low, fretful mutters. She understood little of what they said, but sensed its meaning.

La muerte. Death.

Someone had done something here, something monstrous, with the deliberate intent of trapping her.

Tolling bells drew attention to the church at the end of the plaza. The world seemed to pause as a procession emerged—first altar boys with a crucifix mounted on a tall staff, then a priest in robes of white. A knot of people appeared at the door maneuvering something bulky. They sorted themselves out and emerged carrying three plain, wooden coffins. The first seemed unusually large and heavy, but the other two were scarcely three feet long. She ached with the sorrow of such young lives lost.

Gil stood frozen, unable to breathe. Her life had become linked to those three lost souls. No, four—an infant still cradled in its mother's arms; even in death, she would care for it. Gil's gaze, however, remained fixed on the last coffin. Out of grief, out of reverence, she could not turn away from it.

"*Señor* Lopez apparently forgot about his arrangements with Lena," Petra announced as she approached from the inn. "It took an extra thousand *soles* to jog his memory." Gil scarcely heard her words. Aware of Petra watching her watching the procession, she remained focused on that sad parade as it turned the corner and proceeded down the far side of the plaza. Did they mean to circle the entire plaza, and she at its heart?

"I told you to—"

Petra stopped in mid-sentence as she finally noticed the object of Gil's attention and watched respectfully for a minute. "Such a tragedy," she whispered, leaning towards Gil. "The whole family murdered. They say an American did it."

For the moment, the words had little meaning. A chill pierced the marrow of Gil's bones as she beheld black wisps seeping from the coffins. Like a banner, they unfurled, a smudge across her vision.

The gossamer weaving, unseen, tangled among the mourners. The American artist had packed up his paints and strode now across the plaza. A warning choked in Gil's throat as he passed through that malign barrier, snagging his soul. He was lost to her now, and would not live to return home.

Gil turned as the procession progressed down the right side of the plaza. Once it encircled the plaza, she feared she would be trapped, unable to leave without becoming ensnared in the dark evil it plaited. Her mouth opened and closed, but she could not speak. She was aware of Petra's voice in her ear, of a hand upon her arm, but could not respond. All her attention, her entire being, was drawn to that last small box.

Now the priest turned the final corner, headed for the cemetery mound beyond the church, the smoky banner a wave breaking over her. Screams cut off in death now found voice, buffeting her like a malevolent wind. The water in the fountain at the plaza's center turned to crimson, overflowing its tiled wall to flood the plaza.

Gil gasped for breath and could find none. *It is corruption,* a secret voice warned. *Its touch claims the soul.*

"Gil, what's wrong?" Petra's voice sliced through the din of a mother's anguished wail, a child's scream.

"*Sálvenos. ¡Sálvenos, por favor!*"

Save us. Save us, please!

Petra grabbed Gil by the arms and forcibly turned her about. "Gil, what is it? Gilaishling, look at me!" She was screaming, though Gil heard only a far away whisper.

She blinked and tears spilled down her cheeks. Petra shook her roughly. Gil pushed away. The tide of blood from the fountain lapped at her feet.

"Run!" she shouted. In sheer panic, she raced toward the church. She bumped one of the altar boys as she edged through the gap remaining between the procession's beginning and its end. The crucifix he carried tilted, its shadow touching her like a blessing. She grabbed the staff, jerking it easily from the startled boy's grasp. Slashing at the darkened air, the blackness wafted away. The air felt clean and warm, and she inhaled deeply. She lowered the staff to the ground and a flash of light spread like a ripple from the point where the crucified figure touched the bloody tide, purifying the water. She passed the staff into the priest's hands and fled.

Behind her, she heard Petra apologizing to the mourners as she followed. "Sorry! *¡Perdón!*"

Sorry. Could such a simple word banish the tragedy behind her? Could it restore the lives taken to entrap her? She had no doubt that was the intent. In its weavings she recognized the touch of Supay and of the Other, as well. She was not surprised at her twin's presence, only horrified. Could her sister, her twin, really do so evil a thing? The very idea wedged in her throat like something too hastily swallowed. Supay and Gemella. Was Gemella the pawn or the master?

The conflict spurred Gil on. She kept running, past mud houses and tin shacks until, breathless, she stumbled and fell against a tailing pile. She clutched at the broken rock. Sesha's pendant fell from her shirt, a pendulum of hope and doom. She managed to tuck it back into hiding just as Petra caught up and collapsed beside her. For long minutes, the two could only wheeze and pant, struggling to breathe the thin mountain air. The sharp edges of the rock cut Gil's palms, dug into her knees.

Finally, Petra turned, holding a hand against a cramp in her side. "Gilaishling Minerva Orlov!" Her anger was diluted by her lack of breath, each word punctuated by a desperate gasp. "Just what was that all about?" she demanded. "How dare you disrupt a funeral like that!"

Gil stared at her sister, her gaze searching, asking, *Did you not see it?* But she had no breath for the words.

"Gemella," was all she could gasp, and the name stuck in her throat like tar.

Petra pursed her lips but did not respond.

"She's here. She's responsible for—" Gil waved her hand toward the plaza, for she could not find words for what she'd experienced.

"Nonsense!" Petra responded sternly. "The family was murdered by an American. A *mestizo* saw him leaving the scene."

The news snared Gil's attention, yanked it back to the present and the real. She turned to sit on the ground, back against the pile of rock, too weak to even consider rising. Loose rock skittered down the pile. "Do they know who?"

Petra shrugged. "Tall, thin, light brown hair. He got off the train and followed them home."

"Professor Williams?" It didn't make sense. How could he be here? Yet she felt his presence in Petra's words, the scant description sketching his essence. Picking up an egg-sized stone, she squeezed it tight in her hand, seeking focus.

"How did he get here?" Petra gazed back down the hill toward the cemetery.

Gil opened her hand and stared numbly at the rock she held.

She could not deny that he was involved in the murders.

Petra squinted at her. "Well, we don't have time to sit here and discuss it." She stood and rubbed at her hip. "If we leave here by noon we should make Yanahuance tomorrow."

Gil stood wearily and followed her sister without protest until they came to the plaza. The barrier she had perceived had vanished. The water in the fountain splashed clear against the tiles. She wondered if she had imagined the entire episode.

Yet she could not enter the plaza, fearing the evil remained, hidden and waiting. Smoke didn't really vanish, she thought, it merely spread too thin to perceive. She veered away, seeking a path around the plaza, and instead found herself facing the cemetery mound. The mourners were gone, leaving only two old men to fill in the graves.

Sálvenos, the voices had said, and the word still echoed in her mind. Save us. Guilt clogged her soul like soot, its gossamer weight too great to bear. She sat abruptly on a bench beneath a red-flowered tree. Petra had to stop and circle back.

"Now what's wrong?"

"I can't do it," Gil whispered. For the first time in her life, she found herself questioning her destiny. "I can't face that again."

"What?" Petra remained standing, impatient and severe.

"You didn't see; you can't know." She trembled and hugged herself, rocking back and forth. Words failed. She dared not explain, lest the specter reappear. "I'm not ready for this."

"We've come too far for second thoughts, Gilaishling. It's too late to abandon the mission. By the time we catch up, your sisters will be at Killichaka."

Gil merely shook her head. She pressed one hand to her chest, seeking the comfort of Sesha's pendant beneath her shirt.

The men had finished with the graves. They mumbled something as they trudged past her, but she couldn't understand their words, only their uncomprehending sorrow.

"I'm sorry," she murmured in return. *It's my fault.* That was the unbearable burden—this family had died because of her.

"So what do we do now?" Petra demanded, still standing apart, arms crossed, closing herself off from her sister's affliction.

Gil stared as if Petra were a stranger. Then she stood and approached the fresh mounds of earth. *Having paid the price, can I turn away?* Kneeling on the barren ground, she scooped up a handful of dirt and crumbled it in her fingers. It showered down across the smallest of the graves.

"*Sálvenos*, little one," Gil whispered. "Save me."

GALEN

Carlo was fuming, gesturing at the half dozen horses and two mules in a nearby paddock, then sweeping his arm north as he argued. Eventually he gave up. Calling to his men, he stalked away with a sour frown.

"He doesn't understand why we wait," Miriam explained as she watched the plaza from a shadowed doorway.

"I'm afraid I don't, either. Why come here if we're not going anywhere? Shouldn't we be headed for Killichaka?"

"We came to avoid being seen," Vera responded, and her glance accused Miriam as well as himself.

Four women entered the plaza, leading a trio of mules. "About time," Miriam muttered. "Mules? Why mules?"

Galen recognized Sesha among them. He stepped forward to greet her, but Miriam pulled him back into the doorway.

"Keep away from them, Professor." She adjusted the black shawl she wore to conceal the red of her hair, so much more vibrant among the dark-haired locals.

"We could be riding with them if you hadn't —" Vera cut herself off and in the glance she refused to cast at Galen, there was a clue. Two women mounted mules, and a Quechuan took the third and led the women out of town. "They seem harmless."

"They're my sisters." Miriam made the word sound vile. "They'll do anything to stop me."

"Your family?"

"They're *not* my family! They threw me away like a piece of trash." She spat out the words like venom, yet Galen detected a deep hurt beneath her scar of hatred. As they passed, Miriam pulled him deeper into shadow.

Sesha laughed at something another said. She had a good laugh, one that lit up her eyes. How could anyone with a laugh like that inspire such enmity? Miriam's nails dug into the flesh of his arm.

"They're ruthless, Professor. You can't trust any of them." Her eyes narrowed as if to contain her pain. Galen wondered if this display wasn't simply a ruse to gain his sympathy. Yet there was something he thought Miriam did not intend to reveal. A sense of grief, perhaps. Or regret?

Miriam continued in an intense whisper. "They want what is mine. They'll use the Ritual to destroy me. For now, we must wait upon them to lead the way to Killichaka." Miriam's glance flicked at Vera, accusing her of some failure. "And they chose to lead mules instead of riding horse."

"But I have the map," Galen offered.

"The map is useless until we find where it starts," Miriam retorted and did not disguise her contempt. "I trust it's somewhere safe."

Galen's hand twitched, but he avoided reaching toward its location. Vera clasped his wrist as if to cover even that slight motion.

"Keep it hidden," the older woman warned. "We'll have need of it soon enough, but if Carlo learns of it, he might kill us all."

Galen doubted he could prevent them from taking it, but the map was the slim thread that bound Galen to this group. He was not about to surrender that limited security. Security. Once it had meant a faculty position, a job and a certain amount of prestige. Now it meant survival. He had no delusions about his chances if they were to abandon him here.

GIL

Delays and more delays.

As they entered the *tambo*, a man in a white suit, flanked by two uniformed police, approached and blocked their way.

"*Señoritas*, I am Detective Juárez of the Cerro de Pasco police. If you would come with me, we have some questions to ask concerning a most heinous murder." His manner and stern frown were not nearly so courteous.

Juárez was a hard man, his features set in a perpetual scowl, his manner abrupt and precise. He carried the air of one who had seen much and was not easily impressed or moved. Yet this matter, Gil perceived, had shaken him. His essence trembled with outrage and anger, as much at his own impotence to solve the crime as for the act, itself.

In the police station, walls of cardboard boxes three feet high defined his office, separating it from those surrounding him. Stacks of folders and papers, some topped with a thick layer of dust, lined the outer wall. Gil shifted in her hard, wooden seat. The clutter made her feel stifled and trapped.

Yet Juárez' desk, a heavy wooden thing, ornately carved, was clear except for a single file. Seated as if the desk were a shield between him and his suspects, he brushed a speck of dust from its polished surface. Speaking in passable English, he questioned Gil for over an hour, his mind mired in a set pattern. He would persist until reality agreed with it.

"We arrived only last night, on the train," Gil insisted wearily, for at least the fourth time.

"So you have said. My aide is checking on that. You would have me believe there could be two identical, red-haired women here in Peru, both named Orlov?"

Gil started and her stomach went cold. "Gemella," she murmured to herself.

Petra spoke up. "She has a twin sister."

"Twins, you say? How convenient. This Miriam—"

"Miriam?" Gil repeated, puzzled.

Petra leaned sideways to murmur, "Her middle name."

Juárez shrugged. "And the man? He was heard to call your name."

"Your description is hardly precise; he could be anybody," Petra cut in abruptly, as if she didn't trust Gil to answer wisely. She glanced sidelong at Gil, her tight frown a warning to keep silent. "Perhaps if you had a photograph or a drawing?"

Juárez spread his hands and sighed. "We have our limits. This is not your United States." Then he opened a desk drawer and brought forth an object wrapped in a white handkerchief. "And what of this?" He peeled back the cloth to reveal a pocketknife, its blade unfolded and streaked with dark smears. The ivory handle was chipped and cracked. "Do you recognize it?" He held it out, close enough to examine, but not to touch.

Evil crawled along its edges like a living, black corrosion. It consumed the light so that the blade dwelt in shadow. Gil could no more contemplate touching that befouled metal than she could imagine plunging her hand into molten lava. She hesitated to breathe the same air that brushed its surface.

"*Señorita?*"

134

Gil shook her head and answered honestly, "No, I don't know it. I've never seen it before." Juárez' eyes narrowed as if he would read the truth from her face. Gil fought to hide how the knife affected her. Could he see how she trembled, how she broke in a sweat, pressing against the back of her chair to escape the thing's presence? Would he take that as an indication she was lying?

Though she'd never seen the knife before, she knew it was connected to Professor Williams. His essence surrounded it like the handkerchief Juárez folded back over it as he set it down precisely in the center of his desk. She struggled to mask her confusion as she considered the implications, then closed her eyes to shut out the victims' anguished whispers. Her center of balance tilted.

"Please," Petra said, her voice not nearly as pliant as her words. "My sister and I have had a difficult journey, and it's far from over. The altitude is having its effect."

Juárez turned his hawkish gaze to Petra. "You, too, were seen with the suspect, though reports describe you as much older. Do you also claim an identical twin?"

Petra visibly shuddered. "My Aunt Vera, perhaps. People have always commented on how much I look like her." She said the words as if they tasted of pure acid. Gil knew how she hated the resemblance she held to her aunt. Vera had never been a favored relative.

"Aaah, but of course," Juárez responded, humoring her. "Just as this supposed *twin*—" His gaze dropped to the knife hidden in its white linen shroud.

They were interrupted by a uniformed aide. He nodded toward the far side of the room, beyond the row of boxes, where Sumala stood with a rather stout and self-possessed man. Juárez excused himself to confer with this stranger, and when he returned, he was clearly disappointed.

"My apologies. Your claims are apparently confirmed." His gaze narrowed as he regarded them, still harboring his suspicions. "It seems you have some influential friends. You are free to go."

Petra and Gil rose at once, but Petra stumbled, catching herself on the edge of the desk.

"Excuse me," she said as both Gil and Juárez reached to steady her. "As I said, the altitude."

Gil peered sideways at Petra, who was not normally so clumsy. As Juárez escorted them toward the door, Gil glanced back. The knife was gone; Juarez had apparently swept it back into the drawer.

Juarez shook their hands in parting. "Pardon, please, my harsh manner," he said. "This is a rough town, yes, but murder, especially murder this—" His tongue moved against his cheek, searching for an appropriate word. He shook his head. "Never in my career has there been anything so evil. The man must've been touched by Supay."

The name startled Gil.

"Supay?"

"The devil, you Americans would call him."

Gil halted and clutched at the back of a chair. *Supay. The devil.* It fit, she thought with horror. Before she could ask more, though, Petra herded her forward.

Sumala met them half way across the room. "This is Señor Hidalgo, a friend of the Hubbells."

"Ah, bless Lorenzo and his papers," Petra responded. "We should leave. Quickly."

The man bowed from the waist. "Your servant," he said, escorting them from the building. "May I recommend you continue your journey as soon as possible, before the detective can think of new questions?"

To Gil's surprise, Petra agreed. "Yes, we've wasted enough time here. We have a lot of catching up to do. Sumala, is everything ready?"

Sumala shook her head, then nodded toward an old man dressed in a red poncho, holding the reins of four horses. "He says he will not leave until tomorrow."

And more delays.

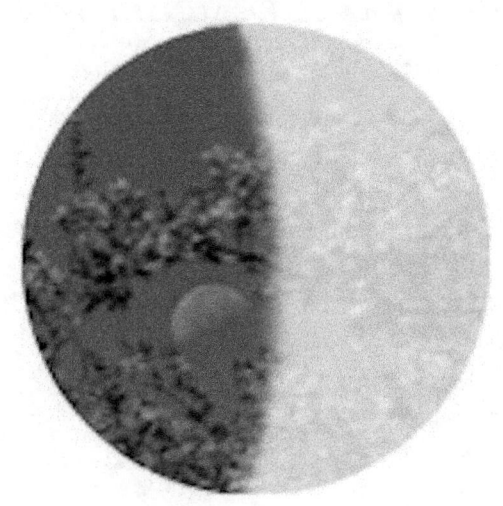

Part Four

The Waning Quarter

MOONRISE: (none) ~ MOONSET: 11:50 a.m. EST
SUNRISE: 6:14 a.m. EST ~ SUNSET: 5:49 p.m. EST
Tuesday, June 1

GALEN

Darkness, motion. Voices and prayers. Music.
Yell!
Someone hovers, dark-on-dark. Reedy pipe music.
Metallic gleam, child's scream, mother's cry.
Move!
The figure turns, face moving toward light.
And still, the music.
"*Salvenos.*"
Move! Scream!
"Nnh."

Not much of a sound, but enough to break the nightmare's grip. The reedy trill of pipe music followed Galen into waking, a far away echo. He stared into the dark space above him, sweating and gasping, until he remembered that he was safe, camped in an abandoned stone hut far from Cerro de Pasco. The nightmare fled to seek other prey.

It's only a dream, he told himself, yet his heart pounded against his chest so loudly, surely it would awaken the others. He peered into the layers of dark upon dark where Carlo's men slept, fearing he would find them slaughtered as well. But no; one snored and another rolled over fitfully, as if Galen's gaze had disturbed his sleep.

Galen pushed back the alpaca blanket and sat up. He combed back his hair and rubbed his face, still trying to scrub away the restless feeling that he could've done something, that perhaps he still could. *Aside from surrender,* he thought.

He had the same dream every night, standing witness to the slaughter, each time more intense and detailed. He snatched at wisps of memory, obsessed with the secrets they carried. What had he witnessed that his mind refused to remember? The image of Harry's knife opened a raw wound. *What did I do?* The words formed shards of ice, sharp as daggers. Each night, the hooded figure moved closer. If he dared to dream long enough, would he see the face concealed in the cloak?

Will it be my own?

Memories and possibilities curdled in his stomach, at odds with last night's stew. The rancid smell of unwashed bodies and stale smoke only made things worse. A coughing fit tickled his throat and he staggered from the hut. Frigid air brought him up short, burning in his lungs. A fit of coughing doubled him over. He felt he might turn inside out before the spasm subsided.

Wrapping his arms around his chest, he held muscles sore from coughing, from the sheer effort of breathing. He hurt all over, bruised and stiff from riding. His chest felt thick and heavy, every breath a deliberate effort.

He was moving too fast. Their steady progress gave Galen little opportunity to acclimate to the thinning air as they scaled a never-ending succession of ridges and escarpments.

Galen dared not lag behind. He understood the leers Carlo passed over Miriam and the meaning of the taunts and sniggers of his men, even if he couldn't translate the words. Among these men, he could not show weakness.

In spite of the cold, Galen lingered. Hopping from one sock-clad foot to the other, he regretted leaving behind the warm blanket but was reluctant to return to the hut. *Not just yet.*

The night was breathlessly clear, quiet and serene, and his alone. In the east, the moon hung above the serrated edge of the mountains like the Cheshire cat's fat grin. It cast surreal shadows, reality drifting into dreamscape hidden from normal sight. It must be around one, maybe two o'clock, if he remembered his lunar phases right.

Stars dusted the ebony sky. Their brittle light limned the peaks with silver and danced across their snowfields. Galen's gaze tracked the thick river of the Milky Way, craning his head back until he staggered off balance.

Moving to the paddock where they had pastured the horses and mules, he sat against its stone wall. Low enough to rest his head upon the top stone, he lost himself in that wondrous profusion of light. He felt the dizzying spin of the Earth as he had as a boy. Back then, he had memorized the constellations and could identify all the brightest stars.

But that was a different hemisphere and long ago. Here and now, he couldn't identify a single constellation, the familiar patterns distorted and misplaced. He felt utterly lost.

Had even the stars abandoned him?

He closed his eyes to their cruel, taunting light.

SESHA

"*Ama sua, ama llulla, ama quella,*" Sesha recited carefully as she emerged from her tent. Don't steal, don't lie, don't be lazy. She pronounced the ancient phrase badly and Tomás corrected her with a bemused but gentle smile.

"*Qampas hinalatoq,*" he responded. To you likewise. Sesha thought this ancient and simple exchange, a common greeting, represented the nature of the Quechuan people far more eloquently than those coca-numbed drunks in Cerro de Pasco.

Tomás had been reluctant to teach Sesha his native tongue, but his command of Spanish was so poor, learning Quechuan became a necessity. She kept pestering their guide with endless "What is that's?" and "How do you say—?" and now understood the language better than she could speak it. She stumbled over the difficult glottal stops and clicks, the explosive, hard *g* of the letter *q*, and the stuttered *tt* at the beginning of a word. She often mangled the complicated syntax. Tomás could not explain, only repeat her words back in the correct manner. She would nod as if she understood and then puzzle it out for herself.

What must he think of us, she wondered. The first morning, when they had exchanged their city clothes for dungarees, flannel shirts and shearling jackets, Tomás couldn't recognize them. Women in his world wore only skirts. Sesha caught secret glances, as if he still sought the women he'd bargained with.

Tomás held himself aloof from these foreigners, but as Sesha's Quechuan improved, he became more open. He talked of his wife Pocha and their five children. He wanted the oldest to go to school in Huanuco. Working the land was hard, with little to spare, he told her, wistfully gazing at the mules. Sesha realized that a temporary convenience for her and her sisters might be economic necessity for their guide.

GALEN

The hooded figure bent over Galen once more, a pale moonbeam almost touching its face. He awoke curled at the base of the stone wall, and someone had draped a blanket over him. The world had gone gray, a fog-shrouded dawn, mountains wrapped with thick wads of cotton-cloud batting.

A distinct snap, loud in the crisp morning air, stilled the chatter of birds. Galen tensed, listening intently. Soft footfalls, another snap, then the clatter of a tin pot.

When he sat up, he saw Miriam hunched over the beginnings of a fire, trying to balance a coffeepot between two stones.

Gingerly he stretched out and stood. "Good morning," he quietly announced, so as not to startle her. She turned with an expression of alarm just the same.

"I didn't expect anyone to be awake yet," she said. "Coffee will be ready soon if I can get this fire going."

Galen spread his hands helplessly as he squatted next to her, offering at least moral support. He was no more prepared for roughing it in the wilderness than he had been for coping with the foreign culture of Lima.

"I'd rather have some of that coca tea, I think." As if to emphasize his point, another spasm of coughing shook him. When he was done, he saw Miriam watching.

"You are having a rough time of this, aren't you," she stated with faint concern. "I hope you'll be able to continue."

Galen nodded. "I'm much better this morning," he said, and hoped that was true. He avoided taking too deep a breath. He watched her face as she kindled the fire. Like a chameleon, she was becoming as hard and stony as the land around them. Yet in unguarded moments, he thought he detected a shadow of pain beneath the bitterness of deep betrayal. The contrast was as incongruous as the red of her hair among the dark Quechuans.

This was the first chance he'd had to talk to her without the silent censorship of Aunt Vera's glowering disapproval. The older woman seemed to consider Galen a threat, though Miriam always laughed off the notion with a self-assurance Galen found vaguely insulting. Vera tolerated his presence, he suspected, only as protection against Carlo and his men, though how Galen could stand against seven armed men, he couldn't imagine.

"So tell me, what does an eclipse have to do with this Killichaka place?"

She glanced at him with an arched eyebrow. "Haven't you

done your research, Professor?"

Galen nodded. "I read your paper, and found the article that went with the map. But it doesn't explain any of this."

Miriam pursed her lips in silent rebuke. "Killichaka is a place of power. In the moon's shadow, that power wakens. It can be claimed, with the proper ritual."

Galen scowled. "An eclipse is just a shadow. How can it have power?"

"How is not important. Being there is."

Galen nodded, pretending to believe her. "And you plan to claim this power, I take it?"

"I intend to," Miriam responded with determined arrogance.

"More daydreams, Miriam?" *More pebbles?* Her classroom persona had not been so ambitious. Galen hoped he was a better judge of character than that.

Miriam's expression turned icy in a way that made Galen shiver. "Such lack of faith could get you in serious trouble." Then she laughed as if to dull the edge of her threat.

"And once you have this power, what will you do with it?"

"Whatever I want. Fame. Influence. *Wealth*," she said in crisp, pointed tones. She gazed into the flames of the fire she had kindled as if watching her future. Her mouth twitched into a bitter smile. "If I desired, I could rule the world."

Her tone, as much as her words, took him aback. She truly believed what she said. Galen decided he should humor the woman, at least until he felt more secure. "So what's my role? Why did you want me along? You mentioned a guardian?"

"An honorary title, in your case." She laughed, and he thought that cruel. "The Guardian merely stands by, protecting the Ritual."

Moving closer, she whispered in his ear. "When we are done, the power will be mine. Mine to share, as I see fit." It was a bribe, he thought. A proffered reward. Or a subtle threat? What had he gotten himself into?

"You could be rich, Professor. Isn't that what you really want? Money—enough that you'll never want for anything again?"

Yes, yes! he thought, yet at this moment, he desired only his small apartment with electricity and running water and a few good books. *Do you really need more than that?* a voice asked, sounding like the Orlov he'd known in Chicago. He longed to have her back.

Miriam smiled, a smile both sweet and false, and her eyes held him, that gold-flecked, green gaze. She reached out to touch his arm, his cheek, to cup her hand beneath his chin and draw him close. Her lips brushed his lightly, as soft as dreaming, her breath warm on his cheek.

He jerked away, almost falling backward, catching himself with one arm. No matter what fantasies he might have harbored, he was certain he didn't want this. Not here, not like this. Nor did the Orlov he knew. *Is that you, Miss Orlov?*

"Who are you?" he demanded.

"Who do you think I am?" Miriam responded, seeming miffed at his rebuff. "Who do you want me to be?"

"Miriam, you're not—"

"*Buenos días, Señor, Señorita.*" Both lurched to their feet. Carlo stood behind the stone wall, still tying his belt. He grinned as if thinking he'd interrupted something important. "Es a good day, today. We can travel far." He came to squat by the fire and poured himself coffee.

"Perhaps, Carlo," Miriam answered, and then added something in Spanish that made the man frown. He glared at her, and something with the tone of an argument ensued.

Galen sensed potential trouble. Carlo and his men were rough in manner and cruel faced. They chewed coca and drank entirely too much *chicha* and *pisco*. They leered at the women, making comments they considered uproariously funny and provocative. Miriam and her aunt pointedly ignored them.

Galen had the distinct impression Carlo was simply biding his time, awaiting the right opportunity. Only Galen's presence kept the men from taking advantage of the situation, but he had no delusions about his ability to defend the women or himself against such odds. The youngest of four brothers, he'd never really learned to defend himself. One or another had always done that for him. Nevertheless, he positioned himself beside Miriam with as stolid a stance as he could manage.

Miriam said something more, her tone tight and hard. Carlo waited a moment, then nodded curtly. His hand flicked toward his belt, and his knife flew to pin a small, squirrel-like *viscacha* to the earth. Carlo grinned at Galen and then sauntered over to claim his knife and his prey—which no doubt would end up in tonight's stew. The message was not lost on Galen, but he stood his ground until Carlo sauntered off.

Miriam casually dusted the dirt from her britches.

"He doesn't understand. We're beset by enemies both before and behind. We must outpace the one without overcoming the other." She walked away before Galen could ask what she meant.

Before Galen finished breakfast, three of Carlo's men rode off. Miriam watched them go, then nodded at Carlo in satisfaction. The man didn't seem too pleased, but he nodded back. Galen couldn't help but feel a certain relief. This cut the odds against him to something almost imaginable.

However, while the men's departure meant a respite for him, it surely meant trouble for someone else. He suspected they followed Sesha and her sisters. Galen touched his jacket where he had hidden his copy of the map. Would Miriam leave them alone if she had the map? Yet the map was key to his own safety. As long as he had it, Miriam needed him.

SESHA

Sesha walked beside Tomás as he led one mule, laden with most of the supplies, including the heavy canvas tents. Lena and Evita rode the other two, Maji taking up the rear and complaining loudly every time one of the mules left a fresh pile of dung. Each woman also bore a pack with food, water and personal belongings. Maji insisted on her make-up kit, though she hadn't used it since Yanahuanca. Evita, an amateur rockhound, collected samples along the way, each accompanied by a lecture on its significance and value. Sesha carried the guidebooks and maps.

They followed the track of the royal Inca road, a uniform eighteen feet wide where it crossed the flat puna. The road was still well-traveled, but use did not include maintenance. Five centuries of neglect had left broken rock littered with rubble and overgrown with the tough grasses and cacti of the highlands.

The landscape here looked very much like the mountains of home, except thatthe agave grew monstrously large. She easily imagined herself back in New Mexico, until a herd of alpaca or flame-leaved eucalyptus or farmers in their distinctive hats snapped her back.

In her reverie, she almost walked off a cliff.

Tomás stopped abruptly, raising his arm against Sesha's next step. She teetered at the edge of a steep drop. Tomás broke into a spate of Quechuan before repeating himself in Spanish. She understood a mere scattering of words—an agitated account of the unwary falling into the abyss.

These deep and narrow ravines sliced the *puna*, carved by fast-flowing streams and nearly invisible until one learned how to see the unnatural edges, the false horizons. A narrow track led down one side and up the other.

"Another *redura*!" Maji complained. "I swear, this land has only two dimensions—up and down."

And each in its way was equally difficult. Lena groaned as she dismounted from her mule. She held one hand to her belly, rubbing it as if to comfort the child within.

Sesha descended the trail gingerly, the muscles in her calves as hard as stone. Her toes were bruised from being crushed against the front of her boots, and sharp pain tore across her knees. Every time she slid on loose stones, she tensed in mild panic, visions of falling twisting her gut.

Climbing out the other side, they paused to check the mules' burdens, adjusting shifted packs and tightening loosened straps. Lena remounted, never mind it was Maji's turn. Sesha watched for symptoms of altitude sickness—nausea or dizziness—but Lena seemed to fare the best of the four. Perhaps she'd been right about the altitude not affecting her—or her baby. By now, they should all be more or less acclimated.

Beyond the ravine, the road climbed relentlessly. *No wonder the Inca never invented the wheel,* Sesha thought as she labored up the steep, zigzag trail. In this precipitous landscape, wheeled vehicles would have been of little benefit, almost useless. People here had little use for vehicles that would require maintenance, parts, and fuel other than grass and alfalfa. She stubbed a toe against a sharp rock—and tires, lots of tires.

She tried to imagine a modern asphalt highway carved into this obstinate rock. How long would it last, compared to the stone road it would replace? Modern travel would be a hindrance here, more hardship than convenience. She eyed the peaks of Cordillera Negra etched with sharp austerity against a sky of breathless blue. It would spoil the harsh beauty and destroy what remnants of heritage the Quechua could still claim.

Evita must've been thinking along similar lines, for when they stopped to rest, she declared, "I will never again complain about having to drive across fifty miles of wonderfully flat, gloriously boring desert!"

"Do you suppose they'll have hot water at the next town?"

"You're dreaming, Maji. We'll be lucky if they have a *tambo* and fodder for the mules."

"Oh, what I wouldn't give for a hot bath!"

"Cheese," Evita added.

"A real bed instead of a mat of sticky leaves," was Lena's wish. Sesha smiled as the list went on, but worried that such talk would only demoralize them. The patter ceased on its own, though, as each woman ran out of breath for anything more than putting one foot in front of the other.

Atop the rise, Tomás stopped by a mound of small stones almost two times Sesha's height.

"*Apacheta*," he stated. "Leave something of yourself." He reached up to pluck hairs loose from his eyebrow and set them among the rocks of the marker. "Offer thanks to the *wamani* for their protection and safe passage. Mountain spirits."

Sesha chose her scarf, one she'd had since she was ten. Gil would recognize it; she would know they had come this way. Maji left a compact from her make-up kit. Evita chose a stone, and Lena, a lock of hair.

Sesha stared back down the valley, seeking.

"Any sign of Petra, Sumala, and Gil?" Evita asked. "They should be close by now."

Tomás expressed confusion with a raised brow.

"Our sisters," Sesha explained in Spanish.

He gestured to the others. "*Turi?*"

"We have other sisters."

With an unvoiced "aah," Tomás expressed both confusion and understanding. He nodded back along the path. "They come now?" he asked simply, as if they merely lingered just out of sight.

"Soon. They'll catch up soon," Sesha told Tomás, with more hope than conviction. She gazed across the landscape with the futile expectation that Gil would suddenly appear.

In this open and empty land, Sesha had the incongruous itch-in-the-middle-of-the-back feeling that someone watched them. But if Gil were close, she wouldn't hide. *Who, then?* Sesha wondered. She rubbed her arms against a sudden chill in spite of the equatorial heat. Tomás stood beside her, watching. She wondered what he could see that she could not.

GIL

Gil was only too glad to escape Cerro de Pasco. Her experience at the funeral haunted her, as if a wisp of that dark evil had snagged on her spirit, dragging upon it with increasing inertia. Only the thought of Sesha ahead and Gemella somewhere between kept her moving.

The horses Gil, Petra and Sumala rode were barely worthy of the name. Underfed and mistreated, Gil wondered how they could possibly endure the trek. Their owner was supposed to accompany the three women, but suddenly remembered "other duties." He had sent his father in his stead, an aged, gray-haired man who nonetheless walked with a proud, straight back and such dignity Gil dared not question his ability to guide them across the rugged mountain terrain. The old man knew no English. He understood a little Spanish, but spoke only Quechuan. He had very little to say.

Their guide would not be hurried, and the horses refused more than a plodding amble, heads drooping to snatch at wisps of dry ichu grass along the road. When the sun lowered toward the stolid peaks of Cordillera Negra, and the old man declared an end to the day's travel, they were still far from Yanahuanca.

SESHA

Peruvians ate only breakfast and a late afternoon dinner. The sun was low and Sesha hungry when they reached a compound of mud-walled huts, too small to earn a dot on her map. The women pitched their tents in a meadow while Tomás built a small fire using branches of a shrub he called *tola*. He plucked fruit from a red flowered *poroqsha* vine, and two women brought a basket of potatoes. Sesha counted at least six different varieties in colors of purple, red, yellow, and white. While they ate, Tomás sat on a rock and played a set of small reed pipes. Their breathy, shrill whistle sang counterpoint to the wind's harsh tune. He gazed ahead as if contemplating where this journey would take them.

Sesha pulled her maps from her pack and traced their progress on the largest of them. Detailed maps were hard to come by and matching one to another almost impossible. They followed the route described in the monograph, from Yanahuanca north to Huaratambo, and then to Angoltuto, a place that did not exist on any map.

Beyond Angoltuto, they entered the realm of the archeologist who had discovered Killichaka. He had left only a few sparse notes and the cryptic, hand-drawn map.

Tomás watched her now, or rather, his gaze fell just above her map, as if it were something of immense curiosity forbidden to gaze upon. Sesha figured he'd never seen a map before. She beckoned him closer and pointed to one of the black dots.

"Cerro de Pasco," she said, trying to connect this piece of paper to the reality of his world. She traced their route, stopping at each labeled dot. "Yanahuanca. Huaratambo." After that, they had followed a steep walled canyon, a rugged, relentless climb. Sesha slid her finger north, then spread her hands in helpless confusion. "Angoltuto?"

"Angoltuto." Tomás tapped the air just west of a long, narrow lake.

"There? That's Angoltuto?"

He nodded slowly. Hope trembled in Sesha's gut, and she pulled out the map of Killichaka.

Once she had thought the map sketched in haste or from distant memory. Now she realized the mixture of lines and symbols must be a devious, private code to protect the site from treasure seekers and rivals. It lacked orientation and labels and had no legend to explain its cryptic symbols. A cryptic *A* sat beside a long and narrow shape labeled with an *L*.

She showed the map to Tomás, smoothing its creases. She tapped the *A* then the *L*.

"Angoltuto?" she asked hopefully. "Lauricocha?" He offered a noncommittal shrug. Undaunted, she moved her finger to an enigmatic starburst.

"We are going here," she said in her fledgling Quechuan. "Killichaka."

Tomás shook his head vigorously.

"*Mána*. Gashapampa." *Mána* meant no. Gashapampa was the village nearest his home.

Sesha lapsed back into her more competent Spanish. "But we need to find Killichaka."

"*¡Máná!*" Tomás insisted, then launched into a quiet diatribe, his Quechuan so fast, Sesha could barely follow. *Chúkara* stood out clearly, and *wamaní* and *huaca*. Something about spirits, then, and a forbidden, sacred place.

"*¡Más despacio!*" Sesha responded, waving her hands and shaking her head. "*¡Ama usqaytachu! Mana intindiykichu.* I can't understand you. You know I can't."

Tomás wound to a stop, his final word, an emphatic "*Máná!*"

"But you promised to take us there." She turned to Lena. "You explained it to him, didn't you? What did you tell him?"

Despair crossed Lena's face like a shadow. "I thought he understood. He spoke so little Spanish, it was difficult enough getting him to understand that we wanted a guide. I figured once we were on our way, we would have time to explain and we could persuade him to go on, that he'd have no choice." She shrugged helplessly.

Sesha turned back to Tomás, who was watching them shrewdly. "We must go to Killichaka," she tried to explain in her limited Quechuan, tangling her words in the unusual syntax.

"We can pay you more," Evita offered in Spanish.

Tomás remained silent. Sesha wondered if this hadn't been his plan all along—to wait until they were in the middle of nowhere to take advantage of them. She should have known better. "How much?" she asked with a resigned sigh.

But Tomás shook his head adamantly, eyes narrowed to a judgmental glare. He muttered something about *huacacerro*, treasure hunters. Did he now think they were seeking Inca gold?

"Explain about the eclipse," Lena suggested. "How the moon will cover the sun and—"

Sesha cut her off with a wave of her hand. They were in enough trouble. In primitive cultures, eclipses were often looked upon as bad omens. It might frighten Tomás enough to abandon them altogether.

"We aren't here for any treasure," she told Tomás. "No gold."

Tomás clearly did not believe her.

"We do not go there. *Huaca.* Forbidden."

"Why is it forbidden? What do you know?" Sesha asked.

Thomás's only answer was a curt chopping gesture.

"Please, Tomás, I need to know."

"A place of the old ones, with great power." Tomás spoke in Spanish, as if the Quechuan words were forbidden. He shook his head. "Now the mountain claims it. It is *chúkara*." He stared off at the snow-covered peaks.

"*Chúkara*," he repeated.

"What is *chúkara*?" Sesha asked.

"Wild place. Place of spirits." Tomás sat back on his heels. "In the valleys, the Lords protect us," he explained in careful Spanish, referring to crosses planted at the heads of glaciers and beside lakes, wherever natural forces might threaten the villages below. "Where it is *chukara*, there are no Lords. Wild spirits rule. They trap the soul in stone. We do not go there."

He put an end to further discussion by turning from them and stalking over to the mules. Carefully lifting each hoof, he checked for stones and thorns. Sesha looked to her sisters for guidance, but they only shrugged. Slowly, she folded her maps and stowed them in her belt pouch. Eventually, they would have to convince Tomás, but it would require patience. One step at a time. Angoltuto, Lauricocha.

Then Killichaka.

GALEN

Carlo made camp on a low hill overlooking the place where Sesha and her sisters stayed. Miriam was in an edgy mood, pacing from one task to another with fierce impatience. She would stop and glare at the compound, muttering to herself like a low growl, as a tiger might stare at those who had caged it. When Galen picked up one of her bags to take it into her tent, she snatched it from him and suggested he collect fuel for the fire instead.

Gathering fallen branches, he met a young child. Shy but curious, she offered him a dried twig. Her dark eyes reminded Galen of Eisabel. Scowling, he glanced to see if Miriam noticed. The woman had no patience with children, insisting they were only waiting for a handout or the opportunity to steal something. Galen remembered Pedro carrying his bag from the train, sharing the fruit in La Oroya. He almost smiled, but the memory of Eisabel, dying in his arms, destroyed that small pleasure. He rubbed at the invisible handprints burning his chest like brands, Eisabel's upon the larger. Might he awake tomorrow to find this child vivisected?

"Stay away from me, kid," he muttered in self-indulgent ire. "I'm fatal to children." He chased her away, even flinging a small stone after her to emphasize the point.

After dinner, the drinking started—a nightly ritual. One of the *cholos* brought out his pipes and started playing, that same mournful melody Galen had heard in Cerro de Pasco. *Was this the only tune in all of Peru?* Galen wondered, and he cringed. He considered going to bed, but feared the flute's song would only trigger another nightmare. He'd rather not sleep at all than relive that horror yet again. Retreating from the group he stood in the darkness at the edge of camp and pressed his hands against his ears to shut out the sound.

Rising voices pierced his isolation. An argument evolved swiftly into a fight. Galen watched from a distance as Carlo and another man drew knives and circled one another warily. Galen noticed thatMiriam watched intently, almost gleefully, eyes alight and cheeks flushed. He moved to her side, raising one hand to touch her shoulder.

The fight was over as abruptly as it had begun. One man fell to the ground, clutching at a knife hilt stuck between his ribs. Galen saw with dismay that the victor was Carlo. The man's bravado would be insufferable now, Galen realized, and even more of a threat. Carlo retrieved his knife and challenged the other men, the blade weaving a dance in the firelight. They muttered but went back to their drinking as if the incident was of no consequence.

Carlo strutted around, holding the bloody knife aloft in triumph. Wiping the blade across his pants, he returned it to its sheath. He bent over the dying man and pulled off his gun belt then pulled a flask and a pouch from his pockets.

"¡Ya no la necesita!" he shouted, and no one objected.

Galen left the circle of firelight in disgust and sat on a low boulder, watching the lights of the compound below and listening to distant llama bells and the bleat of goats. He studied the farm and the simplicity of its life, fiercely cutting off any thoughts of the fight and Carlo and his bloody knife. After a while, he noticed Miriam's presence beside him.

"Do you know," he stated, trying to head off whatever she might have to say. "All my life, I have taught and been taught that growth is the only way to survive, that more is better. A country, a company, or a person who doesn't grow is deemed a failure. But

look at these people. They have what they need, by their stand-
ards, and they are satisfied with it. What to us is necessity is to
them unimaginable luxury."

"They're dirty, ignorant, and poor," Miriam replied sourly.

"But are they really so impoverished? They have enough to
eat and warm clothes and shelter. We want so much we don't
need. Who is the more content?"

"I can be just as content with a million dollars for a mat-
tress."

"Could you really? Wouldn't you be afraid of losing it?
Wouldn't you always want more? Enough becomes an illusion, a
goal you can never reach. I thought money would buy security.
Maybe I was wrong. Security comes in the satisfaction that whatever we have is enough. Wealth is a spider's web. Once caught,
you only ensnare yourself the more. Perhaps we were never meant
to grow rich. It only complicates our lives."

The look Miriam passed to him was both peculiar and un-
readable. He felt foolish for expressing such idealism, opening
himself to her scorn.

"An easy platitude for the poor, an excuse to rationalize their
lack of wealth. Would you still believe that if you were as poor as
they?" She studied him and seemed to come to a decision. "I
could make you rich, Professor." She circled him, fingers tracing a
loop around his shoulders. Galen stepped back, trying to catch his
breath. "I could give you whatever you want. Money and more
money."

Miriam moved in front of him, her hand resting above his
heart, igniting that hidden print like a brand. Galen felt himself tilt
slightly out of balance. He glanced at Vera, standing at a distance
but watching. A warning formed on her lips but went unspoken.

"But I need your map. Carlo lied. These *cholos* know nothing
of Killichaka." The loop she'd drawn tightened.

"*Don't do it.* The hand print itched. Hadn't Vera warned him
to keep it hidden?

"Miriam, I—"

"Trust me, Professor," Miriam said as if reading through his
eyes. Her tone lacked its usual scorn. "I need you as much as I
need the map." Her glance ticked pointedly toward the group of
horsemen now sharing the dead man's bottle of *pisco*.

Galen also glanced at the men, Carlo in particular. He had no delusions about his abilities. Maybe if the others stayed drunk enough, he could trip them up—though it would probably be over his own prone body.

Still he hesitated, misgiving and doubt pricking his judgment. Miriam left too much unsaid and Vera practically held her breath in anticipation. "Then tell me, why don't you have a map of your own?"

"My sisters stole it," she said sharply.

"Why would they do that?"

A dangerous, angry light came to her eyes. *Beware.* "I told you, they want to destroy me." Then abruptly, cunningly, she smiled. "If only I had the map…"

"You would have no reason to keep following them?"

"You catch on quickly." Miriam paused, her fingers sliding up his arm to trace the edge of his jaw, a touch that seemed as much threat as caress. His hand slipped toward the slit in his jacket lining. *Don't trust her!*

"Indulge me," Miriam murmured. "I can make it worth your while." Her eyes made promises that bored through his wariness.

His hand brought out the folded paper of its own accord.

Miriam's eyes glittered with anticipation. Galen thought she would snatch the paper from his hands, but she held still, allowing him to place it against her palm. Her smile barely containing her glee, she stood on tiptoe to kiss his cheek.

"You're wonderful," she said, like a child who'd received a long desired present.

Galen, however, felt no such joy. "You'll leave them alone now, right? You don't need them anymore." He nodded toward the village where the women were encamped.

"Oh, but I do need them, even more than I need you." Her smile made him shudder, and he feared he'd made a mistake. That simple paper had become a part of him, a piece of his identity. Now the space where it had rested felt empty. He had traded away his one asset for the sake of strangers. He was losing himself. Miriam had become the source of all security, of life itself. Bit by bit, he was surrendering to her.

What would she demand next?

Wednesday, June 2

SESHA

Predator stalking prey. Legs fettered, unable to flee.
White, gleaming slash. The scent of terror.
Something screams.
Sesha awoke gasping, sweat like ice on her skin.
Evita rolled over restlessly. Lena was snoring.

Only a dream, she told herself. Yet the scream persisted in her memory. She listened to the night, but heard nothing. Absolutely nothing. The darkness was as thick as the alpaca blanket twisted around her like a winding sheet.

She breathed slowly and dared not move, as if that menace might still lurk in the darkness, waiting. Listening to the night, she passed unknowing into sleep.

GALEN

Miriam and Carlo were arguing again and in Spanish, of course. Galen felt irritated that he was so pointedly left out. He was learning, though, phrases picked up more from context than direct translation—but the two spoke too rapidly and fluidly for him to catch more than a word or two. Vera looked on with an uneasy frown. Galen dared approach the older woman.

"What are they saying?"

Vera glanced sideways at him and passed him one of her persimmon frowns, as if not knowing the local language was an unforgivable sin. "Carlo's men are going to Killichaka."

"What have you done?" Galen demanded in alarm. "Miriam didn't give Carlo the map, did she?"

"Of course not." An odd mix of reproach and hope carved Vera's expression. "If Carlo knew about the map, we'd all be dead. She merely claimed to have *divined* the location." She said the last with a wry frown.

"You don't approve?"

Vera didn't answer right away, as if weighing the value of the

154

truth. "I'm losing control of her," she admitted at last. "It wasn't supposed to be like this. It was never supposed to be about the power—not for the power itself."

"What about Sesha and the others?"

"They'll be safe enough." Her twisted frown expressed doubt.

Evidently Miriam won the argument, for Carlo stomped from the camp scowling. He returned some time later, staggering drunk, and reached out to finger Miriam's hair. Miriam raised her hand against the man, but Carlo grabbed it before she could strike. He laughed and said something that made Miriam's face darken with rage.

Galen stepped forward. "Carlo!" he shouted before he'd even considered what might follow. Carlo released Miriam and backed off. He grinned at Galen, his fingers caressing the hilt of the knife in his belt. He spoke in Spanish, his tone sounding of both jest and challenge. Galen remembered yesterday's fight. Would he last even half as long? He glanced at Miriam, but she was watching with mild amusement. Now that she had his map, he was excess baggage. He realized he'd been drawn into a trap. Perhaps Miriam had staged this confrontation to be rid of him.

Behind him, Galen heard the distinctive sound of a pistol's hammer cocking. Carlo frowned. With a final curse, he turned and strode away.

"You see, the professor has his uses," Miriam said past him. Galen turned, half expecting a small army, but only Vera stood there, still holding her pistol as if he were the threat instead of Carlo. She carefully released the hammer and pocketed it in her coat. By degrees, Galen relaxed, only now noticing his hands clenched in tight fists at his side.

Miriam's gaze shifted back. "I may have underestimated you, Professor. You might make a suitable guardian after all."

"What did Carlo say?" Galen demanded. He turned to Vera. "What did he say?"

Miriam seemed bemused. "He said someday you won't have women to protect you."

SESHA

"*Buenos dia*, Tomás," Sesha called out, and then the Quechuan greeting she had practiced. The early morning air was chill and biting, the thick ichu grass glazed with frost. Thick fog clung to the steep cliffs surrounding the valley where they had camped. The air hung heavy and silent. Tomás was not there.

"Tomás?" she called again, loudly, and was answered with silence.

"What's wrong?" Maji asked, stumbling from her tent, throwing the flap wide as if to tell the others, *If I have to face the cold, so do you.* She stood rubbing hands together, prancing to get warm.

"Tomás is missing," Sesha answered as Lena and Evita joined them.

"So are the mules," Maji noted. She strode toward the spot where they'd picketed the animals the night before.

"Maybe they got loose, and he went to find them," Evita suggested.

"Then we should help him search," Sesha responded, then called again, "Tomás!" Only her echo answered.

"Maybe he stole them," Lena added darkly.

And then Maji shrieked. She was holding a leather strap in one hand, the other raised to her open mouth.

"Maji, what is it?" Sesha asked, already running toward her sister. Then she saw for herself. One of the mules sprawled on the ground, its throat gaping like a wide grin, and its belly sliced open, the entrails dragged onto the frozen ground. One eye, open wide, stared at her, still reflecting terror. The stench of death and decay was already strong.

Sesha spun around, arms spread wide to ward off Lena and Evita as they ran up behind her, but it was too late. Lena dropped to her knees and began to heave, one hand pressed tight against her stomach. Evita knelt beside her until the wretching ceased, then helped her to her feet, keeping them both turned from the grizzly sight. Sesha took charge of Maji, one arm around her waist to gently turn and guide her back to camp.

For a while, they could only sit and gaze at the fog.

"What about Tomás?" Evita finally asked.

"I'll search for him," Sesha suggested. "Maji, start the fire and start breakfast. I think we could use some tea."

Still dazed, the others agreed. Sesha left them huddled together and searched the area. Finding no trace of either the little Quechuan or the other two mules, she returned to a whirl of speculation.

"What if he did this?" Lena was saying. "We should never have trusted him."

"*You* hired him," Evita pointed out.

"The other mules must've run off," Maji suggested diplomatically. "Tomás went after them."

"No, he's betrayed us and stolen our mules."

Their words carefully avoided the possibility that he, too, had been slain. Tomás refused to sleep in their tents. He preferred the open, a self-appointed guardian. Sesha wondered if he slept at all. She rubbed her hands up and down her arms as if that could warm the chill of her thoughts. Was Tomás also staring terror-eyed at the sky?

Sesha's thoughts kept returning to her nightmare. Had reality slipped into her dreaming? Had she slept while Thomás fought? A shiver of guilt shook her shoulders. Memories of the attack in Cerro de Pasco floated to mind. Did that creature—she could not consider it human—follow them? Was it lurking yet in the fog?

She sought a weapon, but could find only the small knife they used for preparing food. A stranger's yell had vanquished the creature—a yell and a stab of light. This creature dwelt in dark and shadow. As dawn erased the dark, she tried to convince herself that they were safe now.

The memory of that transient hero warmed the chill of her fear. Face in shadow, she remembered only his eyes. If she summoned him, would he appear now, as suddenly as he had that night? Wistfully, she imagined him riding a tall, white horse. *And they call Maji the dreamer!* she chided herself.

While Lena prepared breakfast, Sesha mentally cataloged their supplies, thinking, *This we need. That can be left behind.* She felt guilty for doing so and banished such plans from her mind as she spooned up a bowl of *moroya*, a potato mush. They crept back as she sipped at a mug of *maté de coca*. Sesha relished the heat of the cup against her palms as much as the tingling warmth spreading across her chest. A cure for *soroche*, Tomás had brewed it for them every morning. *How will we manage without him?* she wondered with a shudder.

She shook off the thought and forced herself to eat, her gaze still seeking Tomás but avoiding the still, dark mound in the field. Dark birds like crosses circled in the sky.

Her sisters avoided her glance. They knew they couldn't carry all the supplies themselves, yet could not leave them behind. Nor would Sesha consider leaving without knowing what had happened to their guide.

"We should go on without him," Lena insisted.

"He'll come back," Sesha insisted. "I won't abandon him."

"How will we find our way without him?"

"The road must lead someplace. We'll hire another guide, maybe more mules."

Sesha stared at Lena, wondering how she could be so callous. She was forced to concede, though, that her sister was right.

"How long do we wait?" she asked in quiet capitulation.

Lena shrugged, and Evita suggested that they could break camp and sort out the gear while they waited. Sesha saw that as a way to delay their departure and reluctantly agreed.

"What will we do with what we can't carry?"

"We'll cache it behind those rocks."

"What about Fred?" Maji asked.

Sesha blinked in confusion, then remembered that was the name Maji had given the dead mule, claiming his eyes reminded her of an old boyfriend. Sesha pressed her lips into a tight, flat line, trying not to think about those soft, brown eyes.

"There's nothing we can do," Lena stated flatly. "It would take too long even to pile rocks over him. Sesha closed her eyes, knowing that meant Fred would be left to the carrion eaters. *And what of Tomás?*

They started to break camp, because there was nothing else to do, sorting supplies as they went. Two tents and four camp cots. *Evita's rock collection.* Blankets and cook pots. Maji's make up case. Sesha's own collection of travel guides and books, of little use this far from the tourist locales. They divided out the necessary, and then the absolute necessary, and still, it seemed too much to carry. *What about the tents?* Too heavy and bulky, they were also necessary. Neither could they discard the despair weighting their spirits.

GIL

Petra's horse stumbled, almost pitching her over his neck. The poor animal recovered, but limped, favoring its left foreleg. Petra stopped and dismounted, staggered to a nearby rock and sat down.

"Are you all right?" Sumala called as both she and Gil joined her. Their guide remained mounted and took up the reins of Petra's horse.

"Just shaken," Petra assured them.

Sumala turned then to the horse and calmed it. Running skilled hands along the scarred legs with as much care as she gave her human patients, she shook her head. "It's not broken," she announced. "But he can't carry our weight." She retrieved her pack and fumbled through her pouches.

"I can fix him," Gil offered, already approaching the animal.

"No!" Petra countered. "You can't waste your power on a horse." It was the same argument that prevented her from healing the artist in Cerro de Pasco.

"We need this horse," Gil argued. "Without him, we ride double or one of us walks. Either way, we'll be too slow to ever catch up to Sesha and the others."

"And how do you explain it to the old man?" Petra nodded at their guide, who now leaned over Sumala's shoulder babbling in heavily accented Spanish.

"Bruha," Sumala responded. "I'm a healer. So is my sister."

Still, Petra would not let Gil touch the horse. "It'll look like magic," she argued with a pointed glance at their guide. "We'll get another in Yanahuance. It can't be far."

Gil relented, though she seethed with frustration. Someday, she would have to stand her ground, but not today. While Sumala treated and bandaged the horse's leg, Gil paced restlessly, a sense of urgency goading her to keep moving.

To the west, the waning, Earth-lit crescent of the moon sat like a soap bubble atop serrated peaks. This ordeal challenged the spirit as well as the body. It stretched the sinews of her character and forced her to contemplate new vistas. Up and ever up, and she was no longer certain she was prepared for what was to come.

Now was a time of change. After Tuesday, everything would be different. Tuesday. It hovered like the clouds shouldering up the mountains, casting shadows that shifted the colors of the landscape, turning conviction into uncertainty. She would either hold the power to face the Vision or, if the Ritual failed, she would be helpless to alter the future it foretold.

Summoned to mind, the Vision burst the barriers she imposed upon it. The air burned, devouring flesh and searing lungs, consuming the body both inside and out. Voices crying out in horror and anguish, extinguished in a breath. Utter silence and stygian black. The Earth was left in smoke and ashes.

Gil gasped and was surprised to find the air sweet and cool. She blinked away the lingering red glow. So intense the images, she was surprised to find herself unmarked and not reduced to a lump of char.

She was sitting on the ground, Petra next to her. Sumala handed her a packet along with her canteen. Gil accepted it with a quizzical look.

"Just aspirin powder," Sumala explained, and after Gil downed the medicine added, "Mostly. How do you feel?"

"I'm fine," Gil replied, though she trembled and the sense of fire still stung her skin. Sumala urged her to drink more. Gil obeyed, for her throat was parched. She watched with an expression of concern and sympathy, but Petra stood and moved toward the horses and the old man.

"They're getting worse, aren't they," Sumala observed. Gil still felt Sumala's touch on her shoulders. She had shared the ordeal, lessening its impact.

Gil could only nod. After another long drink, she responded, "I half expect to find myself a charred cinder."

Sumala shook her head. "How do you bear it? The glimpses you share with us are hard enough." Her hands trembled and her face was pale.

Gil attempted a thin smile. "I'm sorry, Sumala. I would never share them, but it helps. Thank you."

Sumala bit at her lower lip. "Sometimes I worry that every time you see the Vision, it becomes more real. I fear that when you confront the real thing, it will have become too strong to defeat."

Gil could only nod, the idea a hard knot stuck in her throat. She held the same fear—that the images of the Vision would become so engrained in her memory that she would not be able to alter them.

"What could cause such destruction?" Sumala asked. "Do you know what it is?"

Gil shook her head. "It's something new." She considered all she'd learned in Chicago. "I snuck into a post-graduate physics lecture once. It triggered the Vision—people assumed I was having a seizure. There's a clue there, and I pray I can understand and stop it."

"And if you don't?"

Gil shuddered. "I don't even want to think about it." But think about it she did as they mounted and headed out, Petra and Sumala sharing one horse. Death and fire. Ruin and desolation. It wasn't fair, she thought, that she alone bore the burden of defeating the Vision.

She called out to Petra, seeking diversion from her thoughts. "What will we do, Petra, once this ritual is over?"

Petra looked at her querulously, as if she considered the question inane and obvious. "We go home."

"But what will we *do* when we go home?"

"You'll defeat the Vision." She shrugged as if the answer was inevitable and didn't really matter.

"And you?"

Petra gazed ahead, her mouth pressed into a straight line, as if the road ahead revealed the answers. Sumala had her patients and Lena, her family. Evita and Maji both had lives and interests beyond the Vision. Sesha would stay with Gil. *Pancho Sanchez to my Don Quixote,* Gil thought with wry humor. But what of Petra?

Petra laughed, a hard, clipped sound. "I'm not sure. All of my life has been so focused on this one point, I've never thought about after." The shadows in her eyes, though, spoke of secret desires she had no wish to share.

"Me, neither, I guess." Gil looked away before Petra could read the doubt in her eyes. "I feel like a bride so focused on the wedding, she's never given thought to the marriage that comes after." And that was the crux of the matter. She'd never really considered *after*—not in concrete terms, but only in generalities and fantasies. She would save the world from the future the Vision portrayed. Then what? Cure poverty? End hunger, and abolish hate? Bring world peace?

But now the question: How?

And she had no answer.

SESHA

Sesha delayed as long as she could and would not let anyone put out the fire or empty the pot of *moroya.*

"When Tomás shows up, he'll be hungry," she insisted.

"*If* Tomás shows up," Evita countered, and was answered by a shout out of the lingering fog.

"*¡Ola!*"

The figure emerged slowly, wreathed in mists, so it was another moment before Sesha recognized the distinctive red, yellow and blue stripes of Tomás's poncho. He was leading the two missing mules.

"What happened?" Sesha called out in her limited Quechuan when he was still a dozen yards away. The two mules shied at the scent of their dead companion, eyes gone wild. Tomás turned to control and calm them, and it was some time before he was free to speak.

"*Chinchey*," he replied simply in Quechua, then, "Puma." He stared at the slain mule, mouth and eyes both weighted by a mournful frown. A glance at the packed and sorted gear asked, *would you leave me behind?*

Sesha accepted his explanation. She wondered if Tomás really knew what had attacked the mules, or if he simply named the only animal that could have done such a thing.

Evita and Maji ran forward to help with the mules, greeting the pack animals with grateful and affectionate hugs. Sesha's arms twitched with the urge to do the same for Tomás, but she suspected he would not welcome such familiarity.

"Come and eat," she said instead, and again in Quechuan, then knelt to ladle out the last of the *moroya*. "We have breakfast ready." He accepted the bowl with a small bow and a comment about their cooking skills Sesha thought was a joke, though she couldn't understand all the words. As he ate, she noticed slashes of dark red among the bright colors of his poncho. The mule's blood or his own?

"Are you hurt?" she asked in dismay.

The little man shrugged. He said something in Quechuan, and then "*No es nada*," in Spanish, but Sesha didn't think it was the same thing. She insisted on inspecting the wound anyway. Tomás pulled back his poncho to reveal a set of long, deep gashes, like claw marks.

"Tomás, I'm sorry," she cried, a whole new wave of guilt swamping her. "I should've helped." But he simply replied it was not her fault while his gaze asked why she should blame herself.

It might well have been a puma, she thought as she cleaned and bandaged the gashes, but then Tomás spoke quietly.

"You have dark enemies."

GIL

Gil kept pushing, always bargaining for one more hill, one more switchback, just to that next tree. Her need to catch up to Sesha countered the careful pace set by the old man who was their guide and the limits of their worn mounts. It was late afternoon when they finally reached Yuanahuanca.

She was disappointed that Sesha was not waiting there, and wondered why her sisters continued on. The innkeeper confirmed they had left two days ago. Gemella followed in the company of horsemen and a tall, pale gringo. He had the *soroche*, the man said, and should have stayed behind. The *cholos* had argued over it, but the fire-haired woman had insisted he stay with the group.

Though *cholo* merely indicated a native who had moved to the city, the word was spoken as if he was spitting out something distasteful. Her sense of it was dark and troublesome. Was Gemella aware of the risk she took with these men?

The mention of Professor Williams also troubled her, stirring anxious shadows of concern, intangible but no less valid. As with the artist in Cerro de Pasco, she felt a *wrongness* in his essence. Unaware he was dealing with twins, he was vulnerable to Gemella's influence. She was claiming him for her own, weaving him into her web. The tighter Gemella's hold became, the less Gil could perceive of him, fraying to a pale, worn thread. *And what of Supay? Had it possessed Williams, as it had the coyote and the wind and the man at the hotel?*

Gil fretted, pacing the road and gazing north while they watered the horses. Petra's lame mount would have to be left behind, and no others were available. More delays; more lost time.

If Sesha traveled beyond Huarautambo, how could Gil hope to follow? She touched her shirt, feeling the contour of Sesha's pendant beneath the flannel. Instinct kept it hidden, even from Petra and Sumala.

"How will we find them?" Sumala asked. "Beyond Huarautambo, there's nothing on the map."

Gil glanced at Petra, who said only, "Gilaishling knows the

way. She can follow them." Sumala looked to Gil with a quizzical quirk of her brow.

How to explain what she could barely understood herself?

"Everyone has a unique essence. Neither energy nor matter, it's like a glimmering dust." Shaken off, poured out, and sown like seed. "Spirit, perhaps. Or soul? It leaves a trail I can follow." *If we're not too far behind,* she thought.

Though Petra argued for staying the night, Gil insisted they push on. Huarautambo was only a little further—less than two miles. If they were to ever catch up with Sesha, they had to keep going. Her impatience was tempered, though, by the realization that she would soon have to face Gemella. What would she say to her? What *could* she say?

After nineteen years, she still was not prepared to meet the Other.

SESHA

They continued on, inertia dragging them forward, though reason begged to wait.

"My legs are turning to stone!" Maji exclaimed in English when they paused for a rest before tackling yet another climb. She waved her hand at the stolid outcrops surrounding them, like the tops of lesser mountains all but buried in the detritus of time. "These aren't rocks. They're people." She spoke in short phrases punctuated by deep gasps of the thinning sir. "They climb up here. Slower. And slower. And slower, still. 'Til they can't move at all. They turn to stone. Stone piled on stone, on stone. We'll all turn to stone, and these accursed mountains will be another foot taller."

In spite of their fatigue, Lena and Evita laughed. Tomás glanced their way as if wondering what the joke might be.

"Careful," Evita advised her playfully. "If Tomás understood English, he might believe you. Then what?"

"You might start a cult of stone worshipers."

The sisters laughed again, a tonic against the fatigue weighing them down. But to Sesha, Maji's words echoed Thomás's idea of *chúkara.* A wild place, untamed, where humans were not welcome. She gazed at the surrounding peaks with a small shudder. If the Quechua would not venture into the highest mountains, the realm of spirits and gods, how could she ever convince Tomás to take them all the way to Killichaka? What were their options if he did not?

Tomás waited at the top of the ridge, his red, blue, and yellow poncho bright against the drab gray of the stone. His mule snuffed at the sparse grass. And this was truly and finally the top. A long, narrow valley opened up before them, and as each of her sisters crested the slope, Sesha could hear their relief in long, drawn out sighs and small "aahs" of wonder.

"Down," Maji murmured in delight. "The trail goes *down*. Wonderful, blessed down."

But Sesha's relief was tempered with dismay. At the end of the valley, a wall of enormous peaks, bright with snow, confronted them, austere guardians denying passage. *How will we ever get past them in time?*

Like a storm-wracked sea, one relentless crest after another, the land seethed at the impudence of their trespass. It seemed impossible that Gil could find them. Like two small boats, how could they hope to encounter one another except by the most remarkable chance?

Yet Gil had most remarkable talents, and Sesha was certain her sister could track them, aided by the maps and the messages Lena left in each village. *So why haven't they caught up yet?*

GIL

Crossing the river, the path joined the ancient royal highway, and they followed it toward Huarautambo. The road took them past the remnants of an old mill of colonial vintage and stone ruins far, far older.

Had Sesha had a chance to explore these ruins? Gil didn't think so; the lingering trace of her sister's essence remained on the road. Sesha and the others had passed by, their attention focused only on the future.

On the return journey they would have time to relax and enjoy the scenery. They could stop and explore these ancient stones. She could touch them and summon their ancient builders, just as she did with the handprints back home, and she could sing their songs for Sesha. Thinking of her sisters, she turned her attention back to the trail and the sense she felt of their passing. They were all there—even the faint glimmer of Lena's unborn child.

Sesha's essence ran ahead beyond the range of Gil's senses. She recognized its *color* and its *song*—inaccurate words but the closest she could find to describe the intangible energy she perceived.

Professor Williams' essence was there also, braided with others, some dark and foul. The Other—Gemella—as well. Sesha didn't know Gil's twin was here; she didn't know the danger. How to warn her? Gil touched her shirt where Sesha's pendant rested against her skin. A feeling of *connection* snapped so taut, Gil jerked in her saddle. She could almost see her sister and hear her voice.

Sesha, she thought, as if calling out loud. *Sesha, be careful. Wait for me.*

~ * ~

The sun was near to setting when they caught sight of the bell tower of Huarautambo. Tall and square, built of stone and clay, it stood out among the adobe huts of the small town.

Gil approached with a feeling of dread like a leaden weight in the pit of her stomach. Supay had not appeared for some time, but she was certain it had not yet given up. The possibility was an itch on her soul. She eyed the tower as if it were an omen of doom. Its peaked roof pointed at the sky like the pivot point of some massive scale. What might hang here in the balance?

She clenched the reins tight in her fists to keep from wheeling her horse around and fleeing as she had in Cerro de Pasco. She could not allow such fear to dominate her again. She could not fail again. She couldn't.

Long shadows draped the town while the surrounding peaks and the air glowed with sunset's pink and gold hues. Petra and Sumala expressed their relief in audible sighs, and even the old man seemed energized by the sight. As in Yuanahuanca, the villagers crowded around—first the children, openly curious, then, more warily, the adults.

The villagers showed no sign of leaving. Those closest couldn't resist stroking the horses, running their hands along the packs, and even touching, tentatively, Gil and her sisters as well and remarking on Gil's red hair. Petra eyed them suspiciously, brushing at their hands as if they were annoying insects. Her nervousness transmitted itself to her horse, and the poor, tired creature pranced and skittered. Gil feared someone might get hurt. She reached out to calm the animal, at the same time warning the people to keep their distance.

"Gil, where are we going to sleep?" Sumala called out over the heads of the crowd. "How can we get these people to leave us alone long enough to even eat?"

A woman appeared then and motioned for them to follow, taking the lead rope from Sumala's hand. She wore three hats and carried an infant in a *lliclla*. A dark line crossed her throat like a scar. The crowd separated before them and dispersed quickly, leaving behind dark mutters and furtive signs. The woman brought them to a small rancho where they were greeted cordially by an aged woman and invited into the kitchen to eat.

When Gil turned to thank their rescuer, the woman had left as abruptly as she had appeared. Gil could find no trace or essence of the woman or her baby, only a faint whisper that could have been the eucalyptus trees fencing the fields. Their hostess denied knowing or even seeing her.

"*Almas*," she whispered when Gil described the woman, and then crossed herself. Ghosts. The natives believed the soul walked the earth for a full year beyond its death. Gil frowned in confusion. Why would such a spirit come to their aid? The memory of the funeral in Cerro de Pasco sent a shiver trickling down her spine. She shuddered and turned from the implications.

Perhaps the spirit was instead one of the Inca Atahualpa's servants, charged still to protect his domain and all who traveled within. A pleasant enough fantasy, she thought, one to give comfort while traveling these vast and empty places. There was an enchantment upon this land, Gil decided with a whimsical smile, that summoned such beings to aid the beleaguered traveler and then vanish back into the void. She found it comforting to imagine that something might be on their side, that not all the forces in play were against them.

Offering some of their own supplies in return for the rancher's meager hospitality, they enjoyed what in these parts amounted to a sumptuous feast. Sumala helped cook, carrying on an animated conversation in Spanish. Gil suspected she did more than exchange recipes and the herbs she added were as much for healing as for flavor.

After dinner, the woman showed them a walled-in porch

where they could bed down, and a fenced yard for the horses. For fifty *soles*, they were able to purchase enough alfalfa to feed the horses for two days. The old man tethered the animals for the night and then left them, perhaps to claim hospitality with distant family, to enter where strangers were not welcome.

These people warmly invited them into their kitchens to share a meal, but not into their homes. They drew that barrier between themselves and those outside. *You may share my world, but not my life.*

Petra bedded down as soon as she'd eaten. Gil's sense of her oldest sister was bruised and weary. For Petra's sake, Gil realized, she would have to rein in her impatience. Sumala, however, wandered off to confer with the local *brujas*, to learn about the herbs and remedies they used. She had studied both modern medicine and traditional, the latter nurtured by a tribal shaman. She wasn't averse to combining the two. Gil wondered what new concoctions she would bring back.

Aching and weary from the day's ride, Gil nevertheless found her mind too troubled to sleep. She sat on the porch wall where it met the house, so she could lean back and contemplate the stark silhouette of the bell tower pointing into a moonless night.

The quiet peace of the village lulled her caution, but not the tension that had built throughout the day, a sense of displacement. She felt off-balance. *En casa ajena,* the locals called it. Literally, "In another's house." Figuratively, in an alien place. *More like a house divided,* she thought.

The spoor of Gemella's passing befouled the air. How could twins be more opposite, she wondered. *Or are we?* Did she carry within her the same potential for corruption?

Such thoughts led inevitably to Cerro de Pasco. Here in Haurautambo, she'd put enough distance between her and that incident that she felt safe in examining it. Was Gemella in league with Supay, engineering the murders to trap Gil, to bind her to darkness? If her own twin could fall prey to such evil, what hope did she have? The Ritual would give her tremendous power, and she wondered now if she could wield it without falling prey to its temptations and corruptions. Would she find it too easy to use it to her own ends?

"You're not still brooding over that funeral in Cerro de Pasco, are you?" Sumala asked, coming out of the darkness and taking a seat beside Gil. She carried the scent of strange herbs and potions and the giddy rapture of knowledge gained.

Admittedly, "brooding" precisely described Gil's mood. Her thoughts weighed heavy enough to bear down upon her posture and drag her expression into a frown. She straightened, bringing herself to focus on the present, and considered Sumala's question.

"That family in Cerro de Pasco—they were murdered because of me. If we had come sooner—if we hadn't gone to Pachacamac, they might still be alive." Her hands fluttered, attempting to weave her thoughts into a coherent idea. "The funeral—I should have *done* something. I should have stood my ground." Instead, she had fled, trembling in terror and horror. Could such cowardice ever be forgiven?

Sumala shook her head. "I can't believe Gemella murdered them. She couldn't be that evil, could she?"

Gil licked at dry lips. "Remember the attack in Lima? That entity called itself 'Supay,' and it can possess things and bend them to its will. It's the incarnation of evil"

"But that attack was the same night as the murders. How could it be in two places at the same time?"

"It's everywhere, Sumala, even here. It uses people, manipulates them. I don't know if I can defeat it. It tested me in Cerro de Pasco, and I failed."

And that failure provided fertile soil for doubt and despair. If Gemella had left a trap here, it was no more complex than the weight of Gil's own anguish. "I should have banished that evil, and instead, I fled."

Sumala said nothing, and in the dark, Gil could not see her expression. Was she laughing at her, or holding her in scorn? Did she believe or even understand what Gil was trying to say?

"I was afraid," Gil continued, needing the solidity of spoken words to express the enigma of her turmoil. "Maybe the evil of this world is stronger than I am, and our whole purpose here is in vain. Once I believed I could do anything, but now doubt erodes even the abilities I already possess. It's a quagmire pulling me under."

Sumala let out a long, soft sigh, and Gil wondered if it had been a mistake to confide in her.

"Your power comes from thousands of years of tradition. It's worked in the past, whenever it was needed; it'll work now. You simply have to believe."

"There's nothing simple about it. The world has grown so complicated. You know what happens in the Vision. How am I supposed to stop something like that?"

Gil gazed at the black point of the crumbling bell tower eclipsing the star-mantled night. A balance scale for the soul, she thought. Until now, she had moved with a fragile confidence toward the challenge of the Vision. Her spirit shifting beneath her, her footing became uncertain. She tilted toward an abyss of fear and despair. She held herself still in delicate balance and barely dared breathe. Was this yet another trap, this paralyzing fear, perhaps of her own making?

"Wait for the Ritual," Sumala advised. "It will succeed, and then you'll have your answers." To Gil, her sister's words had a hollow timbre.

"Do you truly believe that?"

"I have to, don't I? That's the trick of this. We all have to believe."

"But *do* you?"

Sumala would not meet her gaze. "I wouldn't be here if I didn't." A yawn escaped her. She stood and stretched. "You're tired, Gil. Get some sleep. Things won't seem quite so bleak in the morning, when you're rested." She crossed the porch to one of the pads of dried grass.

"You have to believe, Sumala," Gil called softly after her, not even sure her sister could hear. "It's all a matter of faith." Words she perhaps intended for herself. "You have to believe," she murmured, like a prayer.

The sun was gone and the moon not yet risen. The night was empty except for these fears she conjured for herself. Angry with herself for granting power to such phantoms, she slid abruptly down from the porch wall and settled in her own blankets. It was easy to close her eyes, not so easy to close off her thoughts. A long time passed before she finally slept, her thoughts slipping edgewise into the stuff of dreams.

Thursday, June 3

GIL

Sometime in the night, somewhere in her dreams, the balance tipped. Gil slid inexorably toward a black maw, a darkness woven from fear and despair. *I can't do this!* she thought before fully waking. The thought became a scream, a child's voice crying out.

¡Sálvenos!

Gil awoke, tearing free from a vivid replay of the funeral, a child riding astride her own coffin. She had turned her empty gaze upon Gil. The image carried over into waking, along with her unvoiced cry.

¡Sálvenos!

Save us.

But it's too late—they're already dead.

What did it mean, then?

The murders had served as bait, their abandoned spirits trapped on Earth. *Almas.* Their role was incomplete, something yet undone. How could she redeem their deaths?

The question nagged at her as she emerged into a morning shrouded in mist, an ethereal landscape, half hidden, half revealed. The bell tower stood above the mist like a beacon.

Sumala and Petra were already up. Sumala was brewing tea, using water from an ancient well and mixing in dried herbs from her kit bag. *Maté de coca*, a remedy for *soroche*. The bitter concoction managed to keep the worst symptoms at bay, but Gil wished they had something—anything—for a sweetener.

She sat on a stone bench, gnawing at a hard roll, her cup of tea tucked between her knees to preserve its warmth. The bench, well, and two stone walls were of Inca construction, remnants perhaps of the *tampu* for which the village was named—storehouses provided for the Inca's messengers and those who traveled on his business. She studied the remarkable precision with which these stones had been placed together, so that not even a blade of grass could separate them. The empire of the Inca had been run with such precision, in some ways cruel, but efficient

171

and thriving. Villages divided the land according to the size of each family, but the fields were worked as a community. Each man paid a labor tax, a time spent working the mines, building roads and cities, or serving in the army.

Pizarro had believed in his right to conquer and dominate these people and to steal both their dignity and wealth. Out of fear and ignorance and misdirected zeal, missionaries had hunted down the mummified remains of the Inca rulers and destroyed them, every one. Nothing they had built in the centuries since had served as well. In time, the new would be gone, but these ruins would still remain.

Was she not taking on a similar role, Gil mused. If the ritual succeeds, she would have the power to topple nations. Did she have the wisdom to use it or the strength and courage to keep that power under control, to keep it from dominating her and becoming the master? Once she'd had no doubts, but the events in Lima and Cerro de Pasco cast shadows across her bright dreams, and the encounters with Supay taxed her faith. Gemella's manipulations cast Gil's own character in a sinister mold. This journey tested the stamina of her soul. Too bad Sumala had no remedies for *soroche* of the spirit.

She shook her head. "I'm not ready for this," she murmured to herself, unaware that Petra was near.

"Of course you are," she said, taking a seat on the edge of the well opposite Gil. They faced one another, elbows resting on knees so that their hands hung just inches from one another. Gil had but to raise her fingers to touch her sister's hand and clasp it in her own, to give comfort and seek assurance in return. But she did not, waiting instead for Petra to reach out.

Gil and her sisters had always been just as these two pairs of hands, within reach but never quite touching, beads strung on the thread of the Vision, separated by knots of conflict. What did she know of any of them? The focus had always been on her and her power. It took all of her concentration to contain and control the restless energy within her. The others were a mere backdrop to her role, bit players in the drama of the Vision.

Of all her sisters, she'd been close only to Sesha, and Sesha was not here. Gil thought of that last day in the canyon behind the rancho, and how Sesha had slipped down the hillside. Now Gil was the one sliding toward the abyss, and she needed Sesha to pull her back. How desperately she needed her now, to listen. To simply listen.

"I'm not as prepared as I should be," she explained now to Petra, trying to describe the turmoil she felt. "I haven't learned the things I truly need to know."

"You've had the best schooling of any of us," Petra responded sharply, a taste of resentment in her voice. With their mother gone and the aunts aging, Petra was the one who planned Gil's education and arranged the details of her life, always with the aim of defeating the Vision. Anything that contradicted those plans was taken as a personal affront. "We sent you to the best university we could afford. Others in the family were not so fortunate." She glanced pointedly toward Sumala, who was examining one of the horses. Unable to afford proper training, Sumala had apprenticed herself to a local doctor and eagerly devoured every medical text and journal within sixty miles. Her education was hardly formal, her practice not exactly legal, but among the poor she attended, such details didn't matter.

"That's not my point—"

"It's important that you learn as much as possible—history, economics, politics, science."

Gil sighed, for this was an old argument. She had always maintained that understanding people was the true key, and her preferences had always run to the arts and humanities. Now she found a new direction to the debate.

"Theories and principles and soulless facts. What about the real world? I should've walked the slums, stood in picket lines, worked in hospitals and soup kitchens. *That's* the education I should've had."

Petra jerked away from the notion, her hands coming to her face in utter dismay.

"No! Oh, no! We couldn't take the risk. If something had happened to you—there's no starting over. You know that better than any of us. We had to protect you."

"From what, Petra?"

"From danger! From corrupt influence."

"But I have no experience! You can't defeat evil by hiding from it! I should have gone out and met it face to face and learned to shake hands and wrestle it to the ground. The funeral in Cerro de Pasco proves that. You protected me so well, I can't defend myself. I was naïve and untried, and the enemy almost won." *Did win, in a way,* she thought. The memory of that sooty veil, the blood flooding the plaza, and the cries of the dead made her shiver. Gil dreaded the certainty of the next ordeal. *Never again,* she prayed. *I can't face that again.*

Petra arched her eyebrows as if she questioned Gil's senses. "Gil, you always had a creative imagination—"

"*What* imagination?" Gil shouted in frustration. "I am the seventh daughter of a seventh daughter, yet you question the very skills I was bred to have. Don't you believe in who I am?"

"Of course I believe!" Petra responded, too quickly to have truly given it thought. Her face revealed her hurt. "I've devoted my whole life to our mission."

"You say that so easily, but you don't have to live with this power—or its consequences. You don't have to control it. You don't really know what I can do. Up to now, it's been mere finger exercises. I could save the world or destroy it."

For a moment, she thought Petra might slap her, the way one does to stop hysteria. She was breathlessly aware that her words had tumbled like stones down a hillside, like Sesha sliding down the cliff. She clawed for an anchor, dragging her thoughts to a precarious stop.

Instead, the lines of Petra's face deflated, her spirit crumpling beneath the weight of Gil's chastisement. But it wasn't really Petra's fault. Gil should've known, perhaps had known all along, and had avoided the responsibility. It'd been too easy to let Petra control her life and make all the decisions, to sit back and let things happen and think *someday, but not today.*

Someday had finally arrived.

"Why does it have to be now?" Gil said softly. "Why can't we wait another year?"

"You know the next eclipses are in all the wrong places. I'm thirty-six years old, and I have no life," Petra responded with bitter anger in her voice. "I've spent my whole life preparing you, taking care of you and the others. I've lived and breathed the Vision. I don't *want* to wait another year. None of us do. If Sesha's right, and this ritual gives you the true power you need, then I want it to be over *now.* I want a life of my own, before I'm too old to do anything with it." She gestured helplessly as if to say, *Look at me; I already am.*

Gil studied Petra's face, truly looked, for the first time in many years, it seemed. She saw weariness etched in fine lines around Petra's eyes and mouth, a dusting of gray among the brown of her hair. Her cheeks sagged beneath the weight of too many years, dragging the mouth into a perpetual frown.

Petra continued, "And what about the others? Do you think Evita wants to continue traipsing around the world to satisfy your whims? Sesha or Maji? Sumala left behind patients who need her. And Lena. How often can you ask her to abandon her husband and kids? We're here now. This is your one chance. You have no right to ask any more of us."

"At least you have the choice!" Gil responded in abrupt and searing anger. She was slipping again toward that dark edge, with nothing to grasp except her own nameless fear. "Lena can go back to her family and Sumala to her patients. This will be the end for all of you, but for me, it's only the beginning. I have no life to go back to, only a Vision, and it's not even my own. I have no choice; I never did. I wasn't born; I was manufactured—conjured from a folktale. No one ever asked *me* if I wanted this!"

Petra stood and walked away from Gil's anger. "I'm sorry," she said from a safe distance. "There are times I envy you, when I think about the power you wield, the prestige of being the chosen one. I forget about the responsibility and the sacrifices that go with it. Maybe I don't want to think about it. But we're here now; we have to go through with this. You know that better than any-one."

"We don't have to," Gil murmured, her voice a soft flutter like the wings of a moth trapped in a jar. She didn't have to do this. She could simply walk away, pretending this was nothing more than superstition, the mutterings of old wives in the gloom of a stormy night. A concoction of hope. There had to be another way to stop the Vision from becoming reality.

"Gilaishling." Petra's voice was unusually soft and gentle now, begging her attention. When Gil looked up, Petra stood be-fore her, her hand extended and open. She stared at it as if the lines and calluses, the marks of age and toil, mapped her own fu-ture. "We can't turn back now; the others are waiting."

Behind Petra, Sumala and the old man stood with the horses. Somewhere in those mountains, Sesha and the others waited, too, and beyond that, all those voices crying out from the future.

¡Salvenos! The word mingled with those ever-present voices until they all took up the same cry.

¡Salvenos!

Save us!

I don't know how!

And now her fear had a name.

Failure.

SESHA

The morning began with dew frozen on the tents and the waning moon proudly riding the zenith. When Sesha crawled from her tent, farmers were already working their fields, tilling steep, terraced slopes on the surrounding cliffs.

They had arrived long after dusk, pitching tents in a fallow field. Now Sesha noted three mud huts crouched on the rim of a steep-walled valley, the white ribbon of a river coursing its floor. To the west, Mt. Yerupaja glowered above its court of lesser peaks. The rising sun turned its snow-draped flanks to flaming magenta.

Sesha stretched as if offering homage to the newly-risen sun. "Tomás, it's a good day to be alive," she said in English as their guide approached and offered her a mug of tea.

"*¿Como?*" the little Quechuan asked. Sesha laughed as she accepted the mug gratefully. She sipped slowly, letting the rising steam warm her face, then translated her comment into Spanish.

Tomás nodded, a wide grin illuminating his face. "*Sumaq p'unchay a.*" he responded in agreement.

While Evita and Lena prepared breakfast and Maji tended the mules, Sesha carefully unfolded the Killichaka map. Tomás squatted beside her and stared at the paper. He seemed to consider it a powerful talisman. Sesha pointed to one of the black dots on the largest map.

"Angoltuto?" She nodded at the three huts then tapped the symbol on the map. "Here?"

Tomás nodded, his brows knitted in concentration. Now was the crucial point. Could she persuade Tomás to stay with them?

"Gashapampa," he said with a broad smile, nodding north across the river. Sesha realized he was thinking of home.

"Not yet," Sesha responded in Spanish. "We have to go here,

to this lake." She indicated the oblong shape on the map. "*Cocha Lauricocha. Mainintata risah Lauricocha.*" Show me the way to Lauricocha. That far, she thought, she could coax him. She didn't want to get into another argument about Killichaka.

But the man shook his head and faced north.

"Gashapampa," he said, and then a string of words that perhaps described the route home.

"But we must go there," Sesha insisted, switching back to Spanish and pointing to the mountains of Cordillera Raura, a snow-crested ridge to the southwest. She avoided mentioning Killichaka. "We need to climb the mountains to see the ocean."

Something passed across the peasant's face, a dark look, quickly hidden. Sesha wished she had Gil's ability to read such things. Did this man whose world was bound by endless stone have any concept of a horizon other than the line of peaks carved like ragged teeth across the sky? Could he comprehend the word *ocean?*

She jabbed her finger at the lake on the map. "You agreed to take us here." *Get him that far, at least, and perhaps a little farther.* "You said you knew the way to Lauricocha."

His expression crumpled, for her words accused him of lying. She feared she'd insulted his honor, insinuating he wasn't a fit guide. Tomás wore his pride as a delicate garment; she had no intention of rending it from him. His face set into planes of stubborn denial, he refused to look at the map. He gazed north.

"Never mind," she told him quietly. "We'll find our own way." She stowed the map in her pack, then stood and walked away to break the news to the others and help with the mules.

"If he won't take us, then we'll find someone else," Lena stated, in Spanish and loudly enough for Tomás to hear. A bluff? "You have the map. We'll find our own way from here."

"Perhaps we should wait for Gil and the others. They must be close," Evita suggested. But this close to his home, would Tomás wait also?

"We need to find Killichaka first," Sesha stated. Only five days to find the shrine and prepare for the Ritual. The eclipse would occur late in the day, the sun setting roughly north by northwest. If mountains blocked the view, their trip would be in vain.

"But they might be only a day behind, or half a day—or an

hour," argued Lena. "It doesn't make sense to keep going now."

Sesha agreed, yet the urge to move on made her restless. Only yesterday, she would've argued for waiting. But now she felt a quiver in her bones, a sense of anticipation and anxiety. It was important to find the place *now*. The need to keep moving welled up like a bubble in her chest, goading her on as one might herd prey. What had changed, she wondered. She turned to gaze at the mountains. What had passed in the night that made haste so necessary? *What lurks out there, waiting?*

"No," she stated. "We have to keep moving."

To her surprise, Maji agreed, rubbing her own trembling arms. *What do you feel?* Sesha wanted to ask, but didn't want to foster unfounded fears. Sullenly, Lena and Evita gave in.

While Maji and Evita loaded the mules, Sesha and Lena searched the town for another guide. But no one was willing. They stared blankly past her as if her Quechuan was beyond understanding. Sesha and Lena returned to the mules. Maji had distributed their gear and supplies evenly between the two animals. Sesha considered leaving some gear behind, but as far as she knew, this was the last village, the last source of food and fodder. In the higher elevations, even fuel for their cooking fire would be hard to come by.

Tomás followed sullenly as they walked through the village and down the narrow track to the river. Would he come with them when they turned upstream or continue on towards his home? At the bottom of the valley, a side trail followed the river upstream. When Maji pulled her mule onto it, Tomás called out "*¡Mana!*" He hurried forward to snatch the lead strap from her hand and turned the mule to face the river.

"Where are you taking us now?" Lena muttered, a rhetorical question spoken in English.

"The mules, they don't fly," he responded in Spanish. His normally somber expression shattered into a grin and a hearty laugh. He seemed as pleased with his joke as the look of surprise on the women's faces.

"Tomás," Sesha yelled above the rumbling voice of the river. "We want to go west."

"No good," he responded in his limited Spanish, waving away the rocky track. A burst of Quechuan and gestures described the lake bound by steep cliffs. "Cross the river, go around," he said at last in Spanish.

The river was not deep, but ran fast and wide and undoubtedly cold. Tomás held one of the mules and gestured for Lena to mount, then told Maji to ride the other.

Maji glanced at the cold, rushing water with a rueful frown and insisted Evita ride instead.

"Twisted my ankle. I'll be fine," Evita explained with an apologetic wince, limping as she approached the mule. *Why didn't I notice*, Sesha wondered with a twinge of guilt. She should have noticed and taken care of her. She felt invisible reins connecting her to each sister, tethers that made her responsible for their well being and safety, and wondered just how and when she had become the group's leader.

Tomás set out first, plunging into the river with Lena's mule. Maji held onto the packsaddle so that the mule protected her from the current. She let out a small shriek at the river's icy touch. Sesha followed with Evita's mule.

Once across the river, the road threaded a narrow canyon, emerging at its head onto a terrace between one set of bluffs and another. Tomás stopped, pointedly ignoring a side trail, a track marked only with the prints of deer and *taruka*, the rare Andean stag. Sesha feared he was leading them home.

"Lauricocha," he said with the slightest of nods.

Sesha regarded the narrow track. How would Gil know to take this route? What sort of sign would her sister both notice and recognize as a message for her? A cairn of stones seemed obvious, like the *apachetas*. No one else would disturb it or even give it a second glance.

Maji helped her construct the cairn while Lena scribbled a hasty note like the ones she'd left in each village and farm. She tucked it under the top stone. Tomás watched patiently, his head cocked at a curious slant.

"For my sisters," she explained. She thought that for Tomás, the three sisters that followed had taken on a mythical quality, spirits that herded them ever onward. She studied the stone cairn. It did not seem enough.

"Maji, where's your lipstick?"

Maji's brow furrowed in a question, but she dug out a tube from her kit and handed it over. Sesha set her right hand against the side of a boulder, thumb pointing toward the trail, and traced around it with the lipstick. She considered filling in the shape, but she had already used half the lipstick.

"Look what you did!" Maji cried as she took back the tube, staring at the mashed stump of red color. "You've ruined it!"

"I'll get you another one. I never liked that shade anyway." She smiled to soften her words. "Gil will know this sign, know it's from us."

"Maji, you haven't worn makeup for three days," Lena pointed out. "Why do you still carry the thing?"

Maji pouted. "It reminds me of who I am."

Tomás faced north, gazing wistfully at the stone road. Sesha held her breath, not daring a word lest it be the wrong one. At last, muttering unintelligible Quechuan and shaking his head, Tomás turned away from home, taking the narrow trail. What must he think, Sesha wondered, of these stubborn women who would brave this wilderness alone? Before Tomás could change his mind, she herded the others to follow.

GALEN

The horse's uneven gait jerked Galen from side to side, and his hips ached from the motion. His legs ached, too, sore where the stirrups rubbed against his ankles. There was more to riding, he'd discovered, than just sitting on the back of a horse enjoying the view. Galen tried to ignore the narrow trail of broken steps, the steep drop to the left, and the way his horse seemed to prefer the edge of the trail to the middle. The horse's left hind leg slipped, and the animal jerked abruptly. Galen could do little more than clutch at the saddle horn. He leaned forward as his mount lunged for purchase on the slick stone, and kept reminding himself the animal didn't want to fall off the cliff any more than he did.

The trail finally topped the escarpment. For a pace, Galen looked back over his past, the ancient road descending one valley to another. He imagined he could make out Cerro de Pasco, a dark smear in the hazy distance. Slipping his hand under his shirt, he rubbed at the skin touched by the bloody handprint. It marked him, an invisible brand. He turned away, from the bitter memory.

Ahead, the road descended a long, wide valley. Beyond, mountains towered in somber elegance, wearing a cape of ermine snow. There was a desolate beauty in the sheer emptiness, the sweep of gray stone, and the utter blue of the open sky, as if that particular shade should define the color once and for all.

It didn't matter that elsewhere it was 1937. Here, in the age-less vaults of the mountains, time lost all meaning. It moved with the slow, ponderous pace of the glaciers perched like epaulets on the shoulders of the mountain crests.

He let the view distract him, pretending thatits beauty left him breathless, not the altitude. The pretense didn't last. His head ached and his chest hurt with the effort of drawing air. He had thought he'd acclimated to the altitude, but a deep, heavy cough had shaken him from sleep. The spasms became more violent and frequent throughout the day. He felt as if the evil wrought in Cerro de Pasco had taken root in him, his cough seeking to expel it from his soul.

Galen tried swallowing to drown the persistent tickle in his throat. The smallest wheeze would lead to a full bout. He prayed for relief, for a single breath that didn't feel like his chest was tear-ing open. For the sake of Miriam and her aunt, he could not allow Carlo and his men to see any weakness in him.

The road leveled out, and the horses settled into a relaxed gait. Galen allowed the even rhythm to lull and soothe him. Vi-sions, though, lurked behind his eyelids, the nightmare returning. Each time, more focused, more detailed, his mind forcing the event upon him one painful layer at a time.

Someone hovered over him, black-hooded, silent, holding a knife at his throat. He waited, helpless, while it took his posses-sions—his bags, his money, Harry's knife. Pedro's shriek became a gurgle. Mama gagged on a scream. Through it all, pipes played an eerie tune.

"¡Salvenos!" Eisabel cried, falling. The pocketknife with the ivory handle seemed the size of a sword. Eisabel lifted her gaze to ensnare him. "Salvenos."

The hooded figure turned. Galen's gaze fixed on the knife in its hand. Blood like a black shadow slid down the blade and dripped to the floor. Within the hood, pale light limned the barest outline of a face, vaguely familiar. Someone he should know? The point of the blade touched his throat, pricking his skin. *I know that knife. I've seen it before.* He tried to cry out, but couldn't. The figure lowered the blade, swiped it across its hand, and pressed the hand against Galen's shirt, just over his heart. Bending closer, it whispered in his ear.

"You are mine."

Galen jerked suddenly as he felt himself sway in his saddle. For a moment, he was confused by the bright sunshine and the open vista. A shudder ran across his shoulders, as if the dream were a blanket he could shrug off and leave behind.

You are mine. The breathy whisper echoed in his head. One of the horsemen was playing his pipes again, threading the nightmare into reality.

"Are you all right, Professor?" Miriam called from behind him. She urged her horse forward to ride abreast.

Galen nodded, a lie. But if he admitted the truth, he feared they would leave him behind.

"I've been wondering," he said, seeking to avoid the subject, "What does *salvenos* mean?"

"'Help us,' I believe, 'save us,' perhaps." She frowned, perhaps at the question. "Why do you ask?" Galen wondered if he hadn't escaped one avenue of danger to dash down another.

"No special reason. I heard it somewhere, and the phrase seems to have stuck in my head." He shrugged it off as meaningless, fearing he had let something slip.

Day by day, Miriam's aloof distance at their first encounter melted into a manner that could only be called seductive. This was not the GeM Orlov he'd known. Did she play out a desire that in the proper decorum of the campus could exist only as fantasy? Had Galen done anything to encourage it?

Yet her advances had a calculated air to them, almost condescending. Her smile could be brittle and hard, as if the cool mountain air had frozen it there. He found himself more repulsed than attracted, as if their relationship had taken a turn somewhere into a darker realm he did not wish to enter.

Vera, too, seemed discomforted by Miriam's behavior, unable to influence it. In whispered discussions he wasn't supposed to hear, she berated her niece, only to earn her scorn and wrath. This morning, she had emerged from her tent with a red mark on her cheek. Galen could feel the older woman's gaze boring into his back even now, as if he were at fault for Miriam's behavior.

"You still haven't answered me about being my guardian," Miriam commented when Carlo called for a rest stop. Galen walked a small circle to ease the stiffness in his legs and avoid the subject. Then he leaned against a rock to take a long drink from the canteen Miriam offered him.

"You still haven't told me why you need me."

Miriam circled behind him and slid her hand across his shoulders. He jerked away from her touch, but she persisted, kneading the tight muscles. It felt so good, Galen leaned into it, hoping she would not stop.

"I have my reasons," she said softly near his ear. "It's a simple task. Vow to stand guard during the Ritual. That's all. As I said, an honorary position."

"Then why would you need one? What could happen?"

"Nothing, I assure you. Your role is merely a precaution, based on ancient legend. Something went wrong once, and the sea god, *Pachacamac*, cursed the tribe with a plague of rain."

"A plague of rain? You'd think rain would be a blessing."

"Think about it. They lived in a desert and built with mud. A little rain is fine, but too much, and a whole culture washes away, quite literally." She stopped massaging his shoulders and moved around in front of him. "They sacrificed hundreds to appease the god—to no avail, of course." That image seemed to please her. She paused to savor it. "Conquered by the Inca, their history all but vanished. Only a few secret sources remain." She leaned closer, her breath on his cheek warm enough to give him goose flesh. "Will you be my guardian?" she whispered. "Will you vow to stand by me, no matter what?"

Once again, Vera circled the edge of his vision, watching him with a sense of anticipation that seemed almost hungry. Miriam's gaze was on the edge of patient. Galen felt a wary itch at the back of his neck.

But, oh, those eyes. They distracted him, held him in their green, green thrall, so that he lost the reins of reason. A persistent ringing in his ears seemed to block any attempt at rational thought. What did a few words mean? Why hesitate so? But even as he opened his mouth to speak, doubts pressed in.

Before Galen could utter a single word, though, Carlo charged at their group as if he'd been eavesdropping and had deliberately chosen this moment to interfere. He stopped in front of Miriam, pointedly ignoring Galen's presence.

Galen shook his head to clear it. The ringing in his ears persisted.

"It can wait," Galen said to Miriam's expectant gaze.

GIL

The weather matched Gil's mood. A storm building to the east chased after them as they pushed their horses along the rugged trail. Gil sighed, all too aware of the risk of imposing her own mental state upon the world around her.

"Is it Sesha?" Sumala asked, and Gil realized her expression must be giving away her thoughts.

"Sesha's all right," she answered with a wistful smile followed by a frown. "No, it's Professor Williams." She peered ahead, beyond the mountains. "I sense danger, but he's hidden. I can barely trace his essence." A frail and tenuous shadow, all but obscured by Gemella's bold presence, carefully hidden.

"Do you think he murdered the family in Cerro de Pasco, like they say?" Sumala asked. Gil shook her head, refusing to believe she could've been so wrong about his nature.

"Then why's he traveling with Gemella?" Sumala persisted, giving voice to Gil's own doubts. She could easily assume Gemella had tricked him as she had Sesha, but perhaps he'd been in league with her twin all along. The murders certainly cast shadows upon his character.

"I wish I knew," Gil murmured, and Sumala retreated. A renewed sense of dread curled heavy in Gil's stomach. Had Gemella twisted him to her own design and claimed him for herself? And what of Supay? Gil still believed Galen was an important key to the success of the Ritual, but his role was shifting, turning like a weather vane in an uncertain wind. If only she could warn him.

SESHA

Far older than the royal highway and concealed by neglect, Sesha could barely discern their trail. Ichu grass and spindly shrubs grew in cracks and shallow pockets of soil, and little else. A herd of wild vicuna, like delicate, miniature llamas, kept pace with them for a time. To the north, a series of bluffs rose to a high escarpment. Rumpled like furrowed brows, it frowned at their intrusion.

Storm clouds were rising in the east, keeping them in chilled shadow, the air a sharp slap against Sesha's cheeks. When the sun finally emerged, it ruled with fierce intensity. Elevation vied with latitude—15,000 feet but close to the equator. The temperature could drop twenty degrees in cloud shadow, and bitter cold nights opposed blazing days.

Sesha considered how such extreme variations must temper the people who lived here, both body and soul. The people were as stolid and enduring as the stone of the mountains. They clung to old ways in silent rebellion against their conquerors. Like the low growing flowers on the windswept pampas, they let the modern world sweep over them, untouched and undisturbed.

Where a high ridge intersected the terrace they found another *apacheta*, scarcely two feet tall. As Sesha bent to place a stone on the pile, she noted how moss grew between the stones and thought at first no one had passed this way in a long, long time. But two stones presented fresh, unweathered faces and another pinned a grass stem, not yet withered. She frowned, stroking the thin cut on her throat where the knife blade had rested. Last night's forebodings resurfaced.

Her glance crossed Tomás's. She noticed the same wary tension. She pressed her lips in a flat line and nodded, once. A shiver shook her shoulders.

To her dismay, the narrow trail veered to traverse the steep, crenulated slope above the lake shore, a shallow pause in the relentless *down*. It reminded Sesha of the trail back home, The memory of her harrowing slide brought her to a halt.

"Are you all right?" Maji asked from behind.

"Fine," Sesha responded curtly and forced herself to move. One step at a time, breath hissing between clenched teeth, she followed Tomás. Lauricocha lapped at the base of the cliff, a brilliant blue.

When they rounded the end of the lake, the ledge became a wide shelf. Sesha paused for breath, turning to check on her sisters. Maji coaxed her mule along the path, silenced by the arduous trek. Evita was a dozen yards behind, the line of her back a study in fierce determination. When her mule jerked against his lead rope, her whole body winced. Plump Lena lagged even farther behind, striding doggedly. Sesha waited. Lena simply glared at her, every ounce of strength and focus spent on drawing breath.

This journey was changing them in more ways than one.

Beyond Lauricocha, a smaller lake filled a steep-sided bowl. At the lake's head, an alpine meadow snuggled among dark stone teeth. Wind-swept grasses were dotted with orange daisies and tiny flowers like blue stars; cactus and moss grew among the rocks that girded the lakeshore. Hummingbirds flitted about, snatching at insects while viscachas protested the intrusion with high-pitched barks and squeaks. Caves or deep niches made ominous black slashes in the surrounding rock. A fitful wind played a song both sinister and threatening.

What might lurk here? Sesha wondered. Did the scent of evil waft in the breeze, the scent from Cerro de Pasco? She shivered and hugged herself against a sudden chill.

Tomás halted and started to unload the mules.

"Tomás," Sesha called out. "What are you doing?"

Tomás nodded toward the lake. "We camp here."

"But it's barely past noon."

Tomás glanced at the sun as if it lied. "I will go no more," he said in Spanish.

Evita, Maji, and Lena set up a twitter of protests.

"But you promised to take us to Killichaka?" Lena argued, both lie and insult. Sesha winced, hoping he would not take offense.

Tomás shook his head. *"Mana. Tomorrow, I go home."*

Now's the time, Sesha thought. Now she had to convince Tomás or lose his aid. Her Quechuan had improved considerably, and she had asked Tomás endless questions, seeking some leverage with which to sway him. She scarcely felt prepared and looked to her sisters. They could offer no more than shrugs.

"We go to Killichaka to ask favor of the spirits," she started carefully, aware she hadn't yet mastered the intricacies of the grammar, much less the voice stops and fricative variants. "My sister is—" she searched for a word. "Broken," was as close as she could come. "We journey to fix her."

Tomás looked to the others, his glance resting briefly on Lena. His expression, when he turned back, said he did not believe her.

"The one who follows. She faces a great task and needs the help of the spirits. Terrible things will happen if she fails." Sesha hoped the meaning, at least, was clear. That she tried so hard to speak his language must surely emphasize its importance.

Tomás shrugged as if it did not matter. His world was here and he could not conceive how anything beyond these mountains could affect him. What happened there did not concern him.

"We can't find it without your help," Lena added.

"It is there." His chin jutted toward the mountains glowering above them.

"Tomás, you wouldn't abandon us here, would you?" Evita asked, her Spanish plaintive and wistful.

But Tomás seemed to have suddenly forgotten the language, turning to the mules as if he hadn't heard her.

"What are we to do?" Sesha asked in Quechuan.

"You have your maps." Tomás replied. His glance darted toward her pack where she kept them.

"But we need you."

Tomás muttered something in Quechuan, too low and too fast for Sesha to follow. He tethered the mules in the middle of the meadow. Her sisters merely looked at one another in wordless dismay. Maji reached out to touch Sesha's arm.

"We'll get there somehow. We've come too far to fail now."

Tomás set up camp at the meadow's edge, in the lee of the massive cliffs that bound the lake, near the shallow caves cleaving their slopes. After erecting the tents, Sesha helped Tomás with the fire. At this altitude, there were none of the *tola* shrubs the natives used for firewood. Tomás showed Sesha how to use grass and dried dung instead.

"The mules need water," Maji said and led them toward the lake.

"Mana!" Tomás cried out. He looked to Sesha in dismay and with pantomime and Quechuan-flecked Spanish, warned of danger.

"He says the bottom drops off and isn't stable. The horses would flounder," Sesha relayed. "I think." Tomás waved instead toward the stream that fed the lake.

"See how we need you?" Sesha noted. Tomás merely frowned.

Blocked by the mountains, the sun followed the moon to an early bed, and Sesha's sisters gratefully followed suit. Sesha listened to them rustling and bumping about in the tents as she sat alone by the fire and studied the Killichaka map, trying to reconcile it with the surrounding terrain.

The map was a coded puzzle, sparse markings, enough to jog the memory without giving away the location. Inverted V's and distorted shapes mimicked landmarks. Sesha had hoped that once here, she would be able to reconcile them with the actual landscape. The mountains cut a black silhouette against a prolonged twilight. Could this crude "M" be that peak there, the one with the notched summit? Sesha shook her head, straining to read by the meager firelight and a kerosene lamp.

As the fire settled into a bed of embers, Tomás came and squatted beside her. The pale light cast restless shadows across his face. He gazed north. Sesha could believe his intense stare saw beyond the dark and the surrounding rock.

"How far is your home?" she asked.

"Lauricocha." He jabbed a stubby finger against his palm with each word, as she had when she first explained her maps. "Gashapampa. Gashacucho. Home."

Sesha nodded. So close, she thought, before she'd forced him here. How sad, to be so near and turn aside.

"You've been away a long time, haven't you." she murmured quietly in English. Though he couldn't possibly understand the words, he nodded.

"Come home with me," Tomás said in Spanish. "I will show you Tunsacancha. Old. Treasure there, maybe gold."

"We don't want treasure or gold, Tomás. I thought you understood that. How can I explain? If we fail, all will be gone." She waved to encompass the valley, the lake, the mountains. "All of this. Can you understand that?"

Tomás gazed past her with a look of cunning that said, "*This is the world. I know it well, and it will not change.*"

He poked at the glowing coals with a thin stick until it caught fire. He watched it burn. When half the stick was charred, he blew out the flame.

"Watch," he said in Spanish and waved a hand along the fanged crests. A final spear of golden light flashed, lighting a pinnacle of rock. "There." Reaching over her shoulder, he used the stick to mark the map with a black smudge and a thin line. "The way to Killichaka."

Sesha nodded slowly.

"*Taitacha pagasunki,*" she murmured. Thank you. Literally,

God will pay you.

Tomás dropped the stick in the dirt and ground it with his sandal, erasing any sign of his aid. "The mules cannot go there. Rocks, cliffs. No food." It was a casual remark, yet filled with hidden meaning.

Something rustled in the dark. Tomás stood and made a slow circle, peering uneasily into the night. Did he feel it, too—the sense of someone watching? Sesha opened her mouth to ask him, but thought better of it, not wanting to spook him. He walked away to bed down as usual near the mules, refusing to share the shelter of their tents.

"Tomás, the mules," Sesha called. He paused but did not turn. "Someone must care for them and show my sister the way, the one who is coming." The night hid his response.

Sesha sat staring into the dark. Whatever waited, she would handle. She knew the scent and touch of its evil, had felt its steel against her throat.

Friday, June 4

SESHA

In the morning, Tomás was gone. So were the mules.

Yet they were not alone. Sesha studied the rocky slopes with a wary eye. Someone watched. She could feel it.

GALEN

Set back from the road, three mud hovels huddled in the bowl of a valley at the edge of a deep river gorge. A fine drizzle, almost a mist, veiled the village in drifts of shadow. Two mules and a half dozen llamas grazed in a muddy yard. They stared insolently at Galen as he trudged by. Someone had said this was Angoltuto.

Gray smoke drew a thin line from one of the thatched roofs into an even grayer sky. Galen stooped to enter through the low doorway, then blinked until he could see through the smoky air. Firelight cast bare walls and earthen floor in hues of sallow ash. Alpaca blankets covered the door and windows. Their colors faded and muddied, the effect was more depressing than cheerful.

It was crowded in the hut. Two of the horsemen stood by the fire pit in the center of the room, drinking their chicha, their belligerent manner demanding twice their physical space. Carlo sat with Miriam and Vera at the only table, talking to a local. Galen worked his way into a corner and hugged himself uneasily. The place was too familiar, too much like Mama's home in Cerro de Pasco. Images curled around the edges of his vision, threatening to unleash the nightmare once more.

But it was warm. Only that kept Galen from fleeing. He rubbed his hands together, then cupped them over his face and blew into them. That set off a round of coughing, which he hid behind his soiled handkerchief. When the spate of wracking coughs finally subsided, the cloth was flecked with red and that frightened him. Hadn't there been something in the guidebook about such symptoms? He couldn't remember, but his sense of it was one of urgency and peril. He stuffed the cloth back into his pocket before anyone could notice. His head throbbed to the beat of his pulse.

Determined to prove himself able, he had managed to keep up with the group most of the day, pushing both himself and his weary horse. But the weather was changing, a heavy cloud layer close and smothering.

If only they would give him a day of rest. He craved one good night's sleep, some place warm and dry. A quiet place, where the snores of the horsemen and his own fits of coughing didn't keep him awake. Somewhere safe from *nightmares*.

But Carlo's pace allowed no time for rest, keeping to some undefined schedule. Miriam insisted on sending a rider to watch their back trail. His reports would cause Miriam to push on for a time even more strenuously. Galen wondered what pursued them.

Miriam continued talking to the local, Carlo translating Spanish into Quechuan and back again. The relentless headache made it hard for Galen to concentrate or even to care.

This new man was small and compact, barrel-chested. His broad face had a large nose and small, almond-shaped eyes. He wore traditional clothing, his poncho and *chullo* cap striped red and blue and yellow. He'd seen that pattern before. Pressing fingers against his temples, he tried to think past the throbbing pulse of pain. Yanahuanca. Yes, with the women Miriam called her sisters, the one named Sesha. Galen tensed, his breath a sharp hiss, and Miriam finally noticed his presence and spoke across the smoky room.

"Tomás, here, seems to have me confused with someone else." She smiled at some private joke. "He claims he left my sisters at a lake west of here. He says they're waiting for us." Irony touched her voice, and her mouth curled into a rather sly smile, as if sharing some jest and Galen should know the punch line.

Galen frowned. If this was Sesha's guide, why had he left them? He was not like these others. His face, though impassive, held integrity. If he was Miriam's spy, why did she send out others? *No*, he decided. *This man doesn't belong. He's blundered into this mess just as I did.*

Miriam was speaking to the others now in Spanish. Galen thought they argued to stay the night here. He fervently agreed, but no one asked his opinion. As in the other villages they had passed through, he considered staying behind—considered it, planned it, devoutly wished for it. Yet each time, he had ultimately rejected it. As long as he stayed with Miriam, he had some hope of getting out of the country. Without papers, money, or a convincing alibi for the murders in Cerro do Pasco, he was dependent on her and whatever diplomatic rabbit she might pull from her hat. Without Miriam, he couldn't even beg food or shelter.

Miriam obviously wanted to push on. A single word stood out in her argument. *Oro.* Gold. What was she telling them that she hadn't told him? What did she promise? Galen frowned. These men were dirty and unkempt, more so than almost anyone else he'd met. Their mean-spirited attitude and the cold glaze of their expressions made Galen think that the dirt and grime permeated their souls as well. He did not think it wise to cross them.

Tomás, Galen noted, also listened to the argument with an intense expression. He watched Miriam closely, as if seeking some detail. Apparently, he failed to find it, for his eyes narrowed and his posture shifted away from the others. When Miriam posed a question, his answer was terse but emphatic. Carlo frowned as he translated, and Miriam's response was harsh. Tomás stood to leave. Carlo stepped into his path, knife drawn so quickly, Galen had not seen the man's hand move.

Tomás's eyes wandered from one face to another, settling on Galen's as if measuring him. Galen pushed away from the wall, wondering how he could defend the Quechuan.

"You don't need him, Miriam. You know where your sisters are headed. You have men watching them."

The look Miriam gave him was chill and calculating. "You're very observant," she said as if that were an accusation.

Miriam turned to Carlo. "*Suéltalo.* Let him go." She strode toward the door, then turned when no one followed.

"*¡Vámonos!*" she commanded. "We have no time for this." She stared at the others as if challenging each individually, then left without waiting to see if they would follow.

Carlo waited, hefting the knife as if weighing the cost of a life. Galen stepped between Tomás and the horseman, glaring at Carlo as if he were an unruly student. The horseman shifted the point of his knife toward Galen.

He waited while his two men followed Miriam out the door, drawing circles in the air with the tip of the blade.

"*La próxima vez, Gringo. Muerte,*" he said in a low growl. Galen needed no translation to recognize the threat. He shifted his weight, feeling Tomás' presence at his back. A moment more, to make it clear this was his decision, not the woman's or the gringo's, then Carlo sheathed the knife as quickly as it had been drawn. He walked away, insult implied in the insolent turn of his back.

Galen waited until Carlo left the hut, then let out his breath in a long, slow sigh. The day was coming when he would have to fight Carlo. Thankfully, not today. He really didn't feel up to fighting anyone today.

Tomás was watching him. A question came to the man's eyes.

"I don't know, either," Galen muttered as if he'd understood. He wished he could say more, but he had no words. He knew even less Quechuan than Spanish.

Outside, Galen watched Tomás retrieve the two mules from the yard as Miriam and the others mounted up. Galen hoped for some kind of delay, but Miriam goaded the others impatiently. They set out, Carlo in the lead, then Miriam and Vera, followed by the two men. Galen came last. The trail into the gorge was rocky and steep, and Galen would've felt more secure walking his mount. But Carlo rode, and Galen dared do no less.

At the bottom, they plunged into the swift flowing river. The dizzying swirl of the current threatened to unbalance him, and he swayed in his saddle. Icy water surged around his legs, inciting a spasm of feverish shivers so intense his muscles all but locked him into a tightly curled knot. Someone grabbed his reins and steadied him. Galen looked up. Tomás watched him carefully. He had waded into the water and positioned his mules to deflect the worst of the current around Galen and his horse.

"*Gracias,*" Galen muttered with a single nod, and then made a feeble attempt at the Quechuan equivalent. Tomás smiled and nodded back.

Across the river and out of the gorge, the group paused at a small cairn of rocks. The top stone held down a piece of paper.

Miriam dismounted and smiled as she read the note, then laughed out loud. "Look! My sisters left us a marker," Miriam announced. She scattered the rocks so that no trace remained.

Tomás pushed his mules and Galen's horse around the far side, near a large boulder. A hand was outlined in bright red on the rock's face. With a nod, he shared the Quechuan's conspiracy, though he had no idea what the mark might mean.

"We're getting close now," she said to Galen with a bright smile. She reached out to squeeze his arm excitedly. Galen frowned. Would her sisters leave a message for Miriam if they hated her so? Did someone else follow? He stood in his stirrups to look back across the river, half hoping to see the cavalry come over the ridge.

"Lake Taulicocha, indeed," she announced, waving the paper like a flag. She pointed west. Tomás stared impassively, but his eyes narrowed and the hand still holding Galen's reins clenched tight. He spoke to Carlo, who translated for the others. "He says we shouldn't go there, that the mountain spirits will take us."

Miriam laughed. "Tell him to go home. Tell him we have no use for old men frightened of their own shadow." She urged her horse forward, and the others followed. As Galen took his reins from Tomás, the Quechuan nodded towards Miriam, then pointed at his eye. Galen wasn't sure what the gesture meant, though it seemed to be some kind of warning. He nodded in return and set out. When he looked back, Tomás and his mules had started up the ancient roadway headed north.

GIL

The storm they had outrun yesterday caught up to them, enveloping them in a world as gray and dismal as Gil's mood. She sat her horse hunched over to make a smaller target for the incessant raindrops. The trail was muddy and the rocks slick. Their pace had slowed to a miserable crawl just when she felt an urgent need for haste. She feared Petra would insist on stopping and taking shelter.

Events were unfolding, unraveling from the skein of time, and she was powerless to affect them. *Professor Williams.* Yes, she sensed an obscure threat. Gemella was weaving her influence as a spider wraps its victim in gossamer silk. Bit by bit, Gil was losing her sense of him. Soon he would be hidden from her altogether.

Beware, she found herself murmuring. *Be wary.*

GALEN

Galen had fallen behind. In the drizzle and mist, he soon lost sight of the others. Their voices, even the sound of the ever-present panpipes, faded. In the flat and waning light, the trail became hard to distinguish, little more than a polished stripe across the rock, with here and there an unnaturally square stone marking its edge. He almost missed where it descended to cross a steep slope. The mist hid the view below, and for that, he was grateful.

The *soroche* had indeed returned, and the more he tried to breathe, the harder it became. On top of that, the mist turned to rain, and his coat was soon soaked through. Miserable and aching, he lacked the energy to force his horse to keep pace with the others and could not bring himself to hit the animal. The horse snatched at the sparse grass growing beside the trail.

He traveled within a globe of grey and gloom, now fading to dark, the landscape lost to him. He let the horse take the lead, assuming it would want to join the others. As Galen considered finding shelter for the night rather than risk losing his way, his horse nickered eagerly. The other horses answered back. The placid surface of a lake reflected stars as if it were a black gash in the fabric of reality. The distant rumble of cataracts contradicted the apparent calm, however. Beneath that flat surface, strong currents must flow, surging to escape the valley in a rage of impatience. How much like Miriam, he thought. What currents seethed beneath her façade of calm? What might he risk to explore those treacherous depths?

He found the camp at the far end of the lake, the campfire's light a flickering beacon. Vera came forward to meet him as if she'd been waiting. He considered that odd, for she generally seemed to resent his presence. She held his horse while he dismounted, then pointed him toward the fire. She seemed about to say something, then the thought faded from her expression, and only a disapproving frown remained.

As he trudged toward the fire he realized how much his body ached and how fever quivered in his bones. The rain had stopped, but his clothes were still wet. He focused on the bright, crackling dance of flame and shuffled toward it, hands held out to the fire's warmth like a sleepwalker.

The horsemen had crowded into one tent. Galen could hear

their drunken song accompanied by a single set of panpipes. Miriam waited for him alone by the fire. She greeted him with an eager smile and a cup of tea.

I shouldn't drink this, he thought when he had tasted it and found it laced with fire. Memories of Mama's pisco floated to the surface, and the nightmares could not be far behind. But the warmth soaked his aching chest, and it felt so good, so very, very good. He emptied the cup, savoring the heat it stoked in his middle, then held it out for more. His aches eased, draining like melting ice. As if that pain were the strings keeping him erect, he sat abruptly on the ground.

Miriam knelt behind him and started to knead his shoulders. His muscles twitched at her touch, and some small part of him wondered at the purpose of this sudden attention.

"Poor Professor Wiliams," she whispered in his ear, seeming genuinely sympathetic. "This trek really has been hard on you. I wish I could say the worst was over."

She refilled his cup and gave him a bowl of thin potato soup. Seating herself on a low, flat rock, she watched as he ate. She had changed out of her riding clothes into a white blouse and flounced skirt, tied at the waist with a bright red sash. Her only concession to the cold was a fringed shawl about her shoulders, as if she were immune to such mundane conditions. Galen thought about the overburdened horses and wondered how she could justify such nonessential baggage. What else might be in that bag she would allow no one else to handle?

"Three more days, and this will all be over." She smiled like a little girl anticipating Christmas. Even her eyes reflected that joy, and for a moment, Galen saw the Orlov he remembered. "Three more days, and the world is mine!"

Galen frowned. The Orlov he knew was not nearly so ambitious.

"You disapprove?"

"You sound a bit melodramatic."

Miriam laughed with tipsy abandon. "You shouldn't take things so literally. It's not as if I'm going to stride into the League of Nations and declare myself Empress of the World. People don't take kindly to such things, even when it's for their own good. No, the world will scarcely be aware of any change. It would hardly be prudent to call attention to my manipulations."

Manipulations. Was that what she was about? A tremor ran through Galen, shaking off an icy snare. He brushed at his hair as if he'd run into a spider's web. Miriam's exuberance seemed to issue from a source of detached calculation, her manner veiling a purpose of dark intent.

"What's happened to you? Where's the student who argued ethics and battled lewd professors?"

Miriam smiled suggestively. "That was there and then. Here, now, I make my own choices and my own rules." She ran her hands along his arms and across his shoulders and around again. Once more he felt the touch of unseen bonds. He tried to shrug them off, but they were not so easily broken.

She cocked her head to listen to the horseman's panpipes trilling like birdsong. Standing, she took away Galen's emptied bowl and tried to pull him to his feet. "I feel like celebrating!" she said with a laugh. "Dance with me."

"Is that a royal command?" he said with as much sarcasm as he could muster, then shook his head, resisting the tug of her hand. "I can barely breathe just sitting here." He wondered what she had put in his tea and how much she, herself had had. He licked at the lingering taste of it still numbing his lips.

"Then I'll dance for you."

Miriam twirled about, her skirt billowing like a white flower blooming, red hair like a flame. As if the piper in the tent knew what she was about, the music picked up tempo. She circled around him, arms and face lifted to the night sky. Galen felt dizzy just watching her.

"I am the moon," she sang. "You are my Earth." She laughed, and Galen couldn't help but smile. She stopped and dropped suddenly to her knees, eclipsing the fire. Backlit, her hair was a crimson halo around the dark silhouette of her face. Galen couldn't see her expression.

"Whew! You're right—that is rough at this altitude!" she exclaimed breathlessly.

She swayed as if about to collapse. Galen lurched forward to catch her up. She laughed unexpectedly, arching back in his embrace, exposing the white of her neck. Before he could even consider what he was doing, Galen leaned forward and kissed the hollow between her collarbones.

Miriam sat back abruptly. "Professor Williams, I'm surprised," she said, but her expression said she was not offended, that indeed, she welcomed it. "I was beginning to think I'd have to make the first move."

Galen opened his mouth to protest. Miriam closed hers over it, kissing him with uninhibited passion. Caught off guard, Galen tumbled backward. Clutching at Miriam for balance, he pulled her down with him. Taking that as encouragement, she continued to kiss him. He found himself yielding to such velvet persuasion. He slid his arms around her, pressing her against him. Her fingers combed through his hair. The warmth of her lips flowed through him, easing his aches and spreading like a warm fog through his thoughts, befuddling them.

"You can have me," she whispered in his ear. "Just give me your vow." The soft touch of her voice, her warm breath, sent a thrill along his spine. "Just promise to guard and protect me. Simple, harmless words."

He became aware of coarse laughter. Turning away from Miriam's kiss, he lifted his head to peer toward the tents. One of the horsemen had apparently poked his head out of their tent, and now the others had joined him. Galen rolled out from under Miriam's embrace and sat up, taking hold of her arms to push her away. He felt exposed, the stars spotlighting this remote lakeshore, summoning the attention of all the world.

"Perhaps this isn't wise," he whispered. "We shouldn't be, uh—" His words floundered in the depths of her eyes.

Miriam pouted. "What's the matter? Afraid your academic friends might find out, *Professor?*" Her voice was soft but held a sharp edge of derision. "Who's to tell them? You? Me?"

Somehow the last word seemed as much threat as assurance.

"You're shivering," Miriam observed. "Come into my tent." She stood and held out one hand to him. "I can make you feel better. I can make all the pain and hurt go away."

This was as unlike the Orlov he knew as was the cold and calculating personage of before, and twice as frightening. Like a dark sea, her presence engulfed him before he was aware of its touch. He glanced at the black slash of the lake and knew it instead to be deadly cold with treacherous currents.

"Come," Miriam whispered, her voice gone throaty and soft. "It's warm there, and private."

Galen hesitated, but his mouth still tingled from the passion of her kiss. Mostly, however, he thought of warm blankets and a quiet night away from the snores and smells of their companions. A woman in his arms might even banish the nightmare. He allowed Miriam to pull him to his feet and lead him toward the tent. The men, still watching, made undoubtedly rude comments Galen was grateful he couldn't understand.

Galen had not been in Miriam's tent before. A guttering lantern cast more shadow than light. Miriam's belongings were scattered haphazardly around two narrow sleeping pallets made up of blankets and mats of leaves.

"Where's Vera?" he asked.

Miriam passed him a simple shrug. "She's guarding the horses. Our friends seem restless of late, and I wouldn't want them to abandon us in the night." When she saw concern in his expression, she added, "Don't worry; she has a gun."

Obviously, Miriam had set this up. Galen shrank back against the tent wall. If he was going to get involved in an affair, he wanted to at least think it was his own idea.

"Come closer. I won't bite." Miriam settled herself on the pallets and beckoned for him to join her. As Galen stepped forward, he tripped over one of Miriam's packs. It fell over, the contents scattering across the blankets. Galen dropped to his knees to gather them up, but Miriam took hold of his hands.

"Leave them," she whispered and drew him close. She pulled off his coat and began to unbutton his shirt. He brushed her hand away, fearing her touch upon the invisible, bloodied print.

"You want me," she murmured, her breath warm in his ear, her fingers tracing fire across his chest. "You've always wanted me. Come now. Be mine."

A fever took him that had nothing to do with *soroche*. He kissed her lips, her chin, her neck. She was fumbling now with his pants, and he pulled at her blouse. Eyes closed as he lost himself in her passion, he took her down, sweeping away the litter of items spilled from her pack. He pulled at some item poking his ribs. His hand brushed against something small and flat. He pushed it aside, but some small tick in his mind sought it out and would not let it go. *What is that?*

Her body yielded to his, warm and supple. *I can have her,* he thought. *I can mold her to my desires, shape her to my image.* This isn't Chicago.

"You can have me," she echoed, her breath warm in his ear. "Only say the words. The vow."

Consumed by his own passion, he barely heard his own response. "Yes," he murmured as his own kisses slid across her chin and down her throat. "I promise."

"Say it," she urged, husky voiced, between kisses that burned his skin like flame. Her green-eyed gaze locked his thoughts in a single direction. "Say you'll stand by me, guard me, no matter what."

Galen gasped, barely able to breathe. "I do. I vow to stand by you. I'll guard you, no matter what."

Miriam grinned but something in that smile made him shiver. A hint of triumph lurked there, as if he'd surrendered something precious. She withdrew to stare at him with those captivating eyes. "Remember that vow. You are mine now." *You are mine.* The words echoed in Galen's mind like a warning bell, but he could not remember. He knew only the taste of her kiss.

Her lips touched his chest in just the spot where the bloody handprint had been. His skin tingled, flamed as if touched by a brand. He cried out, then gasped. The cold air tickled his lungs, setting off a spasm of coughing no amount of passion could overcome. Pulling away from her, he doubled over with the violence of the attack. Fumbling for his handkerchief, he turned from her to hide the blood. He felt her gaze on his back, a mixture of bemused compassion and detached impatience.

When it was over, he crouched on his knees, not daring to move, breathing slowly lest he set off another spasm. He opened his eyes and stared at the nearest object to hand—something, anything, to bring the world back into focus. The *something* resolved into a small, dark blue booklet. Again, the persistent tick in his mind demanded attention. *What is that?*

Without thinking, he picked it up and flipped it open. His own face stared back at him. His first thought was that it was a mirror, but no, he could not be so clean-shaven.

"My passport!" He stared at the familiar photo—his hair slicked in place, clothes neat and pressed—another person, another age, another world. "This is my passport. How did you get it?"

Miriam shrugged. "I found it somewhere. It seemed useful." She moved toward him. He backed away.

"Why didn't you tell me?" Galen was trembling. He could go

home. Right now, he could walk out of the tent and back to civilization, hot baths, and people who spoke English.

"Because I want you with me. You might not stay if you had the choice."

"But where—How did you find it? What about my money, my clothes?" *What about Harry's knife?* On hands and knees, he rummaged among the items he'd so blindly swept aside, but it wasn't there. "How could you keep this from me?"

"Control, Professor." The word was full of spite. "Without it, you have no choice but to stay with me and obey. I planned to return it eventually. When the Ritual is over."

His ardor was gone like a whiff of dust, leaving him suddenly cold and empty. Dizzy, he sat abruptly, arms resting on his knees. In a stupor he gasped, "You lied to me. How could you lie to me? How could you change so much?"

Miriam stood over him. "Fool! That simpering little student was nothing more than a pretense. The time for such hypocrisy is over." She plucked the passport from his fingers before he could even react. "As long as I have this, you'll do as I say."

Galen lunged to take it back, but Miriam spun away. He could not bring himself to assault the woman. Such etiquette was far too deeply ingrained to casually break, no matter how desperate the situation. Whatever cruelties and barbarism he might encounter, and no matter how primitive the circumstances, he was determined that he, at least, would remain civilized.

Fastening his pants, he shrugged into his shirt and coat. "I won't be your puppet, Miriam. Enough of your games." As if a boulder had settled upon his chest, he couldn't summon breath enough to argue further.

"And where will you go? *How* will you get back, even to Cerro do Pasco? Will you walk the whole way, without food or horse?" Her scorn for his predicament was obvious.

The mention of Cerro de Pasco stopped him cold. If Miriam had his passport, she must know something of the murders. She might even know who did them. Was that the hold she had over Carlo and the others? Galen couldn't return without her, he realized, not if she could clear his name.

"Remember this, Professor Galen Williams: you vowed to stay with me, and stay with me you shall, until the end. You are mine now." She waved the passport at him. "As long as I have this, you are mine."

She laughed then, a harsh and bitter sound. Stepping to the doorway, she held aside the tent flap, implying their romantic interlude was finished. She had what she wanted. Galen sidled past, not daring to turn his back upon her.

Slapped by the cold night air, his skin crawled with fever. His head throbbed with the beat of a pulse in double time. He met Vera outside. She looked at him closely, pressing her lips into a flat line.

"So she failed to seal the vow," she said quietly, enigmatically. "Good. It means you can still be free of her."

Galen's chest hurt too much to wonder what she meant. Maybe tomorrow. He clenched his teeth against the urge to cough as he crept into his tent. Blessedly, the two *cholos* had fallen either asleep or into drunken stupor. He had no intention of waking them to face their contempt—even if he couldn't understand the words, the content would be plain. He rolled into his blankets, restlessly trying to understand just what was going on. As he tumbled into febrile sleep, the voice at the back of his mind whispered, *Where is Carlo?*

GIL

Gil rolled over into wakefulness and a feeling of grief. She began to weep without knowing why.

She had not meant to fall asleep. Determined to hold vigil, she had sat outside the tent, staring into absolute dark. At some point, she'd slipped from her watch and failed.

"Professor Williams," she murmured into the dark, but could not sense his essence. He was lost to her, utterly lost.

Despair was a winding sheet—no, a serpent, squeezing her in its coils. How could she go on when so much was lost? She sank into a blackness deeper than the night.

Saturday, June 5

GALEN

"¡Salvenos!" a child screams.

Black with blood, a blade pricks his chin. A bloody hand presses against his chest. The hood slips back, and for a moment, just a moment, light falls upon the face.

Miriam!

"No!" Galen jerked bolt upright, head swiping the pitched roof of the tent. He moaned softly.

Miriam.

He rolled back down, staring at memories, heart pounding, gasping as if there were not enough air in the tent, in the entire world.

It can't be true, he thought. His mind had merely combined two nightmares into one.

Then how did she get my passport? that annoying voice asked from deep in his mind.

He pressed the palms of his hands against his eyes, as if that would rub away the images harassing him. He felt he was drowning. He could not find enough air.

What would Miriam say if he confronted her? What would she do? If she had murdered Eisabel and her family, would she feel no compunction about killing him, too? They were miles from anywhere, and she held his passport ransom. For now, at least, he was helpless. Better to feign ignorance and pretend all was well. Yet how could he face her again without revealing what he knew. His flesh squirmed with febrile tremors at the mere thought of her touch. Surely, he would give himself away.

One of his tent mates muttered in his sleep. The other snorted in reply. Galen groaned and rolled over, pulling knees into chest, trembling. His chest hurt so, he could draw no more than a shallow breath, and it was not enough. No matter how fast he breathed, it was not enough. Coughing brought the taste of blood to his mouth.

How had he gotten into such a mess? Was there some un-written rule that said ordinary guys weren't supposed to get in-volved in such exploits? Was this punishment for breaking such rules, for wanting to add some spice to a mundane existence? *If I ever get home,* he thought, *I'll never leave again. I promise.* He'd stay at home and teach his classes and never again complain about bore-dom and mediocrity.

If he ever returned home—which seemed at the moment a remote and futile dream. He thought about his passport. Numbed by the shock of finding it, he'd let Miriam snatch it from him. He should've wrested it from her, yet knew he could not.

How, then, was he to get it back? He had no assurance, other than Miriam's word, that she would return it. He had lost faith in anything Miriam said. Whatever she had been in Chicago was clearly a fabrication. Whatever he may have felt for her was now pummeled on the rocks of this harsh land.

He was contemplating slipping into her tent to steal it back when a harsh scream shredded his thoughts. At first Galen thought he must be dreaming again. But the other two men in the tent were rousing sluggishly. *And where is Carlo?* Galen disentangled himself from his own blankets and groped for his boots. He pulled on one as he ducked through the tent flap.

The pearly, pre-dawn light cast a spell of serenity, belying any urgency. Galen tottered dizzily, his sudden activity robbing him of breath and balance, and he paused to survey what had been hid-den in the dark. The lake he'd seen the night before was cupped in a bowl of rock, the camp on a small delta at its end. Mist laced the shore and hung in shreds from the nearby rock faces. The thin sickle of a moon floated above the eastern range of mountains.

Another yell, full of terror and rage, caromed off the sur-rounding cliffs.

Hopping forward, he tugged at the second boot.

"Forget it," he muttered and tossed it aside. After a dozen clumsy paces with only one boot, and that one unlaced, he kicked it off toward the rocks.

He ran toward the horses tethered near the lake. They shied at his sudden approach, blocking his view. Hands braced against his knees, he panted, hungry for air. His ribs felt three sizes too small.

No coughing! he thought desperately. *Not now!*

When he looked up, Vera stood facing the lake, gun in hand but pointed uselessly at the ground. Rage and anguish twisted her expression.

Beyond her, a tangle of dirtied white and filthy poncho wrestled at the water's edge. Muddled thoughts pieced out the events. Carlo must have witnessed Galen's banishment from Miriam's tent and concluded Miriam was no longer Galen's woman. Catching her alone, he had moved to claim her.

"You're the Guardian. Do something!" Vera yelled at him, and even in her desperation, she couldn't keep the sarcasm from her voice. Carlo had Miriam pinned, sitting astride her with one hand at her throat. The other fumbled at his pants.

"You have the gun. Shoot him," Galen replied, a perfectly logical solution.

"I can't! I might hit Miriam."

I vow to stand by you. His own words goaded him. *I vow to protect you.* He stepped forward like a puppet, quite unable to stop himself. *You are mine.*

Steps became strides became running—sluggish, as if wading through mud. He felt clumsy, barely able to keep his balance. Was this merely another dream?

Even as Galen approached, Miriam managed to clutch a stone and strike a glancing blow at Carlo's head. He fell to the side, dazed long enough for her to scramble to her feet. She turned to flee in the only direction open to her—toward the lake. Still, Vera would not shoot.

"Carlo!"

Galen's hoarse shout was overthrown by coughing. Frothy pink sputum spattered the rocks.

Carlo turned to face Galen with a scornful, eager grin. His knife appeared in his hand as if from nowhere. Its honed edge gleamed like white fire, the flat of the blade dull with grime. For an instant, Galen wondered whose blood those dark smears might include. He watched that bright line sketch a slow dance as a bird might watch a snake's weaving head.

Behind Carlo and ignored by him now, Miriam fetched a large stone and raised it over her head. She stood poised behind him, ready to crush his skull. Some instinct must have alerted Carlo, or perhaps the expression on Galen's own face. Carlo turned, raising his arm to deflect the blow. He slashed at Miriam. She jumped back. Overbalanced by the rock, she splashed into the water. Carlo followed.

Miriam's head emerged, her red hair plastered dark and flat against her head. Her desperate gaze met Galen's. The start of a scream, a plea, abruptly shifted to a gurgle as Carlo pushed her beneath the surface.

Galen charged into the water. He tackled Carlo, the force of his impact breaking the man's hold on Miriam. The muddy bottom dropped off sharply, shifting beneath Galen's feet. He pitched forward into deeper water. The icy cold bound him tight. Now was not the time to remember that he was, at best, a weak swimmer.

Galen surfaced, gasping for air. He twisted about, seeking aid. The two horsemen watched impassively. Vera paced the slow drift of the conflict down shore.

Finding Miriam, he pushed her toward Vera. The motion forced him back and under. Her booted foot caught him in the stomach, driving the air from his lungs.

Galen flailed, gasping for air. Carlo lunged toward him, knife raised. Galen flopped aside, grabbing Carlo's wrist. The two thrashed about, clinging to one another as much for balance as combat. Galen's attention focused on Carlo's knife, his only thought to keep it away.

Carlo was smaller but stronger, experienced. Galen had never been a fighter. The smallest and youngest, he'd learned to survive by avoiding combat. He managed a flailing punch that hurt his own hand more than Carlo's jaw. Carlo returned the blow. His aim was deflected as he floundered. Galen splashed beyond reach. *Vera, shoot now!*

He risked a glance in her direction. Miriam stood beside her now, one hand resting on Vera's arm. The two watched.

They simply watched.

Carlo's knife slashed at him and in its gleam Galen saw memories. Images hidden by guilt and grief tore free. Mama. Pedro. The flash of steel.

"You killed them." Horror dawned red behind his eyes.

Carlo merely grinned and beckoned him forward.

"You killed them!" Galen screamed. Enraged, he lunged recklessly forward. Carlo charged. Pain flared across Galen's left side. He jerked backward, beyond Carlo's reach. Blood stained the water. *His* blood. Like Edward's washing away in the rain. Like Eisabel's.

Carlo lunged. Galen grabbed the man's arm, twisting the knife away from its target. Together, they went down. Rolling in the water, Galen again caught sight of Miriam and her aunt.

Shoot him! he thought, too occupied to give voice to the words. *Why doesn't she shoot now?*

As if in answer, something zipped through the water close by. Loud pops echoed from surrounding cliffs. Far away, his mind yelled. *About time!*

With a surge of strength born of sheer panic, Galen wrenched Carlo's arm back, desperate to keep the knife away. He didn't think about direction or target. He just wanted it *away*.

At the same time, another bullet *zinged* past Galen's ear—Vera didn't seem to care who she hit. Carlo spasmed into a backward arch. Dropping his knife, he grabbed at Galen, his hand a rigid claw. Terror-stricken eyes begged for aid even as life drained away, leaving only vacant pain. Galen let go.

Red billowed through the water, his blood, Carlo's, mixing in a new nightmare. Galen floundered in fresh panic. Carlo floated face down, the body drifting inevitably north, tethered to the trail of its own blood tracing the hidden currents.

Galen lurched toward the shore, only a few yards distant. The mud shifted beneath his feet, offering no purchase. Barely afloat, he drifted. Vera and Miriam still watched from the shore, but no longer kept pace with him. He reached for them, calling out. His voice was no more than a harsh whisper, his lungs unable to draw enough breath to support it. They watched, slowly receding.

"Miriam, help me!"

Her mouth opened. His cold-numbed mind could not tell whether she was speaking or laughing.

Then she turned and walked away.

"Miriam!"

SESHA

With a groan, Sesha pushed back her blanket and rolled to her knees, half-surprised to find she had not frozen to death in the night. The wind keening over the sharp-edged rocks was the only sound, and when it suddenly died, the silence rang in her ears like cathedral bells. Nothing lived here. Nothing grew but lichens and moss. Only rock and snow met her gaze, gray and white. Were it not for the blue of the sky, she would've thought the world drained of color. She coaxed the kerosene stove to a feeble life and set a pot of water to boil.

One by one, her sisters awoke and joined her. No one spoke as they ate a meager breakfast and prepared for the day's journey.

Yesterday, Tomás had abandoned them, taking the mules. "I sent him back for Gil," she'd said. No one had asked why. No one had dared question her though they knew it was a lie. Numb and empty, Sesha had sorted their supplies—the absolutely essential versus the simply necessary.

Each of the sisters now carried a backpack with bedroll, a single change of clothes, and food, along with enough fuel for one fire. Maji carried a length of rope. To her own load Sesha had added the mess kit, the small stove, and its dwindling supply of kerosene. The thick canvas tents supported with wooden poles were too heavy to carry. Those and the remaining supplies were cached in a cave near the lake. Past the point where they could leave messages at inns and *tambos*, they had erected another cairn for Gil and Petra. With charcoal from the fire, Sesha had left handprints on a boulder, thumb pointing south. Gil would under-stand.

They had quit the trail when it passed the pinnacle Tomás had pointed out. It stood sentry beside a faint track, scarcely a smudge on the bare rock, angling north and west. Sesha had left handprints wherever she could, using mud when she ran out of charcoal and Maji's lipsticks. As their path took them higher and higher still, altitude had finally conquered latitude, the air chilling rapidly. Rain and nightfall had caught them by surprise. Too soon, the sun had disappeared behind the canyon walls, long before true sunset. The light had faded gradually and darkness caught them unawares.

Finding shelter from the wind in a jumble of broken rock and too tired to build a fire, they'd eaten supper cold, then rolled into their blankets and huddled together for warmth.

"We should've brought one of the tents," Sesha had muttered last night as the ground leached the warmth from her body.

"We could've managed one tent," she muttered now as she shouldered her pack. Sore muscles protested and a spot near her collarbone felt chafed raw. *Or at least a piece of canvas big enough for a shelter.*

"*Now* you think of it," she grumbled ruefully. As she left more markers for Gil, she watched her sisters moving about, gathering stamina as if it could be plucked like pebbles from the ground.

Mountains surrounded them, the raw bones of the earth, snowfields glaring white in the sun. Cordilleras Raura and Huayhuash, austere, merciless and simply magnificent. Killichaka bided within that formidable barrier. Sesha felt insignificant in their presence. It seemed impossible that they could surmount that barrier in time.

Now they faced a massive alluvium, flood debris choking the mouth of a narrow canyon, a reminder that Pachacamac held strong sway here. Sesha glanced warily at the cliffs surrounding them. Above the cliffs, glaciers, bright jewels of ice, were as treacherous as they were beautiful. Spalled ice falling into a glacial tarn could send ice and water, mud and rock hurtling down this canyon, sweeping them away like grains of sand.

A plait of small streams trickled among the massive blocks of stone. Sesha led the way along the largest of the rivulets until it merged with the others, surging through a narrow gap carved between two sentinels of cold-faced stone.

Beyond the barrier of fallen rock, a valley opened into a wide gouge penetrating the mass of the mountain. Though Evita had ceased to marvel at the shape and texture of the landscape, and had even given up her habit of picking up samples to examine for a time, then letting them drop, her interest in geology momentarily revived.

"They call it a *quebrada*," she informed them, tracing the distinctive U shape.

Scant remnants of a stone-worked trail lured them on. It followed a torturous path, crossing and recrossing the stream and weaving in and around and sometimes over the broken rock.

No one spoke; even Maji had at last run out of breath for words. Only the stream had a voice, a nonstop prattle that seemed to chide them for going *up* when *down* was so much easier. It reminded Sesha of the creek back home where she'd encountered Gemella. That day now seemed an eternity and a world away.

Sharp peaks surrounded them, serrated ridges caped in snow.

A flock of clouds cast mottled shadow patterns across their flanks. Wind blowing across not-so-distant snowfields coursed the twisting canyon, shrieking at its confinement and chilling the skin. Even shadows seemed blue with cold. The first snow of winter would soon mantle this valley as well.

And above all, Yerupaja. The mountain seemed as capricious as any god—at one moment hiding behind glowering clouds, then peeking through in sunlit benevolence.

What secrets do you hide? Sesha wondered, before turning to more practical paths. She frowned at the prospect of cloudy skies on the day of the eclipse. What if all their journeying, their pain and hardship came to naught? She shook the worry from her shoulders. It couldn't happen, wouldn't dare. *The skies will be clear. They have to be.*

The relentless ridge of crests dipped in a sharp V directly ahead, the pass Tomás had pointed out. Still, it seemed terribly high. Not so far above them, ice and snow draped the shoulders of the peaks with eye-tearing white. There had been no mention of such conditions. Sesha prayed their path kept to the lower elevations, but could not see how they could gain the western slope otherwise.

Ahead of her, Lena worked her way around a fallen stone. She held one hand to her stomach, as if to reassure the child within. Sesha had given her the lightest pack, mostly food, so that its weight would diminish as they went. But Lena was still having trouble. In spite of chasing after children, Lena's life was more sedentary than the others. Add to that the demands of pregnancy, and the trip was exacting a heavy toll. Even from here, Sesha could hear her wheeze. If only Sumala was here. *We should've waited for the others. We should never have split up.*

Sesha signaled to Evita, who had taken the lead, to find a suitable resting place. *Someplace,* she thought, *in the sun and out of the wind.*

She was not the only one concerned about Lena. As soon as Evita stopped, Maji shed her own pack and worked her way back to take Lena's from her. Sesha hurried to catch up.

"I'm all right," Lena told them as if she resented the attention, but she didn't shake off their support. The two of them managed to guide her to the sheltered niche Evita had chosen. More than the others, she was gasping for air, her chest rising and falling in a deliberate rhythm. "It's just the altitude." She sat down and massaged her temples.

"We all need to rest," Sesha responded diplomatically. "My legs feel like jelly, and I've got a splitting headache." Evita handed her a canteen.

"Drink. It'll help."

Sesha obeyed.

"How much farther, do you think?" Lena's question ached with weariness, hoping for a close end.

Ahead of them, the valley curved right, limiting her view. The sharp line of rock against the clear Andean sky promised an end to the torturous climb, but such promises had been broken too often to hold out much hope.

Rather than pull out the map, Sesha looked at the sky as if she could see it inscribed there. She remembered a set of squiggles, as if drawn by a palsied hand. She hoped it was merely an exaggeration, yet feared it might be accurate. At any rate, the trail would inevitably get a lot steeper. The question was: how steep, and how negotiable? She decided not to mention it just yet.

"It's hard to say. The map has no scale," she responded evasively. "Let's go a little farther before lunch. We'll stop early to make camp, so we'll have time for a fire. I certainly don't want to eat dinner in the dark again."

The others readily agreed. With undisguised groans, they pushed themselves to their feet and trudged on.

Beyond the curve, the valley ended abruptly against an escarpment hung like a curtain between two peaks. A small lake colored milky blue huddled against a headwall of sheer stone. Pooled in a deep cleft, it appeared unusually deep for a glacial tarn. A thin cataract festooned with rainbows fed the lake. This close to the end of the dry season, it was little more than a trickle. Long before it reached the lake, it spread into a fine mist, wetting everything. Dark, sulking rocks surrounded the water like beasts come to drink.

The four sisters stared at the glowering rock face, at least five hundred feet high, in utter dismay.

"Where do we go now?" Evita asked. The others turned to Sesha, their faces expressing doubt, even anger.

Sesha knew what they were thinking—Tomás had deliberately misled them. He had sent them on a false trail to keep them from reaching Killichaka. With the obdurate rock face staring back at them, it was hard to disagree. Perhaps they had missed a turning in the trail. They would have to back track and find another way. The question was, how much time had they lost?

Had she failed, then? Had they come all this way to fall just this much short? Was Killichaka simply a deluded fantasy? The thought of backtracking, of time and energy wasted, held her motionless, unwilling to risk even one step in the wrong direction. She felt the sting of tears freezing on her cheeks. The others turned away from her distress and made a point of studying the rocks.

"Look there!" Evita pointed to the left of the lake. "It looks like the trail goes that way." Sesha stared where her sister pointed, and finally made out an edge of worked stone and dark patches where steps were carved into the rock. She took a deep breath, as if suddenly freed of shackles.

Lena sat abruptly on a low boulder. "I can't," she said in a low wail and shook her head. "I just can't." Maji and Evita sat on either side of her and hugged her between them, rocking back and forth. The comfort only encouraged her to release her tensions. She began to tremble and shiver, and then to cry.

Sesha knelt in front of her sister and reached out to close her hands over Lena's and still their fretful twitches.

"We're tired; we are all just tired. We'll stop here for lunch. It won't look so bad once we have rested and had something to eat. We'll even build a fire." She turned her back to the latest obstacle and shed her pack. "A small fire," she added as she calculated the nights remaining until the eclipse and weighed the need to conserve their precious supply of fuel against their flagging spirits. She decided their morale needed the boost and hoped they'd find more fuel when they reached Killichaka. That hope seemed more like a forlorn and desperate desire, but at least it would keep her going.

The fire did indeed help. They huddled around it, soaking up its meager warmth as they waited for water to boil for tea. Though the altitude lowered the boiling point, even a little extra warmth was welcome. They all cradled their cups in their hands, huddled over them to let the steam rise into their faces.

The fire failed to dim, however, the feeling they were being watched. Sesha studied her sisters' faces, trying to discern whether they felt it, too, the prickly sensation crawling up her spine, the almost overwhelming sense that if she turned suddenly, she would catch a face peering over a rock or a shadow sliding across the trail.

Someone waited; someone watched. She could not shake the feeling and built the fire between two boulders and the cliff wall as much for concealment as for shelter. She said nothing, unwilling to frighten her sisters with mere fantasy.

No one spoke as they ate. Lena and Evita pointedly avoided looking at the daunting cliff, but Sesha studied it carefully, and so did Maji. Silently, they pointed out features to one another. The trail went there and there, vanished here to reappear up over there. Beyond a certain point, it seemed to cease altogether. She hoped it merely skirted an unseen obstacle, but what if rock falls had destroyed it? They wouldn't know until they climbed.

Finally, they could delay no longer. Sesha noted the heads of clouds peeking over the eastern horizon like curious children. They needed to reach the top and find shelter before the weather changed. Already, tendrils of mist swirled around the rocks as Sesha shouldered a pack that seemed ten pounds heavier each time she picked it up.

"We'll take it slowly. If it gets too bad, we can always find another way," she promised. *If there is another way.* "When we reach the top, we'll have a feast for dinner."

"Who would ever have thought hard rolls and *chuno* would constitute a feast?" Evita said with a weary laugh.

"I think I have a bit of meat left. We could make a stew."

"And I have some chocolate for dessert."

"Lena!" Maji exclaimed.

Lena shrugged unabashedly. "I've been saving it for a special occasion."

Sesha smiled at their attempt to lighten each another's spirits, as well as their burdens. Reluctantly, she kicked the dying embers of their fire and shepherded her sisters onward.

GALEN

Galen drifted, and the moon kept pace, floating above the frothy pink of dawn. It occurred to Galen almost lazily that he should do something. He listened for his heartbeat, straining for breath between the vise of the water's gelid grip and the incredible pain in his chest. Visions floated beside him—Eisabel reaching for him. His brother, Edward, falling, endlessly falling. Miriam laughing.

The current curved, bringing him back toward shore. One foot touched bottom, and he pushed against it, more reflex than conscious effort. The mud and silt merely sloughed away and gave him no purchase. Pain stitched his side and lanced through his chest.

Miriam laughed. Fool! *her phantom shouted.*

If only he could get one clean, deep breath. Black dots speckled his vision.

Miriam sneered at him from a black corner in his mind. He thought how blessed it might be to let the water take him.

Bumping against rock, he nudged stone. Loud ringing in his ears drowned the gentle lap of water against land, even the imagined sound of Miriam's laugh.

More black specks smeared his vision. Acute pain stabbed his chest, echoed now where Carlo had slashed him. The *black* grew, flowing one speck into another, merging into a dark funnel drawing him inexorably *down*.

"Miriam," he mumbled, and saw her face, laughing, as he slid into utter black.

SESHA

Evita was right about the trail. They picked it up far to the left of the small lake. Narrow and long neglected, in places fallen away, it hugged the valley wall, snaking back and forth—the zigzagging line on her map. The correlation encouraged her.

Now massive stone steps wound around rough spires like the buttresses of some ancient cathedral. Sesha told herself she had hiked more treacherous trails back home. For the most part, as long as she concentrated on her hands and feet, on the next step, the next rock, the climb wasn't so bad. Tomás had been right; the mules could not have managed these narrow ledges. Sesha would've been forced to abandon them below with no food or shelter.

Not a creature stirred among these barren rocks, not even a bird in the empty sky. They were utterly alone; no one was watching.

No one.

For the first time since Cerro de Pasco, she didn't feel the sensation of someone lurking nearby. The mysterious presence had left.

Had it given up? Had she merely imagined it after all? For some reason, that made her feel more uneasy rather than less. She jerked her gaze to the shadows ahead.

By now, they had nearly reached the valley headwall. The small lake waited forty feet below, and the mist from the falls wetted the rock. Moss grew in the cracks. The trail narrowed even more as it rounded a wide shoulder. Shallow, cup-shaped holes had been carved into the rock for handholds. Sesha wondered if this was deliberate—a natural defense against raiders or a test of courage, so only the worthy might pass.

A section of the trail had fallen away, leaving only a scalloped ledge barely a shoe's length deep. Below, the lake winked at them through swirling mists.

Lena shook her head. "I can't," she whispered, or perhaps she yelled, her voice lost in the roar of Sesha's own pulse in her ears and the ever-present hiss of the falls. Was it tears on her face, or only the mist?

"It doesn't look that bad," Evita told her.

"We can use the rope," Maji suggested, already uncoiling it from the strap on her pack.

"Oh, no," Evita said, horrified. "If one fell, she might drag the others with her. We'd never be able to hold her." To her credit, she did not glance at Lena. "Look, it'll be all right. I'll go first." And before anyone could protest, she stepped along the ledge.

"See! Nothing to it!" she called out, an edge of fear trimming her tone of bravado. She moved slowly, digging moss and lichens out of the handholds as she went, kicking away rubble and broken stone. Sesha watched the stones bounce off the rock walls and splash into the lake and tried not to shudder.

"Don't look down," Maji advised, and reflexively, Evita did. She laughed.

"What?" Lena demanded. "What is it?"

"Oh, you should see it!" she called back in delight. "There's a rainbow—it makes a full circle around my shadow! It's beautiful!"

Not until Evita was safely across did Sesha realize she was

holding her breath. Judging by their sighs, Maji and Lena had been, too. On the other side, Evita laughed, a sound expressing both nervous relief and the exhilaration of danger conquered.

"See, it's easy! The trail curves inward here." She leaned right to peer beyond the wedge of rock. "There're steps here, leading to a crevice. Oh, my goodness!" She disappeared around the curve. Sesha waited uneasily. *Where had the watchers gone?*

"Evita?" Maji called out, just as her sister reappeared.

"There's a cleft in the mountain, like a tunnel. This is it! No more *up!*"

She held out her hand. "Come on, Lena; you can do it. But leave your pack. I thought mine would pull me over backward!"

Lena shed her pack and stepped onto the ledge before her courage and Evita's enthusiasm could fail. Sesha watched as if the strength of her gaze could hold her sister's weight. When she was safely across, there was a pause for nervous giggles and whoops and cheers of triumph. Maji followed and then whipped the end of her rope across to Sesha. Sesha tied it to Lena's pack, all the while watching the sky, the rocks. A sense of foreboding settled upon her. *Where is the watcher?*

"I'll scout ahead," Evita shouted as they passed first Lena's and then Evita's packs across the gap.

"Evita, no!" Sesha shouted. "Wait for us!" But it was too late. Evita was gone around the curve of the cliff.

Sesha stared at the foreboding emptiness while her heart beat faster and faster, willing Evita to reappear. *Did the watcher wait ahead?*

"Lena!" she yelled. "Lena, don't let Evita go any farther!" She stepped onto the ledge, sliding her foot along the narrow rim. "Lena, stop her!" The weight of her pack threw her off balance, threatening to pull her backward.

Sesha kept her eyes on the rock she clung to. Her heart seemed ready to burst as her mind perversely replayed the memory of her fall back home. A moment of vertigo forced her to stop and close her eyes, mouth too dry to swallow, heart hammering hard enough to threaten her balance. Eyes closed, she clung to the rock as if her fingers were roots.

The sound of a scream unnerved her. Her foot slipped. *It's only a bird,* she told herself, and her self countered with *No, that's Evita's voice!*

"Hurry, Sesha!" Maji called, glancing over her shoulder. She danced anxiously from one foot to the other, from one option to another. Wait for Sesha. Follow Evita.

Another scream echoed off the uncaring rock.

"I'll go check!" Maji yelled, and before Sesha could respond, she, too, was out of sight.

"No!" Sesha cried out. "Maji, wait!"

Sesha's feet refused to hurry, though her mind screamed, *Run!* She leaned forward to peer around the shoulder of rock and saw the tunnel Evita had described. Maji, Evita, and Lena stood in its shadowed maw, held by three men. *Cholos.*

"Where's the fourth one?" one demanded.

"She's dead," Lena shouted at him with convincing grief, and past him to where Sesha crouched. A message. Stay hidden. "She fell and drowned in the lake." The man motioned to one of the others, and he moved toward the ledge.

"I told you, she's dead," Lena shouted. Her captor slapped her, and she crumpled to the ground.

Maji wrenched free and ran toward Sesha, shouting a warning. One of the *cholos* raised his pistol and fired into the air. The report banged off the stone walls like cannon fire. He lowered his aim and fired again.

"No!" Sesha screamed in unison with her captive sisters.

Maji went down, hugging her leg.

"Maji!" Sesha's hoarse whisper forced past a sob. She lunged forward.

The stone beneath her right foot gave way. For a breathless moment, she seemed to hang suspended while the rock clattered down the cliff face. Beneath the roar of her sudden terror, it seemed soundless.

Her fingers clutched at the stone handhold, but the sudden burden of her weight tore them free. She lurched toward safety. Her left knee buckled.

"Sesha!" Maji cried out, her face, every feature, every line, clearly etched with pain and terror. Sesha's hands scraped across rough stone, nails scratching for purchase. Too far below, rainbow surrounded the blue of the lake.

No! her mind screamed, though she had no time to give it voice. *Gil, help me!* she thought, and, *If I die, we won't be seven. Gemella will win!* She had but an instant to react, even less to plan. An image flashed in her mind—skidding down the slope back home.

A voice whispered within her mind. *Let go.*

Fighting every instinct and reflex, Sesha pushed away from the rock, even as she fell. She spread both arms wide to embrace the mists, diving into the rainbow's ring. Through its center, the bright blue eye of the lake blinked.

GIL

A bright blue eye opened in a gauzy mist. A wave of cold like burning ice slapped Gil in the face. Muscles spasmed, and she curled into a tight ball. She could not breathe, though her lungs burned. Something held her down. She groped blindly with hands numb from cold. Crystal chimes rang in her ears.

A shaft of light slanted through the blue. All but paralyzed by cold, she reached for it. Bubbles escaped her lips. The white sibilance of noise faded gradually, resolved into distant voices calling her name.

"Breathe, Gil," someone told her, and she gasped for air. The deep, rasping breath set off a spell of wracking coughs and muscle spasms.

Breathe, she thought. In. Out. In again.

There was a sensation of coming back to her self, as if she'd been somewhere else. She reached for that other place, but it slipped from her grasp. Movement brought on a chill that curled her into a helpless wad of shivering bones.

"Gil, look at me." A calm, insistent command. "Open your eyes. Look at me."

"Sesha," she whispered, her voice a hoarse gurgle.

"Hush." Sumala hovered above her, eyes filled with concern. "Take it easy. You have *soroche*, maybe even edema."

She must've fallen from her horse. She was on the ground cradled in Sumala's lap. Petra knelt before her, but the old man who was their guide still sat astride his horse, watching impassively. She was cold. So cold, her shivering locked her muscles tight. She curled against Sumala's warmth as a child.

"Was it the Vision?" Petra asked.

Sesha, she thought, *Sesha's gone.* Unable to give the words credence, she could only shake her head. She attempted to get to her feet, but her legs failed her. She crawled forward.

"Gil, you need to rest." Sumala held her back.

"I have to help Sesha."

"Sesha?" Sumala prompted. "What about Sesha?"

"She's gone," Gil whispered.

"Tell me what happened. What did you see?" Gil mouthed words that would not come and finally shook her head. She squeezed her eyes shut to hold in tears and found herself sinking into the darkness behind her eyelids. *Sleep. Blessed sleep,* she thought, but Sumala would not allow it.

"Come on, stay with us." She shook Gil until she opened her eyes again.

"You can't know for sure," Petra responded, and Gil was forced to agree. The images had been vague and incomplete. Yet she could not deny the horror she felt. "Something terrible happened. We have to hurry." She struggled free of Sumala's hold and stood. The abrupt change caused her to all but black out. She clung to her horse's saddle until the dizziness passed. She was not surprised to find Sumala again supporting her. "I have to find Sesha," she insisted.

"You can't. She's too far away." And that was the ugly, horrid truth. Gil strove to recapture the dream. *Sesha!* Her spirit sank deeper into the quagmire of despair. The feeling of drowning persisted, and she could not catch her breath.

"Here," Sumala said, unwrapping a bundle of leaves. "Chew these."

"You don't believe me," Gil said quietly. Sumala glanced at Petra, standing somewhere behind Gil. "You don't believe I saw this." *First Professor Williams,* she thought. *Now Sesha. Both lost.* A wail pushed against the thick grief lodged in her throat, but she swallowed it back down.

Not Sesha. Anyone but Sesha. That thought stopped all others cold. Could she really mean that? Could she truly choose among her sisters? Who would she sacrifice if not Sesha? Maji? Lena and her unborn child? Perhaps it was best that the decision was not hers to make. But why Sesha? Why any of them?

MOONRISE: 3:52 a.m. EST ~ MOONSET: 3:49 p.m. EST
SUNRISE: 6:16 a.m. EST ~ SUNSET: 5:49 p.m. EST
Sunday, June 6

GIL

Rain had forced Gil and her sisters to stop in Angoltuto, for it made the river a muddy, angry torrent too dangerous to cross. In the morning, the old man who had been their guide refused to continue; this was as far as they had bargained. With Petra still trying to argue, he took the horses and left. The three women stood abandoned amid their supplies and gear.

Gil was anxious to be on their way, quivering with urgency and trepidation. She had dreamt of Sesha last night, awakening abruptly with that hideous sense of falling, clawing at the moonless dark. She had spent the rest of the night trying—and failing—to sense her sister, to reenter the vision of Sesha's fate.

Danger waited ahead, an ambush of foreboding. Voices spoke in anxious whispers. *Quickly, quickly, before it's too late.*

Petra tried to bargain with the villagers for one or two of their llamas, but the people turned away. The animals were needed for the potato harvest and could not be spared, one woman explained, not for foolish gringos in search of false treasure. Another warned against angering the spirits of the high mountains, certain the village would be punished for allowing such looters to pass through. Gil wondered just what Gemella had said or done to alienate them so.

In the end, they had no choice but to shoulder their supplies, as much as they could carry, and proceed on their own. Petra had a copy of the map, and Gil could trace the passage of the others. They would find their way somehow.

The villagers watched in stone-bound silence as the three set out on the road descending into the river gorge. A small boy, no more than seven or eight, joined them as if he just happened to be going the same way. He held one hand to his chest, cradling something precious. He said nothing.

When they had crossed the river and climbed out of the gorge, Gil paused. Her sisters' essence tangled here among scattered stones. Whatever Sesha might have left was gone. The trace of the Other smothered all. Gil reached for the pendant, Sesha's gift, hidden beneath her shirt, but touched only darkness. Petra and Sumala looked about in dismay.

The boy tugged at Gil's sleeve and pointed out a broad stone with a bright red handprint that had escaped Gemella's notice. Even before she set her own hand against it, Gil knew it was Sesha's. The thumb pointed west along the broad terrace overlooking the lake, and so did the flow of their essence.

"This way," she told the others. *Yes, this way.* Gil was certain. *Hurry.*

Petra frowned, skeptical, but the boy smiled broadly and marched down the trail as if to affirm her choice. In mutual and silent agreement, the three followed after, but in spite of the flat terrain, he soon faded from sight. Gil could not even sense any trace of his existence.

Wamani again, she mused with a slight smile. Or something more foreboding? Her sleeve, where he had touched it, was stained reddish brown. His eyes, sad and empty beyond the usual indifference of his people, had held a secret plea. As she recalled his image, she thought, too, of the woman in Huarautambo—the one with the baby. The two were linked together and linked also with the funeral procession in Cerro de Pasco. They wanted something from her. Justice? Release, perhaps, from the purpose which bound them here.

But there had been three caskets in that procession. What of the third?

GALEN

Galen became aware first of sound—the gentle lap of water against stone, the *zhing* of a humming bird flitting around his head.

"Miriam," he cried, but heard only a hoarse gurgle. His breath curdled in his chest, lips too cold to shape the word. *Move,* he thought, *before they leave.* Pain wrapped him in sheets of fire. The sun leered at him like the molten eye of a dragon.

He remained still, face turned from that baleful eye. When the pain finally blurred around its edges, he tried again to stand. Too dizzy to rise, he clung to rough stone until his vision cleared and the roaring in his ears subsided. He thought only of breathing, in and out.

"Miriam, wait for me."

GIL

It was early afternoon when they found a hastily abandoned campsite by a rock-bound lake. A sense of both anticipation and dread shivered in Gil's bones. She thought about Huarautambo and the fear and doubt spawned there. She had since banished them, or so she thought. At times she caught them lurking, peeking from murky corners of her mind, waiting.

Now Gil stared at a pile of rocks, another cairn left by Sesha. Gemella had only partially destroyed this one, leaving a message of her own. *I was here first.*

Numerous charcoal handprints marked the surrounding rocks, many scrubbed to smudges. Gemella would not have understood their import. She may have followed Sesha up the canyon back home, but she had never set her hand against those ancient prints, never touched the souls of those who left them, nor listened to their songs. That, at least, Gil and Sesha shared alone.

Petra found a cache of supplies, including tents, cots, and other bulky items hidden in a deep niche in the cliff wall, overlooked by Gemella and her crew. A crude copy of the map etched in charcoal on the crevice wall connected reality to the enigmatic symbols.

Gil read aloud from the note Lena had left, "'…From here you should go on foot. Tomás says there's no food for mules or horses,'" she announced to the others.

"Well, we needn't worry about that." Sumala joked, and they all laughed, as if the old man's desertion had been an act of fortuitous insight.

Petra wanted to move on, and Gil agreed, an urgent dread tugging her toward the trail. A pall of violence hung over the lakeshore, reminding Gil of the incident in Cerro de Pasco. Eager to escape the taint of decay and to find her sisters, she returned to Sesha's handprint and stooped to set her own against it. It pointed south, and Gil gazed in that direction. She felt only cold and dark. *Where are you?* Was that her own question or Sesha's plaint?

"Let's go," she said sharply. "Sesha's waiting."

Even as she stepped forward, *something* held her tethered. The uneasy, discomfited sense she was leaving something behind swayed her balance. *Essence* lingered, a tangled knot she felt compelled to unravel.

It tasted of violence and passion, sang of betrayal and death. A shadow hovered upon the lake and death lapped against the shore. Treachery abided. Gil shuddered. The wounds of Cerro de Pasco still stung, deep scratches across her psyche. Instinct urged her to flee.

I'm not ready. I can't face this again!

"What's wrong?" Petra called to her. Gil realized she'd been circling, lakeshore to trail, back and again, her sisters watching. *Stay. Find Sesha.* The two impulses tore at her.

"Nothing. Let's get out of here." Striding boldly across the broken rock, she headed toward the trail. If Gemella had left another trap, Gil was determined to avoid it. Sesha needed her. She closed her mind to the voice pleading in the breeze.

Sálvenos.

"Gil, wait!" Petra, striding toward her across the deserted campsite, stooped and tugged at an object wedged between rocks. "What do you make of this?" She held up a boot. It was too big for Gemella or Vera, and the locals wore sandals. It could only belong to Professor Williams. Distracted by her concern for Sesha, Gil had not thought of him. Now when she gazed south where the others had gone, she realized he was not among them.

He had not left this place.

GALEN

Shadows draped the rock and demons lurked in every crevice. The sun-dragon breathed its fire, leaving a dry and brittle husk.

Someone, some *thing* came hunting. Closer. Ever closer. He must escape. Forcing himself to his feet, Galen staggered on until he tripped over a shadow.

Stone shifted against stone. A voice called his name. He struggled to flee, crawling over the jagged rocks. Shadow eclipsed the sun. He fell, rolling into its embrace.

"Hush," a voice whispered. A hand touched his brow, cooling its fever.

Open your eyes, he thought, as if the command was required before he could complete the action.

A blur of gray, a smear of blue. Sunlight stabbed his eyes,

making them blink and tear. A silhouette surrounded by a nimbus of molten red hovered over him.

"Miriam," he whispered, or thought he did.

The head turned from him to call out, "Over here! I have him!" Galen struggled to see who approached.

"Be still." Gentle and familiar, the voice soothed the fire in his chest.

"Miriam?" Galen asked again.

"You're safe now." Water poured across his lips, and he licked eagerly at the moisture. He felt like an ember, burning from within, and wondered that the water did not sizzle as it trickled across his cheek.

A second person joined the first. One on either side, they struggled to lift him.

"You have to help us," the second voice said. "We can't carry you." Galen tried, feebly shifting his feet under him. Pain seared his ribs. He gasped, but there was no air. Darkness framed his vision, curling like ash before flame. It roared in his brain like a forest ablaze. He tumbled forward, taking the others with him.

GIL

"Get one of the tents," Gil commanded, pulling Williams into her lap. "We'll use it like a travois." Petra nodded and obeyed.

"And blankets!" Gil yelled after her.

Sumala knelt opposite Gil to examine her new patient. His cheeks flamed bright with fever, but fingers and lips were cast in shades of blue. Gil felt the crushing pain in his chest.

"Cyanosis. He's not getting enough oxygen," Sumala said, pointing out the blue skin. "It's a wonder he survived the night." She opened his jacket. Dark blood colored his shirt. Peeling back the fabric, Sumala exposed a deep gash blotched purple and yellow-white.

"How bad is it?"

Sumala probed gingerly at the torn flesh. "A knife wound, I think. His ribs kept the blade from penetrating." Sumala shook her head. "It's infected. This is your Professor Williams, I take it."

Gil nodded. "Gemella left him here. She simply abandoned him."

Sumala's mouth twisted in a bitter frown as she pressed

against the wound. "What else would you expect of her?"

"I'd hoped for…" What had she hoped for, Gil asked herself. Humanity? Compassion? Gemella had already demonstrated that she lacked those qualities.

What happened here? Gil asked herself. Traces of death and betrayal lingered like an oily sheen at the water's edge. She'd found Professor Williams among the *rock*s at the edge of the meadow, barely conscious and raving incoherently.

She turned her gaze to the south. Sesha needed her. To linger here, even an hour, was to risk losing her—if it was not already too late. Waiting for Petra, she paced fretfully, south toward Sesha, back to Williams. Choices. Sacrifices. Abandon one to save the other. But Williams was here. His need was immediate and certain. "Sesha, wait for me," she whispered, her voice aching with despair and grief.

It took an hour to drag their burden back to the campsite. Williams cried out at each lurch and bump, and Gil flinched from the touch of his pain. By then the sun was nearing not so distant mountains, a sickle moon but a couple hours behind.

While Petra built a fire and set water to boil, Gil helped Sumala erect a tent around Williams. They wrestled him onto a cot, and Sumala stripped his sodden clothes, swaddling him in blankets.

"I'll need to clean and drain the infection, then stitch it closed," she stated. "Fetch a knife." As Gil ducked through the door flap, Sumala added, "Make sure it's sterile."

Petra must have anticipated the need, for she already held a knife's blade in the flames, hilt wrapped in white cloth to protect her fingers. She passed it over to Gil, her mouth a tight, thin frown.

As Gil touched the knife, the cloth slipped, revealing the ivory handle. Gusts of images lashed her mind—mother and infant, a young boy. A girl, no more than four.

"*Sálvenos,*" they all prayed.

Gil's fingers flinched from the accursed blade. The knife would've fallen in the dirt had not Petra grabbed it.

"That's the knife the police in Cerro de Pasco had," Gil cried. "Petra, how could you! That was evidence in a crime."

"It seemed important to keep it," Petra responded with a diffident shrug. "Hurry now, while it's still hot."

"But a child was murdered. It's tainted with her blood."

"And now it'll be used to save a life. Doesn't that balance things out? I sterilized it in the fire. It's the only suitable knife we have."

She held the knife out for Gil to take, but Gil hesitated. Her hand hovered as if pressed against an unseen barrier. Was it the taint of evil that she felt or merely the heat? Her fingers refused to grasp it.

"I'll take it, then," Petra said with a frown that chided Gil's squeamishness. Gil followed her back to the tent with a lantern from Sesha's cache. Its yellow glow turned Williams' blue pallor a ghastly green. His breathing was rapid and so shallow, his chest barely moved.

The girl she'd just seen stood in the corner of the tent, near Williams' head, though Sumala and Petra seemed to take no notice of her. Gil instinctively glanced around, seeking the child's mother. But she was in Huarautambo, rescuing lost travelers. Gil didn't question the girl's presence, but she didn't mention it, either.

Gil didn't want to witness Sumala's work. Throat rigid and jaws clenched tight, she forced herself to stay, kneeling near Williams' head. When the girl saw the knife in Petra's hand, she screamed, shimmering with terror. She flung herself at Gil, rocking her back on her heels. Gil hugged the child, shielding her from both sight and sound. Petra's gaze chastised Gil, unaware of the little *wamani* she sheltered.

When Sumala touched the infected wound, Williams screamed. Gil's stomach lurched and her legs shifted to flee. *What have I done?* she wondered. *What have I brought you to?*

GALEN

Galen drifted between waking and dream and couldn't tell which was which. He didn't much care. A dragon held him captive. Talons raked his spirit, leaving deep furrows, and fire seared his soul.

Galen screamed. His cry brought him awake, yet the nightmare remained. Miriam's face, haloed in red flame. Miriam the deceiver, the betrayer. Miriam the heartless.

GIL

Williams hovered on a nebulous border of consciousness. Gil sat cross-legged beside him. Opposite her, Sumala frowned as she bent to listen to his labored breathing. She straightened and shook her head.

"Pulmonary edema," she announced. She took a small pouch from her pack and pulled out a handful of leaves. "*Muña* leaves," she explained, rubbing them on his chest. "A *bruja* in Huarautambo gave them to me." The crushed leaves gave off a scent like sage, reminding Gil of home. She thought of Aunt Faye, who had carried her illness in secret until it was too late for Gil or Sumala to help.

Sumala was still speaking. "The only real treatment is to get him to a lower altitude, fast. They might have a ventilator in Cerro do Pasco."

Petra frowned. "We can't even get him to Angoltuto." She made a wry smile, as if imagining the three of them lugging the man down the steep trail.

"Even if I can save him, he won't be fit to travel, not for days."

"But we can't just leave him here," Gil argued.

Petra glared at her. "For the sake of our mission, we—"

"For the sake of our mission we *can't* abandon him" Gil countered. "He's part of it."

"He's Gemella's pawn. Why should we help him?"

"Because I must be what Gemella isn't. I brought him to this; I won't use and abandon him like she did."

"While you two are arguing, the patient is dying," Sumala cut in. "If you can help him, Gil, it has to be now. He's slipping into a coma. A flying carpet couldn't get him to a safe altitude fast enough."

Gil looked to Petra. "I have to do this. I have to know that I can."

Realizing Gil's intentions, Petra's expression turned bitter and outraged. "No! You can't do that. You can't afford the risk, or the power—not now. It'll weaken you, and you need all your strength for the Ritual, not to mention facing Gemella."

"I couldn't heal Aunt Faye. The artist in Cerro de Pasco will die before he reaches home. I won't—I can't—let it happen

227

again."

"But you can't save *everybody*. It simply isn't practical. You have a responsibility to the rest of the world."

"I'm responsible to *all* the world, and that includes this one man. I can't help the rest of the world if I can't save him. Don't you understand? We need him."

"We needed Aunt Faye," Petra shot back, but left the rest of the accusation unspoken. There was more to this argument than the old battle over the use of Gil's powers.

"I will do this," Gil stated.

Stubbornly, the older woman shook her head, still refusing to concede. Her disapproval stood like a wall. She left the tent, twitching the flap closed as if she were slamming a door.

Gil sighed. She felt weakened, off balance, as if Petra's withdrawal took away some crucial support. As much as her own faith in herself, she needed Petra's.

She rubbed her hands along her thighs. She had never tried this before with a human. Small animals and birds, Maji's kitten, even a wild rabbit—when Petra wasn't looking. *At least it's not a broken bone,* she thought, picturing the juniper back home and its swollen, twisted knot. Doubts spawned in Huarautambo swarmed now from hidden lairs. The anguish of that night and the terror of Cerro de Pasco cast tainted shadows.

If only Sesha were here. Sesha believed. Sesha would stand by her. But thoughts of Sesha conjured only emptiness. They disturbed and distracted her, filling her with despair.

Sesha, where are you?

"Gil?" Sumala touched her arm, bringing her back to the here and now.

"What about you, Sumala? What do you believe?"

"You're the one doing this. Are you certain you *want* to?" Sumala did not like her own domain as healer challenged. Though she accepted Gil's powers, it must be difficult to concede to them.

In Sumala's doubt, Gil heard the echo of truth. Sumala had witnessed Gil's anguish in Huarautambo. They shared the same guilt over the death of Aunt Faye. Sumala's question opened the wound afresh. Gil bit at her lip and glanced toward Williams. He was connected to the events in Cerro de Pasco—they were at opposite ends of the same chain, both bound and divided by it. Could she face that nightmare again?

The little girl crouched in the corner, shivering with fear. "*Sálvenos*," she murmured.

"I don't have a choice," Gil answered aloud, expecting Sumala to argue, even hoping for it.

Instead, Sumala advised her. "He's too weak to survive what I have to do. You must keep him breathing while I work. His chest is so filled with fluid, there's no room to for his lungs to expand or for his heart to beat. The harder he tries to breathe, the worse it gets."

Gil took a deep breath. Closing her eyes to all that had gone before, she set her hand over his chest. The heat of his fever radiated like a glowing ember, searing her hand. When she touched him, pain coursed up her arm. She recoiled from it.

"What's wrong?" Sumala asked, twitching back the blanket. On his chest, a blood-red hand glowed like heated iron.

"Do you see that?"

"See what?" Sumala leaned past Gil, a question wrinkling her brow. "The skin is chafed—looks like he's been scrubbing himself with raw granite."

"What of a hand print?"

Sumala frowned. "No. Nothing like that." She rocked back on her heels. "What do you see?"

Shaking her head, Gil replied, "Never mind." Sumala wouldn't understand, not like Sesha would.

Sesha, where are you?

Don't think of Sesha now, she commanded herself. *You can't afford the distraction.* Reluctantly, she put Sesha from her mind. She could not help her, not until this crisis was over.

Wait for me, Sesha. I will be there. And if it was too late? If Sesha was already gone? Gil repressed the thought and the shudder it spawned. *Not now. Don't think of that now.*

Gil stared at the mark visible to her alone. It held the essence of the Other and the stench of Supay. *What have you done?* she asked of her twin. Was this another trap, luring her into Supay's evil purpose?

"I can't," Gil whispered, unable to take her eyes from that vision. Sumala grabbed her wrists, forcing Gil to face her.

"You have to, Gil. If you don't, he'll be dead within the hour. You are stronger than whatever you perceive. *I* believe that."

Never before had Sumala spoken directly of Gil's abilities. Gil had always assumed her sisters believed; that assumption was crucial to her own faith. To actually hear Sumala's belief voiced aloud was another matter, a much-needed counterbalance to Petra's angry withdrawal.

"Whatever you fear, conquer it, Gil. Now, before it gets any stronger."

Not my fear, she decided, confronting not Supay, but her own spirit. *Supay planted this. I can't allow it to take root.*

"We are with you, Gil," whispered Sumala, her hand strong on Gil's shoulder. "You're not alone."

Sumala waited and also the child, sitting now on Williams lap, as if that was her place. Petra lingered close by. Far away, too far, her sisters waited, and even the stars overhead. The whole universe waited, holding its breath until she found hers. Sumala was right. She had to conquer this now, not for Williams' sake, but for her own. If she did not banish this fear now, she could not hope to defeat either Gemella or Supay.

The child rested her small hand upon the invisible brand. Her presence muted the awful power there and shielded Gil from its influence. Her shy smile promised hope.

Gil took a deep breath, as if courage were some vapor to be inhaled, absorbed into the blood. She held one hand on Williams' chest and closed her eyes, shutting out all else. Time lost meaning; place dissolved. She let her spirit soak into his.

GALEN

A white tunnel, like an inverted tornado, promised refuge and peace. Galen craved that solace, yearned for it with a deep, innate instinct. Caught in its eddy, Galen circled, ever closer.

But the dragon with Miriam's face wouldn't let him escape. She held Galen secure, trapped in her lair, and invaded his soul. It coiled inside his chest and tore his flesh. It devoured him, feasting on his pain.

Galen screamed.

GIL/GALEN

Gil echoed the cry as Williams' pain stabbed her own chest, his wounds becoming hers. Her body rebelled against what she

would bring into it. Such intimate contact, such pain and illness—
it was a risk she'd never considered. Immersed in Williams' psyche, Gil feared losing her way back to her own.

With every ounce of will, she struggled to maintain the fragile
union. *I can do this!*

Williams convulsed, drawing her with him toward death.

~ * ~

Demons attended the Miriam-dragon. One wielded a knife.
Harry's knife. The knife came down, slicing through his very soul.
Eisabel's blood mingled with his own. From shadow, the child
watched, her small hand upon his chest.

"Hush. You're safe here."

~ * ~

"Hush," Gil murmured. "You're safe here."

Pain coiled around Gil's chest and pierced her ribs. Fever
seared her bones. She bled the liquid from their chest, giving the
heart room to beat, the lungs the space to expand.

The pressure eased and they could breathe again. As one, Gil
and Williams inhaled.

~ * ~

Galen gasped, free to breathe.

~ * ~

Gil borrowed time, spinning thread from minutes, hours,
days, to knit their torn flesh.

~ * ~

Galen dreamed of demons with Miriam's face. One held him
bound, the other promised freedom. Miriam and Not-Miriam. He
could not tell one from the other. They challenged one another,
Galen at their center, the prize of their conflict.

~ * ~

The handprint inked a tattoo upon Galen's heart, soaking
even into his soul. A portion of the Other's essence remained in
that phantom stain, wedging itself between Gil and Williams and
claiming him as Gemella's own.

You can't have him, sister. He is mine.

Smothered in darkness, Gill faltered. Her hold on Williams weakened. He was slipping from her grasp.

Stay with me.

~ * ~

Stay with me.

The Not-Miriam beckoned, but Miriam claimed him, held him fast with a knife through his soul.

~ * ~

Someone drew Gil away, rending her contact with Williams.

"No!" she cried out. "I'm not done!"

"It's enough." Sumala's voice summoned her back to the physical realm. "He'll survive."

"You don't understand. The Other!" Gil clung to Williams' self, but the connection tore like a bandage from a half-healed wound, leaving Williams unguarded except for the child resting upon his chest.

Abandoning him to Gemella's phantom.

~ * ~

Not-Miriam was gone. Miriam remained.

The old nightmare returned. Miriam loomed over Galen. But this time, it was his heart she held, still beating in her hand. Demons waited, eager to devour it.

"You are mine," she said. "Remember that. You are mine."

Then she began to squeeze. Galen screamed.

GIL

"Rest now." Sumala's arms held Gil secure. She felt weary to the very marrow of her bones. Electric fire soaked her skin, every nerve frayed to tatters. Was this how it would be?

Never again, Lord. "Never again," she prayed. "I can't do this ever again."

Sumala passed Gil into Petra's embrace. Gil blinked at harsh lantern light, the edges of the world too sharp and bright after the misty illusion of Galen's nightmare. She tried to stand, but cramped and numb legs would not support her.

Petra took her as if she were a child. She did not carry Gil so much as guide her fall onto a waiting cot. She fed Gil a hot, thick soup, and then nested her in thick blankets. Through the night, they hovered close by, Sumala and Petra and the flickering presence of Professor Williams. His fever still coursed through her blood, and her own cries and ravings and soft, whimpering moans were mere echoes of his own. He was not totally separated from her. Her spirit still cradled his.

"Hold on," she murmured in her dreams while spectres and shadows and creatures of malice floated past. "Hold on and stay with me."

Monday, June 7

GALEN

Galen awoke to heavy darkness and the musty smell of damp canvas. And silence. The silence, he decided, had awakened him. He tried to sit, but dizziness and pain betrayed him. With a groan, he toppled back. Someone lifted his head to pour a warm, bitter liquid between his lips. His stomach refused it. That unseen someone held him as he wretched and heaved, and afterward sponged his face.

He peered up at his caretaker, but lantern light cast the face in black shadow.

"Who are—?"

"Shh. Go back to sleep. We still have far to go." A woman's voice, neither Miriam nor Vera. He settled back into his blankets, too weak for even minor exertions of the mind.

The woman, he noticed, did not follow her own advice. She sat vigil nearby. Drifting back into oblivion, he was aware of her presence, keeping silent vigil.

GIL

Gil emerged from the tent and blinked. Pearly dawn light softened the harsh landscape but held no warmth. She rubbed her arms against the chill and moved close to the small fire. Still wearied from the night's ordeal, she shivered from both cold and memory.

To her credit, Petra had remained with Gil throughout the night, in spite of her disapproval. Petra's voice and presence had been Gil's anchor, keeping her from drifting beyond life's shore. Sumala had spent most of the night brewing her medicines and caring for Professor Williams. All three were exhausted, and they still had a long trek ahead of them. How much longer could they go on?

The healing had spent Gil's strength, draining her both physically and psychically. Miriam's presence through the handprint, her influence, had added to the ordeal, and still Gil wasn't certain of the outcome. The struggle worried her, for if she couldn't defeat a phantasm of Miriam's power, how could she ever face her sister in the flesh? This, she realized, had been another trap, delaying her for Williams' sake.

How often would she have to perform such a healing? Knowing now what it cost her, could she do that again—willingly take on another's pain and illness, even to the edge of death?

She shuddered. Perhaps Petra had been right, and the risk was too great. She swayed, arms folded tight across her stomach to contain the lingering memory. *Never again.*

But when she lifted her gaze to the tent and the solitary occupant within, she knew that, yes, when needed, she would repeat such feats again and again. How could she do otherwise? The harder choice would be to deny someone that aid.

GALEN

When the world emerged again, daylight edged sideways through the tent's door, a cold and misty dawn. A woman he thought was Vera entered, carrying a kettle. Though she frowned, she seemed pleased when his gaze focused on her and he mumbled a greeting.

"Your patient's awake, Sumala," she called over her shoulder to someone outside. Then she set aside the kettle and bent over him to brush the back of her hand across his forehead.

"Your fever's broken," she observed. "And your breathing has improved. You might live after all."

He could see now that she was not Vera, but could've been, twenty years or so younger. She had the same Slavic features, but her brown hair had not yet begun to gray and her face was less creased. Her voice, too, was less harsh.

She poured tea from the kettle into a cup and held it for Galen to drink. It smelled bitter and noxious and unpleasantly familiar. Galen waved it away.

"If I drink that, you'll be mopping up in here again." He could still smell the acid stench of previous upheavals.

"If you don't, Professor, the fever may return. We've lost too much time already; I'd just as soon leave you behind."

Galen studied the hard face as she helped him to sit up. "I bet you would," he muttered, and then aloud he said, "Are you one of Miriam's sisters?"

"Miriam?" The woman's face registered a quick transition from confusion to comprehension, followed by distaste, as if she had also swallowed the bitter medicine. "Ah, Gemella." She shifted away from him, or perhaps from that relationship. "Yes, Professor. I'm Petra Orlov."

"Please, Galen will do." Miriam's biting sarcasm had reduced his title to a mockery he didn't care to ever hear again. Miriam had insisted her sisters were dangerous and spiteful, but his sense of this Petra, though distant, was anything but cruel, and they had obviously gone to considerable trouble to save his life. Another of her lies?

A second woman now entered the tent, this one tall and dark eyed, with long, black hair. Surely, she could not also be related to Miriam, nor was she one of Sesha's group. Where had these women come from?

"It looks like your patient will recover, Sumala," Petra said quite matter-of-factly and without any particular pleasure. "I'll fetch him some breakfast."

As Petra left, the one named Sumala knelt next to him and moved to lift the blanket. Galen clutched at it, realizing he was in an embarrassing state of undress and uncertain of her intentions.

"Your clothes are drying by the fire, and I'm your doctor." With calm detachment, she pried the blanket from his grasp and folded it down to his waist. He felt her lift a bandage and probe gently at the wound in his side. He raised his head. What should have been an open wound was puckered scar tissue crossed with neat stitches.

"Just how long have I been out?" he asked.

"We found you yesterday. I can't take full credit for the healing, though."

Her manner was reserved but competent. She replaced the bandage, then helped him to sit and offered the cup Petra had left behind.

"I'm not drinking that. I've had enough." Indeed, he thought, he'd had enough of swallowing anything offered in the naïve belief it would do him good. That went for words as well as tea. "What is it, anyway?"

Petra, slipping back through the tent flap, let loose a single laugh. "You really shouldn't ask." She carried his clothes over one arm and held a bowl in the other hand.

Sumala, in turn, let slip a teasing smile. "It's medicine made from mold. I grow it myself."

"Mold?" He let his head fall back on the cot. *I've fallen in with witches and lunatics!*

"I told you not to ask," Petra remarked as she dropped his clothing next to the cot and offered the steaming bowl. In spite of his previous resolution, he realized he was hungry—ravenously so. The bowl contained a thin gruel, which she fed him at a slow, even pace until he had swallowed every drop. He felt better by the mouthful, his thoughts turning lucid and solid.

Petra's manner, however, remained aloof. She leaned away from him, her posture rigid.

"You don't like me much, I gather," Galen observed.

"You were with Gemella," she said flatly.

"You mean Miriam? That was a mistake." Galen shook his head. "She certainly isn't the woman I knew in Chicago."

"Of course not." Petra seemed surprised.

Her attitude made him angry, and that felt good. It gave him strength. He'd been shuffled about and manipulated, and lied to. It was time for honest answers.

"Where is Miriam? What's happened to her?"

A slash of daylight entered the tent, followed by someone lost within its glare. Galen shielded his eyes until the tent flap fell closed, then blinked against the sudden gloom as the newcomer exchanged words with Petra and then took her place.

"Is that you, Miriam? Where did you go?" Galen propped himself up on one elbow. "Why did you leave?" He struggled to sit, determined not to appear weak in Miriam's presence, not ever again. A wave of dizziness caught him, and his hands clenched the blanket until it had passed.

"I'm not Miriam; I'm her twin sister. Call me Gil."

"Sister? Twin?" The blunt words shoved Galen back as forcefully as a gust of wind. He peered closely at the woman, the familiar red hair and green eyes.

"I'm the Orlov you knew in Chicago, the one who gave you the map and ticket. I'm sorry this has become such an ordeal. We've been trying to catch up to you ever since Cerro de Pasco. Our plans have gone so awry."

"Twin?" Galen repeated numbly, testing the word to see how it fit. He stared hard at her, seeking some proof, some subtle difference. "How do I know that? How do I know you're not Miriam trying to trick me again?"

She tilted her head as if to approach the question from another angle, and such an attitude was familiar. "That, Professor Williams, you must decide for yourself."

"Call me Galen," he replied with a plaintiff note.

She smiled at that, and there was none of the calculation that seemed to accompany Miriam's every motion and gesture. "Ask me a question. Something I would know and Miriam would not."

He considered the challenge, then shook his head. What would it prove? Besides, he realized he could not recall a single significant event. That world seemed to belong to someone else, someone he no longer knew. He realized he'd even lost track of the days. Was this Sunday? No, Monday. It must be Monday. The eclipse would happen tomorrow.

"So why the deception? Why didn't you tell me before?"

"You're not the only one deceived. Had I known she existed, I would've warned you. It was in Miriam's best interests not to. So long as you believed there was only one 'G. M. Orlov,' you would never question whether you were with the right person. She sought to divide us and claim you for her own. Now tell me what happened in Cerro de Pasco."

Galen glared at her, thinking, *Don't you know?* But this was not Miriam, or so she claimed. Her gaze was both desperate and bleak. "It started with a family on the train." He found himself describing that night to her without hesitation, as he had never told Miriam. Perhaps, he thought, it was the way her eyes invited him to speak, the way she listened and did not pass judgment.

"...When I woke up, my passport, my money, everything was gone." *Except for Harry's knife in Eisabel's back.* "The family had been—" Galen paused to swallow his grief. "—slaughtered. I went looking for you and met Miriam instead. She took me in—in more ways than one, I suppose. She claimed to know nothing of the murders, but she has my passport, perhaps my money as well. I believe Carlo, her guide, was the real murderer." He glanced at the wall of the tent as if he could see through it to the lake. "Carlo is dead," he added flatly. "I don't know what happened to Miriam. She just walked away." He scratched at the mark on his chest, the invisible tattoo that could not be erased. He saw the gesture re-flected in Gil's eyes and had the feeling she *knew*. He rubbed his palms one against the other as if to wipe away something sticky.

"I can't understand, though, why she would do such a thing."

"It was a trap." Gil's eyes brimmed with grief and guilt. "She used it to lay claim upon you, so you couldn't serve as my Guardi-an."

"I'm tired of hearing about Guardians!" Galen yelled, and surprised even himself with his anger. Guardian was another title he wanted nothing more to do with. "I don't want to hear about secret rituals and hidden shrines and schemes to take over the world. I want to know what is going on!" For a moment, there was a pause in the world. Only his words echoing in his own mind broke the silence.

Gil studied him until that silence passed and the world began to breathe again.

"No more lies," he said as if he could shape her decision.

She shook her head.

"No lies. Never. But are you ready? Are you strong enough for what it will require of you?"

Galen waved away such concerns. "I need to know what this is about. I *deserve* to know.

"You've certainly earned it," Gil responded, nodding slowly on a course of action. Like someone shrugging into an over-sized robe, she squared her shoulders and drew herself up into a regal posture, a difficult thing sitting cross-legged in a canvas tent. Her entire demeanor changed, becoming a new persona, and she spoke in formal and carefully shaped tones.

"I am named Gilaishling, which means 'Servant of the Vi-sion,' and Minerva, the goddess of wisdom. I am the seventh daughter of Amani, whose name means 'Promise.' She is the sev-enth daughter of Wikima, which means 'being guided ahead.'" She broke the tone of formality with a giggle.

In response, Galen shook his head, dissatisfied. "That's all very interesting, but it really doesn't explain anything." Again she regarded him with that appraising, cocked-head look that seemed so achingly, distantly familiar.

"A hundred years ago, my great-grandmother had a dream. She saw both the end of the world and the means with which to save it. Her people decided it was a gift from Taiowa, the Creator, a final warning before he would destroy this world. They gave her the name Tuawta, Hopi for 'Vision,' and sent her into exile. She journeyed as her ancestors had, to the south, the east, the north, and west. In each direction, she found others who had the same Vision. Together, they began the Mission, of which I am the culmination." Her cheeks colored and her mouth twisted wryly, as if she were not entirely reconciled with that destiny—a curiously humanizing gesture.

"And Miriam? Where does she fit into this story?"

"As I said, we are twins. But I was born first, and therefore I am the seventh. When Gemella—Miriam—was born, my aunts were confused and distraught; nothing in their lore covered such a turn of events. It had apparently never happened before, and they didn't know what to do. In a panic, they decided to get rid of her and pretend she had never existed. My Aunt Vera said she would take care of it, and everyone assumed that ended the matter. No one realized she had kept the child for herself, raising her alone. She kept to herself after that. My other aunts thought it was out of shame, and were just as glad to avoid the reminder of their own guilt."

"So now I know your family's dark secret," Galen said sourly, impatient with what he considered delaying tactics. "What does it have to do with the eclipse?"

"I was born during an eclipse, but my abilities were diminished, not enhanced. We're not sure why, but we're hoping this eclipse will restore the power I need to fulfill my mission."

"You make it sound like the end of the world."

Gil stared at him, head cocked thoughtfully to one side. "It is," she murmured, and there was both wonder and despair in her voice, as if the idea gelled into certainty.

"And why is Miriam here?"

Gil answered with a shrug and a rueful shake of her head. "In truth, you know her better than we."

"She spoke of revenge. She described you as vile monsters," Galen offered.

Another shrug. "Aunt Vera, herself, would've been the seventh daughter, had it not been for a stillborn child. No one realized how that spawned such dark hatred."

"Miriam talked of ruling the world. What's your angle?"

Gil allowed an indulgent smile. "I hope to save it. Throughout history, seventh daughters have used their power to mold the course of events, to guide humanity—some for the better, some not. It isn't an easy thing to accomplish, you realize. Never before has the world truly needed such a guide. There's so much at stake, events shadowed in the future that could well destroy the world— quite literally." She closed her eyes for a moment and shuddered, as if she witnessed something he could not, and it terrified her.

"Like fire? That's what Miriam showed me."

She studied him with a melancholy gaze. "Suffice it to say that *Now* is a critical time. The world could come to an end without guidance."

"You mean manipulation," Galen responded brusquely, remembering Miriam's own words.

"That may be Miriam's plan, and why it's important she does not succeed. The consequences are terrible to contemplate. She doesn't understand the true significance of the Vision."

"I'm still not convinced you're not Miriam," Galen responded sourly, then demanded, "Name a student in my class."

He could see her eyes tracking memories—up one row and down the next. It wasn't a fair question. At the moment, he couldn't name one, himself, and she had never paid much attention to the other students, anyway.

"Smith. Or Jones," she finally responded with a quirky smile to emphasize the futility of the question.

Galen considered the ramifications. At some point, he would have to choose between the two. "You should know that I vowed to protect her, to be her Guardian." He winced at that, the word sour on his tongue.

Gil looked away as if absorbing this information, testing its fit. "If you vowed to stand by Miriam, it may be that you cannot serve me. I've seen her mark upon you."

Galen touched his chest, where Miriam had placed her hand, the mark of innocent blood staining his skin, perhaps his soul, as well. It remained; he could not escape it.

"There's another print, though," Gil said, an offering of hope. "A child's."

"Eisabel," Galen responded with a pang of grief.

"I believe we met," Gil whispered. "She offers a counterbalance." She paused and shook her head. "I don't know. The lore is passed down, woman to woman. Much has been lost." She stood abruptly, brushing the matter from her lap like breadcrumbs. "Rest while you can. We still have a long way to go, and time is running out." She, herself, appeared pale and in need of rest. Her balance drifted as she stood, and she caught at the tent pole for support. Vague dreams floated in Galen's memory, and she had been part of them. What had she done to him, and what had it cost her?

Of only one thing was he certain—that he should quite probably be dead and he wasn't.

GIL

Shreds of cloud dragged shadows across the lake. Gil watched Petra and Sumala sorting through the gear Sesha had left behind in the cave. How much more could they carry than what they already had? Food, of course, and fuel for the kerosene stove, she thought, gazing at the barren peaks surrounding her.

None of them had yet eaten. Water was boiling in a kettle on the fire. Gil made tea and dished up the remains of the porridge Sumala had prepared for Galen. She called her sisters.

"What of our Guardian?" Petra asked with ill-disguised contempt. "Will he be able to travel?"

"I should think so," Sumala answered before Gil could respond. "Gil advanced his healing by four, maybe five days. He'll be weak, but should regain his strength now that the infection is gone and his lungs are clear."

"Perhaps we should leave him here," Petra suggested. "We can collect him on the way home."

"You speak as if he's simply another tent or a cooking pot," Gil argued. "We can't just cache him in a cave. He's our responsibility."

Petra made a sour face. "Pah! He's more a burden, and he'll only slow us down. We don't even know where his loyalties lie. He could still be working with Gemella."

"I don't think he much likes Gemella—Miriam, that is. Not after what she's done to him." Gil didn't mention the vow. She gnawed at that dilemma as if it were one of the hard rolls they shared. "He still has a role to play." She forced her gaze to remain constant and certain, emphasizing once more that she knew things her older sisters did not.

"So you're taking charge now," Petra responded with a bitterness that did not agree with her words. "You're making all the decisions, as you did last night."

"You're still upset over that, aren't you. Petra, how can you be so callous?"

"You should not have done it," Petra blurted out, as if spitting out a seed that had been caught in her teeth. "We almost lost you both."

"Would you rather have sat there and watched him die? Petra, you must understand. It's not the so-called important people who change the world; it's the common, ordinary people struggling to survive. Each and every one of them has their place in events, and you cannot judge that place by the rank society assigns them. You have no way of knowing who is important and who isn't. That's why I have to be healer for all, the least as well as the most important."

"What about Aunt Faye? Was she among your *least*? Was she not important enough?"

For a long moment, Gil could only stare at Petra, stunned as much by this sudden twist and its implications as by the bitter vehemence with which Petra had spoken.

"Is that why you don't want me healing other people—because you think I could've saved Aunt Faye?"

"You should've known. You should've done something." Like an ice-laden wind, Petra's anger made Gil shiver.

"Gil was in Chicago when Aunt Faye died," Sumala argued. "Blame me if you must. Aunt Faye begged me not to interfere. She was old and weary. Planning this mission was her way of atoning for an ancient sin. I see now, she hoped to set things right, not divide us. She wanted reconciliation, not conflict."

"Reconciliation?" Petra cried. "With Gemella? You don't know her!"

...*like I do*. Gil could read the words sitting unspoken on Petra's tongue. She stared at Petra, seeing both a puzzle and its solution. She blinked, hoping she was wrong, but the answer remained the same.

"You were there," Gil said. "When we were born. You've known all along."

Petra's silent regard confirmed her answer. Her mouth pressed into one of those frowns so much like Aunt Vera. "They were wrong to get rid of her. Only Vera understood," she said as if to vindicate herself.

"And you've been helping her," Sumala added. "That's why she knew of our plans. That's why the others left without us, and why Gemella—Miriam—turned Professor Williams against us."

"Was that the scheme, Petra?" Gil turned on her sister, the heat of anger rising in her throat. "Did she plan to take my place?" Sesha's pendant rested heavy beneath her shirt. Was that why Sesha's presence was dark now?

"I don't know. I only sent one message. Just one."

"Petra, how could you?" Gil wasn't sure if her shock and outrage was more directed at her sister or herself for not seeing the truth.

Petra's gaze flicked between Gil and Sumala like a cornered animal. "Believe me, I would never jeopardize our mission," she said defensively. "But I was afraid of what she would do." She paused, her anguish so keenly etched upon her face, Gil wanted to hold her and tell her it was all right. But it wasn't, and Gil was not ready to forgive her just yet.

Petra continued, "I never intended to betray you. I don't know her plans or where she is. You can trust me on that."

Trust. That would be hard now. Though she knew Petra spoke the truth, her trust was now tarnished. Gil chewed at her lower lip, mulling over things said both now and past.

Petra stood, turning on Gil as if seeking vindication. "You were always so wrapped up in yourself, you never paid attention to anyone else. Things happened right under your nose, but you were too busy being the *Seventh Daughter*, the Chosen One." She strode away angrily, and neither Gil nor Sumala dared call after her. Gil followed only with her gaze.

Was all this true? Had she willingly been blind to Petra's resentment? And if Petra felt so strongly, what of Lena and the others? Did they also consider her cold-hearted and vain? Was she truly so concerned with herself and the Vision, she had lost awareness of those closest to her?

"What do you believe, Sumala? Should I have saved Aunt Faye?"

"If I believed that, I'd be just as guilty. I could've kept her alive, but not as the woman she was." Her glance asked if Gil could've done better.

"And the others? What do they believe?"

Sumala shrugged. "We've managed to avoid the subject."

"How could I have been so blind to my own sisters? Sumala, how am I to save the world if I can't heal the wounds in my own family, if I can't even see them?"

Sumala reached forward to rest a hand on her arm.

"It's hard to focus when you're too close." Sumala paused, leaning closer. "Gil, you have such tremendous power, it must take all your concentration simply to contain it. I never fully understood that until last night, when I watched you use it. I wonder that it doesn't consume you like a torch. I've often thought it must be very difficult to be Gilaishling Orlov."

Sumala turned away, embarrassed by her admission. Before Gil could find a response, a small cough wedged into the silence. Professor Williams stood just outside the tent, dressed and watching. *How much had he heard?*

"I don't suppose Miriam left my boots behind." He lifted one sock clad foot.

Sumala stood. "You shouldn't be up yet."

"Some things, I'd rather do for myself, if you don't mind." He waved toward a cluster of bushes. "And in private."

"You're obviously feeling better," Sumala noted. She passed a practiced gaze over him and nodded approval. "And in fact, we do have your boots. We found one yesterday, and that led us to finding you. Petra found the other this morning near the lake." She paused, awaiting an explanation. When Williams didn't respond, she moved toward the caves. "I'll fetch them."

Gil remained seated, ignoring Galen as she mulled over what had been said, weaving it into the pattern of her previous fears. Her failure to save Aunt Faye now seemed like a betrayal to the clan. Had she been afraid to put her power to the test? Did she doubt even then?

And what of Petra's betrayal? Her sister's words were like wounds, only now beginning to sting.

She doubted even her power could heal the rift between Petra and herself. It was a sad thing to contemplate. She stood and gazed south beyond the mountains. Beyond tomorrow and the day after. But the future remained out of focus, blurred by events she had chosen to ignore.

GALEN

"Miriam must've been in quite a hurry to have missed these," Sumala said as she handed Galen his boots. *Why did she leave you behind?* The unspoken question was clear in her eyes.

"I guess she had no use for them." Galen took the boots and made them wait while he pulled them on. "Carlo attacked Miriam. We fought." He frowned at his own words and his gaze wandered to the lake, so placid now, the water clean. It seemed such a simple thing to say. *I had a fight. I killed a man.* The words betrayed the tragedy of the event. Whether it was the knife or Vera's bullet that had actually killed Carlo, he would never know. Either way, Carlo had died beneath Galen's hand. Galen couldn't reconcile that with all he believed about life and death and one's power over the other.

"Miriam apparently believed we both drowned." It was a lie; from the look on her face, Gil knew. She was gazing at the lake as if she could see the events unfold even now. Were they really twins, or had Miriam merely reverted to her classroom persona? If so, where had these other women come from?

Sumala and Petra took charge of packing supplies, insisting both he and Gil rest. He sat on a rock drinking tea laced with Sumala's medicine. He could breathe without pain now, and periodically took a deep breath simply because he could.

Gil sat close by. She seemed weary, in a way he still felt to the core of his bones. *What had she done to him?* The idea thatshe had invaded his mind seemed a violation far more devious than Miriam's machinations. He remembered little—dream images enhanced by the argument he'd overheard this morning. He puzzled over the meaning of what had been said and the tension between the women.

Their relationships had shifted somehow, and the bonds between them had not yet adjusted, like rubber stretched tight here, loose there. That he was at the heart of their contention both puzzled and dismayed him.

Galen let his gaze wander to the lake. The still, incredibly azure water reflected the far mountains and the sky with crystal perfection. *If I had a photograph of that,* he thought, *I'd be hard pressed to tell which way is up.* It seemed a perfect metaphor for his situation. Which was the real G. M. Orlov, and which the reflection?

They packed swiftly, taking only what they could carry. They left the tent standing and stashed what remained in the cave. When they were ready, Petra approached him.

"It's your choice. You can stay here until we return." She gestured at the cache of supplies and the tent, indicating that staying would not be a particular hardship. "Or you can come with us." She looked as if her words were more a challenge than an invitation, but Galen was grateful that someone, at last, was giving him a choice in his own affairs.

Sumala was shouldering her pack as if his decision was of no consequence, but Gil paused, one arm awkwardly tangled in the straps of her pack. Petra had apparently overstepped some boundary, and their gazes fought an unspoken battle. When Gil turned toward Galen, he caught her glance and locked it to his own while he considered his options. In spite of his ordeal, he found himself determined to see it through. Miriam owed him plenty—a lengthy explanation at the least. For that matter, so did Gil, and he was still not certain the two were not the same person. He'd never get any answers sitting here.

"I came to see an eclipse," he said is if nothing else mattered. "I certainly won't be able to see it from here." He gestured at the towering mountains surrounding him. "I'll go with you, but I want answers. I've been strung along on this as far as I'm willing to go."

"Fair enough," Gil responded abruptly, glancing sharply towards Petra as if daring her to disagree. "We never intended to hide anything from you. You'll get all the answers you want, though you may find some difficult." A warning lurked in her words that made him want to shudder.

"That includes Miriam. When we catch up, I want to deal with her."

This time, acceptance did not come so readily, not even from Gil. After some time, she responded vaguely, "We'll have to wait and see. You're not the only one she has wronged, and you may find that what you want now is not truly to your liking or best interests."

There was not much Galen could say to that. He was fairly certain he knew exactly what he wanted of Miriam. He would let the matter pass for the moment, determined he would not change his mind.

"So where's my pack?"

"You need to conserve your strength, Professor. The route will certainly be more strenuous ahead," Sumala responded.

"Please. Don't call me 'Professor.' It makes me feel old, and after this last week, such a notion scarcely needs reinforcement." *Besides,* he added in his own thoughts. *It reminds me of Miriam.* "Galen will do quite well."

Petra cast him a look of misgiving, but nodded. She handed over a small pack, mostly food and firewood, along with a blanket roll.

"I get the impression you don't much approve of me," Galen remarked to her as they set out. Gil took up the lead, seeking out the trail as would a bloodhound. Sumala followed behind, the better to keep an eye on her two patients, Galen surmised.

"You were with Miriam, under her influence. How do we know you're not still helping her?"

Galen stared at her. "I could ask the same of you," he countered, admitting he had overheard their argument—it would've been difficult not to.

Petra pursed her lips in imitation of Vera's persimmon frown. "What I did was for the sake of the mission. What did Miriam promise you? What will you gain as her guardian?"

"She promised me wealth," Galen responded honestly. "Once that meant something to me, but after this, I think I can survive on a lot less. As for this guardian business, no one asked if I wanted the job or if I was even qualified."

Petra pursed her lips as if agreeing with the statement. "It wasn't my choice," she said as if she felt vindicated by his admission. "I have to trust Gil's judgment."

"But you don't have to like it, right? Well, we're on even ground there. I've been lied to, tricked, coerced, framed for murder and stranded in a foreign country. Dragged up and down mountains, knifed, and nearly drowned." *Not to mention seduced by a woman out to conquer the world.* He kept that part to himself. "You promised me answers. Tell me more about this seventh daughter thing. I only remember seventh sons."

"Sons have power, yes. But it's relatively easy to produce a seventh son—a virile man could accomplish it within a week." Her glance seemed to take his measure. "Seventh daughters, though, take time and careful planning, as well as a lot of luck. They are therefore more potent, so much so, the lore has been kept secret. This is a man's world, after all, and the idea of a woman having power over it would be disturbing, to say the least." Petra paused to gauge his reaction, as if hoping to raise his ire. Galen chose to reserve judgment. So far, this was no more than folklore.

"So why tell me? Aren't I the enemy?" He added a grin to soften the accusation.

Petra nodded toward Gil. "According to her, you're more involved than you know."

Sumala took up the story, reminding Galen that she followed, watching him for any sign of weakness. "The last seventh daughter was burned as a witch some three hundred years ago. Our own clan includes Hopi and African shamans, a Chinese princess, and a Jewish priestess. Even an English *wycham*."

Galen glanced from Sumala and Petra to Gil, noting the unusual mix of features. He remembered puzzling over Orlov's nationality but had never imagined such a diverse parentage. "How? I mean, socially, such things are simply not done."

"Intermarriage, you mean? It wasn't always by choice. One of my great grandmothers was a slave raped by her owner's son. As for the rest, Aunt Ada used to say, 'Only in America.'"

The women laughed, as if that were a family joke, and the sound, like bubbles, floated on the wind. It was the first truly pleasant sound he'd heard since Eisabel's giggles.

Eisabel! his heart echoed, and all the bubbles burst. He turned to indignation for comfort. "Even in America, such things are *not* done. It's illegal. The miscegenation laws—"

"Is that what you believe or what you've been taught?" It was a challenge. Petra's gaze studied his face, seeking betrayal.

He opened his mouth to retort—what's the difference. But the words didn't come because they tested false. Often prejudices confused him, and racial slurs caused a mental twinge, a note out of tune. "America is supposed to be the Great Melting Pot, equality for all, but realty contradicts the Ideal. People aren't willing to accept all that implies."

"So much for society in general. But I asked about you."

Galen puffed up his cheeks and blew them out. "I, uh—I'm honestly not certain. I've always considered myself a tolerant man, but I confess it's difficult to ignore the pressures of society."

Petra nodded, acknowledging his honesty. "Our little clan settled in New Mexico to hide from such judgment. Love and duty can overcome a lot with so much at stake."

Galen nodded. "And what about men? Surely they've been involved in all of this."

"Oh, very much so. They, too, shared the Vision and supported the mission."

"So where are they now? Why do you need me? And what mission?"

"To defeat the Vision and keep the world safe."

"And the rest of us become her puppets, is that it?"

Petra cast him a sharp glance. "Which rankles you more—that she has such power or that she is a woman?"

Galen paused to consider. "I don't like the idea of one person manipulating the world, male or female." Galen expected her to say something about Napoleon and Julius Caesar, but she appeared to swallow such thoughts.

"Not manipulating. You've listened too much to Miriam."

Petra kicked aside a rock. "Gil will only guide. A nudge here and there. But time is running out. Gil says certain events could quite literally destroy the entire planet." She shuddered, closing her eyes for a moment.

"And who decides which way to nudge?"

"That's the tricky part. Understand, Gil is not the only one. We've learned that another Daughter will come to power in the Middle East, and one in China—women with less regard for the state of the world as a whole. They will each serve the interests of their own country. Like the three Fates of Greek mythology, these women will shape the future. Gil must influence the weaving or their dark designs will eventually take over. Without Gil to balance their power, the future looks bleak, indeed."

"Gil will serve America's interests?"

Petra shook her head impatiently. "Tuawta gathered people from all cultures, so that Gil could serve the world. She represents all of humanity, not just a single race."

"So if Gil possesses so much power, why did you object to her healing? Isn't that what this is all about?"

"She healed you by taking the illness into herself. She gave you some of her life, and that life is not something to be lightly spent. Gil has limits, and now she has weakened herself when she needs to be strongest. Aside from that, she has diminished her own life, reduced the span of her power. Because she saved you, sometime in the future, she may not be able to save someone else. Someone of more importance."

"I'm not important enough?" He tempered the question with a sideways smile.

"You are," Gil called back from her lead position, obviously listening to the conversation. She turned to pace backward. "It's something Petra's never understood—that every individual is important. If I can't help the least significant, how can I expect to save the rest of the world?"

"Oh, so now I'm the least significant?" Galen presented a wide grin to show he was merely teasing.

"Not by any means," Gil responded with a light laugh, leaving Galen to ponder just what it was she expected of him. *You have potential*, she had said. At least these women were more willing to share information, though he had the impression they still held back.

Gil stooped to point out a smudge of charcoal on a stone face. "This is Sesha's."

"How do you know?" Galen asked. This was the third one they had found. "Maybe Miriam's trying to throw us off track."

By the look on her face, Gil had no doubt. She set her hand against the print. "Oh, this is Sesha's all right." In spite of her smile, her face looked troubled.

"What's the matter?" Sumala asked.

Gil shook her head. "When I reach for Sesha, I find only darkness. I can't touch her. We need to hurry."

"Miriam wouldn't harm them," Galen offered. "She said she needed them."

Gil frowned. "It's not Miriam's doing, though she passed this way, too." She stood to survey the landscape, one hand raised as if seeking something.

"They left the trail here," she announced as if she spoke of something other than the narrow track they followed. She pointed out a stone pinnacle raised like a fist. "They went that way." She set out along a faint trace that could've been no more than a deer trail. *Vicuna*, Galen corrected himself. Petra and Sumala followed without question. Galen could only shrug and follow in turn.

For a time they were silent, and Galen found that uncomfortable. Just to hear his own voice, he remarked, "Sesha, Sumala, Gilaishling. Such unusual names."

"They were all carefully chosen," Gil responded as if the observation were mildly insulting. "My sisters are named for the six elements of the Earth."

"Six? But there's only four—earth, air, fire, and water."

Gil noded. "Petra is stone, Sumala is air, Maji, water, and Lena, light—the Greek elements. The Chinese include wood and metal. But my great grandmother had other ideas. In her honor, Sesha is time and Evita is life."

Galen could only shake his head, chuckling softly.

"I shouldn't laugh, if I were you. Your own name is also of great significance."

"Galen? It means 'healer.'"

"Ah, but your middle name is Septimus."

"How do you know that?" Galen blurted out in surprise, feeling his face go hot. He hated that name and couldn't understand how his father could've saddled him with such a pompous moniker. He held it the greatest secret in the universe.

"It means 'seventh,'" Gil continued as if he'd not spoken.

"Who told you? Harry?" *No, not even Harry knows. Especially not Harry!*

"You are the seventh son."

Galen shook his head. "I'm only the fourth. I have three brothers and two sisters." Galen felt a moment of triumph and relief. Gil was fallible after all.

"There are three other sons."

Galen frowned and shook his head. "Not a chance," he insisted, yet the statement somehow evoked a faint memory— something when he was four, maybe five years old. A mysterious woman and her sons—cousins, he'd thought, from the comments of the adults—half-heard and even less understood. Two were older than even Edward, but the youngest was closer to Galen's age. For a long time after that, his parents had fought bitterly. He'd been too young to understand why.

"Even if that were true, my father was an only child. I can't be a seventh son of a seventh son."

Gil acknowledged that with a single nod. "No, but your own son could be."

Galen shook his head, rejecting such a notion. "But how did you know?"

"Research." Her enigmatic smile was as disconcerting as the word.

"You've spied on me?"

"It was necessary to check your background. I didn't choose you for Guardian because of your teaching style."

Galen chewed on this new information. He didn't much like the idea that Gil had been *checking* on him, that she knew things about him even he didn't know. Somehow that took on a cast more sinister than Miriam's treachery. This version of G. M. Orlov was more forthcoming, but seemed no less devious, in spite of her smile.

GIL

Gil fell into silence as they continued on, mulling over the events of last night and the morning. Her clash with Petra still tasted sour. As much as she craved independence, she still needed Petra's support.

Still weak from healing Galen, the urge to find Sesha forced her on. She pointed out signs of her sisters passing. "They spent the night here," she said at one point, and stared at the spot, a niche among rocks with no sign of a fire. How could she expect this of her sisters, this ordeal that sapped both body and spirit? Pangs of guilt tore at her.

Within another mile, the trail ended beneath an expanse of fallen rock. While Petra rested upon a boulder and Sumala passed around a canteen of water, Gil paced restively. She found muddy prints scattered among the rocks—Miriam had apparently given up trying to erase them.

"Sesha wanted to make sure we got this message." Gil pointed to the handprints, thumbs all pointing at the rubble-choked slot cleaving the valley wall. The essence of her sisters trickled across the slope like a creek flowing uphill.

"Sesha went this way. She's up there."

GALEN

It was a rough climb, challenging Galen's recovering strength. Clambering over the rocks caused him to twist and turn, every motion pulling at his wounded flesh. When they had finally worked their way through the gap into the valley beyond, Sumala insisted on examining his wound.

"A good place to rest," Petra announced, eying the angle of the sun, then pulled off her pack to rummage for water and food. She offered Gil the canteen yet glanced pointedly at Galen.

Sumala peeled back the bandage and gently probed his side. "Healing nicely. Let me know if it gives you trouble" As if, Galen thought, she hadn't been watching his every move, calling for a rest every time he'd set his hand to his side.

Petra pulled out their small kerosene stove and Sumala coaxed enough heat to brew more of her bitter tea. It was barely tepid, for the stove burned fitfully in the thin air.

"No more foul concoctions," Galen complained as Sumala doctored his cup with thick brown syrup. He tempered his words with a teasing smile.

"Last dose, just to be safe," she said, returning the smile. "I know it's putrid stuff, but I'm still refining the process, and I'm not certain of the dosage. It would be more efficient to inject it, but I have no syringes."

Galen shied back. "You're experimenting on me?" The idea he was being used as a guinea pig caused more than a little consternation.

"Not at all. I've been feeding this stuff to my sisters and the locals back home for years." She settled into lecturing posture. "An Englishman named Fleming discovered that the *penicillium* mold inhibits bacterial growth. He published his findings back in 1928. Personally, I think it shows great promise, but no one else seems interested."

"Haven't you published?"

"Who would listen?" she replied with a shrug.

"You *are* licensed, aren't you?"

Sumala winced. "Of a sort."

"Meaning not legally?" He spoke out of curiosity, but the woman seemed to take it as an accusation. She retorted with more than a hint of ire.

"Meaning that just because I don't have a scrap of paper to hang on the wall doesn't mean I don't know twice what the standard family doctor knows. Do you object to a woman having an education?" She glared at him, clearly hurt by such attitudes in the past.

Galen held up his hands in defense. "I only wish more women would. My classrooms are full of women whose only thought is to marry someone else with such abilities. They fail to see their own potential."

Sumala nodded. "Inertia," she said. "We have thousands of years of custom and culture to bring to a stop and turn around. But we'll get there."

"Is everyone a fortune teller?" Galen cried out in melodramatic jest. Even Petra managed a thin smile.

"Your sense of humor seems to be healing nicely," Gil commented from where she sat on a nearby boulder. Then her gaze traveled up the valley, seeming to look beyond rock and sky.

"So explain this Vision. What do you have to do to fulfill it?"

"Not fulfill," Gil explained as she turned to him. "Defeat. The Vision is the end of the world. I don't know if it's even possible. But that is my purpose, so I have to try."

"Show me," Galen said quietly.

She studied him shrewdly.

"Miriam made me see images of fire and horror." He couldn't repress a shudder. "I need to understand." *I have to be prepared to choose.*

Gil nodded with a grim frown.

"Are you sure you should do this now?" Sumala's look of consternation withered whatever humor Galen was trying to weave from his situation. Petra backed away from the issue.

"There may not be another chance. Events are unwinding." Gil's fingers seemed to snatch at fraying threads. She sat down beside Galen.

"Close your eyes; it's less confusing," she instructed, taking his hand. "It's not easy, but I'll be with you."

In the space of an eye blink, Galen once more witnessed the ghastly horror. Brilliant light paled the sun and strange clouds darkened the sky like vile and noxious flowers. Flame swept past and through him, searing his soul.

Empty land, void of life and color, a place where nothing existed. Only blackened ruin. Smoke and ash choked his lungs and darkened the sky.

Gil's voice whispered in his mind. "This is the Vision that created and drives my clan. The future of the Earth." Her presence both guided and sustained him. Unlike Miriam, she created a buffer against the full brunt of the horror.

Just as he could bear no more, the smoke wafted into tattered shreds and distant clouds. Rock returned, and snow and the blue, blue depths of the sky. Vanquished, his mind refused to accept the horrors he'd witnessed. Nonetheless when he held up his hand, it trembled.

He stared at the blue of the sky, as if that color had been absent from the world for a long time. The barren landscape, however, only reinforced the Vision, a small token of remembrance. For a moment, Galen feared that when he returned home, he would find the prophecy had indeed become truth.

Gil continued. "I don't understand what the Vision is or how it comes about or if I have sufficient power to stop it. That's why the eclipse and the Ritual are so important. I need you to make sure nothing goes wrong."

Galen kept silent as they gathered their energy and resolve to move on. The women honored that, recognizing his need to reconcile these images with his concept of reality. They were watching him, though, all three of them. Whenever he met their gaze, their eyes mirrored the same dread horror he felt. He could not recall a single image, as if the shapes were beyond the grasp of his mind. Only the horror remained, and after a time, it, too, became abstract and surreal.

The landscape widened into a U-shaped valley, a creek meandering down its middle.   The trail followed a creek toward a curve in the valley. Galen's side ached, and if he moved wrong, his wound sent pain shooting like fire across his ribs. Chagrined that more often than not, he had been the cause for delays, he refused to let it show. Still, he felt better than he should. Just to prove it, he dared more conversation.

"Why perform the ritual here? Surely there are better places to watch the eclipse—more accessible and amenable."

"Didn't you find the article that goes with the map?"

Galen hadn't thought about that article in a long time. "It didn't give a lot of detail, and experts decided the man was delusional."

"An easy judgment when one wants to avoid a truth. What did Miriam tell you of Killichaka?"

Galen shook his head. "I want to hear your version."

Gil gazed up at the snow-mantled peaks surrounding them.

"It's a place where the forces of the Earth gather. They focus and concentrate the energy released by the corona. A thousand years ago, long before the Inca, local tribes built a shrine there. When Sesha realized it was in the path of the eclipse, she thought we could use it to restore the power lost at birth."

"Look," Petra called out with abrupt alarm.

Birds like dark crosses circled in a narrow funnel.

"Condors," Sumala said. "Scavengers."

Gil stared at the birds with a look beyond consternation. "We need to hurry." She took the lead, breaking into a jog when she could. Her sense of urgency was as palpable as a scent.

At the head of the valley, a thin waterfall fed into a small lake. Four horses huddled together, browsing on short grasses growing along the creek. Sumala wondered aloud how they had managed the avalanche chute.

Petra cried out, pointing to where the funnel of condors touched ground. A mule's corpse lay at the base of the cliff among the litter of its pack. Remnants of its load marked its fall down the steep face.

"The fools!" Sumala exclaimed in anger as she knelt beside the animal. "Who would force a mule up that?"

"Miriam," Galen muttered. "That's one of her mules."

GIL

Gil ignored the mule and broke into a run, past the horses to the lake's edge. She stared at the milky blue water, then knelt beside it to touch its placid surface. Terror clutched at her heart.

"Sesha," she whispered, nearly a sigh.

Gil cast glances of confusion and dismay to the cliffs like a child realizing she's lost. "It happened here." A veil of mist drifted across the rock, wetting the stone so that it seemed to weep. Though cloaked in afternoon shadow, Gil saw a circular rainbow, a figure falling through its center. But the lake's milky water revealed nothing.

"I can't find her." She turned to Galen, stricken with plaintive despair. "I can't find her. She's not here." She paced back and forth, seeking her sister's essence. She would've leapt into the lake had not Galen restrained her.

"Who?" Galen asked as Petra took Gil into her embrace. Unable to bear her grief, Gil collapsed to the ground, slipping through Petra's hold. Sumala joined them.

"If you can't find her, it means she's not here. She's up ahead somewhere."

Gil could only shake her head. Sesha had fallen, of that she was certain. But there was no sign she had emerged.

GALEN

"Who?" Galen asked again.

"It's almost nightfall. Perhaps we should camp here," Petra suggested. "You'll feel better when you've rested."

"No!" Gil stated. "I have to find her. We've lost too much time already." She glanced at Galen but said nothing.

Because of me, Galen realized, though Gil did not voice the thought. If it hadn't been for him, they would've been here yesterday. Her urgency bordered on panic.

Galen turned to Petra. "Who?" he demanded.

"Our sister Sesha."

Galen stopped abruptly. *Not Sesha!* he thought. He barely knew her, but felt responsible. Had Miriam caused this, he wondered.

"Let's go. We should reach the top before dark."

They were forced to a slower pace in spite of Gil's urging, hampered by failing light. Galen noticed the three women maneuvered to keep him between them, one hand always ready to steady him, covert glances gauging the strength of his stride. He was determined to make it to the crest, even if it took half the night.

"Someone's been here," Petra commented, nodding at a displaced stone.

"Lena and the others, I should think," Sumala offered. No one mentioned Miriam, though Galen was certain they considered her also. Where was she, and when would she show herself? *What will I do when she does?*

Galen caught a shudder from Gil that the others failed to notice. He followed her gaze upward toward the cliff top. The sun had passed the canyon's rim, and they had no hope of catching it, the ridge a torn edge of sky already shading toward night. Galen forced himself into the lead.

The trail narrowed to a bare ledge, handholds carved into the sheer rock face. Parts had broken away, the fresh rock a pale gleam in the dusk. Here, too, were signs of passage—moss scraped away and gouged by hands and feet. Galen dared to look down, but the bottom was lost in the gloaming. Beside him, Gil stared at the ledge, trembling.

"I'll go first."

"Are you strong enough, Professor?" Petra called from behind Sumala. "We could rest again."

Galen took a deep breath, aware of sweating palms and shaking knees. "I can make it," he called back. "And stop calling me 'professor.'" Determined to prove himself, he shed his pack and gingerly stepped forward. Fighting an urge to close his eyes, he inched his way across the gap.

He was half way across when he heard a half-suppressed gasp behind him.

"Be careful," Gil whispered, her voice like a hand on his back, holding him steady. "There's a—"

Galen's foot slid off the ledge. He lurched, clutching handholds, hugging the rock like a lover. Pain lanced across his ribs and his legs felt like jelly. His senses went numb and his vision whirled. *Not now,* he thought fiercely, gritting his teeth. The phantom pressure of Gil's *hand* supported him until his foot could find purchase again and the spell of vertigo passed.

"Are you all right," Sumala called.

"I'm fine," he called over his shoulder. "Just fine." He kept his face away from them to hide the pain—and the terror. When he reached the far side where there was room to turn and stand secure, he told Gil to toss him their packs. Then he collapsed onto a stone step and watched his hands tremble.

He should help the others, he thought, but what could he do? He felt heavy and awkward, and in spite of his protests otherwise, lightheaded. Better to stand clear, out of the way.

He watched as Gil started across the ledge, holding his breath as her feet touched the spot where he'd almost fallen. *Careful,* he thought, but did not voice the word aloud for fear it might distract her. She seemed all too aware of the danger, anyway. For a moment, she hesitated, eyes closed, whitened fingers gripping the cup-shaped handholds.

In that moment of utter silence, Galen heard something behind him. A small cry, or perhaps a whimper, distorted and amplified by the uneven walls of rock, but decidedly human.

He turned his attention to the way ahead. Steps carved in the stone led to a narrow but open fissure, a slash of black. Galen stared into that gloom, blinking to adjust his vision, straining to hear another sound. Now that he was listening for it, he thought he heard a shallow gasp—or was it merely the wind?

"What is it?" Gil's whisper and her touch on his shoulder startled him.

"I thought I heard something." He didn't turn from his scrutiny of the passage, lest he lose acuity, but sensed Petra and Sumala coming from behind. Considering how this might be an excellent place for an ambush, he waved them back.

"Wait here," he commanded, but Gil tried to push past him, her expression both eager and anxious. He swept his arm across her path. "Wait!" he repeated with his sternest teacher's voice.

Within the passage Galen could barely make out the edges of raw stone. He kept to one side, pressed against the wall. In that way, he found a narrow crack at such an acute angle, it almost doubled back. He was about to pass it by when he *felt* someone. Not a sound, but a softness that absorbed the echo of his own steps. A current stirred by a shallow breath.

He shook his head. *Their fantasies are getting to me,* he thought. Squeezing through the narrow opening, he felt jagged stones like teeth press against him. One scraped across the wound in his side, causing a moment of dizzying pain. Beyond, he sensed the space widen into a sizeable chamber. The darkness was all but absolute.

Galen pushed into the open, one arm groping ahead .

Something hurtled out of the dark. Caught off balance, Galen toppled beneath its weight.

Tuesday, June 8

SESHA

She's dead!

Lena stared at Sesha. You're dead.

Sesha had almost come to believe it. Cold seeped to the very marrow of her bones, the darkness all but absolute. She was dead, entombed and unable to escape, barely able to move. She was dead, and she could not warn Gil. She could not save her sisters. She could not find Killichaka. Played in both dream and conscious thought, she no longer knew if she were awake or asleep. Endlessly, helplessly, she watched Maji collapse and Lena shout. *She's dead!*

Darkness bound her in its gossamer shroud. Worse, though, was the silence, a heavy pressure upon empty ears she dared not banish. *The* cholos *are coming. The* cholos *will hear you.*

She had awakened with a cry, unable to stifle her terror.

Another dream, she had thought, blinking at darkness that would not go away.

But something had disturbed her sleep. She'd become so attuned to this place, she could sense the subtle change in air pressure, the minute shift in gravity. Someone had entered the outer tunnel.

The cholos *are coming!* She mouthed the words to the intangible object at the core of the chamber. *Did I yell when I awoke? Do you think they heard?*

Be quiet. They will go away, it responded.

What if it's Gil? she asked of her companion. *I need to warn Gil*

Quiet! They're coming.

GALEN

The same nightmare, altered once more. Miriam laughed as Galen's own hand wielded the knife. He held Sesha—

Galen started awake, holding Sesha. Reality and dream merged. When Sesha shifted, moaning in her sleep he sighed, exhaling the dream's cold grasp. He rubbed his eyes as if that would

261

erase the images from his mind. But he couldn't escape the dread it inspired.

He remained where he had toppled beneath Sesha's rush. Gil had squeezed through the narrow gap before he could warn her. Together, they had held Sesha between them, limp and cold—so fearfully cold—while he issued commands. Bring blankets and water. And light!

Lantern light had revealed crystal spears set in the narrow gap to impale anyone trying to leave. "Find something to smash those crystals!" Galen had ordered, and Petra had worked with uncommon, almost manic zeal. Shattered remnants littered the floor beneath broken stubs.

Now a small fire guttered at the entrance, where the outer passage acted as a natural flue. A pot simmered. Gil and Sumala fed Sesha water and soup whenever they could rouse her near conscious.

They took turns holding Sesha to warm her, needing the tangible assurance that she lived, Galen no less than the women. There was little else to do now but wait for morning. In this place of perpetual night, that seemed but a futile promise.

GIL

I almost lost Sesha. The thought was unbearable. If Galen hadn't found her, if he had not *heard*...Gil shuddered, certain Sesha would not have survived one more night of cold and solitude.

Gil took her turn holding Sesha. Sumala and Petra stood sentry in the outer passage. Restlessly, Galen circled the chamber before settling down next to her.

"You should rest," he told her. "You'll need your strength."

"You sound like Petra," Gil responded with a laugh, then grimly added, "So will you. Miriam's waiting."

Galen's mouth pressed into a thin frown. "Miriam believes me dead," he admitted, staring into the rock as if he could see beyond it. Gil cast him a sidelong glance, half curious, half suspicious, but waited for him to continue.

"Even so, I feel I'm at the end of a tether. She's reeling me in." Galen's hand went instinctively to his chest, to that invisible brand. His expression turned grim and determined. "She can't control me. I won't let her."

Gil sensed the shift as new strengths settled into place. She had watched him take charge, casting orders with a stern authority she'd not seen before, not even in the classroom.

"Get some sleep," he told her now. "Rest."

Sleep, however, was not in her mind. There would be time enough for sleep after the eclipse.

Gil let her gaze explore the chamber. The lantern cast barely enough light to reveal details. Until now, she had noted only objects to be avoided, stepped over or around; all her focus had centered on her sister.

Now the structure in the chamber's core snared her curiosity. It stood no more than three feet high, including a base of carved stone, and scarcely four feet long. Quartz crystals had been fashioned into a translucent case. A corpse rested within, visible only in fragments refracted through the surrounding crystal.

New whispers joined the voices perpetually haunting her thoughts. Ancient and obscure, sand patterns drawn by a capricious wind. The past lingered, beyond any sense of time. Latent power abided within the crystal matrix, so potent she dared not approach. *Piezoelectric.* She couldn't recall where she had heard that term. It was one of the unique properties of quartz. Crystal radio sets depended on it. She retreated until she felt solid stone at her back. Here, too were memories, preserved in ancient pigments, safe to handle. Ancient dreams brushed the edges of her mind. She retrieved the lantern to study them closer.

Hues still vivid after centuries sang the story. A priestess, long, black hair, a robe of white and spun gold sat upon a radiant throne.

Sun balances moon, touching the edge of the world. Moonlight bleeds across water, a bridge spanning heaven and earth. Power feeds the huaca. *Energy warms the soul.*

A cherished face, knife raised—the silver knife used for healing—only for healing. She has no time to scream.

The girl's dying breath caught in her throat, Gil sank to her knees, clutching the reality of stone until the images faded.

Bad dream, she thought and wondered when she'd fallen asleep. Yet the images held such intensity and clarity, she could scarcely deny their reality. Ancient dust choked her throat, and the imprisoned corpse stole the air from her lungs. Voices sang of betrayal and loss.

Gil had no time for such matters. She had the future to worry about; the past could not be reshaped. She fled, slipping past a dozing Sumala to stand at the far end of the passage, inhaling the clean, chill air. The dark of night was almost as absolute as Sesha's hidden chamber. It suited her mood.

No moon tonight. It would rise with the sun.

SESHA

The arhythmic crackle of fire roused Sesha, the first true warmth she'd felt in days.

They are here, whispered the voice at the core, awakening the fear that had become the core of her being. *They found us.*

Sesha wrestled a swaddling tangle of blankets. *Someone* held her—a man by the scent and bulk of him. In mad panic, she beat against him, struggled to break his hold. The more she struggled, the tighter he held her.

"You're safe, Sesha." Was that Petra's voice, echoed by Sumala?

Sesha paused in her struggle, and Petra continued. "This is Professor Williams—Galen. He rescued you." Rescued. For so long had she feared capture, she could scarcely comprehend the word.

"Where's Gil?" she asked. *Where's Gil?*

"She's close by," said one, and the other, "She's sleeping." And neither was quite the truth. Another persistent worry poked like a sharp rock, nagging her until she jerked awake.

"What day is it?"

The man gazed upward as if gauging unseen stars. "It should be Tuesday by now."

"The eclipse!" Sesha renewed her battle with the blankets.

"There's time enough and not yet morning. Here, drink this." Sumala's voice accompanied a canteen of water, a bowl of thin soup.

GIL

Supay manifested itself in the chuckle of pebbles falling. Yes, it would be here, lurking in the darkest pools of night. It would not surrender so easily. Had that malign entity lured them here for its own designs?

She considered the dark shadow upon Galen's essence. Was he now Supay's tool? Why couldn't she foresee that? Had she told him the entire story at the start, Miriam couldn't have tainted him, branding her mark upon him. She had planned to tell him on the ship, but he wasn't there to hear the story.

The essence of the Other spilled across the velvet night like spindrift. *Why are you here? Why can't I touch your soul?* Images skittered like fallen leaves—too ephemeral, too swift, to focus upon any one, too ethereal to perceive.

A tepid light seeped into the dark. Mountain peaks became silhouettes against the paling sky. Snowfields and glaciers reflected the palest shades of rose and amber. Supay's presence failed. A peace settled across the landscape. In the mystical space between night and day, a respite had been declared and turmoil banished. She sensed it in the frosty tang of the air.

Someone held sway here, a force equal and opposite to Supay. She was not quite as alone in this struggle as she had thought. She wrapped that assurance about her like a warm blanket. For the moment, Supay could not touch her. For this moment, she was safe.

Darkness faded, revealing a landscape of drab red and lifeless gray. Low clouds lidded the sky, their shadows casting mottled patterns to distort the true contours of the land. Gil frowned at the prospect of cloudy skies. What if all their journeying, their pain and hardship came to naught, obscured by cloud during the precious three and a half minutes of totality? She shook the worry from her shoulders. It couldn't happen. If sheer will and determination accounted for anything, the skies would be clear.

Shadows oozed down the mountainside to bide beneath blankets of morning fog. Mountain peaks floated above the mists, glowing in shades of cherry pink and autumn gold. To the east, a pencil-line sliver of moon announced the dawn. It soon paled, yielding dominion to the sun.

From the passageway came a near hysterical shout.

"Let me out of here!"

SESHA

"Let me out! Let me out! Let me out!" Each cry was louder

and louder still.

Petra blocked the narrow crack that was Sesha's only escape. Sesha fell to her knees. She rocked back and forth, hugging herself and moaning softly.

She had known *something* occupied the chamber's center, as if weight were a property that could be sensed. She had talked to it and imagined its answers, telling her to wait, that help would come.

But she had never been able to touch it. She had circled the chamber, one hand trailing along the wall like an anchor, but she couldn't reach it. Awakened by the careless bang of a pot against stone, her curious gaze had sought it out.

Seeing the crystal case, the form biding there, she feared the essence of that corpse had permeated her body and she had inhaled its very soul. She could not breathe deep enough to expel it, to cleanse death's taint from her lungs.

You're dead. The sight awakened her nightmare. *You're dead, you're dead, you're dead.* Lena's words became a manic mantra.

"I need out," she demanded, but they failed to understand. Her hands danced nervously as she balanced on the brink of panic.

"Let her go," Gil called from somewhere behind Petra. Sesha lurched to her feet and squeezed through the narrow gap into the outer passage. She lunged toward the promise of light, one hand trailing the outer wall out of habit. After three days in total darkness, the pale light beyond the passage made Sesha's eyes tear.

The stranger—Galen—went with her, his arm around her waist, aiding her. "It's all right. Just a little farther."

The words echoed a dim memory. She leaned into the comfort of his touch.

"I remember you," Sesha said. His fingers tensed on her arm. He was watching her. What did he see? She touched her face, wondering how the dark had changed her.

GALEN

The far end of the passage emerged in the middle of a steep slope. A fold in the rock formed a pocket where they could avoid the brittle wind. Galen guided Sesha into the enclosed space. The others followed. From this sheltered balcony, he scanned the surrounding rock with a narrow gaze. The idea that someone might be watching was an itch in the center of his back.

Galen studied the scene while Petra passed out hard rolls and sun-dried *charqui* for breakfast. They perched at a geographic boundary between merely relentlessly steep and unscalably-precipitous *up*. At their backs, near-to-vertical cliffs; below, a broad skirt of broken rubble. In between, boulders from the heights, like a tumble of children's blocks, created a hide-and-seek landscape where a dozen men might hide.

Knife-blade ridges of red and brown divided U-shaped valleys, filled near to the brim with a river of cloud. Galen fancied he could discern the blue-gray smudge of the sea. To the north, Yerupaja's peak crowned Cordillera Huayhuash with solemn, snow-mantled majesty. Glaciers and snowfields cast a diadem of sunlight while pennons of snowdrift flew from jagged peaks. *Thank the Lord we're not up there,* Galen mused. This group was not equipped—mentally or physically—to handle snow and ice. He was relieved to see their trail meandering like a thin scar across the apron of loose rock below.

Sumala brought him a cup of tea.

"No more concoctions!" Galen protested, only half in jest.

Sumala responded with a flat smile. "*Mate de coca*, and some herbs for the altitude."

Galen waved it off. "I'm fine; no more edema. See?" He took a deep breath, held it a moment, then let it go.

"This will keep it from returning," Sumala responded, unimpressed. "We're all at risk. Tell me if the pain returns, or if you have headaches, drowsiness or trouble walking."

"Is that all?" he asked, begrudgingly accepting the cup.

"Irrational behavior. Hallucinations. Symptoms you won't notice in yourself."

"Thanks for your confidence," Galen answered with a sarcastic bite, finding he resented any insinuation that he wasn't fit. He was still the outsider, even if he had taken command. His place in this group had shifted. Like walking on uncertain footing, he felt wary.

As Sumala moved on, Galen turned to study Sesha over the rim of his cup. She was the one they should be worrying over, he thought, glad Sumala had a new patient to occupy her. Sesha sat hugging her knees, rocking back and forth. *So fragile,* he thought.

She might shatter at a touch.

He tried to compare this Sesha to the woman he'd encountered in La Oroya and rescued in Cerro de Pasco—how many ages ago? But he couldn't picture the face. As with all of them, the trek had taken its toll. Her skin was well tanned, sunburned across the cheeks and nose. Once round contours had become hollow and thin, and drifting shadows haunted her eyes. He remembered those eyes, their bright and inquisitive fire. That fire smoldered now, a dusky ember.

At her sisters' urging, she began to tell her story.

SESHA

Her sisters plied Sesha with persistent questions. She answered them, but not the way she wanted to. She wanted to tell them it was her fault, that she had let Gil down and abandoned Lena.

"He shot Maji. Maji!" This she uttered in an anguished wail, trembling at the memory, still unbearably fresh. "There were too many of them, and they all had guns, and I was so afraid, and then I fell." Her fist pounded against her knee in a steady, manic rhythm as her words picked up speed. She'd lost her pack, the maps ruined. Was there anything else? "Stupid, stupid! It was all my fault!"

"How did you survive the fall?" Gil asked. "I couldn't sense you. I thought you had—" She bit at her lip to quell the words.

"I dove into the lake. The water was so cold, I curled into a ball and that saved my life. My pack wedged between two rocks, and I almost drowned before I could get free of it. I was so cold, I couldn't move. By the time I climbed the cliff again—" she paused to shudder at that harrowing memory. "They were gone, but they left a sentry. I couldn't get past him.

"There's no one there now," Gil said matter-of-factly. Sesha gazed past her, not so certain.

"He was there! I wanted to sneak up and hit him over the head with a rock." Her right hand gestured to complete the story. She shook her head. "I couldn't do it. I hid instead."

"That's how you got trapped," Petra noted. Sesha nodded.

"The entrance felt like no more than a tight squeeze. It wasn't until I was past that I discovered I couldn't get out again." Sesha paused to rub her hand across her stomach, bruised and scraped from her trying. "There was no way to break out. All I could do was wait. I felt so helpless! I should've been with them! I'm sorry, Gil. I let you down."

"You did the right thing," Gil assured her. "If you hadn't escaped and waited for us here, we wouldn't have known what happened. We would've walked into their trap, too."

Sesha was unconvinced.

"Did you see Miriam?" Petra asked. "She was ahead of us."

"Miriam?" Her gaze questioned each face in turn.

"Gemella. Gil's twin."

"Gemella's here?" Sesha shuddered.

"She calls herself Miriam. She's been following you."

Sesha jerked upright and peered at Gil. "Prove you're Gil, then, and not Gemella," she insisted.

Gil glanced at the others, lingering upon Petra. She took Sesha's hand and rested it casually over her heart. "You know I'm Gil. You can feel it here."

Sesha nodded, feeling the shape of the pendant under the fabric of Gil's shirt. *What's going on?* she wondered, but aloud said, "After a while, nothing was clear." She rubbed her arms and closed her eyes, but then quickly opened them again. "The darkness," she murmured, and then said aloud. "They might've passed by." *Did I dream that?* she wondered. "Maybe the bandits captured her, too."

"It's more likely they're working *for* Miriam," Petra responded. She glanced at Galen, who nodded affirmation. Sesha stared at him, wondering why he would know that.

"It doesn't matter," Petra continued. "We must find the others and then the shrine. We have to be ready for totality."

GALEN

Totality. For the first time Galen turned his mind to practical matters and his attention to the horizon. They were roughly ten degrees south of the equator and near to summer solstice. At the time of the eclipse, the sun would be low on the horizon, about twenty degrees north of due west.

"How do you know we'll be able to see it from the shrine?" he asked and wondered if they were even still in its path.

"We will," Gil said with a certainty no one questioned. "Kil-lichaka was used for lunar rituals. There's a clear view where the moon touches the horizon."

"And the clouds?"

Gil smiled at some hidden joke. "I'll see what I can do."

Sesha still trembled, shaking her head and muttering. Her anguish made Galen angry.

"How can you do this to her—to any of them?" he yelled at Gil. "You're all exhausted, half-starved, and near frozen. Your sisters have been shot and beaten and who knows what else by now." The last words were a mistake. He saw by their reactions that they were trying to avoid thinking about such consequences. Sesha trembled anew. "How could you drag your sisters—your own family!—to this place? How could you put them through this ordeal for some ancient superstition?"

Gil looked stricken with pain. Her face reminded Galen of Carlo's when he had died. But it was Sesha who spoke.

"Please, Professor Williams—"

"Galen," he cut in wearily. "Just Galen."

"Galen, it's not her fault. Aunt Faye found the Ritual. I convinced the family we had to do this. *I'm* the one to blame for being here."

"We thought you understood," Sumala added. "This was our choice. We have to do this—"

"To defeat the Vision—yes, you told me. But is your Vision worth what you're putting yourselves through? Is it worth the suffering, worth Carlo's life, Eisabel and her family, and whomever else might die before this is over? Who gave you the right to interfere in mankind's affairs, anyway? We've done well enough until now."

"*Until now*," Gil shot back. "We've had one global war, and we're on the brink of another. The horrors Hitler inflicts are unimaginable." She paused, shuddering. "We're still recovering from the worst economic disaster in history. But until now, *man*kind wasn't able to destroy the entire planet."

"Absurd," Galen countered. "There is no such power."

"You've seen the Vision."

Galen considered the images she'd created, but they were so far beyond the context of reality, the memories crumbled, phantasms of dust. A deep, infinitely weary look came to Gil's eyes, allowing Galen a glimpse of the burden she bore. It quickly vanished, as if she'd drawn a mask over her soul.

Sesha reached out to touch his sleeve, drawing his gaze to meet her own. "We've all seen Gil's Vision, and we know the consequences if we fail. We committed ourselves to this journey. We have to do this. We *have* to."

Galen looked into a face sketched in lines of stubborn will, eyes still tortured with guilt. Sooty smudges highlighted the strain her ordeal had etched there. Her desperate tenacity took hold of him then, seized him around the middle and shook him to the core of his being. More than anything else, more, even, than Gil's vision of global destruction, Sesha's resolve moved him. His will teetered off balance, and then settled around a new center.

His chest began to itch, and he clenched his hand tight around his cup to keep from scratching it. Jaw muscles tensed as he swallowed any remaining doubt. If Sesha believed so strongly in this venture, he would do anything to see it through.

"Okay, so here's what we'll do…"

~ * ~

It makes sense, Galen told himself an hour later, convinced of the logic of a plan that could nonetheless jeopardize the entire mission. It was both simple and inevitable. What could go wrong?

Sesha insisted at least one *cholo* waited to ambush them. She still wanted to sneak up and bash him with a rock. Galen had fiercely vetoed the idea, recalling Miriam's fight with Carlo, and how the same move had gone awry.

They had spent the better part of an hour arguing over it. Sumala had suggested forcing the sentry to lead them to the missing women. That casual remark had inspired Galen's own plan. Let the *cholos* capture Gil, Petra, and Sumala. Then Galen and Sesha could follow and free all of them.

Petra, of course, opposed the idea. "And what if you can't? Then Miriam has us all." She glared at him, daring him to deny that was his intent.

"I know as much about Miriam's plans as you," Galen responded pointedly. She was using him to mitigate her own guilt and he wasn't about to be anyone's scapegoat.

Gil stared towards the horizon with that *otherwhere* look Galen knew so well. An uneasy tremor shifted through Galen's gut. *What does she see,* he wondered, *that casts such a doleful shadow in her eyes?*

"If someone waits, he's well hidden, even to me," she declared, yet her manner left something unsaid.

"That settles it," Petra stated. "If Gil can't find anyone, they must've given up. We should stick together."

That's not what she said, Galen thought. *She didn't say he's not there.* He stared at the trail winding across the slopes like a toboggan run, one with no brakes.

"We have to reach the temple before the eclipse starts," she reminded him as they prepared to set out. She obviously fostered a reserve of suspicion toward his motives. "We have much to do, and the eclipse lasts only about three and a half minutes."

"That's just the total phase. First contact begins about an hour before."

"First contact?" The term clearly perplexed her.

Galen held up both hands, touching forefingers to thumbs to form dual rings. As he touched the two rings together, top to bottom, he addressed them all, slipping into the garb of teacher. "The eclipse begins when the leading edge of the sun meets the trailing edge of the moon. You'll see shadow bands, crescent suns whereever light shines through a pinhole..." But there were no trees to cast such images, no dogs set to barking, no birds to roost.

"Second contact occurs when the two leading edges meet." He slid the two rings together until they overlapped. "*That's* totality." How to describe it? Words and memory failed him. "Totality ends when the trailing edges pass—third contact. And when the sun passes the moon's leading edge, the eclipse is over."

He aimed his gaze directly at Petra. "If you want everyone in place on time, I need to know when the eclipse starts."

Petra pursed her lips, as if she didn't trust him with the information. "According to the astronomers in Cerro de Pasco, totality should occur around 5:18. Remember, all seven must be there for the Ritual to succeed." She clearly considered his presence superfluous.

"What about Miriam?" Sesha asked.

"I'm not the one you should ask," Petra responded. "I wasn't in her camp." With that, she volleyed the accusation back to Galen.

Galen didn't answer. His sense of commitment was still too

fresh, too tenuous to risk such a challenge. *Even concrete needs time to set,* he thought, rubbing his shirtfront.

Petra left the subject hanging, hoisting her pack and setting out on the narrow trail. Sumala and Gil followed. Galen gazed at the barren landscape, wondering if Miriam could sense his presence. She might already be working her treachery on him, luring him along paths of her choosing, steering his thoughts to her own ends. Could his plan, so logical and inevitable in his own mind, be the manipulation of Miriam's desires? How could he tell, and what could he do about it?

"What did she mean by that?"

Sesha was staring at him with frank curiosity. The doubt he read in her eyes stung more than Petra's blatant accusations. He took a deep breath, letting it out slowly.

"I met Miriam in Cerro de Pasco. I had no reason to suspect she wasn't my student." He scanned the boulder field. If a sentry did wait for them, he could still put his plan into effect; ha had only to delay a minute. If no one appeared before the other three reached the open scree slope below them, then he'd think of something else.

"You're not the only one she's fooled," Sesha responded with a rueful frown. "So what happened?"

Galen slung the straps of his pack over his shoulders and adjusted the fittings before answering.

Reluctantly, he sketched out the events that had brought him to this place, using the telling of his story as an excuse to lag behind and to keep Sesha with him. *If I give her this much, she'll be satisfied. She won't think I'm hiding anything.*

"That was you, then," Sesha exclaimed suddenly. "When I was attacked in Cerro de Pasco, you rescued me."

"A fortunate coincidence," Galen cut in, and wondered if it really had been. He started to rub absently at his chest, caught himself and self-consciously lowered his hand.

"I didn't get a chance to thank you," Sesha persisted. He waved it off as a minor matter and set out, concerned someone might turn and call after them.

He had omitted the part about Mama and her family. Sesha didn't need such details to add to her concerns. *Miriam won't harm the women,* he thought. *She needs them, too.*

The memory of Miriam and her evil treachery squirmed in

Galen's gut like a serpent feeding on his soul. What would he do when he faced her again? Would he have a choice or would all his convictions and determination melt beneath her gaze? *You are mine,* her voice whispered.

The others had crossed half of the boulder field without incident. Galen hurried his pace to close the gap. Fallen boulders and rock outcrops afforded plenty of cover—for both Galen and for any watcher. *This is insane,* he decided, now that it was too late. No wonder the others had rejected his plan.

As Gil, Petra, and Sumala crossed onto the barren talus slope, he relaxed. The wide skirts of broken rock were too open to harbor a hidden watcher. So far, nothing had moved.

He paused to give Sesha a hand down a particularly high step. Sesha, however, pushed him aside. Galen's glance caught a man as he emerged from behind the last boulder.

"*Ola, Señoritas,*" the man called out to the women, his back to Galen and Sesha.

Sesha started to charge forward. In a single motion, Galen snagged her around the waist and dodged behind a boulder. Before she could utter a sound, he covered her mouth with his hand.

"Shh," he whispered as she bucked against his restraint. Pinning Sesha with his knee, he dared peek over the top of the boulder. The man brandished his rifle with casual menace.

Petra's eyes went wide with alarm. She raised one hand to point, but Sumala grabbed her arm before she could give away Galen's presence. Gil merely regarded the man calmly, as if he were expected. Galen expected her to transform into Miriam's persona. *Is that really you, G. M. Orlov?* he wondered. *Is that you, GeM?*

Sesha struggled against his grasp.

"Be still," he whispered.

She shook her head, her eyes bright with fury.

"This will work. Trust me."

She tried once more to twist from his grasp, then relaxed and nodded. Galen released her.

"Stay down," he ordered as he slipped closer.

The man spoke in Spanish, seeming both relieved that his wait was over and angry that it had taken so long. Galen didn't need to understand the words. The *cholo* pushed Sumala, causing her to stumble. Petra caught her. Gil stared at the man for a moment, then turned and started down the trail.

Once we find the others, we won't need him anymore. Hands clenched tight, Galen relished the image of a solid roundhouse punch. But flashes of his fight with Carlo gnawed at his confidence. He resolved that next time, he would fare better.

"What should we do?" Sesha asked, startling Galen.

"I told you to wait."

"You're not leaving me behind," Sesha responded. "We need to rescue them." Sesha's whisper was as fierce as any shout.

"It's all right. I have a plan."

"Not without me." The corner of her mouth twitched and her eyes teared. "I promised myself. I'm going to free my sisters, and we don't have time to argue."

Galen studied her face and its expression of haunted desperation, and he thought of his brother, Edward. How often had Galen relived their final conversation as if, if he could only find the right words, everything would change? He understood something of Sesha's distress.

"Come on, then. But keep quiet."

The trail meandered across the treacherous, barren shoulder of broken rubble, a slope that seemed too steep to maintain its repose. Galen wondered that the narrow path had not been buried long ago or swept away by shifting scree. With virtually no cover, Galen and Sesha were forced to hang back lest the *cholo* turn abruptly. Lingering shreds of cloud drifted across the mountain, occasionally both concealing and hindering them.

Without apparent cause or warning, a clatter of stones heralded a rockfall somewhere above, disrupting the empty solitude. Galen shoved Sesha flat to the ground, covering her with his own body. Caught near the edge of the slide, small rocks thudded against his back. Larger ones bounced over him. Galen flung his arms across his head and pushed Sesha tighter against the upslope side of the trail, as if they could root themselves in the mountain, itself. The broken rubble shuddered and shifted. Galen feared the entire slope would give way; that they would tumble headlong, faster and faster and never stop until they spilled into the sea so many miles below.

Abrupt silence. Galen dared to breathe. With dust settling around him, he raised his head, fearing the others had been swept away. The slide left a wide gash across the trail. Safely on the other side, Petra and Sumala stared in horror, obviously fearing the same fate for Galen and Sesha. Or Sesha, at least. Galen was fairly certain Petra couldn't care less what happened to him. Gil, however, cast her glance directly at them, offering a nod and a half smile in relief.

Gil's captor also scanned the terrain with a sharp-eyed squint. Only partially concealed by the angle of the slope, Galen dared not move. Trapped beneath him, Sesha tried to wiggle free. Her elbow jabbed his stomach.

"Hold still," he whispered, his lips brushing against her ear. She moved her head but a fraction, and her cheek touched his. The effect was like fire and ice trickling through his gut.

A twitch of a glance showed the horseman gazing directly toward them. Even a breath might give them away.

Galen's nose itched.

GIL

"*Chúkara,*" Sumala said loudly. "Spirits."

Galen and Sesha were close—there at the edge of the rock fall. Gil turned away, lest her gaze direct the *cholo*'s attention. The man held his rifle at the ready as he scanned the scattered rocks and boulders.

"These mountains are untamed," Sumala continued in Spanish. "The *aukikuna* are angry. You trespass in their holy places."

Gil followed Sumala's lead. "Do you not feel the ground tremble? Pachacamac will punish you for coming to this place." Sumala and Petra cast properly fearful glances at the heights above, directing the man's gaze anywhere but towards where Galen and Sesha crouched scarcely twenty feet away.

As if on cue, Gil felt a slight shudder, just a wisp of motion. The sigh of a sleeping giant. So faint, she wondered if she had imagined it. Or caused it? She didn't think her abilities extended to moving mountains, but then she'd never tried before.

"Pah," the man responded in disgust and false bravado. "I don't believe in spirits." He swung his rifle, gesturing for them to move on. Gil, Sumala, and Petra let out pent up breaths as one.

"Chukara?" Gil whispered to Sumala.

"Wild place. I learned it from the *brujas* in Huaratambo."

Their attempt at misdirection almost backfired, though. In

spite of his denial, their captor now kept a vigilant watch on his surroundings. His nervous glance twitched sporadically. Gil and her sisters did their best to distract him with an unending list of questions, complaints and requests. They took turns at annoying him to the brink of anger.

It troubled Gil to exploit the superstitions lurking in this man's soul, insulting whatever ancient god this site might once have served. She considered the presence she'd felt at Pachacamac. A vengeful, angry god, Pachacamac's influence had spread throughout the Andes and endured for centuries. Earthquakes were considered *castigo*—punishment for those who displeased him, visited upon guilty and innocent alike. Could the tremor be a warning?

The new set of voices whispered long-forgotten stories. She thought that if she could sit still and listen, she might understand them.

Their captor would not let her, though. He kept them moving as their path curved down and around. They had reached the valley floor, a rocky defile bound by ridges of rubble. Nothing grew here; not even lichens colored the rocks.

Gil stepped carefully, almost delicately, anticipating another tremor, expecting the ground to roll beneath her feet. Power lingered in this place, potent but dormant, waiting. It vibrated through the soles of her feet and made her teeth itch. She fingered the weft of the air and shuddered, uncertain whether she truly wanted this much power. Now that they were so close, did she really want any power at all? *Too late to back out now,* she told herself.

Sun and moon weighed heavy overhead, one inexorably overtaking the other, like two lovers rushing to embrace. An absurd metaphor, she thought, considering the nature and orbital mechanics involved. Most of the world would be unaware of the event. Indeed, it was only a shadow. That it should briefly cast a narrow stripe across the Earth's surface should have no consequence.

Yet it did. At totality, the moon would swallow the sun's light, revealing its delicate corona. Beyond the ability of mankind's limited science to explain, beyond even its comprehension or notice, the moon's presence would focus energy normally overwhelmed by the sun's outer atmosphere. That energy would in turn transform something within her own soul. Even now, she could feel a magnetic yearning in the deepest core of her being. She moved carefully, lest the slightest jar unleash it, consuming both body and spirit.

So close now. Restless souls whispered to her in their ancient tongue. Welcome or warning? She couldn't tell.

GALEN

"What will we do when we find the others?"

Galen could only shrug, wishing Sesha would stop asking questions for which he really had no answers. *One thing at a time,* he thought.

"Are you sure this will work?" Sesha continued. "How do you know we can free my sisters when we find them?"

"We don't have much choice, do we?" Galen replied flatly, trying to avoid the subject, but Sesha persisted.

"What do you have in mind?"

Galen pressed his lips in a flat line. *You really don't want to know,* he thought, and wondered why he should. One idea picked up another and then another, like a tumble of pebbles. They slid down a shadowed canyon toward a dark and unknown end.

"We'll have to wait and see," was the only answer he offered aloud.

As they followed the trail into the valley, the sun finally cleared the canyon walls, pouring harsh, flat light over the rim. Like a sponge, it absorbed his energy, leaving Galen feeling dry and brittle. Gusty winds carried the touch of ice from the glaciers not so high above them. Beads of sweat trickled down the back of Galen's neck even as his face and bare hands felt chilled. Light was a physical burden, to be carried like a weight upon the back, balanced upon the head. The glare bouncing off every surface gave Galen a headache and struck his eyes a vicious blow.

It was the sun, Galen kept telling himself, that caused his headache. *It's the sun.*

SESHA

The valley might have been a meadow at a lower elevation. Littered with boulders dropped by long-vanquished glaciers, the bare and polished stone bore deep gouges. It was bound and bisected by ridges of glacial rubble, as if some giant had attempted to sweep the valley floor clear and had just left to get a dustpan. A steep, narrow arete bisected the valley where two glaciers had parted ways. Nothing grew here; there were no insects, no birds. The silence seemed absolute.

Galen led her up the side of the moraine, the rubble ranging in size from pea-sized gravel to boulders as big as houses. From the top, they could survey most of the valley.

Sesha noted a pattern in the stone litter. Random scatter became lines, then squares. Centuries of exposure had softened sharp edges, but there was no mistaking the work of a primitive hand. Remnants of stone walls, like rows of worn teeth, sectioned the flat valley floor. Further on, broken walls became structures, a maze of rooms and roofless buildings huddled against the far ridge, ending abruptly against a backdrop of distant mountains. She was looking upon the roots of a village, perhaps a small city. Quarried from the same stone, the ruins blended with the mountain as if grown rather than built.

"I know this place," Sesha whispered, levering herself up for a better view. A current of exhilaration pulsed through her as she pictured the criss-crossed lines of the map like a poorly woven plaid. "The temple, Killichaka, it's—" She paused to orient herself, to consult her mental copy of the lost map.

"This can't be right." Her hands waved, trying to erase the scene before her. She fumbled for her compass. "North is there. The sun will set—" she glanced north by northwest. The ridge blocked her view.

"No! No, no, no." All their plans, their hopes, crushed beneath a mountain's weight.

"There's no temple here." Galen pointed out dark holes and open pits scarring the cliffs, hedged by ridges of rubble and debris. "Those are mines. Killichaka's somewhere else."

Oh, please be right, Sesha prayed. She couldn't bear the thought of failure. Not after everything they'd been through.

Galen grabbed her by the arm and pulled her down behind a table-sized block.

"What—?"

Galen hushed her, pointing down the center of the valley. At the edge of the ruins, brown canvas tarps formed makeshift shelters surrounded by a careless scattering of equipment and supplies. The ring of a pickax cleaved the air, and a man in poncho and pointed *chullo* hat squatted before a low fire stirring the contents of a small pot. As they watched, Gil and her sisters, prodded by their captor, strode into the camp.

Three men gathered to surround the women. They argued, mostly in heavily accented Spanish too rapid and angry for her to follow. This venture had obviously not brought them the riches they sought, and the harsh conditions were taking their toll, fraying nerves and honing tempers.

GALEN

The men were arguing, the words distorted beyond understanding. With Carlo gone, they had no leader to make decisions or to keep them in line. It made them all the more dangerous. On the other hand, Galen decided, it might be used to his advantage.

That idea channeled his thoughts toward the dark chasm where the serpent lurked. Shadows whispered. *Join them. Take over.* They had, after all, witnessed Carlo's death at his hand. That counted for something in such groups. Carlo had killed one of his own, and the others had accepted it callously. Once Galen had control, he could do anything. *No,* he thought brusquely, banishing the temptation. That's what Miriam would want. Sesha would neither approve nor understand, though it might be key to their success.

"Are you all right?" Sesha asked. "You look a little pale."

Galen touched his chest, wondering if the sharp pain signaled a return of the edema or the stigma of Miriam's mark. "I'm fine," he muttered.

In the ruins below, the argument seemed to dissolve when the man who had captured the sisters set off through the ruins, carrying Gil's pack. The others settled into more relaxed postures. Galen didn't like their expressions or gestures, nor did he like the way they edged closer to the women each time they shifted their weight from one foot to the other. Anger fed the plans festering in his mind. When one of them reached out to touch Gil's hair, Galen shifted forward, ready to charge recklessly down the hill. Only Sesha's hand on his shoulder restrained him.

SESHA

"We need to get closer," Sesha said, and cast about for a better vantage point. Galen pointed out a small, isolated room imbedded into the moraine below and to their right. Only twenty or thirty yards from the camp below, it was still high enough to survey most of the valley. They would be able to watch over the front wall with little fear of being seen from below. The side had partially collapsed, tapering down to a single stone's height where it burrowed into the side of the moraine.

Pulling free from Galen's grasp on her arm, she edged out from their cover.

"Sesha, where are you going?" Galen called after her in a loud whisper. "Sesha!"

She responded by skidding across the slope.

GALEN

"Sesha, wait!" Galen anxiously watched the men below, then scurried after her, muttering imprecations. He caught up when she paused behind a massive boulder. "Do you want to get us both caught?" he berated her, gripping her arm so tightly, she winced and tried to twist away from him. "You move only when I tell you to. Understand?" His anger ebbed into a pool of fear, and he relaxed his hold. "I promised Gil I'd take care of you."

They took turns, one keeping watch while the other dashed ahead. Galen pushed himself from boulder to ruined wall to toppled stele. The short trek seemed unusually arduous, and his chest ached and burned. Reaching their goal, he tumbled over the low side. Slumped against the slope, eyes closed, he concentrated on simply breathing. He noted with some degree of vindication that Sesha appeared equally affected.

As soon as his gasps settled into deep, measured breaths, Galen rose to peer cautiously over the front wall. Petra sat on a stump of a wall, Sumala standing beside her, but Gil paced with restless passion. One man stood guard, but the others had retrieved pickaxes and were poking halfheartedly at the obdurate stone. Galen recalled the argument in Angoltuto. *Oro,* Miriam had promised the horsemen. Gold. How would they react when they found none?

GIL

Trying to contain her own quivering mix of anxiety and anticipation, Gil sat next to Petra. In spite of her fatigue, though, she couldn't rest, could not remain still.

Foreboding overwhelmed her, pushing her to pace restlessly, as much as her captors would allow. Miriam was close, the acrid miasma of her essence simmering among the stones.

Gil spun away from such thoughts, to the ruins before her. Voices cried out—spirits trapped by ancient cataclysm. *Almas.* The souls of the dead. They whispered of treachery and punishment and warned of evil abiding.

Supay.

Its voice the hiss of sand sliding over stone, it lingered, awaiting new victims.

No wonder these men avoid the ruins, she thought. *They sense what abides there, even though they don't understand.*

But opposing that dread and trepidation, penetrating and stifling it, buoyant anticipation.

Killichaka was here!

Killichaka. So near, it brushed her senses with electric potency. It filled the air with the scent of lightning. Her whole being drifted toward that potent core. Her pacing became a tide, surge and ebb, desire and restraint.

GALEN

There was nothing to do but wait. Galen rested his chin on his arm, atop the stone wall, watching the small group. The men kept to the open, and Galen wondered why they hadn't made camp sheltered among the more intact walls. What was there to fear? What spirits might guard this place?

A sense of silent waiting compelled Galen to hold his breath in anticipation. A herd of small, wispy clouds browsed among the ruins. They drifted along deserted streets, lost wraiths seeking home. Shadows lurked, whispering of treachery and guile.

Nonsense! he chided himself. To counter such musings, he studied the ruins, parsing out their structure and purpose. Here were the miners' housing and buildings of practical use. Beyond, more substantial buildings would be priests' quarters and temples.

How had the ancients ever found this place, he wondered. Surrounded by steep, towering mountains, it was as hidden and inaccessible as Hilton's Shangri-La.

And why did they stay? The expense and labor of maintaining a settlement with no resources of its own didn't make economic sense, no matter how much gold they might have produced. No, the gold would not be enough. *Killichaka, then?* What power did the temple hold?

Even more intriguing, what had caused its end? Some ruins seemed to have simply melted into their stone base; other walls had toppled like children's blocks. To the north, it ceased abruptly. The city wasn't abandoned. It had been destroyed.

"There's one missing," Sesha whispered.

"One what?" Galen asked. He retrieved his thoughts from the distant past, chiding himself for being so easily distracted.

"There were three men when my sisters were captured. That one there and the one that captured Gil. I don't know that one." She pointed out a man slightly shorter than the others, wearing a red and green *chullo* cap and a dark brown poncho.

Galen knew him, though. He'd last seen him standing on the lakeshore watching Galen fight Carlo in the water.

"He's one of Miriam's men. They all are. But you're right. There's one—no two—missing."

Sesha cast him a sidelong glance that asked how he knew, but he pretended not to notice.

So where are Miriam and Vera? he asked of himself. *Are you with us today?* Aloud, he said, "One must be guarding your sisters, but the other could be standing lookout somewhere. Keep your head low." Here where both ruins and rock falls provided plenty of cover, the missing man could be lurking anywhere. The feeling he was being watched fed a growing unease, the very air tainted and vile.

"Can't we do something?" Sesha asked, her voice low.

"There's too many, as you said, and they're armed. We can't risk you or your sisters getting hurt. We'll wait a while longer. If they don't move, we'll go on to Plan B."

"What's Plan B?"

"I don't know yet," he lied. The shadows distracted him, whispers that nudged him toward a dark abyss.

"But it must be nearly two o'clock by now. We're running out of time, and we still haven't found Killichaka." Galen glanced toward the sun to confirm her guess. It blazed so fiercely, Galen wondered if they had miscalculated the day. Surely such brilliance could not be overcome so easily. Yet the moon lingered, patient hunter, hidden in the light of its own prey while the sun drifted closer.

"Here, use this," Sesha said as she dug into the pouch hung from her belt. She handed him a small rectangle of dark green glass, a faceplate from a welders' helmet.

Galen held it up. The glass reduced the sun to a cool, pale green circle. Mention of the eclipse reminded him of their purpose here. "Miriam wants your sisters at the Ritual, too. We can wait until they bring them out, then follow them to the temple, itself."

"And Miriam would have control" Sesha counter argued. "Who knows what she has in mind?"

I know, thought Galen, but it was only half true. Miriam expected to take over the ceremony somehow and turn it to her own purpose, but she'd kept the details to herself. He doubted even Vera knew her true intent. Miriam also planned for him to participate. He had made a vow. *I will stand by you.* The words clogged his throat, making it difficult to breathe.

"Until they make a move, there's not a lot we can do." Galen rummaged through his pack. He handed Sesha a hard roll and a bit of dried fruit.

How much food is left? he wondered. Suddenly, Angoltuto seemed terribly far away. He wondered how much food the *cholos* had. Had they bothered to feed the other sisters? Sesha seemed to be following the same thoughts; she stared at her portion as if she considered rejecting it.

"We have a long way to go yet. We need all the strength we can muster," Galen advised her gently. Survival, he realized, might well depend on at least the two of them keeping strong enough to care for the others.

"So what will you do when this is over?" Galen asked abruptly, seeking to divert further questions and his own dark musings.

"Lena and Evita both have families, and Sumala will continue her work as a doctor. Petra, I think, wants to be a nun. And Maji—" She paused to consider, then continued with a fond laugh. "Maji changes her mind with the seasons. This year, she wants to be an actress." A shadow of pain crossed her face. "They shouldn't have shot her."

"What about you?"

Sesha stared thoughtfully at a rock beside her toe. "Oh, I'll stay with Gil. We were always close, and someone will have to watch out for her while she's watching out for the world. She can be so absent-minded at times."

Galen nodded slowly, picturing Gil gazing out the classroom window. *Are you with us today?*

"What about you? Why did you come here?"

Galen thought he'd come for the eclipse, but looking back, he saw differently.

"Broken dreams," he said at last.

Sesha cocked her head to one side and echoed his words back to him as a question, encouraging him to continue.

"I thought the Depression took everything I valued, but your sister was right. I'd only locked the pieces away. I hoped this trip would make them whole again."

"That could still happen. Gil would not have invited you if she didn't believe you would gain something from this."

Gil or Miriam? Galen still wasn't sure which one sat in his classroom that last day. Nor could Miriam have fooled him for so long if she and Gil weren't somehow the same person.

As for Sesha, he found himself comparing her to the GeM he'd known in the classroom—a woman neither Gil nor Miriam. Sesha was more down to earth. Gil, he'd always thought, was only half grounded in reality, as if she were constantly distracted by other voices, even while listening to his. Sesha, when she turned her gaze upon him, was fully, utterly, *there*.

He shifted his weight to avoid a stone poking his thigh. Sesha leaned against him, turning so that her face was mere inches from his.

"Can't we get closer?" she asked. Her breath warmed his cheek.

Galen thought that any closer would require a marriage license. But when Sesha used his shoulder to push herself up to peer over the broken wall, he realized she was referring to the camp below.

"Miriam might sense our presence here," he noted. "She seems to have that ability. I would prefer she continue to believe that I'm dead—that we both are."

"But we could search the ruins."

Galen considered the maze of streets and rooms. "The more we move around, the greater our chances of getting caught. Give me time. This plan will work."

Sesha snuggled down against him once more. "I hope you don't think I'm being forward. Trapped in that chamber, what I wanted most was someone to hold me. I don't ever want to be that alone again."

She shivered, though in this shelter they were protected from the wind. Galen shifted in turn to bring his arm around her. He closed his eyes, trying to imagine what it must have been like, trapped, utterly helpless and alone. She had courage, this one. He wondered if, when the time came, he would be able to match it. If events turned, could he betray it?

That idea, so unbidden and spontaneous, startled his thoughts toward Miriam once more. In the dark behind his eyelids, she beckoned to him, and the serpent began again to gnaw at his gut. How could he fight a woman he had almost made love to? What of his vow? And the bloody sacrifice in Cerro de Pasco— that, too, bound him to her. How was he to escape whatever shackles that work of evil forced upon his will?

Questions crowded around him like children begging for handouts. And he had nothing to give them.

SESHA

He's hiding something.

That was Sesha's thought as she listened to Galen. She studied his face, as he must've watched hers the night before.

His own ordeal seemed to have hollowed him out and drained him. His skin held little color beneath the dry, ruddy hues of too much sun and wind. His eyes were gentle, but they sheltered secrets and revealed a tortured heart. Darkness settled upon him, like the shadow of some unseen entity.

He's not bad looking, though.

The thought startled her. He was, after all, Gil's professor and her chosen Guardian. Gil had mentioned him in her letters, though their relationship seemed purely academic. Gil had no interest in marriage; such a commitment would only inhibit her work. What possibilities did that open?

Sesha, what are you thinking? she asked of herself.

She held back a deep urge to sigh, though the feeling welled up within her, a balloon inflating in her chest. Carefully, she let the sigh escape in a long and slow breath. She didn't want to attract any questions right now, especially those she was reluctant to answer, even for herself.

Such matters would simply have to wait. Tomorrow, after the eclipse, there would be time to sort things out. Tomorrow, and all the tomorrows after that.

GALEN

Galen was aware of how Sesha watched him. He turned to the wall and rested his chin on his fist as he studied the layout of the ruins.

"So if this isn't Killichaka, where would it be?"

"Gil gave you a map, didn't she? Mine was lost." She shuddered, adding, "In the lake."

Guilt twisted in Galen's gut. "I gave it to Miriam," he admitted.

"You *what?*" she responded, but at least had the presence of mind to keep the exclamation to a fierce whisper.

"Miriam had men following you. I thought if she had the map, she would leave you alone." He glanced at the camp below, and his fist closed around a small rock. "How was I supposed to know she'd pull this? No one told me anything." The serpent in his gut fed on his anger. *You belong to me.*

"But you can find it, right?" he asked.

Sesha offered a shrug, then a reluctant nod. She picked up a stone and scratched at the stone floor. "These lines are the ruins here. This loop must be that ridge." She closed her eyes for a moment, consulting memory, then marked a series of tight, nested V's. "This could be a gorge or canyon, but there must be a way across, here." She scratched a line across. "Here's the temple." A half circle with a starburst design at its heart.

"Is that the only way?"

Sesha pursed her lips, studying her map, then the landscape beyond. "That gap in the ridge." She pointed across the ruins to a narrow gorge cleaving the steep arête. "You might be able to climb through there."

Why does everything have to be up? Galen thought.

Before she could say more, voices raised in the camp below caught their attention. Galen peered over the wall.

The first *cholo* had returned. He gave orders to the others, then took Gil by the arm and pushed her toward the ruined city. Petra and Sumala tried to stop him and were shoved aside. Galen shifted, ready to move but uncertain which direction to take. He felt uneasy with this turn of events; his plans didn't cover this separation.

Gil glanced back over her shoulder once, staring directly at their hiding place as if she knew exactly where Galen was. *Free my sisters,* her expression demanded. *Take care of Sesha.*

But what about you? Where is he taking you? Galen silently responded.

"What do we do now?" Sesha asked, echoing his own thoughts. Galen pursed his lips as he considered his options.

"You follow Gil. I'll find the others."

"But I want to go with you; I *need* to. They're *my* sisters!"

It's my fault they were captured in the first place.

She didn't say it out loud, but Galen could read the words clearly in her eyes. He set his hands upon her shoulders.

"I understand that, believe me I do. But one of us has to stay with Gil. I can't be in two places at once. Understand?"

Gil will protect you, he thought, but didn't speak of his concerns. Haunted by the images of his dream, he was afraid of what might happen if he and Sesha remained together. He didn't want to see the hurt in those dark eyes should he betray her.

Sesha nodded reluctantly, almost absently, and Galen wondered if she had really heard him.

"But how will you set them free?"

Galen stared down at the horsemen, wondering how they would react to his presence. Would they accept him in the group? Had Miriam given them instructions?

"I have something in mind," he answered cryptically. Sesha wouldn't like what he was thinking; she wouldn't understand. He wasn't sure he did, himself. He felt manipulated, as if someone tugged his thoughts in certain directions and barred them from other ways. He rubbed at the mark on his chest.

"Do you trust me?"

No, was the answer he read first in her eyes, but she swallowed that thought and nodded.

"This will work out," he told her. "You have to believe that."
Believe it for both of us.

Sesha nodded and reluctantly gathered her pack. She was about to climb over the low side wall when more commotion erupted from below. Petra was yelling at the *cholos* in Spanish.

"She's asking where her sisters are," Sesha translated. Petra had evidently decided to force their hand. When the men refused to respond, she started out as if she would find them on her own. Only the *click* of a revolver's hammer stopped her. She glared at the man who would dare to threaten her so.

"*¡Llévenme a mis hermanas!*" Petra demanded.

Again, the men argued, but finally, one of them shrugged and waved his rifle toward the ruins on the far side of the valley. Sumala grabbed up her pack and scurried to catch up.

"Watch them, Sesha! We have to see where they go."

GIL

When the man touched her arm, Gil had flinched as if burned. *This is not the way,* she thought as he pulled her toward the main body of the ruins. Her sisters were the other way, back in the mines by the cliff. She knew exactly where, their essence burning like a beacon. Lena, Evita, and Maji. She dared to glance back where she sensed Galen and Sesha hiding, willing them to stay and find the others.

A broken gateway guarded the entrance to a broad avenue, walled on both sides. Her escort marched her down the precise middle, glancing to left and right, a sweaty, clenched grip on his rifle.

This had been a privileged route, restricted to a select few. She sensed the faint vibrations of their steps in the stone beneath her feet, escorting her in procession. Priests and acolytes, she decided, those who served Killichaka. She imagined statues and banners, gold from the mines flashing in the sun, robes of white decorated with gold and bright feathers.

Yes, this leads to Killichaka, and with that thought, a tremor of anticipation and joy charged her nerves. Her steps hastened, but the man's grip on her arm held her to a slower pace.

Her confidence waned, though, as they neared the end of the

avenue. Between the promenade and the ridge, a rock fall piled up against a listing pillar, across the avenue into a steep defile. Gil gave it little notice except that she had to pick her way across the stones. Beyond, a hollow shadow pierced the ridge. The ever-present wind sounded a low moan as it passed across the dark tunnel entrance.

Gil hesitated, glancing at the peaks surrounding them. Like rumpled sheets, glaciers rested in their beds, slumbering threats of instant death should even a small part of them tumble down the steep valleys. Her escort pushed her forward, none too gently.

Supay's dark laughter hung in the air like a persistent echo. It waited, one magnetic pole luring another. In spite of Killichaka's lure, she feared to enter that dark passage, to face the shadows lurking there.

"I can't go in there," she told her captor. "This is a place of death. It waits there to steal your soul." She let a shiver shimmy across her shoulders.

"It's dangerous to scare the locals. They might blame us for the sun disappearing when the eclipse begins."

Gil started at the familiar voice. A dark-clad figure stepped out of the tunnel's shadow carrying a guttering torch.

"Aunt Vera!"

"It's really not so bad," Vera said in greeting, the tight line of her lips neither a frown nor a smile. "Come with me, child." She turned to Gil's escort. "Go fetch the other women and bring them here. I will be back shortly." He nodded sullenly and shoved Gil forward. Vera took hold of her by the arm, her grip like a talon's, firm and sharp. Gil went with her because there was nowhere else to go.

As she entered the passage, shadow touched Gil like glacial ice. A persistent murmur, more felt than heard, circled her in a vertiginous swarm. Disoriented, she reached out for support and touched the stone of the entrance. The rock vibrated like the burr of an electric current.

She stepped across the threshold, certain she could hear Supay laughing.

GALEN

"Someone's coming," Sesha whispered, but Galen ignored

her as he watched the women enter the labyrinth of ruined walls.

"Follow Gil," he commanded, but kept his attention on the two women and their escort. "I have to see where he takes Petra and Sumala." This was the critical point in his plan. He was counting on the *cholos* leading him to the other sisters. This had to work; it simply *had* to. The alternative was too risky. *But what about Gil?*

"I can't," Sesha replied in an emphatic whisper. "He's headed this way."

"Who? Where?" Galen asked, though he dared not shift his gaze from his target.

"Over there."

"*Watch* Gil, then." A boulder now blocked his view, so he edged over the broken corner of the wall. Intent only on the women threading their way between tumbled walls, he counted on the angle of the wall to keep him hidden from those below. On the far side of the valley, the ruins became a warren of structures, most roofless but more or less intact. Eventually, they merged with the folds of the rugged cliffs. The dark holes of mine adits pocked the ridge walls.

"He's getting closer."

Galen risked a quick glance where Sesha indicated. One of the men was indeed coming up the hill.

"What's he doing?"

At any moment, the man might look up and spot Galen, exposed as he was outside the shelter of the walls. But Galen had to see where they took Petra and Sumala. If he lost sight of them now, they might disappear with the others.

"Keep an eye on him," he whispered to Sesha. He turned his attention back to the ruins again, and for a moment could not find the sisters. He feared he'd lost them, but they emerged from behind a wall, Sumala's dark blue coat distinctive against the gray and reddish brown rock.

"He's still coming," Sesha reported.

"Shh!" He had to know exactly where they were holding the sisters. Nothing else mattered.

"Galen!" A desperate whisper.

"I know!"

Which one? Which room held the missing sisters? It wouldn't do to affect a rescue, only to burst into an empty room. There wasn't time to search blindly. *And where are they taking Gil?*

Sesha pulled him down just as the procession turned a corner. He pushed her away and popped back up, but the two sisters were out of sight. *Where? Where!*

Sesha's elbow jabbed into his ribs, inadvertently hitting the half-healed knife wound. He almost cried out at the unexpected pain. Before he could otherwise react, though, Sesha reached across the wall to grasp his chin and force his gaze down the near slope.

The man was closer than Galen had expected—less than twenty feet away. Galen recognized him—one of the horsemen he'd last seen watching from the lakeshore as he'd fought with Carlo. The man's intention was plain as one hand fumbled at the front of his pants. If he looked up instead of at his feet, he would surely see them.

Sesha, at least, was still concealed inside the ruin. Galen pushed her head down behind the wall, but he dared not follow after. Movement would certainly attract the *cholo*'s attention.

The man finished up his business and refastened his pants. Galen hoped he would return to the camp, but instead, he sat down and took a long swig from a bottle of pisco. His back was to them now, but he was still too close.

"Now what?" Sesha whispered, her voice scarcely a breath above the wind.

A slow, deep anger bled an icy current down his spine. He'd had enough of being manipulated, of being played for the fool. He was tired of being cautious, of worrying over consequences and fearing failure. It was time to take action. "Wait here," he answered, barely mouthing the words. "And I mean *wait!*"

With one last gesture for silence, he leaned toward the shelter of a block of stone jutting out of the steep hillside. Never taking his eyes off the man, watching for the slightest wary twitch, he slid behind the rock.

There were no dried leaves to crunch or twigs to worry about snapping, but as he moved toward the next boulder, Galen's foot kicked over a stone. He froze, glancing sideways at his target.

The man set down his flask and began to turn.

Galen charged.

The *cholo* reacted faster than Galen anticipated. Before Galen could close half the distance between them, he was staring into the bore of the man's pistol. He skidded to a half-crouched stop.

Now what? Carlo's knife had been challenge enough. What was he supposed to do against a gun? He straightened to full height, a good eight inches taller than the other man.

"*Ola, José.*" Galen forced a wide grin. "It was José, wasn't it?" Probably not, but it sounded good. He grinned as if greeting an old friend on the campus quad. "Hey, remember me?"

José stared wide-eyed and made a frantic sign of the cross, obviously surprised to see him alive.

"*¡Almas!*" José cried out, and something about *muerto*. He backed away.

"*No muerto,*" Galen said with a satisfied grin. "I'm not a ghost." He couldn't help but feel a certain triumph in this man's panic. Galen stepped downhill to angle the man away from Sesha's hiding place.

Stay hidden, he thought, as if Sesha could hear him. Even as he thought it, though, Sesha swung a leg over the low wall, stone in hand.

No!

He couldn't help but compare this to his fight with Carlo. The memory made him queasy. Had Miriam succeeded, perhaps the fight could have been avoided and Carlo would still be alive.

He couldn't let this one end the same way. He wanted no more blood on his hands. He kept his gaze intently upon José's face as Sesha advanced.

Look at me, he wanted to scream, not daring to watch Sesha's progress, lest his glance give her away, as it had Miriam.

"Uh, a fine day for an eclipse, don't you think?" *Don't look behind you; look only at me!* Even as a teacher, he had trouble holding his students' attention. How could he do that here and now, when he couldn't even speak the man's language? His gaze flicked inevitably to the pistol aimed at his chest, eyeing the open bore as a bird might a snake's eye. His confidence faltered. "Can't you point that somewhere else?"

The man only grinned. "*No inglés, gringo,*" he said, mocking Galen's feeble Spanish. He waved the pistol casually.

I should watch his eyes. But Galen's gaze remained locked on the man's finger curled around the trigger. If he saw that finger twitch, could he duck in time, he wondered with a touch of manic absurdity. How much time between the pulling of the trigger and the bullet hitting its target?

José motioned down the slope. "*¡Allá!*" He cocked the hammer.

"I don't think so," Galen responded. His gaze involuntarily clicked to José's right, and the man began to turn. Too late, though.

Sesha closed the gap between them and brought the stone down hard on the man's head.

As José crumpled to the ground, Galen made a grab for the pistol. It struck a rock and went off, the sound cracking like thunder in his ears.

"Well, they'll know we're here now," Galen said. He and Sesha each grabbed an arm and dragged their prisoner over the wall and into their shelter. Galen glanced down slope. The other men gathered at the campfire, rifles and guns held ready, momentarily confused by the echo caroming from peak to peak.

"Is he alive?" Galen asked.

"I think so." Sesha laughed, a nervous, light sound. "Oh, you can't imagine how much I've been aching to hit someone."

"You could've gotten us both killed!"

Sesha opened her mouth to reply, then pointed wide-eyed at his chest, her mouth forming a babble of unspoken words. Galen glanced down. The fabric of his coat was slashed across its front. Instinctively, he pressed a hand to his chest, even as he realized he felt neither pain nor blood. The bullet had only grazed his coat. A slightly different angle and—

Suddenly dizzy, his knees melted beneath him, and he sat down, hard.

"They're coming," Sesha reported, peeking over the wall.

Frantic whispers accented quick movements.

"Tie him up. No, wait. Give me his poncho."

Sesha tied the man's hands with his own rope belt.

"Gag him."

"Get his gun."

"Gun?" Galen wrestled into José's poncho, grimacing at the sour smell and the itchy, crawly feeling that he wasn't alone in the garment. He took the man's hat, too. The tall, pointed *chullo*, earflaps curling away from his cheeks, felt silly. Sesha hiccoughed as if trying not to giggle.

"We could pick them off, one by one," suggested Sesha.

Galen took another peek over the wall and shook his head.

"Too many." He peered at Sesha. "Could you really do that?"

Ruefully, she shook her head. "No. I guess not. What do we do then?" She handed him the gun, but he set it aside to delay handling it. The shadows stirred, and the serpent hissed a suggestion.

What about Gil? The thought nagged at him as he hastily revised his plans. His plans or Miriam's? he wondered.

"I'll lure them away, then you follow after Gil. They're probably taking her to the temple."

Sesha glared at him stubbornly. "I want to go with you."

"Find Gil and the temple," he repeated sternly. "Don't do anything; just watch. *Just watch.* Understand? I'll meet you there."

"But my sisters—"

"I'll bring them." *To whose end?*

"Did you see where they are?"

"I saw enough," he lied. In truth, he'd missed the last crucial moments. But he knew where to start looking, and they had been so close to the edge of the ruins, there weren't many options left—unless they had gone up the side canyon. He refused to consider that possibility. Sesha appeared dubious.

He reached out to squeeze her hand, a gesture of assurance, a means of getting her attention.

"Sesha, you have to trust me. No matter what I do, trust me. This will work. I promise."

It has to work. Something *has to go right.*

There was no more time to argue. Already, two men were climbing the slope in their general direction; he had to act before they came any closer.

If this doesn't work, he wondered, *how many can I shoot before they kill me?* He had no delusions about his marksmanship. He bit at his lower lip in consternation. This *had* to work; he simply had no other options.

Sesha opened her mouth to protest. Galen leaned forward and kissed her. Grabbing the pistol, he turned from her before she could react. Before she could tell him no, and before his own courage could fail him. The image of her face, eyes wide with surprise, mouth a small, puckered "*oh!*" stayed with him as he slipped over the side wall.

A dozen feet from Sesha's refuge, he scooped up José's bottle of pisco. He glanced toward where Sesha hid. *Just watch,* he'd told her, and he prayed that this time, she would obey. His chest felt tight. He feared a return of the edema before he realized he was simply holding his breath. Slowly, he exhaled.

Then he stood and waved the bottle over his head, hailing the men below.

"Hey, guys! Remember me?"

SESHA

Just watch, Galen had told Sesha. And then he'd kissed her. That action had been so abrupt, she'd barely reacted. *Why didn't I say something?* she berated herself. *Why didn't I kiss him back!*

Just watch. She jerked her attention back to the present. She stared in stunned silence as he abruptly stood and waved at the three men below. She thought he was going to pretend to be José—surrounded by boulders that concealed his height, with his face obscured in shadow, he could pull it off as long as no one came too close. But instead, he made no effort to disguise his identity. These were Miriam's men. Just what was he up to? What was his connection with Miriam?

Petra had questioned his loyalty; something must've justified such suspicion. Galen's telling of his own story had left a hollow feeling in the pit of her stomach, as if he'd omitted important details. Something garnered her distrust, in spite of the attraction she felt. She could see his face, framed by José's cap. A dark storm shadowed his eyes, masking whatever secrets lurked there. Even without Gil's talents, Sesha could see how warring elements battled for Galen's loyalty. In spite of his spoken convictions, she was not so sure which way he might eventually turn. She had the impression he didn't know, himself, or that some external power might force his hand, regardless of his own intentions.

You have to trust me. His words echoed in her thoughts.

"I wish I could," she muttered to herself. Her fingers twitched nervously around the stone she held as she crouched at the corner of the wall. It wasn't much of a weapon, and she wasn't sure just who would be her target. If Galen did intend to betray her and her sisters, she had no intention of letting him get away without at least an expression of her anger.

The closest of the men shouted a question.

Galen responded with a phrase he must've picked up from

the *cholos*. He didn't seem the type to use such vulgar language, and Sesha wondered if he actually understood what he was saying.

The man with the rifle repeated his question, and Sesha realized Galen probably had no idea what the man was asking.

This time, Galen dismissed the question with a shrug. "Didn't Miriam tell you I was coming?" He attempted to repeat the question in fractured Spanish, but gave up midway. The men continued to loiter, faces dark with suspicion and mistrust. One of them asked Galen why he was wearing José's poncho. Sesha shifted forward, wanting to translate the question for him, but he seemed to have figured it out for himself. He pointed toward the ruin— toward her—and waved the pistol in the air.

"*Ya-no-lo-ne'sita. ¿Problemo?*"

He ran the words together as if trying to mimic something he'd heard, and then said something else. The wind stole his words away. She wondered if he had intended for her not to hear. He held up the bottle of pisco and invited the others to join him. Sesha pressed back into her corner as if she could become part of the stone wall and closed her eyes as if that would make her invisible. Her heartbeat thudded in her ears as her reality tilted and veered into new directions. *Galen, what are you up to?*

Sesha couldn't see the men below, nor could she hear their words. *What's happening?* She clutched her stone harder and waited, barely daring to breathe, expecting one or more of the men to come around the corner at any moment. When nothing happened and she could bear to wait no longer, she moved to peek over the wall. The men still waited, but they had lowered their rifles and holstered their pistols. Galen, himself, let out a long sigh; Sesha could see the collapse of his shoulders, even from here, as he glanced her way. He passed her a surreptitious thumb's up, then started down the hillside.

Sesha returned the gesture hesitantly, still shaken by the incident and feeling uncertain of his motives. She watched Galen saunter down the hill. He offered the bottle of pisco, and they passed it around. When it came back to him, he waved it off. The man holding the bottle laughed, only too glad to drink Galen's share. Galen shrugged. He glanced toward her hiding place and muttered something lost to distance and the wind. Sesha caught only the word *chúkara*—wild place—as if warning them away. Perhaps he hadn't betrayed her after all.

The others laughed like men made nervous about something they pretended not to believe. They returned to whatever tasks Galen had interrupted. Galen watched them, then set off for the far side of the valley. *Follow Gil*, his final glance told her.

She was tempted to follow Galen. She wanted nothing more than to see her sisters again, to hug them all, and all at once.

Sesha shook her head. Soon enough, she promised herself. For now, it was, as Galen had convinced her, more important to follow Gil. She checked José's bonds to make sure that if he came to, he could not escape and warn the others. With a wary glance at the men loitering below, she slung her pack over her shoulder and left the safety of the ruin.

She couldn't walk across the valley, accepted but ignored as Galen now did, nor could she follow down that broad, walled avenue—she would be too exposed and vulnerable. Instead, she made her way across the moraine, then down to the main body of the ruins. She marked out a route to the far side of the city. From there, she could intersect Gil's path.

The need for stealth hampered her progress. The men were edgy and kept glancing up. It took longer than she'd planned to reach the more substantial walls and structures where she could walk unimpeded and unseen.

She soon regretted her choice, though. The pattern of the streets seemed designed to frustrate her. Only the peaks towering overhead kept her from getting hopelessly disoriented. She paused for a drink of water and glanced sideways at the sun's relentless progress. *Slow down*, she told that insentient orb. *You don't have to be in such a hurry.*

How far ahead was Gil? Fifteen, twenty minutes, by now? Sesha trotted down an alley. Once she was through this maze, she thought she could make faster progress. It couldn't be much farther, because steep cliffs loomed not far ahead. Just past this last building, she thought, for she saw no more walls beyond it. She reached the corner and almost stepped into empty air.

Sesha lurched back and froze, trembling and dizzy. Inches beyond her toes, the valley floor simply ceased. A gulf of air and cloud severed the far mountains from the valley.

Memory replayed the sickening feel of the ground falling from beneath her—her foot slipping, hands scratching at bare rock. The frantic, futile scramble for support that wasn't there.

The old juniper's branch reaching out. The blue eye of the lake opening through the mist. Her mouth went dry, her hands sweaty. She expected the ground to give way beneath her now, plunging her a thousand feet and more.

If I fall here, there's nothing and no one to catch me. No tree, no sister. No lake. Dizzying vertigo swept around her, nudging her toward gravity's embrace. She pressed against the solid stone of the ruined wall, her fingers scraping at it as if gouging soft clay. Eyes shut tight, she waited.

GIL

Gil felt loathe to let the dark touch her. Darkness was Supay's domain, and the very air seemed thick with its presence. The torch created an ephemeral bubble, a haven of light, but it also cast fitful shadows dancing like tortured souls.

"Aunt Vera, where are you taking me?" she asked, using her voice to keep the murmurs at bay. Was there an end to this passage, or did it merely tunnel into the mountain?

"To your goal, child. Your precious Killichaka."

"What about my sisters? What have you done with them?"

"They're safe. They'll be joining you soon."

"Why, Aunt Vera? Why are you here?"

"It's necessary," was all Vera would say, with a bluntness that discouraged further discussion.

Gil persisted. "Why are you doing this?"

Vera's tight, persimmon frown was so familiar, Gil knew it even in this dim light. "You'll find out soon enough," was all she would say.

Time ceased. Minutes and eons passed before a smudge of light appeared ahead. Gil hurried her steps, wondering if she could hold her breath until the end of the passage.

Emerging into daylight, she released her pent-up breath and staggered to a low boulder where she sat. When her trembling had shaken off Supay's dusty touch and her lungs felt clear of his shadow, when she had stopped blinking and tearing at the sudden, harsh light, she looked up to see where the passage had brought her.

The valley spilled into a deeper quebrada in a series of scooped out cirques. A fissure, perhaps twenty feet wide, split the valley's rim. Gil thought the path would skirt the crevice, but instead it descended in a series of steep, carved steps to its brink. Far, far below, through layers of depthless blue shadow, the froth of a tumbling stream stitched a white scar. A massive column of rock spanned the gap. Whether placed there by nature or the work of men, Gil couldn't tell. Its felling had caused it to crack, but it held its place, much like a keystone arch. The top of the span, roughly five feet wide, had been planed flat and polished.

Killichaka was close now. Ever so close. Its presence beat like a warm heart in the cold stone of this mountain. The trill of anticipation wound to a high-pitched humming. As she stepped onto the span, Vera called her name. Gil paused to look back. The older woman's mouth worked its way around words that were not easy to release.

"I truly did love your mother," she confessed. "More than the others and in spite of what happened between us. I couldn't let my sisters throw away her daughter—either one of them. They were wrong. But I never intended for Miriam to be tainted by my own bitterness. Now it's grown to surpass my own." She paused. "I'm sorry, Gilaishling, that this has to happen."

Gil stared at her aunt, uncertain how to respond. Was Vera asking for understanding? Forgiveness? Or was this a warning?

"Go on, now. It's not far," Vera ordered abruptly, nodding beyond the span at Gil's feet. Gil needed no urging. Killichaka's summons rang as sharp as crystal, and Gil could no more ignore it than she could cease to breathe.

She crossed the narrow span warily, testing its stability. The stone shuddered beneath her weight. It would not take much to dislodge it. The tremor she had felt earlier came to mind. She vanquished the thought lest it form reality and concentrated on keeping her step light, ignoring the hazy *nothing* beyond.

Beyond the chasm, the path skirted the brink of the valley to where the final cirque, a bowl halved by the canyon beyond.

Like a hand cupped to hold a brilliant, liquid sapphire, the cirque sheltered an oval-shaped tarn. The lake trembled at the edge as if the slightest disturbance might pour it out to tumble down the sheer, thousand foot drop. Gil found herself holding her breath lest even that slight vapor might disturb the delicate balance.

This is the place, she thought, unwilling to give voice and break the spell of absolute silence. *This is Killichaka.*

She circled the tarn eagerly. What did she expect? Stone ruins, a pyramid? She hadn't really given it much thought. What vague images she had imagined seemed impossible in this place of utter isolation.

Contrary to every expectation, what she found was a deep, oval-shaped grotto encrusted with crystals, some as thick as tree stumps. An immense geode, halved by the ancient glacier, it was roughly fifteen feet wide and seven feet tall at the opening, and perhaps eight feet deep. The ruins of three buildings flanked the grotto, and walls, reduced by time to mere stubble, crossed the basin.

Shadow still draped the opening, though sunlight grazed its edge. Spirits lingered in its hidden corners, whispering their ancient songs. The crystals vibrated with bright scintilla, power stored and awaiting release.

Forgetting Miriam and Galen and her sisters and even the impending eclipse, and ignoring Vera standing at the cirque's edge, Gil approached. At the grotto's heart, a half dozen quartz crystals formed a gigantic fan set in a stone base covered in gold that caught the lowering sun's light and splashed it upon the crystals. By design or nature, a hollow formed a narrow bench, as much throne as altar. It vibrated with power, more felt than heard.

The slender spears—as much as five feet long—were as clear and pure as starlight. Fine growth lines within the crystals' matrix seemed a sort of script, telling a story she could not decipher. The gold, poured molten over the base, spilled down the sides to form an intricate web, like archaic runes softened by time.*Out of focus,* Gil thought, *like the futures I see.*

Here Gil would sit when moon claimed dominion over sun. She would accept its power. What future would she weave? What might Miriam spin if she succeeded in Gil's stead? A shudder spawned deep within her soul broke the spell of the moment.

That shattering revealed a knot of *wrong* marring the crystalline perfection. A reddish-brown stain defiled the bench and the far right crystal.

"No!" Gil gasped, horrified by the implication. This had been a place of healing, not sacrifice. No matter how primitive, the ancients would not have desecrated this delicate beauty with bloody rites. Shivering, she rubbed her arms, but the chill came from within.

A whisper of hope and longing brushed Gil's thoughts—the entombed priestess from Sesha's cave. She remained, abandoned and trapped by her own blood. This was the tragedy told in the paintings in Sesha's cave, the tale of betrayal and blood. A zephyr sang of lost destiny, betrayed dreams.

Gil set her hand upon the bench. "I am here," she whispered, seeking permission to share in the honor of the coming event.

"I wait," answered an echo. *Si*. Not word but image—the moon at the edge of the lake, its reflection bridging the water.

The power of this place had been corrupted, turned from its purpose. Supay transposed the ancient songs to a dark and sinister key. It circled Gil and whispered of lies and treachery. Had she been lured to this place to fulfill the Vision rather than destroy it? Gil shivered at the portent of failure, and despair threatened to overwhelm her.

The whisper that was Si sang counterpoint. Sunlight touched the first of the crystals at the edge of the geode. The light shattered, casting rainbow shards at her feet. Hope burst in their pure, spectral colors. She turned west, toward the sun nearing its destiny at the bottom of the sky. A path of dazzling sparkles danced upon the small lake. Eyes closed, Gil raised her arms to that blessing.

A footstep scraped the stone behind her, a stone shifted, and the unmistakable tang of the Other drifted through the air. Gil's heart thumped against her ribs. She turned, expecting Vera. Instead, her own image stepped from the ruins to the left of the geode.

"Happy Birthday, Sister," said a voice—her voice.

GALEN

This has to be the place.

Galen wandered down a narrow alley between partially tumbled walls of stone, still amazed that Miriam's men had accepted him so easily. Had Miriam been so sure of his death that she hadn't bothered to give them instructions if he should show up? Or was this part of her trap? Once again, he felt himself sliding toward a shadowed but inevitable fate.

The quiet of the ruins was unnerving. Only the wind and the shadows moved, brushing across barren stones, sweeping aside the whispers of ghosts and spirits. His ears kept seeking voices—men shouting orders or calling to friends, laughter. Music and singing. Children? No. Children had never lived here. These were barracks for miners and other workers, quarters for priests and supplicants, and storehouses.

Then why did he hear the voice of a child and the shrill breath of a flute? Why did he catch flickers of motion at the edge of his vision? He wanted something to move, to live. But the city was dead, long dead. *So why do I feel watched?*

Ghosts? Galen didn't believe in ghosts, only memories. His brother Edward. Eisabel. Blood on the sidewalk; bloody handprint on his chest. Carlo's blood in the water. Memories were worse than ghosts, because they abided in hidden chambers of the mind. Galen shivered beneath José's warm poncho and moved on.

His hand gripped José's pistol so tight, he could feel every scratch and nick on the worn grip. He'd never held a gun before, and he didn't like the way it fit his grasp so naturally or the way his finger curled around the trigger like an embrace.

This had to be where the sisters were, or was it farther on? Up close, perspective shifted. Walls that from the overlook had appeared only a few feet high were well over his head. Distinctive stones he'd marked as guideposts now appeared quite common.

Couldn't Petra have left a trail of breadcrumbs? he thought, and thinking that, began to look for some sign of her passage. There was no soil here to leave footprints, only stone in varying degrees of decay. Here, in a patch of gravel, he spotted a depression that might be a bootprint, and there, an overturned stone, its fresh face contrasting with the darker, weathered rock.

Again, a flicker of movement caught his attention as he approached an intersection. Galen glanced to the side but saw nothing. *It's this cap,* he decided. The earflaps cut off his vision like blinders on a horse. He considered taking it off; the wide earflaps and tall, curved point felt ridiculous anyway. But it kept his ears and head warm. He was reluctant to give that up, no matter what crawled among the fibers.

What had he seen? A face? A child?

Eisabel?

Galen stopped abruptly, and in doing so, avoided the man crossing his path. Galen froze, holding his breath as the other hurried past the corner, looking neither right nor left. *Haunted by his own ghosts?*

This was not the one he'd seen herding Sumala and Petra. Galen guessed he'd been guarding the other sisters. He waited until the man had rounded another corner and was safely out of sight.

He was almost out of the ruins. They ended at the base of the ridge. A mile up the canyon, the broad skirt of a glacier glared bright in the sun. The light pierced Galen's eyes in flaming splinters. He lowered his gaze to the stones at his feet, but flashes of brilliant purple and blue taunted him, disappearing whenever he shifted his focus upon them.

Coming around the end of a wall, Galen almost walked into the other *cholo*. Galen jerked back, pressing flat against the rough stone. He held his hand against his chest as if that would calm his thunderous, aching heartbeat.

When nothing happened, he leaned sideways to peer around the corner. The man was piling stones in a gap in the opposite wall. His rifle leaned against the wall an arm's length away. The structure merged into the cliff wall, with only a narrow gap at the top. This had to be where the sisters were imprisoned, and now Sumala and Petra had joined them.

How was he going to get them out?

The guard was there, of course, to keep the women from escaping; he wouldn't be expecting a rescue attempt. That gave Galen a small advantage. However, the man was José's buddy, the second man watching from the lakeshore. He knew Galen was responsible for Carlo's death and had witnessed Miriam abandon him. The ploy he had used on the hillside would not work here.

Wearing José's poncho and hat, how close could he get before this man realized he was not? He glanced down at his feet, and never had they seemed so far away. He was at least a head taller than the tallest of the horsemen, and José had been even shorter. He had no doubt about the outcome of a face-to-face confrontation, nor did he want to risk more gunfire.

Galen retreated to a broken section of the wall and clambered to its top to consider the problem from a better angle. The stone wall was almost two feet wide, and Galen was able to creep along it until he was positioned directly over the guard and opposite the sisters' prison. *Now what?* he wondered. *Tom Mix, you're not.*

This is crazy. Tom Mix was a movie actor; his stunts were carefully set up and rehearsed. The bad guy stuck to the script. Even as Galen crouched at the edge of the wall, he kept telling himself it wouldn't work.

But he leaped anyway. The landing was awkward, but he managed to take the guard down with him, and that was all that mattered. Before the man could roll over, Galen had grabbed his rifle and stood over him, feeling a little like Gary Cooper. He'd never pointed a weapon at another human being, but he wasn't about to let this man know that.

Galen motioned toward the partially blocked doorway. "In there."

His prisoner shrugged indifferently and bent to pull away the stones he had piled up until he could step through the narrow gap. As Galen followed, he heard a series of grunts, a groan, then a heavy thud.

"Anybody home?" he called out. Before his eyes could adjust to the dusty murk, he was grabbed and pushed. Something hit him across the shoulders, and he sank to his knees. The rifle was snatched from his hands, and his arms were pinned behind him.

"Hey!" he called out. "I'm on your side!"

"Galen? Is that you?"

"Of course it is, Petra! How many of these *cholos* speak English?"

Petra hesitated before she commanded, "Release him." The hold on him slackened. He shrugged it off and stood, pulling off his hat and tossing it aside. Scratching his scalp, he blinked to adjust to the low light slanting through the narrow gap between the wall and the rock roof. Petra stood imperiously before him as if she might still question his identity—and his loyalty. The guard was curled at Galen's feet like a rumpled pile of laundry. Two women, both strangers, moved into sight on either side of him. One was fair and blonde, stoutly built, the other black-haired and olive skinned, but both were intangibly and undeniably *Orlov*.

Petra leaned to the side to peer past him. "Where's Sesha?"

"I sent her to follow Gil. What about Maji?"

"She's over here," Sumala announced from the shadows. "Her wound isn't serious. She'll be all right." She stood, swiping her hands across her pants. "I hope we don't have to hike very far, though," she added, helping another woman to her feet.

"I'm Maji," this last Orlov said. A fresh, white bandage

showed through a wide slash in the left leg of her pants. She was short and round-faced, her hair dark and curly. She offered a smile that quickly passed to a grimace when she put weight on her injured leg.

"Call me Galen," he said quickly, before anyone could name him otherwise. "Can you walk?"

"Of course," Maji answered, though she winced as she stepped forward. "Where's Gil? She said she'd be back for us."

For a moment, Galen was confused. "Not Gil," he finally said. "That was Miriam—Gemella." He glared at Petra, wondering why she hadn't explained.

"I was just getting to that," she said.

Galen eyed his new charges. They were all suffering from exposure and hunger, much as Sesha had been, but at least they hadn't been alone.

"Let's get out of here." He grabbed the rifle from the woman on his right. "You help your sister. You," he said, turning now to the woman on his left, "Tie up our friend here." He nudged the unconscious guard with his foot, then gestured with the rifle toward the back of the chamber.

"I don't suppose that leads anywhere."

"It once was a mine," one of the women responded. "But the ceiling collapsed about twenty feet back."

"Too bad. I was hoping for a short cut."

While they gathered their belongings, Galen cleared the rest of the stones from the entrance. Soon they all stood in the open, the women shading their eyes from the sun after so many days confined to darkness. Petra started back toward the ruins.

"You'll never get past the men at the camp," Galen warned.

"You did," she responded with a degree of suspicion.

"I have a certain advantage."

Now is the time, the shadows whispered. He shook the words from his mind, but his hand shifted its grip on the rifle ever so slightly. *Not yet.*

"But there's no other way," Petra observed.

Galen studied the cliff rising above them.

"There's a break in the ridge up there. Sesha thought we could get through there and come down the other side." He gestured with the rifle. "That way."

"We've wasted enough time already with your dubious

plans."

Galen stared down Petra's doubt while the shadows taunted him and the wind nudged his back. *Take them now.* "I'm taking charge," he stated and hefted the rifle as a subtle warning, then swung it around like a signpost toward the canyon. "We'll go this way."

Tight-lipped, Petra turned and set out, and the other women followed. No one questioned him, and for that, he was grateful. He had the rifle and José's pistol, but he didn't want to resort to force. Not yet.

Sumala glanced back, eyeing him suspiciously. Galen avoided her gaze. What he planned was not something he cared to share. Petra wouldn't understand. He only hoped that when it was over, they would see he'd made the right choice. *If it's my choice I'm making.* The shadows laughed.

As he followed the last of the women, Galen glanced up at the sky. The sun barely hovered over the ridge. He pulled out Sesha's welder's glass and raised it to peer at the bright orb.

A small chip dented the bottom of the sun's pale circle, just slightly off center.

The eclipse had begun.

Part Five

Bridges to the Moon

Eclipse—First Contact

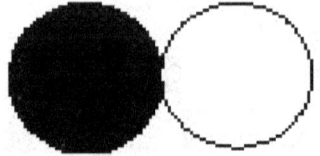

GIL

This was the Other—the phantom haunting her life, always present, ever unreachable. At last it had a face, and it was Gil's own.

Gil watched Miriam approach, carrying Gil's pack and another. She set these down on the stump of a ruined wall and stopped about five feet from Gil. She wore leather sandals and a long, white robe with wide sleeves and a hood draped around her shoulders. A gold cord cinched her waist, and her hair was loose, the wind teasing it like dancing flame. But none of that mattered. Gil's attention settled on Miriam's face.

It was like looking in a mirror. Yet just as no mirror casts a true reflection, there was a difference, an indefinable distortion that both bewildered and disoriented her. The two of them stood in counterbalance to one another while Vera hung back at the edge of their circle of presence, a silent witness. Once again Gil felt poised upon some pivot with no idea which way she might tumble. Tentatively, she raised a hand, half expecting Miriam to mirror the movement. When she did not, Gil let her own drop again to her side. She searched her twin's face, seeking some flaw, some difference, as they circled one another, as wary as they were curious.

"Well, *little* sister," Miriam said with bitter sarcasm. "Aren't you going to return the sentiment? We are twins, after all. Today is *our* day. The world awaits our pleasure."

What to say? What *could* she say? After all this time, knowing the inevitability of this moment, Gil did not know.

"I even brought you a present," Miriam continued, retrieving the two packs. "You should be dressed appropriately for the occasion." She pulled out a pair of sandals and a second white robe.

Shaking it out, she tossed it to Gil. "One for you, and one for me. Twins should always dress alike."

Gil automatically caught the garment. It was woven of alpaca wool, incredibly soft and warm, and she hugged it to her.

"Put it on," Miriam ordered. "It's a gift, and a gift must be accepted. Isn't that what Poppa used to say?" She spoke with a cruel sarcasm that made Gil shudder.

How would you know? Gil wondered. Her fingers twitched toward Sesha's pendant. *Keep it hidden.*

Gil saw the germ of Miriam's plan. With both of them wearing identical clothing, her sisters would have no chance of telling them apart. Her hands slid along her arms, then touched her face, seeking something, some scar or mark, which would set them apart. Details of her life? In her desperation, memories scattered, feathers tossed into the wind. Miriam's deception in the canyon back home proved that even well-guarded secrets were no longer secure.

How many times might Miriam have played Gil's role? How many memories were shared with Miriam instead of herself? Or had that incident been a single event, the yeast to ferment such doubts? Gil's sense of self frayed at the edges, unraveling.

Sesha will know, she thought. Of all her sisters, Sesha would know. She felt the pendant's weight against her breastbone. If she kept it hidden from Miriam, it could prove her trump card.

"I said, put it on!" Miriam yelled.

"And if I refuse?"

Miriam pulled a knife from a pocket in her robe, a folding knife with an ivory handle. Gil glanced at her pack sitting now at Miriam's feet. Petra must've stowed it there. Now Miriam used it against her. "If I cut you now, it will make no difference. Who could say who cut whom?"

"It shouldn't be like this," Gil said, watching the weave of that tainted blade. There was blood there, old blood and new, and in that blood, the power to ensnare her. As in Cerro de Pasco, it dizzied and sickened her. Supay's cold breath brushed the nape of her neck.

"You will wear that!"

Gil removed her jacket and slipped the robe over her head.

"Your clothes," Miriam demanded. "Remove them."

"Allow me some dignity," Gil responded, gesturing at their

audience of stone and cloud. "Besides, it's cold." Beneath the robe, she began to undress. "We're not enemies, Miriam. We're family."

"I have no family. They threw me out like unwanted trash."

"I'm sorry that happened. No one told me—"

"But you knew. *You* did." An accusation. "You knew something was missing, a piece torn from your soul. You were as much aware of me as I was of you."

Gil couldn't answer, not in words that would calm her sister's rage. Miriam was the Other, the invisible companion she was never certain truly existed.

"I spoke to you in dreams, and you heard me. I *know* you did. But you never came. You didn't want to find me." Hers was the voice of a lost child, pain annealed into cold iron.

Gil shrugged off her shirt. Beneath the robe's cover, she paused to touch Sesha's pendant before pushing her arms through the sleeves. Its presence reassured her. *I am me. I am not her.*

"Do you know what it's like, to be shunned by your own family? To spend every birthday and holiday alone and apart? To be six years old and abandoned on Christmas Day because your family hates you?"

"We never hated you, Miriam. You can't hate someone you don't know. It was Vera who kept you from us."

Gil stepped out of her pants and sat to exchange her boots for the sandals, and with each change, became more like Miriam. *We are not the same.* There had to be a difference.

"I had no choice," Vera said, stepping now into their arena with the pretext of gathering up Gil's discarded clothes. "My sisters talked of murdering the second twin or abandoning her to avoid complications. Had the child lived, she would never know her heritage. I couldn't take that away from her." She faced Gil. "Sometimes I imagined bringing Vera home for your birthday, wrapped up like a present with a big bow. I could just imagine the surprise on your face, the delight. But I was afraid the others would send her away again—or worse."

"Oh, I wish you had," Gil said softly, fervently.

Miriam stabbed at her aunt with a glance that made the older woman shrink back. "She came home from parties and family gatherings and described my sisters—what they were doing and how each one looked. Mostly, she talked about you—every detail, every word."

This isn't going well. A few minutes of conversation could not prove antidote to nineteen years of festering hate. Hate now boiling over, erupting in gouts of anguish and pain, too great to contain. Let her rant, Gil decided. Let it all spill out until there's room for reason.

Gil glanced at Vera. Her aunt had always been aloof, her frown and narrow gaze unapproachable. Gil and her sisters had learned to ignore her, even callously avoided her.

"I spied on you and learned to mimic your gestures and expressions until I knew you better than myself. I practiced until not even precious Sesha could tell the difference. But I could never pretend that they cared about me. *Me!* Not you."

"They would have, given the chance," Gil insisted. "But you left Sesha hanging from a tree. *You* chose to abandon her." Miriam was silent, as if considering a new concept. *Would they?* Gil could read the question in her eyes, sensing a soul deeply wounded.

"No!" Miriam said with a sharp wave of her hand, severing the possibility from reality. She gripped her hatred with stone-fisted anger. Gil reeled beneath its force, her sense of self splintering anew.

"Our aunts were wrong," Gil argued. "I can't change that—neither of us has that power. But Vera was wrong, too, when she said you weren't wanted. You could've been one of us."

"'One of us?'" Miriam repeated bitterly. "Hah! I'm eighth in a set of seven, a spare part at the back of a drawer."

"We could work together," Gil responded, even as she sought desperately for something that would separate them again, a uniqueness she could cling to as her own. She caught herself reaching for Sesha's pendant hidden beneath the robe and disguised the gesture by crossing her arms instead, holding her *self* close.

"But you would be the seventh. You would still be the Gilaishling, and I, the *also ran.*"

Gil studied Miriam's bitter frown and realized the difference was nothing so superficial as outward appearance. The distinction between them centered in the core of their being. In Miriam, Gil perceived her darker self, the shadowed planes she had never explored.

She clung to that difference, using it to create a rift between her own self and the Other. She was still the seventh, and even Miriam had just admitted that. "You acknowledge, then, that I am the seventh?"

"It doesn't matter," Miriam responded with a sneer. "I'll take your place, and the power will be mine."

"It won't work. They know you're here."

Miriam strode away from Gil and returned to face Vera.

"We should throw her off the cliff and be rid of her."

"I told you, you need her.

"I don't need anyone—including you."

"She's your twin. You can't—

Miriam slapped her aunt, a vicious blow that sent the older woman reeling away. "Don't tell me what I can't do, old woman!"

All semblance of shared identity turned to ash on the pyre of Miriam's fury. To what power had she surrendered? Supay? Was that maleficent creature Miriam's pawn or her king?

The rainbow fragments shimmered, their colors bleeding across the stone pavement. The eclipse had more to do with darkness than light—were they doing the right thing here, or playing into Supay's schemes?

"Why are you doing this, Miriam? What do you hope to gain?"

"The world, dear sister. The world at my feet."

"My purpose—*our* purpose is to save the world, not conquer it. The world at your feet would be nothing but dust and ashes. Doesn't that frighten you?"

Miriam laughed, a single, sharp bark of a sound, full of contempt and pride. "Not at all. I intend to control the Vision and use it to my advantage."

Gil shuddered.

"Think of the power, Gilaishling. Do you really want to be the servant, when you could be master? Do you want it at all?"

This was the very question that had haunted Gil since the incident in Cerro de Pasco. Now came the moment when she had to face it squarely. She knew that she did *not* want Miriam to have the power, but as for herself...

Beyond the desperate need to save the planet from the fate of the Vision, what did she want? The voices silenced themselves, awaiting her answer. Could she abandon them? Would they forgive her?

Gil took a deep breath.

"Yes," she said finally. "Yes, I do." And she realized that she truly did and always had. She had been born for this, her destiny encoded within her. As much as she might resent that, she could imagine no other fate.

Miriam studied her for a long time.

"An honest answer, at least," Miriam said at last. "But are you willing to fight for it? Do you want it that much?" She squared off, knife at the ready.

Not here, Gil prayed. There mustn't be blood here. But if not here, where else? Until this journey, she'd never had to fight for anything. Now she'd battled Supay, the elements, her own doubts and weaknesses. But was she prepared to battle her sister?

Miriam made a passing swipe that Gil dodged.

"Why do you want this so much, Miriam?" she asked. "Revenge? That's a flimsy excuse to risk the future of the Earth." They circled, Gil putting the lowering sun behind her so that Miriam had to squint.

"I want my birthright, my—" Miriam paused suddenly, and her eyes narrowed shrewdly. "You keep calling me Miriam."

"It's your name." Gil responded, trying to mask the quivering realization she had made a vital mistake. Another feint, another dodge.

"Professor Williams is the only one who calls me by that name."

Gil stared back at Miriam, mouth open to deny the truth, but the words would not come. *How do you lie to your own twin, to your Other who might as well breathe the same air and think the same thoughts, no matter how distant you become?*

"Where is he?"

Gil set a pose of defiance. "He was too weak." Which was the truth at one point. "We left him." Another partial truth.

"Oh, I don't believe you would have done that. He is, after all, your chosen Guardian, your *hero*." The knife wove a figure eight. "But it's of no consequence. I'll fool him as easily as the rest—I already have. I daresay he even *preferred* my version of 'G. M. Orlov.' Do you know he made love to me?"

That's a lie, Gil thought, wanting to scream it at Miriam's face. Yet she could sense a portion of truth in the words.

"He didn't know we are twins," she argued. "He won't be so

gullible now."

"Ah, but he's already vowed to stand by me; you can't change that." A lunge.

"Don't be so sure," Gil dared to say, dodging the wicked blade.

Miriam held up her fist, clenched tight around Galen's knife. "He is mine. He can't protect you, no matter what he intends." The color of her words paled, and Gil realized Miriam was bluffing, no more certain than Gil of Galen's loyalty. He would remain an unknown factor until the end, the force that would tilt the balance. Gil had to believe she'd made the right choice, whatever the outcome. *He has a purpose here.*

Miriam raised the knife, ready to charge. Vera stepped between the two, grabbing Miriam's wrist.

"Enough of this. Miriam, put that away. We're wasting time." She pointed to refracted images scattered on the grotto floor, fat crescent suns. "The eclipse has started, and your sisters aren't here yet."

Gil thought Miriam might start another tirade. Instead, stared down her aunt, then laughed, folding the knife and slipping it in the pocket of her robe. "You'll have to fight eventually, Gilaishling."

Eventually, but not now. For that, Gil could be grateful.

"So let's take a look at you," Miriam said, circling Gil with a critical eye. "There must be no difference between us."

SESHA

For a long time, Sesha could not continue, and she wondered what would happen if that time did not end.

When she could control her breathing again and her heartbeat had ceased its rampant stampede, she forced herself to look down past her feet. The quebrada intersected a deep canyon, its bottom lost in mist. The wall she leaned against crumbled at its edge. Time was consuming the city, not with the patient etching of wind and water, but in massive, calving chunks.

Gil needs you, she told herself, and only that thought could coerce her into moving. She forced herself, one step at a time, to edge away from the rim, clinging to the false security of the solid wall at her back.

When the sharp edge had merged with the cliffs beyond and she could no longer see the vertiginous depths, when she could breathe normally instead of gasping for air as if doses of courage, she paused to study her situation and rework her plan.

Sesha doubled back, seeking the walled avenue. Scaling that wall, however, was out of the question. The quarried stones were too smooth and fitted too precisely; she could not find any hand or footholds. No buildings or rocks came within fifteen feet of it. The city's edge angled toward the wall, creating a wedge that forced Sesha to its brink. By the time she reached the end of the wall, the canyon was only a half dozen feet away.

A rock fall had breached a gap between wall and mountain, a wide chute of rubble tumbling into the depths. A fallen pillar had wedged itself to dam the flow of rock. Sesha edged around the wall's crumbled end, clinging to it like a shadow. It wasn't that bad, she told herself, refusing to look down. She was all too aware that rock falls were inherently unstable. A slip or stumble here would mean an uncontrollable tumble *down*.

The open avenue, when she reached it, appeared deserted, and she stepped cautiously into the open. If anyone came along, there was no place to go, no place to hide.

An archway pierced the high ridge. Once more, the ancient, pre-Inca people had taken advantage of a natural fissure, widening it, smoothing the walls and filling the floor. She couldn't tell how far it penetrated the sullen mountain. To its left, a singular monolith canted precariously in the rubble, stemming the flow of broken rock that poured down the ridge. Vague contours suggested a great bird—a condor perhaps. Whether a trick of light and shadow or a carved likeness, the suggestion of a watchful bird was overwhelming. Someday, it, too, would slide down the rubble slope and into the void, but for now, it stood a stalwart sentry.

Sesha turned to the tunnel. The dark closed around her like a trap. The memory of her days in the chamber was still too fresh. Something brushed lightly across her cheek, and she swiped a hand across her face. Were there spiders at this altitude?

From one extreme to another, she chided. *You're never satisfied.* She automatically trailed her fingers along the reassuring solidity of the tunnel's stone wall.

Gil went through here, Sesha reminded herself. She had to follow. *If only I had some light.* As if thought conjured presence, a

317

yellow glow appeared and gradually brightened. It swung side to side, casting shadows that pranced along the wall. Voices drifted, amplified and distorted by the rock walls of the tunnel. She could neither distinguish words nor judge distance. Footsteps echoed, so that one or a dozen might approach.

Sesha turned and hurried as quickly as the dark would allow. She paused at the tunnel's entrance, blinking in the abrupt sunlight. Two men strolled down the avenue. She slipped to the side of the tunnel before they could spot her.

"But what of the demon?" one of them was saying. "The woman said it would eat the sun if we don't obey them." He eyed the tunnel's maw as if a dragon might emerge. Sesha pressed into the shadows.

"Fool!" the second man responded. "They lie to keep us from the treasure. There is no demon." But he flinched as if he feared retribution for his doubts. Behind her, the garbled voices echoed in the dark. Sesha's gaze scratched at the surrounding rock, seeking a place to hide.

GALEN

Galen glanced back along their trail, but only shadows pursued him. He skidded on a scattering of loose pebbles, caught his balance, and hurried on, not daring to slow down. With every step, fire pierced his side where the knife wound still healed. His head throbbed as flickers of motion teased his vision like imps playing among the rocks. The air was much too thin for so much activity—fifteen, perhaps eighteen thousand feet, he guessed.

He promised himself a rest at the next bend. When he looked up, he saw the women waiting for him, seated among a cluster of boulders. Ten more steps, he told himself. Five, and then three.

The change in momentum, from hurried pace to standing still, staggered him. Sumala reached out to steady him, and he flinched away from her. *Don't touch me,* he thought.

"Breathe slowly," advised Sumala. "Hyperventilating will only make it worse."

Why didn't someone tell me that five days ago? Galen wondered, but did not waste air to voice the thought.

The one named Lena passed him a water bottle. He accepted it with a nod of thanks but drank sparingly. They had little left, and it would take at least two days to return to Angoltuto. According to Lena, Miriam's men had taken what little food the three sisters carried. Galen wondered how long they could survive, though he kept his concerns to himself. Had these women even considered what would happen *after* the eclipse?

The shadows whispered to him, a keen tinnitus scratching his mind like the hiss of steam. *Now, do it now.*

Too soon, he argued. *Wait.*

Evita held out her poncho so that sunlight through the loose weave cast tiny crescents on the rock. The bite of the moon's disc pushed relentlessly across the sun's disc, heedless of the puny trials of men. The light already held a surreal, twilight quality smearing shadow edges.

I shouldn't be here, Galen thought bitterly. *I should be sitting comfortably in the company of astronomers, making observations, taking notes, maybe even photographs. I should be enjoying the eclipse, not running around mountaintops playing at hero.*

Galen blew out his resentment in a forceful sigh and turned to study the path they followed. The canyon walls seemed to be closing in, just as his thoughts were running down ever narrowing paths with fewer and fewer options, channeled toward a dark maw. The wind whispered in familiar voices. Eisabel. Edward. Carlo. He couldn't linger; he had to stay ahead of the memories.

Take them now. The voices grew more insistent.

"Not yet," Galen murmured to himself.

"We should move on," he told the women. *They're waiting for us.*

"Maji needs more rest," Sumala responded. "We all do."

Maji was indeed ashen-faced, her pallor enhanced by the penumbral light. She grimaced as she stood and put weight on her injured leg, but she offered Galen a thin, determined smile. Her limp was getting noticeably worse. Galen wondered if she would make it. Would any of them? He, himself, felt the familiar pain in his chest, a burning lance through his ribs.

Lena pushed herself wearily to her feet. She, too, looked pale, and her hair clung to the sides of her face in sweaty tendrils. She held a hand to her stomach as she took in slow, deliberate breaths. Galen had noticed how Sumala and the others watched over her with whispers about pregnancy and an unborn child. Were these women truly so dedicated to this Vision of theirs, or simply foolish? Galen shrugged off the thought because it made him question his own convictions. He didn't want to examine those too closely right now. His stomach felt queasy as the serpent stirred.

"We should be close," he offered, trying to picture Sesha's map and compare it with his surroundings. "A little farther and everything will get easier." The shadows urged him on, their voices like the wind nudging him toward darkness. They grew longer as the sun descended toward its destiny.

No one questioned him, though Petra eyed him suspiciously. Galen avoided her gaze. Petra would never understand. He kept José's pistol tucked in his belt and held the rifle so that anyone watching might assume he held the women captive. He told himself it was only a ruse.

"Galen?"

They had stopped again, and the women were watching him. *How long?* he wondered. His chest felt tight, and the skin burned.

"Galen, are you all right?"

Take them now! They are yours!

He shook his head to clear it, a mistake.

"You don't look well," Sumala observed, studying him closely. "Are you sure you're all right?" Again, she reached out to touch him, but Galen flinched away.

"I'm fine."

Sumala's gaze narrowed, and Galen knew she was looking for signs of the edema returning. What had she said? Headache, hallucinations, irrational behavior. He pressed a hand to his chest where the handprint burned. It must certainly be visible, a glowing reminder of the vow he'd made, the stigma of Miriam's treachery. How could they trust him if they saw that mark?

"I said I'm fine. Don't touch me!" If she touched him, she would know the truth.

If that isn't irrational, what is?

I'm not irrational, he insisted. *But they don't trust me. They won't understand. I know what I have to do.* They would not like what he had in mind. But it was the only way. He was convinced of that.

"You should slow down." Sumala advised.

"Ha! Tell that to the sun. We don't have time." He stalked away from her to avoid further discussion.

Sparks flickered at the corners of his vision, images playing hide-and-seek. Eisabel appeared in a rock face. Edward floated among the clouds. Hallucinations?

The wind blew like the reedy sighs of a flute while shadows lurked in crevices and crept behind rocks, waiting. Waiting for moonshadow to give them substance.

He felt a tug on the rifle.

"Perhaps I should carry that," Sumala suggested.

Now! Now is the time! Whispers shrieked until all rational thought fled. Galen jerked the weapon from her grasp. He backed away two steps and leveled it at the women.

"I'm in charge! You'll do as I say."

Evita was the first to comprehend; her sharp gasp alerted the others. One by one, he watched the bewildered sense of betrayal dawn on each face. Petra's expression, in particular, passed from surprise to fear to a smoldering rage. She glared at him with undisguised hatred and would probably kill him if he gave her the chance.

Galen shrugged off their anger and told them with intense calm, "It's better this way. You'll see."

Trust me, he wanted to tell them, but the lie refused to be spoken. He herded them on, glad to have those faces turned from him. But even the set of their shoulders accused him.

SESHA

Sesha crouched in the space between the archway and the bird-shaped pillar. Rubble shifted beneath her boots, echoed by a shiver in the stone of the pillar. She felt its delicate balance as she focused on the tunnel entrance, listening for the scrape of footsteps. Seconds later, a figure stepped into view.

Gil!

Sesha almost shouted out loud at the sight of the familiar red hair. She shifted to move forward, but her left foot had wedged between two stones. In the moment it took to work it free, Aunt Vera emerged close behind, one hand at Gil's back.

Gil or Miriam? From here, she couldn't tell. *If the two stood side by side, would I know the difference?* She studied the woman closely, seeking some clue that would verify whether or not this was the sister she thought she knew so well. This woman wore a long, white robe tied with a gold cord. Her hair was loose, combed out in a dance of red flame. They had not brought any such robes with them, of that Sesha was certain, but Gil might have bought one later. It was the sort of thing Petra would choose. Or was this part of Miriam's plan, to dress alike? But Miriam didn't know about the pendant. Only Sesha and Gil shared that secret.

The women paused as the two horsemen strode toward them. Vera glanced askance at the second of the men, then called out in Spanish. "Rico, where are the other women. I told you to bring them here."

The man shifted to a more defiant stance. "They're gone. The gringo took them." The two men stepped sideways to flank the women. Vera did not seem to notice.

"Time is running short. You must find them and bring them now."

"I think you are trying to cheat us. You tell us if we hold the women, you will bring the gold. Then you send the gringo to free them." Rico shifted his rifle.

Vera faced him imperiously, but Sesha noted also a quiver of panic. "You will have your treasure."

"So far, all we have are rocks. Rocks and more rocks. You promised gold."

Instead of answering, Vera muttered something to the red-haired woman, who altered her posture and expression, became haughty with a hard frown and narrow gaze. "How dare you," she demanded. "You'll have your gold soon enough. Be patient."

"Carlo was patient. Now he is dead."

"Carlo was a fool! He had no patience."

Sesha bit at her lower lip. Miriam or Gil? For now, she considered her both.

"You have your orders. Bring my sisters."

The two men edged closer.

"I think you already have this treasure, and you have no wish to share it." Rico glanced at the tunnel's entrance. "What is it you are doing in there?"

Now Vera was visibly nervous. "We're only preparing for the ceremony. We told you—"

"I think you told us lies. I want to see this place for myself."

Gil/Miriam responded imperiously, "You will anger the spirits, the *aukikuna*." Rico stepped closer, his face inches from hers.

"I do not believe you. Take us there now. Then I will show you real treasure." He leered, rocking his hips suggestively.

Sesha leaned forward, resting one hand against the pillar for balance. It seemed to sway, ever so slightly.

The *cholo* took the woman by the chin and forced a kiss on her. She jerked from his grasp, one hand raised to slap him. He batted it aside. Vera pulled a small pistol from her pocket, but Rico knocked it free. It skittered into the tunnel.

Sesha started from her hiding place, but caution overrode will. She could do nothing against the men's rifles. She beat her fist against the stone in frustration. When Galen had ordered Sesha to *just watch*, he couldn't have anticipated this turn of events. She had to do something; she couldn't simply watch. Not again. She eyed the mammoth pillar, gauging its stability.

GALEN

Galen followed the five women, where he could keep an eye on them. Their quiet voices drifted back to him, and he knew they plotted treachery. The shadows warned him. The voices whispered, *Beware!*

He felt dizzy and close to collapse as they came around a sharp curve. Shadows slipped like wolves among the rocks, hazing him first this way, then that, ever toward that darkened trough. It seemed nothing could turn him from that path.

At least the serpent of Miriam's treachery was quiet now that he had set this course, though he could feel its weight curled within his gut. It slept for now, awaiting the time when he would be forced to choose, ready to morph into a dragon, to devour him in flame and darkness.

The canyon had opened into a wide valley descending in a series of scooped-out bowls like beads on a string. The trail followed its flank around fins and pinnacles. For a moment, the women were out of his sight. As Galen rounded the curve, they burst upon him armed with rocks. Petra snatched the rifle from his grasp and backed away.

But he still had José's pistol, hidden in the folds of his poncho. Even as they raised arms against him, he grabbed Sumala, one arm around her throat. He held the pistol against the side of her head.

"Back off!" he snarled, and his rage slashed his mind like talons and pinched his face into something not human. Its ugliness reflected as terror on the women's faces. They lowered their hands and let the stones fall, some more quickly than others. Petra, he noted, was the last. She set the rifle on the ground and stepped back. Her rage mirrored his own.

He released Sumala and pushed her into their midst. While they caught her, he stooped and picked up the rifle. Then he turned on Petra, pushing her up against the rock, closing his fingers around her throat.

"Try that again," he growled, "and I will most certainly shoot you." Though she glared at him, he had the satisfaction of watching her ire die like a flame beneath a jar.

Petra again led the way, Galen bringing up the rear. Between them, the sisters kept silent, each in her own thoughts. Maji leaned heavily on Evita's shoulder, and fresh blood seeped through the bandages Sumala had applied. Galen worried they might end up carrying her.

He strode doggedly, expression grim, not daring to stop. Darkness stretched across the rock, gliding like a serpent. Could the women see it? Were they aware of the gathering shadows? Shadows spun a shroud around him. Whispers brushed his cheeks.

Sálvenos.

If he spoke of it, they would think him mad. Sumala would call it edema and feed him more vile tea. He said nothing and pushed on, one step after another, each accompanied by a deep, chest-aching breath. Right foot, inhale; left foot, exhale. Never stop in the middle, someone had once advised him. *What if the middle never stops?*

But it did, abruptly, at the edge of a deep crevice. Like the chasm in his mind where his thought tumbled into chaos.

At first, Galen could see no way to cross. Then Evita pointed out a slab of rock bridging the gap.

"Do we have to cross that?" Maji asked, her voice quivering.

"I can't do it," Lena whispered. She rubbed her belly and sat upon a fallen rock.

Galen stared across the gap. "Killichaka is over there." He pointed across the chasm. "There's no other way." *No other way,* the shadows jeered. *There's only one path.*

The women touched one another, seeking courage in that contact. None offered him such solace. Galen sent them across, one at a time. Even Maji, who could barely walk by now. Petra, he sent last where he could keep watch.

Once across the bridge, the trail skirted the rim of the cirque and descended to its floor. A shallow lake rested in delicate repose at the brink, its twilight blue surface ruffled by the rising wind. A clutter of rocks spilled across the basin and created two miniature islands in the lake. Sheer cliffs circled the basin, and beyond— Nothing. The valley ended at the rim of a deep canyon gouging the mountain range almost to the sea, opening an unimpeded view.

A pillar of dark hovered on the horizon—the shadow of the moon, skimming across the sea at almost two thousand miles per hour. A shudder curled around Galen's heart, and a paralyzing sense of dread. Once he had craved to stand within that beguiling umbra. Now he feared its sinister touch.

As the group moved around the lake, Galen at last caught sight of Killichaka. For a moment, he merely stared at it, as if, until that moment, he hadn't really believed any of this was truly going to happen.

SESHA

This isn't going to work, Sesha thought as she shoved against the pillar. The stone that appeared so precarious was proving more stable than she had anticipated. She glanced at the group below. *If only they weren't so close together.*

"Carlo thought he could have his way," Miriam/Gil warned in a deep, even tone. "Carlo is *dead.*"

Rico shoved Miriam/Gil backwards. Sesha still could not decide which she was. "I'm not Carlo," he promised with a lecherous grin, then nodded toward the tunnel. "Let's go." *Not yet,* Sesha thought. *I'm not ready yet.* She rammed the obstinate stone with her shoulder.

"Rico, what about the others?" the second man asked.

"Would you rather divide the treasure between two or five?" the first man responded. "Fetch them if you want; I'm going to find the gold."

Sesha pushed all the harder against the stone. Rico shoved the women toward the tunnel, and Sesha feared she would be too late. They would pass by before she could accomplish her task.

Then what? She kicked at the stones around the pillar's base, but regretted it when they skittered down the slope. The others glanced up. Sesha ducked behind the pillar

"Listen," Gil/Miriam said in Spanish. "You have disturbed and angered the spirits." She pointed at the rock fall for emphasis. "The mountain trembles. Leave before I banish *Inti* from the sky." She passed one hand across the sun. A gust of wind tugged at Rico's poncho.

A skittering of pebbles accompanied a low, grinding moan. Stones shifted beneath Sesha's boots. The massive pillar hovered for a precious, timeless second as if trying to make up its mind. Then it tumbled slowly, inevitably forward.

Sesha glanced towards her sister and aunt. *Too close,* she thought. *They're too close!*

The pillar tobogganed down the slope, taking the rubble with it and Sesha as well. She charged sideways across the shifting mass. At the edge of her vision, she saw the four people dodge the oncoming stone. Sesha leaped as the falling block plowed across the avenue and fell with awesome silence into the gorge.

Like a dam breached, the rest of the broken rock followed, bouncing down the side of the gorge. Their glancing blows echoed like distant cannon. Sesha tackled Vera and her sister, pushing them into the tunnel. With a deep rumble, the ridge collapsed behind them as if it had been waiting for this moment to shed its burden. The women stumbled farther into the tunnel as the entrance disappeared beneath stone and dust. A section of roof collapsed, too, exposing the tunnel to the sky. Light seeped through the dusty air.

Vera crouched within a hollow in the tunnel's wall, and Rico sprawled on the floor close to the rubble-choked entrance. He moaned softly but did not move. Sesha ignored him; he was no longer a threat. She lunged instead at her sister.

Miriam/Gil, caught off balance, collapsed beneath the momentum of Sesha's charge. Sesha straddled her sister, pinning one arm with a knee. She grabbed up a large stone and held it over her head. Her sister tried to raise her free arm, but it was entangled in the folds of her robe. Her struggles faltered, then ceased. She stared at Sesha with hope and confusion.

"Sesha," Vera cried out in surprise. "What are you doing?"

Sesha held her position, the stone still poised.

"Miriam or Gil? Which one are you? Prove you're not the one who had Maji shot!" Rage flared and then as quickly, it was quenched. She had no energy for such anger now. She let the rock drop, missing her sister's head by mere inches.

The woman eyed her warily but said nothing. Her face held a lost, hurt look, reminding Sesha of her encounter with Miriam in the canyon back home. Nostalgia or envy? A chill crept across the back of her neck.

Gil or Miriam? Sesha glanced at Vera, but knew she couldn't trust any answer her aunt might give.

"Prove to me you're not Miriam." In the dim light, Sesha could barely make out her face

"You really can't tell, can you." It was a statement, not a question, echoing her one encounter with Miriam. "If I said I'm Gil, would you believe me?"

"I don't know," Sesha admitted. She pushed herself to the side, allowing her sister to sit. "Prove it."

The woman opened her mouth, but for a long moment said nothing. At last she spoke. "I'm Gil. What more can I say?"

"You don't have to *say* anything," Sesha responded pointedly.

Gil touched the front of her robe. "Miriam has the pendant. She found it when I changed clothes."

Could that be true? Or could this be Miriam, guessing now at the significance of something overlooked earlier. Knowledge, even possession of the pendant meant nothing. How foolish to think something so superficial could distinguish the two! *I should've made her get a tattoo.*

"Sesha, I'm the one who pulled you out of the tree when Miriam left you hanging."

"Why the change of clothes? Where did you get the robe?"

Gil passed her hand down the fabric. "Miriam's idea. She's wearing another just like it. But I found you in a cavern last night. Miriam wouldn't know about that."

Would she? Miriam's ruse put even that in question. A shudder tickled Sesha between her shoulder blades. Could she ever trust Gil again?

"Sesha, either way, we have to go. The eclipse has already started. We have less than an hour."

Sesha turned toward Rico. "What about him?"

"He's no threat. His rifle is gone." The cold and distant tone in her sister's voice made Sesha pause to study the twin once more.

"You are the real Gil, aren't you?" Sesha couldn't keep a plaintive note from her voice, a prayer that she made the right choice.

Her sister sighed and stared into the dark of the tunnel. "You'll just have to trust me. We need to reach Killichaka before Galen and the others. Miriam's waiting for them."

She stood and started into the tunnel; Sesha couldn't stop her.

GALEN

"It's a hole in the rock," he murmured, both disappointed and awed by the natural beauty of the grotto.

"What did you expect—the *Taj Mahal*?" Petra responded scornfully. Galen had the impression she was also disappointed.

Galen ignored the ruined buildings and focused on the open chamber that must be the heart of Killichaka. Crystals studded roof and walls, and fallen shards littered a floor planed smooth. To call the place a temple in the sense of a man-made structure was an injustice. Its natural artistry rivaled any cathedral.

"It's a gigantic geode!" Evita exclaimed with obvious delight, even as she labored to catch her breath. "Quartz! Of course. Quartz crystals are used to tune radios. They can—"

"Please, Evita, we're not here to listen to Benny Goodman." Lena was staring in awe at the shrine as she spoke. "Can't you simply enjoy the beauty?"

Light danced among the crystals, casting a profusion of rainbows and diamonds, paled only slightly by the eclipsed sun. As Galen moved forward, colors flashed in his eyes—spectral blue, verdant green, followed by purest yellow, orange, and red. At the chamber's heart, long spears of pure quartz fanned out from a gold-mantled base.

All was pristine, but for a dull patch marring the bench. A flaw, Galen thought, then realized it was blood, absorbed into stone and metal so that nothing could erase its presence. *Must everything be tainted by blood?* he wondered, clenching fists against the whisper of shadow. *Was nothing left pure?*

"But where's Gil?" Sumala asked, and the others, too, turned to seek their sister. "She should be here."

Movement attracted Galen's eye. In the ruined building to the temple's left, a patch of white stood out against the mountain's relentless gray. Galen motioned for the others to stay put, then stepped to the side, rifle held ready, and edged toward the opening. A woman in a white, hooded robe sat on a block of stone, bound hands in her lap, a gag tied across her mouth. She turned at his approach, and shook back the hood, revealing hair like flaming burgundy. Miriam or Gil? Galen thought he should be able to tell. There should be some mark or blemish, an intangible difference he could *feel*. Her expression remained calm as she watched him, but she leaned forward with tense anticipation. Her gaze tracked from his face to the rifle and back, questions obvious in her eyes. Then she raised her arms, and he saw that her wrists were tied, as well as her ankles.

His first impulse was to throw down the rifle to free her. He took a step in her direction before he could resist. Not until he was sure which of the twins he faced, he cautioned himself. When the sisters saw the woman, they, too, surged forward. Galen waved them back with a sweep of his rifle.

The sisters gathered in a cluster, except for Maji, who sat down on a boulder to rest her injured leg. Without Galen's permission, none dared approach. He scanned the surrounding terrain. *Where's Sesha? If this is Gil, where is Sesha?* With no other recourse, he told Evita to remove the gag.

"I was beginning to think you'd never get here." The woman twisted her hands as if she could loosen the ropes binding them. "Untie me quickly, before they return."

"Before who returns?"

"Vera and Miriam, of course. They left me tied up here while they went back to fetch you."

Gil—it had to be Gil; why would Miriam be tied up?—gazed at him steadily. Galen remembered the look from the classroom, yet there was also a remnant of Miriam's harshness to it. Gil or Miriam? He couldn't tell, and so he fell back on his secret nickname. GeM. Never had it seemed more appropriate.

Finally, he nodded at Evita and let her untie the ropes, then ordered her back. Gil—*GeM*, Galen thought—stepped out of the ruins. The threat of Galen's rifle held the sisters as might a leash, though they strained toward the red-haired woman.

"What are you doing?" GeM asked, her voice carefully neutral. She rubbed her wrists.

Galen let his gaze circle the small basin. Sesha should've reached this place long before he did. Was she hiding somewhere, watching, as he'd ordered her? She must realize now that he had betrayed her—betrayed them all—for the vow he'd made to Miriam. That hurt more than Petra's hateful stare or GeM's bewildered query.

"Galen?" she asked again.

He ignored her and turned to the others instead. "Where is Miriam? If this is Gil, where's Miriam?"

"Gil just said she went to fetch us," Sumala remarked.

"Does it seem likely that she would be gone this close to totality? She risks missing the whole show." *Why isn't Miriam here?* He stared at the red-haired woman. *Or is she?*

Sesha would know, if she had been watching, if this was Gil or Miriam. He considered calling out for her, but decided it would be unwise at this point.

As if in answer to his unvoiced summons, a great, cracking roar rumbled somewhere in the deep valley. It sent shivers across the surface of the lake and thrummed among the crystals in the chamber. A handful broke loose to shatter on the floor.

Sesha, what have you done now? Galen wondered

SESHA

"Fool! What have you done?" Vera screamed.

Sesha wondered that herself as she glanced into the darkness that had just swallowed her sister. A vague uneasiness worried at the edges of her thoughts.

"Was that really Gil?"

"What difference does it make now? When she gets to the temple and they're standing together, even I won't be able to tell them apart. We have to stop her."

"Stop who?" Sesha asked, wary of her aunt's motives.

Vera labored for enough breath to speak. "Miriam, of course. It was never my intention to harm Gil, but I've lost control. I couldn't leave them alone together."

The threat of Miriam harming Gil jolted Sesha to her feet. She offered Vera a hand. Vera refused it and struggled to her feet on her own. Sesha noted how much her aunt had aged. This trip had been hard enough on Sesha and her sisters. How had Vera managed to survive this far? "You have to stop Miriam. I don't have the strength to run anymore."

Sesha expected some hint of treachery in Vera's gaze but found only weariness. Her sad and bitter face, so much like Petra's, had gone gray.

"Hurry, child. I'll be right behind you." Vera paused to scoop something from the floor and tuck it in her pocket.

The pale light from the collapsed ceiling was soon occluded. Sesha held her breath, listening to the wind blowing its dirge to the fading sun. The memory of her ordeal trapped in the hidden room was still too fresh. Her feet shuffled along, testing every step, as she dragged her fingers on the cold security of the tunnel wall. The glow of light that finally marked the tunnel's end was a relief. She hurried toward it.

Beyond the exit, Sesha skidded to a halt, blinking at the sudden light. Overhead, the sky had deepened to twilight blue. The sun was still too bright to look at directly and would remain so until the instant of totality. Sesha prayed for the extra minutes she needed to reach the others.

A sense of urgency pushed her, though the trail was too steep, the air too thin, for anything more than a hurried walk. *Where is the lake and the shrine?* she wondered. *Where is Killichaka?*

A deep chasm split the ground before her, bridged by a trestle of stone. Sesha halted, staring in breathless dismay. *No more cliffs, please, no more cliffs!*

GALEN

The sun appeared as a quarter crescent. Galen lowered the green glass. The light had dimmed to a ghostly gray, as if the sun had already set. The air felt chill, and the wind blew briskly now. A matter of minutes, and nothing was right.

"If this is Gil, where is Miriam?" he asked again. Her absence made him uneasy. Something was wrong, terribly, fearfully wrong.

"*That's* Miriam," called a new voice. Galen turned to see a second GeM approaching at a breathless trot.

"I'm Gil," she announced.

The newcomer stopped no more than ten feet from her twin.

They stared at one another with expressions both intense and lost. What thoughts passed between those twin sets of eyes?

"You really are twins."

Jolted by seeing the two side by side, Galen realized that, up until this moment, he had not been so certain. He had still retained the notion there was only one woman caught up in a twisted dementia. He stared at the fiery red hair, the green eyes and white robes. What minor flaws Galen could detect, he could not ascribe to one or the other. A freckle marked one chin; a similar one on the other. If they were not precisely the same, still Galen could not ascribe *that* mark to Gil or that feature to Miriam.

One seemed bemused, the other curious. Miriam kept her face as impassive and innocent as Gil. How could they look so much alike and be so different, unmarked by their divergent fates and natures? He rubbed one hand across his eyes to clear his sight. *If only the rocks would stop ringing,* he thought, *I could think clearly. If the shadows would stop taunting, I could see which is which.*

"Don't believe her." The first *GeM* stepped forward and pulled at a silver chain around her neck, bringing a circular pendant from under her robe. "See, I have the pendant."

The newcomer glared at her twin. "She took it from me. Ask who gave it to her."

Galen looked to Petra for her opinion. Petra shrugged.

"I've never seen it before."

"Sesha must've given it to her," Evita suggested, spoiling the question—if Sesha ever showed up to verify it.

Where is *Sesha?* He searched the surrounding rocks in a slow pan. He didn't want to ask out loud. There had to be some reason she remained hidden now that the twins were together. On the horizon, the curtain of moonshadow raced toward them.

"It's up to you to choose," said the first GeM, rubbing her wrists to remind him that she had been the one tied up.

The other drew closer, her glance taking in Galen's rifle still covering her sisters. "Have you chosen then?"

"Perhaps I'm merely being cautious." The rifle barrel now swayed between the two women and finally settled between them. Until he played his hand, neither woman would admit anything. It wouldn't do to claim to be Gil if he had taken Miriam's side.

Galen turned to the other sisters. "Which one is Gil? You're her sisters; you should be able to tell."

"That one, obviously," Petra announced, much too quickly to have given it much thought. "Why else was she tied up?"

"Too obvious," Lena countered. They reconsidered and disagreed and in the end, could only shrug and shake their heads.

Petra stepped forward, in spite of the threat of Galen's rifle. Her glance flicked from one set of features to the other as if counting off details. At last, though, she, too, shrugged and shook her head reluctantly.

"It's up to you," she admitted with rue and spite. "If you are the Guardian of the Ritual, you have to choose."

Guardian of the Ritual. The words troubled him, their significance a puzzle he must solve. But he didn't have time now to ponder it. His chest burned where Miriam's handprint had touched him, and his lips stung with the memory of her kiss. Fever chilled his veins. *You are mine.*

"What of your vow?" one GeM asked in a carefully controlled voice, betraying nothing. "Which of us do you honor?" She could have been reminding him of his commitment or testing his resolve.

"I have no choice," Galen stated. *You are the Guardian of the Ritual.* "However, the vow I made was to the G. M. Orlov who sat in my class." *The one who questioned Keynes and dredged up broken dreams.* "If that wasn't Miriam, then she stood in as mere proxy. So the question remains, which of you is *that* G. M. Orlov? If it's a test you want, let's try this."

GIL

Once again Gil faced Miriam. The two stared at each other as if no one else existed. The wind blew chill through the weave of her robe. She rubbed her arms as Galen studied first one, then the other.

She read only turmoil in Galen's thoughts. Bringing him here had put him in jeopardy. Supay shrouded Galen in shadow, ready to claim his soul. Would Galen prove Supay's pawn or nemesis?

She considered the blood staining Killichaka, healing turned to treachery. She shuddered and glanced at Miriam, who smiled thinly as if in triumph, reveling in a truth revealed. In her quest to defeat the Vision, she had played into Supay's hands. It had won Miriam's soul before Gil had known there was even a battle to wage. But the wind promised solace while stone spoke of hope. This temple of healing, betrayed, begged redemption.

Galen was the key, determining whether Supay triumphed or failed. His purpose and fate, then, was to tip the balance. Would Miriam's treachery win out? Gil refused to consider it. She must believe her choice had been right, and the Vision could still be defeated.

All depended on Galen now.

GALEN

If it's a test you want, let's try this.

The words hung before Galen like an accusation. He had made the challenge; now he must follow through. Both red-haired women gazed at him, waiting. Assuming Miriam had followed the same course of study, what could he ask that one would know and not the other? *Name another student in the class.* He'd tried that already, and it proved nothing.

And if he determined that the G. M. Orlov who had sat in his classroom was Miriam, would he be irrevocably bound to honor his vow and betray Gil? The stain of blood sat heavy upon his chest, a weight he could not shed.

You are the Guardian of the Ritual. Petra had said that, and in those words, he found function. The Guardian's duty was not to the seventh daughter, neither Gil nor Miriam, but to the Ritual, to see it through and maintain its purpose.

He licked at dry lips as he considered options and settled on a choice. "A test, then. You have only to answer as you did in class." Gil and Miriam—whichever they were—glanced at one another. One of them flexed her fingers as if drumming them on a table. Was that Gil's habit or Miriam's? Galen took a deep breath and only as he spoke did the question truly come to him—the question and the solution.

"Nothing difficult; in fact, a question from the mid-term examination." He paused to confirm his logic. "Who first anticipated the class struggle between labor and capital?"

The other sisters muttered at the apparent inadequacy of the question. Galen ignored them, centering his attention upon the twins.

The first GeM smiled confidently and seemed relieved. "Sismondi di Sismondi, of course."

Galen steeled himself not to react, one way or the other. Not yet. He nodded, acknowledging the answer, but not its accuracy. *What if this doesn't work?* He turned to the other. "Would you agree with that?"

The second GeM responded with a nod. "She's right of course." The tip of a smile played at one corner of her mouth. "I might have said Karl Marx."

Galen paused, deliberately letting the tension hang in the air while he slowly scanned the basin, looking for some sign of movement. *Now, Sesha. Now!*

Only the wind responded, moaning among the rocks like demons awaiting release. Galen stared at the two women as if he could read what was hidden in those twin pairs of eyes.

Gil, are you with us? he wondered.

"Interesting," he said aloud. "It's the wrong answer, of course."

She gave nothing away. The other sisters surged toward her twin with smiles and relieved sighs. Galen waved them back. Petra glared at him, threatening to charge, rifle or no. Galen sidestepped closer to Gil and Miriam.

"What are you doing," Lena asked, confusion washing across her face. "You've proven who's really Gil. What more do you need?"

What indeed? Playing this role skirted dangerously close to yielding to Miriam's manipulations. He wondered if he could shed the façade, or if the guise had come to fit too snugly.

"Sismondi might be the right answer." *Did you miss it on purpose?* "Karl Marx, however, is the answer the real Orlov gave on the test." *Someday you'll need it,* she had said.

Gil—the real Gil—smiled, a gentle curve, and he wondered how he could ever have been confused. He brought the rifle around to center on Miriam, right through her stolen pendant.

"You are not my GeM." He felt his finger twitch with eager anticipation. It was so simple—you point; you shoot. He frowned. It shouldn't be so easy to kill. Guns should be complicated and difficult. A person should really have to think about what they were doing to pull the trigger.

Did he really hate her that much?

Maji was the first to catch on. "Miriam had Vera tie herself up to make us believe she was really Gil."

"And you're really on our side?" Evita added with a gasp of hope.

"That remains to be seen," Petra commented sourly, her eyes still blazing with anger and mistrust. Galen didn't respond.

Miriam glared at him with passive ferocity and asked, "What of your vow? You can't break your vow." Galen felt the pressure of her fingers upon his heart.

You are mine.

"I'm not breaking it." A whisper forced between clenched teeth was as much as he could manage. "As I recall, my exact words were 'I'll guard you, no matter what.' That's what I'm doing." The words freed him, bonds slipping loose. It could not be so easy, he thought. *She is not through with me yet.* Still, he took a deep, unfettered breath and allowed a smile to express the irony he felt.

Miriam hissed with vexation. "You promised!" she screamed as she lunged at him. Fingers like talons raked across his chest. Even through layers of poncho, coat, and shirt, he felt the burning sting as if she'd flayed his skin. He had to drop the rifle to grab her arms. Her fingers flexed as if she would slash his face. Galen swayed under the onslaught of her fury but held his ground.

"You're mine," she screamed. "You're still mine!" She screeched with hatred, a sound twisted by pure, cold fury into something no human throat should voice. It roused the brand upon his chest. *You're still mine.* Abruptly, her anger deflated. Miriam let slip a smile, feral and foreboding, and shoved her hands into the pockets of her robe.

Galen allowed himself to relax. He raised one hand to comb his fingers through his hair and turned toward the other sisters. He owed them both an apology and an explanation. Maji had picked up the rifle and held it uncertainly. Her glance shifted between Galen and Miriam.

The moment his attention turned from Miriam, she lunged at Gil. He caught the movement at the edge of his vision—raised arm, inhuman rage, and a flash of metal and ivory.

SESHA

Sesha stopped cold, one foot upon the fallen stone that

bridged the chasm. Her other foot refused to budge. No amount of will could force that next step. The span was wide enough, the top planed smooth and even, and it was wedged tight in its place, surviving untold centuries. Yet Sesha relived how the ledge had dropped beneath her feet and that eternal moment when falling became inevitable. If she fell here, there would be no blue-eyed pool waiting. Only stone and more stone. *How far would I fall? Where would I stop?*

"It frightens you," Vera noted as she caught up.

"I've had a couple of bad falls of late," Sesha answered softly, as if to make any noise at all would send the stone bridge sliding into the crevice.

"So I heard. I'm glad the reports were in error."

Sesha cast a look of disbelief.

"I never intended for any of you to get hurt. You are all my family, after all."

"What about Aunt Faye? What about Maji?"

Vera pressed her lips in a flat line. "For Faye, death was a blessing—and not my doing. As for Maji, that was beyond my control." Her gaze wandered out over the gorge, and she spoke wistfully. "I've lost control over everything, it seems. Even Miriam. She's given herself over to something else, some—" Vera shivered, then shook her head and stepped past Sesha onto the bridge. "We don't have time to discuss it. Let me help." She offered her hand. Sesha stared at it, the lines and wrinkles and brown spots.

"Trust me, Sesha," Vera called, backing across the stone, hand still offered. *Aunt Faye had trusted Vera.* "Keep your eyes on me, and you can make it."

For the moment, Sesha convinced herself that her aunt truly wanted her to cross. With a deep breath, she took her first step. Such a narrow gap—a mere twelve feet, maybe less. Yet it might as well be twelve miles. She imagined the stone shifting. Visions of it cracking and splitting in two eroded her resolve.

Sesha shook her head. "I can't."

Vera lowered her hand and spoke with abrupt and icy scorn. "Crawl across on your hands and knees, then."

Sesha considered doing just that as Vera turned and strode boldly across the bridge. Another wave of vertigo rolled past her, and she dropped to her knees, hands braced against the cold stone. The rock seemed to roll under her as if the mountain shrugged.

"You have to cross, Sesha," Vera called from the other side. "Gil needs you for the Ritual."

"I thought that was the idea. If something happens to me, won't Miriam be the seventh?" Sesha stood. *One step at a time.*

"No," Vera responded, shaking her head. "You all have to be there, Gil and Miriam together. That's the way I planned it."

"You planned it?" Another step, and another. "Aunt Faye found—

"Faye found what I wanted her to find. In truth, I planted it, just as I planted the article where you could find it. Miriam believes we had to follow you. She doesn't know I have my own map. I've waited for this event. This is *my* plan, my work! Your aunts found their solution nineteen years ago, when they gave me a newborn infant to 'dispose of.'"

Sesha felt her stomach go cold. She continued, five steps, six. "You lured us here? This is a trap?"

Vera shook her head. "No, not a trap. An opportunity!"

GIL

Miriam's attack caught Gil by surprise. She scarcely had time to react. The blade slashed across her arm as she grabbed for Miriam's wrist. Then they were on the ground, tangled and hampered by their robes.

Gil needed a clear space to breathe and catch her wits. She had never fought for anything in her life, never had to. That was her weakness, while Miriam found strength in her fury. Yin and yang, they were. Dark and light.

In the wind's shriek among the crystals, Gil heard a warning. Si's essence shimmered with anguish. Gil kept one hand clasped on Miriam's wrist, holding the knife at bay. Galen's knife—the one that slew a child and saved a life. It jerked back and forth, missing her throat by inches. Seeking leverage, Gil clutched Miriam's robe. Miriam grabbed Gil's hair. Gil didn't want to hurt Miriam, but her twin held no such disadvantage.

Distant thunder protested the violence. *Huaca.* Sacred place.

GALEN

Galen stared at the knife with the familiar ivory handle. Harry's knife.

The pause cost precious time. Before Galen could react, the two were a tangled heap of dirtied white robe and red hair. Petra lunged forward, but Galen swung his arm to hold her back.

"Stop them before Gil gets hurt!" Petra demanded.

"Let them fight." *Only once had Galen had to fight as a boy, when a school bully ambushed him. Galen's brother had said the same thing.*

"But Miriam has a knife. She's stronger."

"Whose fault is that?" *Edward had done nothing. Enraged, Galen had fought back, catching the boy off guard. Only when he was sitting on the boy, pounding his face, did Edward step in.*

"Gil doesn't know how to fight."

"She needs to learn."

"Why didn't you stop him?" Galen had demanded, wiping his bloodied nose.

"You should learn to fight for yourself," Edward responded. "I might not be there someday."

GIL

"Why are you doing this?" Gil gasped when the fight paused to rearrange tactics. "It makes no sense."

Miriam backed off, but her eyes were full of Supay's darkness. With a howl, she lunged again. Gil fell backward on the hard stone. Miriam leapt at her. Though Gil held Miriam's arm at bay, Miriam had better leverage. The blade inched toward Gil's throat.

Why doesn't someone stop this? Gil wondered, angry that no one interfered. She pushed that ire into strength. If no one else would stop it, she must. It was about time she learned to fight for what she valued.

Releasing her hold on Miriam's robe, she used both arms to wrest Miriam to the side so that the knife struck stone. It jarred loose from Miriam's grasp.

Gil swung her fist, catching Miriam on the jaw. Miriam reeled back, and Gil pushed herself up, shoving Miriam aside and down. Now it was Miriam on her back, Gil astride her. She had the knife now, Miriam's throat bared.

The ground rolled, ancient power aroused. Si vibrated like a swarm of bees, a summer storm, agitated and horrified. Gentle and innocent, never knowing malice, she urged Gil to stop. *No blood. Not here.*

Gil paused, gazing into Miriam's eyes and seeing herself reflected in loathing and hate. The knife slipped from her fingers to clatter upon the ground.

GALEN

"Enough!" Galen declared, grabbing the fallen knife. The serpent in his gut fed on his rage and in turn fueled its flames. Fresh blood dripped from the blade. *Whose blood now?*

Both GeMs sat on the ground, gasping for breath, both bloodied, white robes soiled and torn. Blood ran from a gash on Gil's arm, staining her robe.

Galen held the knife for all to see. "No more! There's too much blood; it surrounds us all. It must end."

"Galen," Gil called, quietly penetrating the haze of his rage. "It's all right. It's a minor wound." Sumala knelt beside her, but Gil waved her off.

"It's not all right," he raged plaintively. He swiped the blade across his sleeve, painting it with Gil's blood. "It's not," he murmured. Folding the blade into the handle, he held it tight, determined to keep it from doing any more harm.

Ignored by the rest, Maji raised the rifle, aiming it at Miriam.

"We should kill her," Maji said with frightening calm. Her finger pressed against the trigger.

"You can't," Galen countered with all the authority he could muster. He stepped between Maji and Miriam, wryly aware he was as much a target as she. "Killing Miriam will only taint the Ritual. I can't allow that. *No more blood!*" The last was a cry, as much a prayer as a proclamation. He saw the infant in Mama's lap, Pedro staring at his own heart, and Eisabel reaching for him. He shuddered and dismissed the vision to focus on the woman holding the rifle.

"Maji." He spoke softly, his voice tight as he swallowed against the urge to shout. "You can't shoot Miriam. She's your sister. She is *still* your sister. She is Gil's twin."

Maji's face puckered with confusion. The end of the rifle sank, then bobbed up again. "But she tried to—"

"Galen's right," Gil said. She stood, accepting a hand up from Sumala. Except for that motion, she ignored her own wound. Slowly, Maji lowered the rifle, its weight too much to bear. It was Petra who took it away from her and offered it to Galen. Their gazes locked for a moment, a truce signaled between them.

"We should tie her up so she can't interfere," Evita suggested. Petra began to retie Miriam's wrists.

That felt *wrong* in a way that made Galen itch and squirm. He glanced at Miriam, and his lips tingled with the memory of her kiss. She stood in simmering quiet and glared at him with a cold, reptilian stare. He leaned toward her, her attraction like a magnet.

You are mine.

"No!" Galen called out, denying both the voice in his head and the sisters' actions. He stepped forward and pulled loose the ropes from Miriam's wrists. "No," he repeated softly, yet with more emphasis. He ran his fingers through his hair, trying to capture an elusive thought. Sisters. Twins. This family had lived with this conundrum for nineteen years. If there were a solution, surely they would've found it. Or had all other paths closed the day they chose to discard a newborn infant? Had their sin blinded them to any other possibility?

The mark upon his chest throbbed to the beat of his own pulse, burning like a fresh wound. The serpent within coiled around his thoughts, setting off lightning flashes that seared his mind until he was certain his head would burst from the pressure. Images skittered in gusts of whispers, eddied and pooled and settled finally into a pattern.

They must be one.

SESHA

"Hurry, Sesha!" Vera called out. She pulled a pistol from her jacket pocket and checked its chambers.

Sesha paused mid-step, arms held out for balance. "Aunt Vera?" she asked, afraid to voice her thoughts.

"I can't let Miriam harm Gil."

Sesha licked at dry lips. "What will you do?"

Vera smiled wryly. "Don't worry, child. This is just for persuasion."

Foreboding swept away Sesha's vertigo. She moved forward,

her gaze on Vera, half expecting her to wave a hand and vanquish the stone from beneath Sesha's feet.

"Sesha, run!" Vera yelled abruptly, pointing the pistol across the chasm.

Sesha sprinted for the safety of solid rock. Turning, she saw Rico on the far side. Twin shots filled her ears with thunder, sent her and Vera sprawling.

Sesha pushed herself up. Across the chasm, Rico curled in on himself as he tumbled over the brink.

Vera sprawled at the very edge of the chasm. The world rolled with a belabored groan. She scrabbled for purchase as she slid toward oblivion

Sesha lunged forward. Her fingers closed around Vera's wrist. Her aunt's fingernails scratched Sesha's skin as the hand slipped from her grasp, eyes wide with terror. *I never noticed they were green,* Sesha thought. Vera tumbled back and down, her mouth open in an unvoiced scream.

Someone was screaming, and Sesha couldn't make her stop.

GALEN

The sound caromed off the surrounding cliffs and smashed down upon Galen and his group, rolling over him like a physical weight. A barrage of echoes hammered him. For what seemed an eternity, nothing existed but sound, all the more intense for knowing what it meant. Knowing and denying until, in the utter silence that followed—

"Sesha," Gil whispered with grim certainty, collapsing to her knees and clutching her stomach. The word crystallized his fear, seeming to freeze his heart in mid-beat. Its echo screamed in his ears like the wind.

"Stay here!" Galen ordered, sweeping a pointed finger past each woman to pin her in place. He ran towards the stone bridge. Altitude didn't matter, nor the steep terrain, not even the shadows that swept across the path to trip him up.

Near the chasm, a figure sat against a block of stone. Heartbeat faltering, Galen dashed forward.

"Sesha!" he called. She stared at a single spot on the rim, and her head barely twitched in his direction.

"Aunt Vera," she murmured over and over as if her mind had

become snagged on a single thought. Not until he touched her did she seem aware of him, whispering, "She fell. I couldn't save her. She fell."

Galen coaxed her to stand.

"I'm all right," she said, clutching at Galen's arm. "See, it's only scratches." She held out her arm. Long, thin gouges ran down her wrist and across her palm, blood welling in tiny, dark beads. Yet her face was taut and shadowed gray. *It's the light,* Galen told himself. The waning light turned everything gray. Where Sesha had been sitting a puddle of dark shadow declared the thought false.

No! Not like Edward; not Eisabel or Carlo.

Sesha looked at Galen with a thin, empty smile. "It's not so bad; it hardly hurts at all."

He scooped her up and struggled along the path, his vision dancing a jig. He held her close, fearful she might scatter across the rock like beads from a broken string. She seemed heavier than her slight body should be. *How much does guilt weigh?*

GIL

Sesha's hurt, Sesha's hurt, Sesha's hurt. The words built a wall blocking all other thought. They became a mantra wrapped around a single, fundamental core.

Sesha's dying.

Gil followed Galen, defying his order, and the others came after. Maji alone remained behind to guard Miriam, though what harm could her twin do worse than what had already happened?

Galen strode past, ignoring her. His face was drawn in grim, tight lines, and a quiet, searing rage worked along his jaw and sizzled in his gaze. He did not stop until he reached the rock where Maji had been sitting.

"Where's Vera?" Miriam asked with the quiet dread that knows the answer.

Galen swung to a stop, swaying with the momentum of his fear. He couldn't find the breath to speak. Sumala and Petra pried Sesha from his embrace. Petra cradled her while Sumala knelt to peel away bloodied layers of clothing. Dark blood flowed from a single wound. *How could so much blood come from such a small hole?*

Sumala's face went pale and empty with helplessness. Some-

343

one handed her a wad of cloth. She pressed it to Sesha's wound to staunch the flow. One hand drifted over her bag with its meager supply of herbs and medicines, even as she shook her head.

"Where's Vera?" Miriam asked more insistently, plucking at Galen's sleeve.

"She's dead," he responded with merciless ire. Miriam's spirit crumpled beneath the weight of grief. Galen pushed her aside to confront Gil.

"You knew this would happen, didn't you! You knew, and you *let* it happen!"

"*You* were supposed to protect her."

Galen rocked back as if accused of shooting Sesha himself. Guilt alloyed with anger hardened his expression into something she'd never seen in him before. She wondered what demons could twist him so. The struggle for his soul continued. Not all the prescience in the world could foretell its outcome.

"Do something!" Galen demanded.

Gil nudged Sumala aside, but when she passed her hand over the wound, Sesha's pain burned through her. She gasped and jerked her hand away.

I'm afraid. Unbidden and unwelcome, the thought was no less true. The memory of healing Galen was still too fresh, the cost of it not yet paid in full. *Not again,* she thought. *I can't go through that again, not even for Sesha.*

But she could not lose Sesha. Wavy bands of light and shadow rippled across the rock, reminding her they were running out of time. The wind rose, its dirge making her shiver.

"Stop the bleeding," Sumala begged. "Just stop the bleeding."

With renewed determination, she set her hand upon Sesha's wound. The fine, silvery dust of her essence poured out. *Too fast, too fast!* She could no more staunch the flow of that essence than she could hold a moonbeam.

"I can't," she whispered, reluctant to give such words voice. Then, "I can't!"—a howl of despair and futility, as if sheer volume might shatter those words and make them untrue.

Galen took her by the shoulders and shook her. "You healed me; you can heal her, too. Do it now!"

Gil shook her head. "It's beyond my power." Her voice dropped to a broken whisper, then faded, even from her own hearing. "There are limits to what I can do!"

Limits, she thought, *Yes, limits.* And she saw that her mission had a cruel duality of triumph and pain, sacrifice and joy. She would never be able to accomplish one without accepting the other. She couldn't hope to save everyone, and there would always be sacrifices to make, choices to bear.

But not Sesha.

The weight of a shadow fell upon her. Gil looked up.

Someone had stolen the sun.

Totality—Second Contact
First Minute

GALEN

Moonshadow engulfed Galen in twilight gloom. Totality claimed his rapt attention, and all else ceased. Childhood memories could not match the awesome beauty of totality; no partial eclipse could compare. It was an event utterly unique.

Attended by Mercury and Venus, the black disk of the moon seemed more a hole in the purpling, star-specked sky. An aura of palest green, soft and pearly, escaped the black maw. Its reflection bled across the unsettled lake in long shards like broken glass. He wanted nothing more than to stand gaping at that spectacle until its image was indelibly tattooed upon his memory.

How could I forget? he wondered.

The Ritual. Whether someone said it aloud or the thought merely whispered in his mind didn't matter. He was Guardian of the Ritual; he must see it through. They must complete the rite, even at the cost of Sesha's life. The truth raked at his heart with cruel claws.

And for the sake of Sesha's life? If all Gil had told him was true, she would have the power to heal Sesha. He must believe. If he banished all doubt, belief could become truth.

Galen shook himself. How much time already? How many seconds wasted before anyone had even noticed? Yet the women stood in totality's thrall, unmoving and silent.

"The Ritual," he commanded. The women turned to him, blinking away the image of the hidden sun. "It's what you came here for."

"Complete the Ritual, Gil," Sesha whispered, a fading echo. Her face was as pale as ashes, her breathing a ragged wheeze.

"While there's still time."

And Sesha is Hindu for time.

Galen scooped Sesha into his arms and brought her to the grotto. Lena and Petra took her from him, a reminder that he was not part of this. Gil did not move, her expression lost and uncertain.

"You must do this," Sumala said, gently guiding Gil toward the bench. "You, above all, must believe. We came here to accomplish something worthwhile. You can save Sesha."

Galen inhaled the words, taking them in to make them true. He watched as the sisters sorted out their places, each claiming one of the tall crystal spears. Petra as oldest stood on the left, and Sesha on the far right, the last crystal, slanted so that she could lean upon it. *The one already stained.*

Yet the arrangement seemed incomplete.

"And what of me?" Miriam asked quietly, her voice hollow and lost.

The shadows whispered. *They must be one.*

"Miriam, too," Galen announced, even before he'd thought out why. "She has to be part of this." Even Miriam reacted as if he'd gone insane.

Galen spoke quickly, his thoughts bubbles he must capture before they burst, before anyone could interrupt and scatter them, delicate beads strung on tenuous thread. "Gil became seventh daughter not at birth, but at conception. At that point, the two were still one. You're *both* the seventh daughter."

He turned to Miriam, who had the decency not to gloat. "Unless you stand together, the Ritual will fail; neither can do it alone." To the group, he said, "Vera understood that; that's why she brought her here now—to unite what had been divided."

"He's right," Sesha said, her voice a rasp of quiet pain. "Vera tried to tell me, before she—" Her words failed.

The sisters protested. Miriam was evil, corrupt. She was the enemy.

"Not so!" Galen insisted, slamming his fist against a stone for emphasis. The pain helped him focus. "She was never your enemy. But abandon her now, and evil will surely claim her." His gaze took in the shadowscape, the moon's dark disc. "See how the demons crouch, waiting for a victim?"

He saw Sumala mouth the word *edema.*

"No! No," Galen said, denying with a sharp wave of his hand the pain in head and chest. Shadows lingered at the edges of his vision. He laughed, bubbles rising from deep in his core, carrying his pain and fear. "Your aunts abandoned Miriam to Darkness. Don't make the same mistake. Include her now or lose her forever."

Galen pointed at Miriam. "You made me Guardian." And back to Gil, "You said Galen means Healer. *That's* my purpose, then; to heal the division. What was one at conception must be one here!"

GIL

...while there's still time.

Time dripped from Gil's fingers in bright red drops. *Sesha is time.* Gil closed her fist to hold Time fast. The world paused, awaiting its release.

Gil stared at Galen, mouth open but wordless. The sun's corona crowned his head with a nimbus of pale green fire. She glanced at Miriam, a dark mirror reflecting herself. Galen was right. Miriam was the *Other*, a void in her spirit like the hole in her mother's mandala. *Fill the center with whatever you are.* Miriam was that center.

But to take evil by the hand—no, she mustn't think that. Miriam wasn't the only one who had to change. Gil must surrender her own fear and prejudice. Did she truly hate Miriam? That thought, itself, felt tainted, and her fight with Miriam revealed her own capacity for evil. No, she could not condemn Miriam any more than herself.

Miriam turned to Galen, her expression both confused and suspicious, her mouth a sullen, twisted frown.

"This is what you truly want, Miriam," Galen explained. "To stand *with* Gil, not against her."

Gil studied Galen, trying to pierce the mask of his madness. Did Supay finally possess his soul, harnessed now to its purpose?

Miriam nodded, not in agreement, but surrender, and moved to sit beside Gil, but shied from her touch. The size of the bench forced them close.

Si's ethereal spirit enveloped them, a mantle of wistful anticipation. So long had the girl waited—a thousand years or more—

to complete this rite, to accept her role as healer. Gil wondered if Miriam was aware of the spirit's presence.

The other sisters hesitated now only in attitude, in the glances they cast at Galen.

"I am stone," Petra began, still reluctant. "The element of *earth...*"

Totality
Second Minute

GIL

Miriam held herself taut, physically close but mind distant. Her hands were clenched in tight fists, a manifestation of the grasp she held on her anger and hate.

Miriam's presence was a black hole absorbing the light their sisters generated. In her dark twin, Gil had admitted a portion of Supay into the circle. How could she defeat Supay when its own servant sat within her circle, shared this seat and held her fast? *Not servant,* Gil thought. *Victim.*

"I am neither." Miriam's words but a faint murmur Gil felt more than heard.

"Then be free of it," Gil whispered. "Let go, Miriam. Hatred gives control to Supay, to evil."

Though Miriam's response was an obdurate silence, Gil sensed conflict. New concepts butted against a wall of engrained habit.

Could Miriam be redeemed or was evil rooted so deep, it could not be removed without shredding her soul? Could Supay be banished without destroying Miriam?

Gil whispered to her twin, "You use hate to avoid pain and fear, but it binds you to the past and robs your future. In the end, it will consume you like the cancer that killed Aunt Faye."

"It's all that I have," Miriam responded bitterly.

"Then you have nothing. Hands full of hate can hold nothing else. So long as you cling to hatred and anger, you are Supay's tool."

"I will not be anyone's tool. Not Supay's and not yours."

"I don't want a tool; I want a sister. We could work as a team, sharing both triumph and burden. Let it go."

"And what will you surrender?"

Gil glanced at her own fist, holding tight to Time. Past Miriam's shoulder, Sesha clung to her crystal as if it were her own life. *Sesha!* Gil faltered, hating the Vision for bringing her to this choice. In that moment of denial and doubt, the hole in the sky claimed her soul.

"I offer strength." Petra's crystal resonated with her words, drawing energy from the corona and channeling it to the center where Gil and Miriam sat. Gil felt that energy coursing through every nerve, electric fire. Si's essence began to glow like a golden aura about them. Finished, Petra sagged, a vessel emptied. *What of Sesha?* Gil thought with alarm. Would she survive the crystal's demand?

SESHA

Pain bound Sesha in fire. She clung to her crystal and willed herself to stay erect. *A little while longer,* she thought. *I can hold on another minute. And a minute after that.*

Her strength ebbed, flowing out with the blood that still seeped from her wound. Her hands were numb, and her feet were cold, so cold. She feared she would turn to a pillar of ice. Instinct urged her to let go.

No! she thought in response. *I promised Gil I would hold on. I have* to hold on or Gil will fail—

The dark of the moon promised warmth and peace. *If I could rest for but a moment, I'll be fine.* She struggled against the compulsion, knowing it a lie.

She was skidding down the slope toward the old juniper, the massive rock, the void beyond. *Let go*—a whisper promising salvation. She tumbled, out of control. She jerked, waking from the dream memory.

GALEN

Strands of unraveled time held Galen immobile. The bloom of the sun's corona seemed fixed in an eternal instant. Galen imagined the sun captured forever in the moon's embrace, perpetual dark.

"I am air..." Sumala took up her chant even before Petra had finished, trying to make up lost time.

Galen stood outside the circle but close to Sesha. Her blood mingled with the ancient stain, marring the pristine crystal. Galen stared at the dark blemish. The Ritual went on, as it must, while the wind howled a dirge. He was Guardian. His was the duty to secure the Ritual, to defend it against the Darkness, and he must see it through. It became a focal point for his sanity as reality shredded. Twilight shrouded all. Shadow clogged his lungs.

Within the grotto, light remained, an aura, twin to the sun's corona, embracing the women. He feared it could not hold against the shadows prowling the dark. Shadows with teeth and claws with which to rend the soul. They circled, snarling and snapping at the globe of light.

Bright blue streamers danced around the duet of sun and moon. Three scarlet beads bled from its edge. The black hole in the sky threatened to devour Galen's soul. Demons danced among the clouds while their shadows rode the wind, bold in the dark of totality.

Galen waved his arms and stamped his feet, and the shadows skittered to the edge of vision, vanishing whenever he turned to face them.

That was how he kept the shadows at bay, by turning to them, for Evil could not defy direct confrontation. Evil flees truth.

GIL

"Lena is light, the element of fire..." Gil's sisters hurried to finish, a chorus of overlapping verses, pared to the bare essentials.

All the while, the energy from the corona poured upon her and in her and through her, so keenly focused through the crystals, she wondered that she did not burst into flame.

Here was the paradox—the light of the corona could not be seen without the dark of the moon. Light and dark together. Good and evil. The two existing as one, separate but dependent. She could not accept one without taking in the other.

Gil raised her free hand and held it open to the light. It filled her palm and spilled over, electric fire running down her arm and spilling into her mind. Beside her, Miriam mirrored the gesture. Gil was aware of every point where her body touched Miriam's, every cell and molecule, every atom. Miriam's thoughts, too, abutted her own, and her twin's anger and hatred permeated Gil's being. They shared love and grief, joy and anger.

Light and dark, good and evil. In this place, at this moment, the two must be one. She felt herself melding with Miriam like the Siamese twins she'd seen in a circus sideshow. Twins indeed, joined at the soul. She feared they would truly become one. She would lose her identity and become a hybrid of the two. *No! I am Gilaishling. I will remain.*

GALEN

Six crystals, six women, Galen thought, watching the Ritual unfold. At the core, Miriam and Gil, vulnerable and open.

His vision blurred, the two women merging into one image. *What was one at conception must be one here.* He feared his proclamation might become literally true, the two a single entity. A spasm of panic shook him. Was he right to put them together, or had Miriam manipulated him once more? He set one hand against his chest where Miriam's brand still burned.

SESHA

Sesha leaned against her crystal seeking breath that would not come. She focused on the black hole before her.

If you let go, you might live.

The dark hole in the sky, the blue eye of the pool. Corona and rainbow. *Sesha stood on the cliff, looking down on the blue lake.*

"—Swahili for water…" Maji's voice washed over her, cool and blue and clean.

Did she stand in this place and remember the fall or fall from the cliff and dream of here?

GIL

"You consider me flawed," Miriam noted with bitter scorn. Sitting beside Gil, Miriam struggled with her own demons.

"Not at all," Gil said too quickly. There was a partial truth in that accusation. Not flawed, Gil decided, but abused. Not your enemy, Galen had said. Supay had planted the seed of his influence, and Vera had fed it with her contempt. "Miriam, mistakes were made, and we can never correct them. But we can start anew. I would—" She searched for a word to describe what she felt. "I think I could cherish you as a sister. No one else, not even Sesha, can understand what the two of us endure."

As she spoke, Gil was aware of Si echoing her words. Did the ancient priestess reinforce Gil's thoughts or did she speak to another, seeking redemption for her own murder? Gil wished she knew more of the girl's life and who had brought it to an end.

Accept the gift, Gil thought but said nothing. So delicately balanced were Miriam's thoughts, so precarious her state of mind, Gil feared uttering the wrong words.

Totality

Third Minute

GALEN

Galen raised his hand to the spectacle of totality and found it smeared with blood.

Whose blood this time, he wondered almost absently. *Sesha's? Gil's? What of Eisabel?* He scrubbed both hands together.

Mama appeared on a rock in the middle of the lake, still cradling her baby. Pedro sat beside her, holding his heart as a priest holds an offering. Shadows clawed and pecked at them, shredded tatters wafting across the water, beyond Galen's reach.

¡Sálvenos!

Eisabel ran across the bridge of totality's reflection, but never came nearer. She opened her mouth to scream. Galen reached for her, but she remained beyond his grasp. Sooty air clotted into the spectre of a demon. It swooped toward Eisabel, a knife—Harry's knife—flashing in the dark.

Galen moved away from the circle and the security of its light. Darkness engulfed him, a silent howling of hatred and rage, but he would not let the demon take Eisabel. She was the sacrifice binding him to Evil; he had to redeem her. Shadows slashed at him, baring his soul.

A pale red glow suffused the horizon and bled into the lake. Carlo drifted slowly, turning toward Galen, the dead, dead eyes accusing him. Galen could not touch that befouled water; he could not cross it to reach Eisabel. She was too far. Too far, and the demon drew closer still.

Sálvenos!

A figure swooped from the sky, falling, perpetually falling. It wore his brother's face, eyes haunted with regret and guilt. "Edward!" Galen called out. "Help me!"

I failed you, Galen. I'm sorry.

It's not your fault.

Edward drifted away.

"Don't leave, Edward. Don't abandon me again!"

SESHA

Sesha felt herself drifting, slipping toward the corona's light. *If I pour myself into that hole—*

But first the Ritual. Finish the Ritual.

"I am Evita…"

Sesha took a deep breath, though the pain of it almost made her swoon.

"I will be Evita." Her strained voice brought Evita's words to a halt. "Take my middle name, Tetsu."

"Sesha, don't do this!" Gil's voice held a desperate plea. The others, too, shifted focus, murmurs rising to protests. *Please don't argue,* Sesha thought. *I don't have strength to argue.*

Evita glanced from Sesha to Gil in both confusion and grief, yet the true import of Sesha's demand escaped her. She shrugged as if names were trivial. "Then I am the Chinese elements. Karmita, Tree." She hesitated. "Tetsu, iron…"

Surrender. The urge was gentle but insistent.

Now it was Sesha's turn, the moment of choice. The black hole summoned her, the blue pool beckoned. She took a deep, slow breath, though it required strength she didn't have. Speaking required even more.

"I am Sesha, which is Time." A shudder ran through her soul, loosening its moorings. *The ledge fell away, leaving her no anchorage.* She looked to the green corona, a promise of refuge. "I claim the name Evita, which is Life. I give them both, for it is all that I have."

GIL

"…I am below," said Sesha, completing the Ritual.

Gil wanted to scream denial and frustration, but could not find her voice. She shifted to abandon her place, but Miriam's fingers remained closed around Gil's wrist, pinning her there. *And what will you surrender?*

Not Sesha. Please not Sesha!

GALEN

Edward hovered, forever falling. Pursued by demons, he

swooped low across the lake. Like a redeeming angel, he swept up Eisabel in his arms, by that act himself redeemed. The shadows howled with rage and strafed him with cruel talons, shredding his ethereal form. A comet with a blood red tail, he fell toward Galen.

The moon's black hole threatened to consume Edward as he fell across the sky. A trail of his essence spiraled toward totality. The demon with the knife pursued him. But this blade couldn't be Harry's knife. Harry's knife was safe in his pocket. Galen pulled it out, opening the ill-used blade. *This* was Harry's knife. It had saved his grandfather's life, but taken the sniper's. It had murdered Eisabel and wounded Gil. Cursed, it seemed. Could it, too, be redeemed by an act of salvation, a sacrifice?

Edward released Eisabel into Galen's embrace. Galen tried to catch her up, but it was like holding a wax figure as it melted. The spectral demon wheeled around the sky and dove.

"No!" Galen yelled, enclosing Eisabel within his arms, as if she was every child in the world who would ever need protecting. The demon's knife pierced Galen's skull straight through to his heart.

GIL

The Ritual was over, yet the ceremony felt incomplete.

For a gift to be given, it must be accepted. This gift was not a pendant hung about the neck, or a robe worn as needed. It must become part of her. And she must learn to control it lest it consume her instead. Energy ran like fire along her nerves and her voice melted in her throat. The sky shrieked and the wind bled a rainbow of fire. Rock, lake, and sky shimmered, blurring as if the world spun too fast for the eye to discern.

Fearing she might explode like a star gone nova, Gil closed her eyes, shutting out the spectacle. Si's gentle pressure urged her to open herself, to accept the gift. The spirit led the way, and with a slow, cautious breath, Gil followed, inhaling the power, absorbing it into her being. Beside her, Miriam did the same. The fire settled down to a fierce glow, banked embers awaiting but a breath to re-ignite.

Now the pale light of the corona caressed her in blessing. Yet if Gil accepted only the light, then only dark would be left to Miriam. Her sister would be lost forever. Only in accepting both light and dark, acknowledging that both must exist, could she bring them both under her control and defeat Supay.

She thought again of the mandala, and her mother's words...*for you to fill, with whatever it is that you are.*

Gil poured herself into the dark, all her doubts and misgivings, her weakness and failure. In that way alone could she hope to save both Miriam and herself.

Gil sensed motion as her sisters lost focus. Unaware of all that went on, they relaxed, distracted by things outside the circle. Evita turned to Sesha. Sumala stepped aside.

"Don't break the circle!" Gil warned, for Supay waited.

Sumala objected. "Sesha needs me and Galen's hallucinating."

"Leave Sesha to me," Gil commanded. "As for Galen, don't be so certain." However, she eyed their guardian with concern. He was vulnerable, raging against unseen demons and berating the sky. Yet she had to surrender him to focus on her own survival. If Supay overwhelmed her now, they would all be lost.

Supay raged beyond the glow of light surrounding their circle, unable to enter. It had nothing here to use against her, only shadow and wind. A whirlwind centered upon the fragile refuge of light, shrieking with utter silence. The light would prevail, so long as they held true and the circle remained complete.

Totality
Fourth Minute

GIL

Totality was not yet over. They still had, Gill guessed, about thirty seconds of preternatural darkness to endure. The ordeal continued.

"Hold on, Sesha, just a little longer," Gil murmured. A whisper, a demand. A prayer.

SESHA

Promises of hope surrounded the well of moonshadow. *I would be safe there,* Sesha thought.

She could wait no longer. She abandoned the ledge and dove through rainbow circle and green corona. Her soul unfurled in gossamer wings. She let herself fall into the moon.

GIL

A breach opened in the circle.

Sesha!

Gil struggled to rise, but her legs had forgotten how to move. Her feet became entangled in the hem of her robe.

"Stay," Miriam whispered. Yet Gil sensed no malice, only bitter loss. "You have what you wanted. Be prepared to bear the price."

"No!" Gil screamed. *Sesha, you promised you would wait! Don't abandon me now!*

Sesha's essence drifted toward the moon, a fine, glimmering dust. Beside her, Miriam took a deep, slow breath and whispered softly, as if speaking to someone within.

Supay crowed in triumph as it sprang after Sesha's soul.

SESHA

Sesha had expected peace. Instead, darkness seized her with

cyclonic fury. It shrieked and roared and spun her in circles. Shadow demons assaulted her, claws slashing her soul. She bled diamond streamers across the sky.

Something pursued her, a creature of dark and fire, its voice like the grinding of massive stones. She tried to flee, but there was nowhere to go. She could not find the moon.

In a pool too shallow for such a dive, icy water caused a spasm that saved her life. She did that now, curling her soul into a ball. Still the shadow beast pursued her. Like a dragon, its tail swept the stars from the sky. Its maw gaped wide, ready to devour her.

A globe of light floated below her, impossibly far away. A single ray pierced the raging dark. *A shaft of light pierced the water's lucent surface, drawing her to the surface.*

Catch me, Gil! Sesha thought, seeking that nacreous beam. *You promised you'd always catch me.*

I'm not Gil.

GALEN

He was falling, would fall forever, he thought, the Earth far, far away. Then someone caught him up, holding him holding Eisabel. He looked into his brother's face.

"Edward," he whispered, though he had no breath for speech. Edward brought him back to the ground.

"You can't reshape the past," Edward told him, falling back up into the sky. "It's done and set in stone. That was my mistake, thinking I could escape the guilt of the past by abandoning future's hope."

Galen held Eisabel now as he had before, on a crowded train, in a dismal hut. Her blood caught stray bits of light in crimson gleams. He hugged the child to him, rocking back and forth. She placed her small hand against the bloody print upon his chest, as she had before. Galen's chest tightened, and he gasped for breath. Miriam's brand burned like ice.

Red streamers shot out from the sun's corona, swirled through darkness, a whirlpool drawing him in. His vision blurred, tears stinging his flesh.

"No more!" he cried out weakly. He screamed, "Enough!"

The demon circled, wrapping them in darkness. In desperation, Galen stabbed with Harry's knife, striking at the moon. The demon bled into the hole the knife made, like water down a drain.

GIL

Bright red streamers from the sun's corona ignited the power within her. Gil lurched to her feet, tearing free from Miriam's grasp. She gathered energy from the surrounding rock and the water of the lake and from the crackling air, even from the light, itself. She held it in the palm of her hand, a sphere of intense, searing light.

With a scream of rage and denial, she flung it at Supay. The creature shattered into a million fragments.

Third Contact

GIL

Light banished the darkness. Supay was gone.

The wisp that was Si danced upon the air, shimmering light in the remaining gloom, but tethered still to the stain of her blood upon the bench.

GALEN

A flash of light shot out from the corona, and within an instant, the sun reclaimed sovereign rule of the sky. The shadows shattered into a hundred rainbows. Light fell upon Galen like rain.

It was over.

The black hole of the moon became a memory already fading into obscurity. Darkness retreated, pouring off the rock. Shadows oozed back into the cracks where they belonged.

Galen closed his eyes against the glare of the new sun. Within his mind, a clot of darkness remained, blinding him to all else. He still felt the burden of Eisabel's slight weight in his arms. But when he opened his eyes and lowered his gaze, it was Sesha he held, as if the two had become one, their blood commingling, one sacrifice in recompense for another.

The women stood in hushed silence, reluctant to break the spell of wonder. Someone at last breathed a deep sigh, and all relaxed into nervous fits of motion and whispers, movements begun and abandoned, sighs of relief, whispers of awe. The tumble into abrupt silence signaled the moment when they noticed Sesha in his care.

They gathered around him, but he focused only on Sesha, on the sweet face resting against his chest. Sumala knelt beside him, and behind her, Gil. She looked as if she would take Sesha into her own embrace, but this time, Galen refused to surrender her.

"It's too late," he said quietly. "She's dead."

Gasps and sobs. Maji and Evita sank to their knees, grief and exhaustion too much to bear. Petra remained standing, fists and jaw clenched tight, glaring at Galen as if he were at fault. They wept, the sound a gentle counterpoint to the roaring blackness still screaming through Galen's mind.

"Your ritual's complete now," he said to Gil, voice harsh with fierce contempt. "You've had your sacrifice of blood."

Gil rocked back on her heels, shaking her head to deny the accusation. Tears leaked through closed eyelids to course down her cheeks, the muscles in her throat working to swallow her anguish.

GIL

"She's dead."

Gil heard Galen's voice, the words muffled as grief filled his mouth like ashes.

"No!" she cried out, reaching for Sesha and finding only emptiness.

"You can still save her," Miriam whispered. "Heal her now."

Gil shook her head, lost in despair. "It's too late. She's gone."

"She remains, but I cannot hold her much longer." Miriam slid from the bench to the ground beside Gil.

Gil stared at Miriam, who regarded her with a dispassionate gaze. Her posture was rigid and her mouth tight, as if her whole being concentrated on a single task. "What have you done?"

Miriam's expression was an echo of Aunt Vera's persimmon frown. "An act of redemption, I suppose."

SESHA

Sesha! Not a voice, but a summons. A presence, familiar yet unknown.

The storm had ceased. Sesha existed as a single star in endless nothingness, infinite black. Time and space did not exist—neither up nor down, nor then, now or will be. She *moved* with no sense of motion, drifting in a current of abiding peace.

Air escaping in a stream of fine bubbles. Sesha's pack, wedged between rocks, pinned her to the bottom. The more she struggled, the tighter its grasp.

She felt comfort here, a sense of welcome and love, but as a diver longs for air, she longed for the embrace of reality—for space and light and the touch of stone and flesh.

Sesha! That presence anchored her. She could not move on.

"Gil?" she wondered.

"Miriam," the entity responded with rue and disappointment.

"Where's Gil?"

"She's waiting." Threads of iridescent light spun toward her like a hand reaching out. "Come with me."

Sesha hung from the limb of the juniper tree while Miriam walked away. "Why should I trust you?"

The same memory shaded Miriam in hues of regret. "I won't abandon you again. I'm not so heartless as that." *Sesha's grip slipped.*

"Trust me," Miriam whispered, still reaching out. *Miriam, not Gil.* Yet the sense of peace and welcome held Sesha as rocks had held her pack in the lake. *Against all instinct, Sesha surrendered, letting herself sink to slip free of the straps.*

"Come with me, Sesha, before it's too late." Miriam's presence wavered. "If I stay much longer, I will lose the way back."

GIL

Recklessly, Gil summoned her new power. It surged through her. *Control this or it will consume you,* an inner voice warned. Si's presence flowing through and around her urged caution and offered guidance.

How can I do this? Gil wondered and in that moment of doubt, felt her skin tingle and every nerve quiver with electric flame. *Not again,* she thought, remembering Galen's healing, the pain and fatigue. In panic, Gil rejected the power, forcing it down to a small seed that burned like a hot, white star within the core of her being.

Yet Sesha needed her. Gil took a deep breath and felt Si enter, a zephyr inhaled. Like a parent with a child, the ancient spirit guided thought and motion. Gil summoned the power anew, slowly this time. She formed it like a balm in her hands and set it against Sesha's wound. Releasing the energy, she shaped the healing. Rent flesh became whole, unscarred. Yet there was no life.

Miriam sighed. Her breath went out of her, warm and alive, and enveloped the cold of Sesha's body.

And Sesha took it in.

She shuddered, gasping like a diver coming up for air. Her eyes opened to gaze at the faces hovering over her.

Si rose transcendent, a swath of diamonds across the sky. Released at last, one soul traded for another.

"She's alive!" Sumala pronounced with breathless wonder. While her sisters laughed and wept with relief, Gil collapsed to the stone floor, drained, longing for nothing more than the blessed oblivion of sleep. Miriam did likewise, and they almost clung to one another—almost, but not quite. There was still too much between them. Gil held out her hand and Miriam did likewise, a whisper apart.

What did you do?

As if Miriam could read the thought—or perhaps only her expression—she replied with a pretense of *no big deal*. "I walked away before. Now the scales are balanced."

"Why?" The word burst from Gil in joyous wonder.

Miriam seemed as confused as she. "You said Sesha would love me if I let her. Perhaps I needed to test that for myself."

Gil nodded, taking this in, adjusting the fit. She smiled, longing to hug her twin.

"There's hope for you yet," she replied and caught a startled, sidelong glance from Galen.

"Don't expect a repeat performance," Miriam warned, the bitter ice returning to her voice.

GALEN

Even as Sesha opened her eyes, the world rolled under Galen. A deep vibration rumbled, grinding his thoughts to powder. Too caught up in Sesha's recovery, no one else noticed.

"She's alive!" Sumala announced. Relief and joy bubbled into laughter. Another tremor passed like a wave beneath him.

"Hush!" Galen commanded. "Did you feel that?" Breaking crystals jingled like wind chimes.

"Was that an earthquake?" Lena asked, and others echoed.

Gil nodded. "Pachacamac. He's angry."

"But we didn't do anything wrong," Maji argued. "Did we?"

"The discord among us," Gil explained. "Supay's corruption." Unfortunately, Pachacamac was known for punishing the innocent along with the guilty."

"Regardless of cause, this place is no longer stable," Galen announced, pretending he could see through the red haze masking his vision. "We should get out of here, fast." He struggled to his feet, and Sesha stood with him. She listed dizzily until Lena stepped to her side.

"Sesha's still too weak."

"Gil needs time to recover."

"We don't have time," Galen answered. As if to emphasize his point, the ground heaved like a floundering ship, sending them all staggering and clinging to one another for support.

"Let's go!" Petra's voice? Maji's? It didn't matter.

They started around the lake, Sumala helping Sesha and Petra taking Gil. Again, the mountain shrugged. Maji lurched, her injured leg taking her weight, and she cried out in pain. Galen caught her, one arm about her waist for support.

I can make it, Galen thought. *I can get this far, and this far, and a little farther.* Then he halted.

"Where's Miriam?" he yelled over the roar in his head. He'd forgotten her in the fuss over Sesha. Turning about, he saw her slumped against the bench.

"Keep going!" he ordered, passing Maji off to Evita and turning back. Miriam did not move as he approached.

"Miriam!" he yelled, and she lifted her head.

A slab of rock broke away from the cliff overhead. Galen swept Miriam to the side as it slammed down upon the grotto, sealing it. The ground shuddered as a crack appeared, splitting the bowl. The entire cirque slipped. For a timeless moment, the lake trembled at the brink of the chasm, and then spilled over in a plume of liquid diamonds.

Miriam in tow, Galen ran, ignoring the searing pain in his head, the laboring of his breath. The ground dropped again. Galen stumbled but kept his feet, racing for the rim. Reaching the edge, Galen shoved Miriam forward, all but flinging her toward her sisters. He lunged forward, barely catching the edge as the stone dropped from beneath his feet. Petra grabbed his arms, hauling him to safety.

On firm ground, Galen turned to watch the entire cirque collapse. How far, he wondered, would it plummet, and were villages in its path? Gil's grim frown asked the same question.

The slab spanning the chasm had shifted, the flat plane of its top canted to one side. The near end had slipped about three feet, leaving a patch of fresh rock face scarred with deep gouges. It rested precariously upon a rock snag that seemed itself none too stable.

"It'll never hold!" Maji wailed.

"We'll cross one at a time," Galen responded.

"Let me go first," Gil offered, already climbing down. Deep fatigue weighted her as she studied the bridge. "I'll support it from the far side."

"You can do that?" Galen asked. Her expression asked if she had a choice, but an aura of energy shimmered around her. Galen shuddered to imagine such power loose and uncontrolled.

"If this collapses, we're trapped here."

Galen glanced at the glaciers poised above them. "*Here* may not last too long, either."

He nudged Miriam. "Unless your powers include flight, you'll have to help her. Can you do that?"

Her gaze lashed him with contempt tempered by terror. "Give me some credit, Professor. I'm neither inhuman nor suicidal," she responded, both hurt and prideful. "If Gil can do it, so can I."

Galen had his doubts. She looked to be as weak as Gil. What had happened, in those moments after he had pronounced Sesha's death? What had they done to bring her back?

"Go!" Galen commanded the sisters. "I'll stay with Miriam." He stepped to her side, hand upon her shoulder to steady her. For a brief moment, their gazes locked, the irony of his vow to stand beside her linking both of them. It seemed fitting that if she didn't make it, neither would he.

GIL

Gil crossed the span gingerly, feeling the precarious shift in tension beneath her feet. She held her breath, as if that would make her lighter, and demanded stability from the stone. Reaching the far side, she knelt to place her hands on the span and saw Miriam mimic her, a mirror reflection.

Together, their energy melded into a weaving around and through the bridge, an extension of their own beings. She quietly exalted in their shared effort. If only it could be like this always, the two them working as one.

As each sister crossed, she felt their added weight upon the stone. When the last was safely across, Galen lifted Miriam to her feet, leaving Gil alone to hold the span. Without Miriam's aid, a terrible fatigue began to drain every muscle and bone. She still had limits, and she had severely taxed them already. She could not hold out for long and must bear double the added weight.

Miriam could barely stand, her face pale, hair clinging in damp ringlets to her cheeks. Fatigue and shock bruised her eyes and made hollows in her cheeks. She gasped for breath as Galen half-carried her across the bridge.

Halfway across, the bridge cracked—Gil saw it crack, and felt it in her own bones. A section dropped several inches. *No!* she commanded, and it held its place. Miraculously, inevitably, it held.

Panic widened Galen's eyes.

"Don't look," Gil called. "Come to me." She lifted one hand to hold them within her palm. A stain of blood remained on the stone. Every muscle strained as if she physically hefted the weight.

Evita and Lena pulled them to safety even as Gil's strength failed. The stone slipped from her command. In utter silence, the bridge fell until it struck the bottom of the chasm breathless seconds later.

The mountain groaned once more. Pachacamac's ire, it seemed, was not yet sated. Boulders leaped with abandon, like lambs skipping down the steep precipice into the depths of the canyon. The mountain itself capered and danced.

"Be calm," she told Pachacamac. "I am here." She held out her hands over the chasm, willing the tumult to cease. Silence followed, as deafening as the roar of the avalanche, and stillness, like the world catching its breath.

Fourth Contact

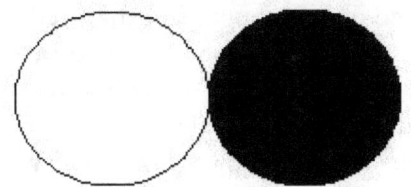

GALEN

The sun had set, still locked in the moon's embrace. Its surreal crescent snuggled down into a blanket of cloud, painting them with molten gold. The colors of sunset seemed garish after the moon's gentle display. The light faded rapidly from moonshadow to twilight to dark.

Pachacamac had ceased his tantrum, and the world was once more calm. With little strength to travel, the group took refuge in the entrance to the tunnel. As soon as mind told body it could stop, Galen's legs refused to take a single step farther. He collapsed to the hard stone as if it were a feather bed, yielding to fatigue and pain.

Someone cradled his head, Sumala's voice saying something about cerebral edema. Had it all been hallucination, he wondered. Eisabel and Edward, demon and shadow? He couldn't accept that, for it would deny their sacrifice and salvation.

Even as Gil's touch eased the pressure in his head and the terrible ache in his chest, he felt her own exhaustion. Feebly, he tried to push her away, but other hands took his own.

"Shh," Sumala whispered as she pressed dry coca leaves into his mouth.

"No vile concoctions," he muttered, but he hadn't the strength for protest.

GIL

Finished with Galen, Gil moved among her sisters, easing their hurts. But she could not conjure food or water or warmth. The sisters huddled close together, sharing their warmth and the comfort of their touch, needing that assurance that the world still existed.

Miriam kept apart, a tangible space about her no one dared breach. She seemed quiet enough, as exhausted as the rest.

Gil eyed her with regret as she returned to Galen's side.

"What will you do with her?" Galen asked in a quiet whisper. She was surprised he was still awake.

Gil shrugged. "It's her choice, not mine. We'll take her home, though I doubt she'll stay. Miriam, I fear, will remain Supay's agent, someone I will always have to contend with."

"There's no hope for her? After all, she helped you save Sesha. That should count for something."

Gil regarded him with a wistful smile. "You're very perceptive. But one act of redemption won't change a lifetime of habit. It's a start, perhaps, but only that."

"And did you get what you came for?"

A spark of passion overcame her fatigue as she considered the changes she felt. "Before, everything seemed out of focus and faded, the future out of tune. Now it's clear and sharp, colors so intense, they burn my mind. And the music—Oh, how the world sings! Did you know that? Time is a symphony." She held out her hand in offering, but her mood sobered. "I feel such power now, Galen. I could do anything I desire. Yet if I lose control of that power, I fear it will consume me like a burning bush. It's a delicate balance, both wondrous and terrifying."

"And the Vision? Do you snap your fingers and make everything all right?" A trace of scorn tuned his voice to a bitter key.

She grimaced with chagrin. "Not exactly. I understand the Vision now, and I believe I can stop the destruction. But I can't fix everything that's wrong in the world; there will always be events I can't prevent and people I can't save." Her eyes focused upon other places and times—scenes of both tragedy and triumph. *So much potential for both.* "You'll have to trust the choices I make. But you'll never know what doesn't happen."

She paused, veering from future burdens. *Later. There'll be time later.*

"What about you?" she asked. "Have you found your broken dream?"

Galen stared beyond the tunnel where stars sparked new promise. Gil knew the answer, but intended the question for him to explore. "You can't put the pieces back together again; they don't fit the same. But you can make something new."

Gil nodded. "And what will you do with that something new?"

Galen sighed, then shrugged. "Too soon to tell. I doubt my life will change all that much, but I think I have a new angle to teach. Security is more a state of mind than a bank account, and there's a certain value in risk. You have to let go of the past to reach the future."

Wednesday, June 9

SESHA

Sesha thought they must make a wretched sight. All were coughing and wheezing now. Maji could barely walk, and Lena kept rubbing her hand across her stomach. Sesha favored her freshly-healed wound as if any sudden movement might tear it open. They plodded slowly, listless and empty, pushing one foot in front of the other only because someone said they must.

The Ritual had wrung from them all their energy, leaving them but dried husks. Sesha, herself, had little memory of the event. That she had stood in the circle, that she had taken Evita's name and offered herself as sacrifice, all was beyond recall. She knew that she had died, and that Gil had healed her and Miriam had retrieved her soul, but even that was hazy dream.

The quake had collapsed most of the tunnel. They were forced to follow Galen's trail up the valley and through the cleft in the ridge.

Just a little farther, she promised her body. *Another twenty feet, and I'll rest.* At least they were moving downhill now, though certain muscles protested that that was no less strenuous. *To that boulder, and then the next.*

Melt water from the glaciers above them drained through the gravel floor, present but unreachable. The smell of it, the sound of it trickling through the rocks, was maddening, honing her thirst to an acute, all-consuming obsession. Sesha tried to suck the moisture from wet pebbles, but it wasn't enough to satisfy her aching thirst. She licked dry lips and prayed there would still be food and water at the camp in the ruins. How much farther could they go? She couldn't imagine how they would ever get back to Angoltuto.

Sesha worked gingerly down a series of blocks like a giant's stairway. Stepping down off a particularly high stone, she turned to offer a hand to whoever was behind her, but hesitated when she saw it was Miriam. Miriam frowned at the small gesture and refused it. Sesha kept her hand raised, though, poised to catch Miriam if she should stumble.

372

The others still did not trust their sister; Petra had wanted to tie Miriam's hands, but the trail was too rough, and she needed freedom of movement. She seemed subdued, recognizing the need for cooperation if they were to survive the trek back.

Sesha paused to rest, propping herself against a large boulder. "You helped save me," she remarked to Miriam. "I only remember faint images—floating mists and sparks of light. But you were there."

At first, Miriam did not answer. When she spoke, her words seemed too thick for her throat. "Of all the sisters, I hated you most because you were Gil's favorite. But I couldn't walk away again. Consider it a debt paid."

"Still, it was a brave thing to do. Thank you."

Miriam frowned now as if she regretted her act. At the next step down, though, she accepted Sesha's hand and in turn, offered hers to Petra behind her. Petra ignored it.

They reached the valley, a high point where they could look down on the ancient city, and paused to stare in dismay and disbelief. Most of the city was gone, simply gone. Even the walled avenue had tumbled into the quebrada. What remained was scattered like children's blocks. The horsemen's camp was a ruin of torn tarps and scattered supplies.

"Maybe there's still some food," someone suggested, and that hope nudged them on. Sesha imagined the aroma of cooking food, a mirage created by hunger. She stoically ignored it. But near the *cholo's* camp, someone squatted by a small fire, stirring a pot.

The stranger stood, and his eyes seemed to count their number with a frown until his gaze paused on her face.

"Tomás!" Sesha called out, recognizing the colors and pattern of his poncho. She rushed to greet the little Quechuan guide with as much of a hug as she could manage. Evita and Lena joined her, and then Maji, much to Tomás's consternation, it seemed. He backed away, as if he feared they were attacking him. Then he released a hearty laugh and returned their hugs.

"Come. Eat," he called out in Spanish, gesturing to the others who approached more warily. "I have food for all."

"Where are the other men?" asked Petra. "The *cholos*?"

Tomás answered with an ominous shrug. "They are gone," he said, and nothing more. He turned again to Sesha.

"A good morning is this," he said in slow, careful English, a proud grin fracturing the solemnity of his features. Now it was Sesha's turn to correct his syntax and to delight in the truth of his words.

"It certainly is, Tomás!" she replied gleefully. "It's a wonderful day."

MOONRISE: 11:51 a.m. MST ~ MOONSET: 11:50 p.m. MST
SUNRISE: 5:01 a.m. MST ~ SUNSET: 7:22 p.m. MST
Monday, July 16, 1945
New Mexico

Epilog—Trinity

GIL

Jornada del Muerto. Journey of Death. Could there be a more aptly named location for this undertaking? The bleak volcanic wasteland had a long history of blood—Apaches and Conquistadors, armies and outlaws. Nature, too, was particularly ruthless in this area. But nothing could compare to the legacy today's event would spawn. Lightning flashed against distant mountains, for a brief moment illuminating the tall steel tower and its deadly device five miles to the north.

The first light of dawn smeared gold across the eastern horizon and touched the mountain peaks surrounding the flat expanse of desert. It reminded Gil of Peru. She fingered the piece of welder's glass in her pocket and allowed a small smile. She had come a long way since then, developing and mastering the power she had gained there.

Sesha had done a miraculous job of getting her here, past Dorothy McKibben in Santa Fe, through the checkpoints on The Hill, and here to Base Camp. She would've liked to be closer, out at one of the bunkers. But closer meant fewer people, and someone would surely ask, "Who are you?" Besides, this was where all the important people were—Fermi, Oppenheimer, Segre.

Gil had kept vigil here throughout the night. It was still too dark to make out the face of the man standing next to her. All the better, for darkness cloaked her in anonymity.

Sesha waited in Santa Fe, as close as Gil would allow her to come. *As if anywhere would be safe if this goes wrong.*

And if it goes wrong, how long will it take? How long before Santa Fe is incinerated, and Albuquerque, and the family ranch near Gallup, one hundred eighty miles northwest? Would they see it coming and know she had failed? What about Lena in Telluride and

Maji in California? Would the news spread faster than the fire-storm?

It had been easier in Germany. Tweaking calculations just the slightest bit had convinced Heisenberg, and more importantly, Hitler's advisor, Albert Speer, that an atomic explosion might well turn the Earth into a second sun. The German effort never really got off the ground. At the same time, Heisenberg, himself, had helped Gil to understand the principles of quantum mechanics. Between his own uncertainty theory and Schrödinger's cat, Gil had found the answer she needed here. All outcomes were possible until the event, until they looked in the box. Then the scales would tip.

Would doubt outweigh certainty? Would the negative surpass the positive? Even Fermi spoke aloud of the possibility of igniting the atmosphere, infuriating Bainbridge and General Groves. Of course, she could clear their doubts with a thought. *Beware of arrogance,* an inner voice chided.

Gil simply had to believe in success more than all the doubters believed in failure. A simple matter of faith. Simple? Sumala's words echoed in her memory. *I fear that when you confront the real thing, the Vision will have become too strong.*

The Vision danced at the edges of perception, tantalizing her with their possibilities. She fought them down, stuffing them into the dark corners and hidden pockets of her mind. They could not emerge today. She could not allow the imagined to become the real. If she saw the Vision today, it would not end. The world would not return.

For a time, she had thought today would not be necessary. Early calculations had predicted temperatures hot enough to ignite the atmosphere. They had almost quit. But then Enrico Fermi had tweaked the parameters to allow for the cooling effect of the surrounding ground. The project continued.

I could still end this with a thought.

But what good would it do? She would only delay the inevitable and be forced into an unending succession of scenarios, each more difficult than the last. This would happen someday, if not today. If not here, then somewhere less accessible to a red-haired American. The Americans had no idea just how close the Russians were to testing their own bomb.

Yes, it had to be now and it had to be here. *Here* she would draw the line. She would set the parameters for all time, and once set, they could not be changed.

This far, she thought, imagining a boundary line. *Let it be this big.* Bigger than their expectations. Big enough to scare them, to instill a sense of awe and horror. To make them vow this new energy would never be used for evil. Images of the future seared her thoughts. Suffering and death. Destruction.

The thunderstorm that had threatened and delayed the test was breaking up now, as if Nature, herself, had given up trying to dissuade these men from their folly. Robert Oppenheimer paced restlessly. He was thin—less than one hundred pounds—and pale and seemed close to collapse. As he passed Gil, she touched his sleeve and brushed his mind with a silent, healing thought. He paused to stare at her, and she held her breath. *Who are you?* asked his expression. *What are you doing here?*

Saving the world, she thought in response. He nodded slightly, then lit another cigarette.

No one knew for certain whether this test would succeed or if they were about to fire "the flop heard 'round the world," as a popular piece of doggerel put it. People worried about their reputations. They were concerned about wasting eighty million dollars chasing a chimera. They justified their work in the name of *Ending the War.* No one wondered what would happen *after* the war or asked if they should do this at all.

Look beyond, Gil wanted to yell at them. *Look at the future and the consequences you create.* If they could see as she did, they would dismantle and bury that thing in the desert, burn this place to the ground, and tremble with terror at what they had almost wrought. Yet it had to be. This beast would make war an abomination to be feared and avoided. In the end it would bring true peace—if only humanity can survive until that end. A long, dark path, and Supay lurked in every shadow.

The countdown approached zero. Tensions adjusted, postures shifted. Next to Gil, physicist Emilio Segre imagined the explosion setting the atmosphere on fire, as if the Vision had forsaken her to attack a more vulnerable mind. She smothered his doubt with a reassuring thought.

Fermi tore a piece of paper into small and smaller pieces.

Outside, the world held its breath, not even knowing the terrible balance of its future.

Three. Two. One.

Too late now. Too late to change, to stop. Too late for regrets. The countdown reached zero.

Fermi dropped his bits of paper.

A premature dawn flashed in the desert.

About the Author

The stories we tell arise from the stories we are. Where we come from and who we are and what we've done with our lives.

Ronnie Seagren's story begins with a grandfather who left Italy at the age of seventeen to set sail in the Merchant Marines. The other side of the family helped settle Colorado. Moving to California when she was seven, she missed the mountains. But when she returned nine years later, she found she loved the ocean.

The original Star Trek series inspired a passion for both science fiction and astronomy. She aspired to be an astronaut, but in 1970, married Frank Seagren, just six years before NASA opened the program to women. They now have three sons and three granddaughters.

Fascinated with total solar eclipses, she's traveled to Mexico, Austria, and Tahiti just to spend a few minutes standing in moon shadow. It's an awesome, mystical, incredible experience to suddenly see a hole in sky where the sun used to be. In 2017, the path of totality will traverse the country from Washington state to South Carolina, and Ronnie threatens to drag the entire population of Colorado to Casper because ninety-nine percent just doesn't cut it.

Now mix in a love of hiking and nature's grandeur, of photographing the wonders of creation. Add a dash of adventure, inspired by the likes of Indiana Jones, and a fascination with the powers of the mind.

All this combined is the recipe for Seventh Daughter, a trek through the inner landscape of the mind as perilous as the physical travails found in the mountains of Peru.

Ronnie is currently working on the sequel and hopes to have it ready in time for that 2017 eclipse.

Coming in 2017 – the exciting sequel to
Seventh Daughter

From *Seventh Daughter:*

"You are the seventh son."
Galen shook his head…. "Even if that were true, my father was an only child. I can't be a seventh son of a seventh son."
Gil acknowledged that with a single nod. "No, but your own son could be."

It took Galen sixty years, but he finally has his seventh son, a boy named Anthony. It means *priceless*. But the child is not what Galen expected.

On the other side of the world in the Philippines, a young girl stands before a towering wall of water and bids it stop.

These two disparate lives are coming together, each to fulfill what the other lacks and racing to save mankind from disaster.

Get ready for more adventures with these fantasy books from WolfSinger Publications.

Call of Chaos – Carol Hightshoe

The exiled daughter of a minor noble, Kyrianna Dalynne, finds herself trapped in a temple dedicated to Thynitic, The Lady of Chaos.

She and her companions are charged with finding an ancient artifact before the ones guarding the portals out will allow them to leave.

As their search continues, Kyrianna begins to question if there was a specific reason she and the others were brought to this place.

The Twelve – James K Burk

Valtierra, a city-state, is governed by archetypes. Every two years they choose twelve men and women to wear the masks and to become the Wise Old Man, the Fool, the Mother, the Harlot, the Warrior, and the rest of the council. But now Valtierra faces hunger, decay, and an enemy on their border and, when the need for leadership is greatest, one mask is worn by a foreigner and one mask hides a traitor.

High Rage – James K Burk

Scarface, on his way back to a clan stronghold after assassinating a legate, meets and falls in love with a woman even more ruthless than he. To win her, he must reunite an empire and create a kingdom. His only allies are his wits, his sword, and the power in his scars—black marks like the taloned finger prints of a demon.

To achieve his goals, he must deal with old enemies, gods of dubious worth, and his own family—who may be the most dangerous of all.

Taking Hope – James K Burk

The power he once held depleted, Scarface has found contentment as Morgan. No longer seeking power or building kingdoms, he is happy with his current life and with his wife Topaz.

However, when what he most loves is threatened, Morgan must again become Scarface to correct past mistakes. He must defeat a king and a god. Knowing one god can only be beaten by another, he seeks an alliance, but what price will be demanded?

With only a few allies, one of them mad with rage, and the power in his scars returned, he must confront old enemies, including one who knows his deepest secret and greatest weakness. Will he be able to lay to rest his past, defeat his enemies and return to the life he has made for himself? Or will he lose everything and everyone he has come to truly care about?

The Road to the Golden Griffin Series – Jason J Sergi

The Dragon King and The Golden Griffin. It's an ancient story, created back when the world was still wild. A story of a wise but fierce ruler, and a bold usurper. A story of strange beings, and fabled treasure. A story with origins lost to legends, wars, and the taming of the world. A story that has attracted hundreds of adventurers and treasure hunters to the dangerous lands of the long-dead dragon king. A story that has intrigued young Bathmal Arined since the day he heard it and now that very story has sent him down a road which passes through cosmic strife, bitter loss, horrid evil, and uncertain friendships.

The road can only end with The Golden Griffin…
or Bathmal's death.

Book 1: The Hero of Twilight

Millstand held very little for young Bathmal Arined. Aside from his mother, the village held nothing for him at all. And yet, he was trapped within its confines. Born fantasizing of grand adventure and of places wholly unlike Millstand. Places where everyone had a voice, and everyone mattered and cared for one another regardless of caste. He often spent long hours wandering the worlds of his imagination, battling evil singlehandedly, rescuing cities and nations from hordes of gruesome demons, and returning to countless glorious homecomings.

But when the fantasies faded and reality crept back in, Bathmal knew he was just a bastard; and in his world, that equaled to nothing. Then, on a cold winter day on the outskirts of the village, Bathmal's life changes forever. He encounters a knight from the north, who tells Bathmal that there is more to the world than being a bastard, and that even bastards can become knights. Bathmal becomes obsessed with the idea and follows the knight from the village and commences on a life journey that will take him into the frozen mountains, across the sea to an ill-fated kingdom, and into the depths of The Black Realm of Hadez itself, there to face his true tests where success would grant Bathmal the chance to obtain everything he'd dreamed of, and failure meant endless death.

Bathmal's journey also leads him to the tale of The Golden Griffin, and sets him down the first few steps of the road towards a possible meeting with history…and a legend come alive.

Book 2: The Threat of Saint Flesh

Bathmal, now a knight of a defunct Order, returns home to revel in his accomplishment, and to rescue his mother from the backbreaking misery offered by Millstand's fullbloods.

But upon returning, Bathmal and Nojo find Millstand deserted and ransacked, his mother and everyone else gone. There is little evidence as to what had happened to the townfolk, but of what evidence there is, it all pointed north. Together, Bathmal and his con-squire charge north through Anfaria's badlands in a desperate attempt to find answers. Along the way they unravel a hideous plot that must be stopped before it can go any further. They also find an old friend of Sir Odon's, whose loyalty is suspect; and a demon far worse than anything Bathmal has ever faced before.

Bathmal needs to find his mother if at all possible, but his duty as a knight may suck him too deeply into the cosmic battles being waged by Deus and Malus. And to compound all else, betrayal and a new war awaits him across the sea in Twilight—but another danger, one which lies much closer, threatens to destroy him and all that he hopes to achieve…

Another detour along a Road where nothing is guaranteed. The Golden Griffin will wait…Bathmal needs only to survive.

Book 3: The Hunters of Shadow

The Battle of Delldoan is over; The Demon Saint Flesh is dead; the threat to Anfaria defeated; but, even with all this good fortune, Bathmal is left feeling lost and anxious.

His friend Sir Kasper is still among the missing long after The Battle of Delldoan has concluded, as is the vile dark-elf Zenlem Sidor. And, perhaps most troubling of all, Nojo-his trusted and faithful con-squire-continues to display signs of Dangerous Instability. If a solution to the problem cannot be found soon, Bathmal fears he may have to do the unthinkable…

Once more he will head into darkness, in hopes of finding Sir Kasper, and ridding the world of the dark-elf Sidor. But unseen forces will try to prevent him from doing both, and Bathmal will soon find out the taint of Hadez lasts far longer and doesn't go away just because he is no longer within the fell realm; but when the time comes, will he decide to fight against the taint, or will he embrace it?

The Golden Griffin waits for Bathmal…possibly forever…

Find out more about these and our other books at
www.wolfsingerpubs.com

www.ingramcontent.com/pod-product-compliance
Lightning Source LLC
Chambersburg PA
CBHW061511020726
47502CB00006B/2025